READERS LOVE
One Enchanted Evening

★★★★★
'The best novel I've ever read'

★★★★★
'Totally enchanted with this book'

★★★★★
'A brilliant story'

★★★★★
'A brilliant debut novel with class, drama and dancing'

★★★★★
'I adored the glamour, gossip, intrigue and descriptive storyline'

★★★★★
'A first class debut novel!'

★★★★★
'A charming book'

★★★★★
'The story is woven with the elegance and grace'

★★★★★
'Full of intrigue, wit, secrets and lies'

★★★★★
'This book is sure to win the hearts of many!'

Praise for

One Enchanted Evening

'This **sweeping**, **engrossing** story offers **glamorous**, high-society **entertainment** and promises to **delight** the reader'

DAILY EXPRESS

'A **sparkling** debut'

WOMAN MAGAZINE

'The consummate storyteller, adept at **captivating** audiences will now captivate readers as he whisks them away to worlds of **dance**, **intrigue**, high society and **scandal** . . . bringing the golden age of dance to life, page by page'

WESTERN MAIL

'As **enchanting** as the title suggests'

CULTUREFLY

'*Downton* with dance, **perfect**!'

SANTA MONTEFIORE

'The characters and stories are **beautifully interwoven** to provide a really **fabulous read**'

JUDY MURRAY

One Enchanted Evening

To
Elizabeth

Happy Mothers day

Lots of Love

Anton Du Beke xx

Elizabeth (2)

Happy Mother day

lots of love

Auntie Debbie xx

ANTON DU BEKE

One Enchanted Evening

ZAFFRE

First published in Great Britain in 2018
This edition published in 2019 by
ZAFFRE
80–81 Wimpole St, London W1G 9RE

A CIP catalogue record for this book is available from the British Library.

Paperback ISBN: 978–1–78576–482–0
Hardback ISBN: 978–1–78576–480–6
Trade Paperback ISBN: 978–1–78576–481–3

Also available as an ebook

3 5 7 9 10 8 6 4 2

Typeset by IDSUK (Data Connection) Ltd
Printed and bound in Great Britain by Clays Ltd, Elcograf S.p.A.

Zaffre is an imprint of Bonnier Books UK
www.bonnierbooks.co.uk

ANTON DU BEKE is one of the most instantly recognisable dancers today, best known for his role on the BBC's *Strictly Come Dancing*, which he has featured on since its conception in 2004. His debut album reached the Top 20, and his sell-out Dance Tour has been running for over a decade.

A household name and all-round entertainer, known as Mr Debonair, Anton brings all the wit, charm and style he's famous for to this, his *Sunday Times* bestselling debut novel.

http://www.antondubeke.tv/

To Hannah, George and Henrietta,
the loves of my life

Prologue

31 December, 1936

The Grand Masquerade Ball

FOR THE LORDS AND LADIES of London town, the dukes and duchesses of every English shire, the counts and countesses of the continent – and even beyond – there is only *one* place to be seen on this New Year's night. The doors of the Buckingham Hotel are open, for this is a night to be remembered.

It is an age of splendour. It is an age of magnificence. For some, it is an age of elegance and grace – and here in the Buckingham's Grand Ballroom, crown princesses and sirens of the silver screen have come to toast the New Year, government ministers and landed gentry have come to forget, if only for a moment, this year of wars abroad and the increasing threat at home. The band is playing. The dancers are swaying. The hall is filled with the great and the good. Others watch discreetly from the sidelines . . .

In the heart of the ballroom, the principal dancer, hidden behind his Venetian mask, twirls away from his partner and seems to glide as he crosses the dance floor. The orchestra prepares to strike up another serenade but not a soul in the ballroom notices the silence in between songs. They are transfixed, every eye trained upon the mysterious dancer who approaches the mahogany stairs and, lifting his hand to the Crown Princess of Norway, beseeches her to join him on the dance floor.

'Your Highness,' he ventures, in a rich, dulcet tone, 'shall we?'

Some of the faces around him flicker. There is surprise, even consternation, in their eyes.

On the other side of the ballroom, the band strikes up their new number. It is time for the waltz to begin.

The dancer takes off his mask . . .

Five Months Earlier . . .

August 1936

Chapter One

THE GRAND BALLROOM SEEMED TO lie under an enchantment on this balmy summer night. The ballroom's wooden floorboards shimmered, as if beneath a haze; the guests bedecked in their pristine dinner jackets and lavish gowns of satin, rayon and ivory silk were open-mouthed in anticipation, and the silence was broken only by the scurrying of footsteps outside the doors – for, though the ballroom seemed frozen in time, life still went on inside the Buckingham Hotel. Guests still came and went, lovers still fought and made love in the hotel's magnificent suites, the generators still turned, the kitchens still buzzed, old Maynard Charles – the hotel director himself – still paced the Buckingham's opulent halls, waiting for the moment when he might be needed. Yet, once the ballroom doors were closed, the Grand was a world apart from the rest. The spell of silence held – until, finally, the Archie Adams Band began to play. Only then was the spell broken, and a completely different kind of magic woven in its place. The magic of music. The magic of dance.

Listen . . .

Raymond de Guise, lead demonstration dancer of the Buckingham Hotel, had been patiently watching the bandleader, waiting for the first note to strike. Archie Adams, a distinguished-looking man in his late fifties, with his bow tie and immaculate hair, had been playing in orchestras for all of his life and had picked up a thing or two about dramatic entrances. His orchestra was making one now. The first notes of 'A Californian Serenade' echoed across the ballroom, the trombones stabbing out the melody and bringing the guests to attention. Archie Adams himself led them on the ballroom's grand piano, his twenty-strong orchestra made up of trumpets, trombones, saxophones, violins and even a double bass, with a single percussionist keeping the beat. Behind the double doors that led to their dressing rooms, the hotel dancers waited. Then, on Raymond's cue, the doors flew open and they whirled, together, out onto the floor.

Raymond, a man of imposing stature that belied his elegance on the dance floor, was the first through. His dinner jacket was midnight blue, his collar high and starched so that his black curls, which were rebellious and refused to be tamed by even the strongest pomade, came close to touching the fabric. Hand in hand with his partner Hélène – resplendent in her sea-green gown, hand-stitched with a million tiny pearls like scattered stars – he reached the centre of the dance floor and together they turned to welcome the rest of the company.

'Shall we?' he whispered, as he did before every routine.

Hélène, who was always ready, smiled in return. 'We shall, Raymond. Let's show them how it's done . . .'

As 'A Californian Serenade' reached its climactic finale, they fanned out among the guests, nodding heads and clasping hands. Out of the corner of his eye, Raymond saw Hélène taking the hand of a regular guest at the Buckingham – a gentleman with slick black hair; Hélène said he came to London from his native California to make movies, and every time he graced the Buckingham he requested her hand on the dance floor. He was not, Raymond knew, the only one. Hélène oozed elegance; she was a beauty so classical that, in a different age, sculptors would have lined up to recreate her in marble and bronze. As her partner took her in hold, Hélène flashed a smile at Raymond; this man would be no match for her on the dance floor, few were, but she would dance with him all the same.

The dance floor was already filling up, but Raymond had not yet met his own partner for the evening. As the Archie Adams Band struck up a Viennese waltz, he stood with his hands folded at the edge of the dance floor, awaiting his turn. Moments later, a finger tapped him on the shoulder. He glided around to see a familiar face peering back up.

'Looks like you may have been let down, Mr de Guise.'

The girl in front of him – because, at scarcely eighteen years of age, a girl she was – had rich auburn hair, cut short as a boy's to spite her father, and spoke with the unmistakable accent of her native New York. Her green eyes had something almost feline about them, and she had evidently spent the afternoon in the hotel cocktail lounge, for her breath smelt sweet, of exotic pineapple and rum. Her ball gown set her apart from even the wealthiest patrons of the Grand Ballroom tonight. Wherever Raymond looked there were the most magnificent gowns, but this girl's simply screamed ostentation. The golden satin silk was textured, the capelet around her shoulders trimmed with feathers, the brooch on her belt a mountain of pearls that glittered as if set with diamonds; perhaps it was . . .

'I'm taken, Miss Edgerton. If you're looking for a partner, you'll find suitors aplenty everywhere you care to look.'

'You made me a promise. Don't you think you should keep it?'

'I will. One day, my dear, I'll show you the quickstep, or the foxtrot. I'll have you waltzing around the Grand . . . but tonight I'm at the beck and call of our guests.'

'Your guests, Mr de Guise,' she corrected him. 'The way I see it, if your partner is not here, then . . .'

Raymond was about to resist further when another finger tapped him on the shoulder and, stepping back, he saw his partner for the evening. At seventy years old she was more than twice Raymond's age, diminutive but elegant in a Madeleine Vionnet gown that flared gracefully to the floor.

Raymond heard Miss Vivienne Edgerton saying his name, heard her repeat it – and after that heard nothing as, disgruntled, she retreated to her table and, with a click of her fingers, summoned a waiter in white and gold brocade.

'Mr . . . *de Guise*?' the lady ventured. 'Raymond?'

'Yes,' he replied, smoothly, finding his voice at last. 'Mrs . . . Adelman, I presume. Lovely to make your acquaintance.'

Mrs Adelman held out a hand, as wrinkled as a glove but adorned with an emerald ring that glittered in the light of the Grand's chandeliers.

Raymond delivered her one of his most practised smiles. 'Shall we?'

As he swept her into hold, Mrs Adelman looked back and saw the eyes of the auburn-haired girl piercing her from the side of the ballroom. 'That girl, is she . . . ?'

'Oh,' said Raymond, trying not to be distracted as he brought Mrs Adelman close and began turning into the waltz, 'nothing of the sort, Mrs Adelman. The young lady has been staying in the hotel for the summer. Vivienne *Edgerton*. You know the name?'

'*The* Edgertons?'

'The same,' said Raymond. 'She has requested that I teach her to dance and . . . well, I wouldn't want to get on the wrong side of her father, our benefactor and lord . . .'

'Can anyone dance, Mr de Guise?'

'Anyone who desires it.'

Soon, Raymond had given himself to the dance – and Mrs Adelman, more reluctantly, perhaps fearful that she might make a fool of herself in this most elegant of ballrooms, had done the same. Mrs Adelman must have danced before, because soon her feet were remembering the steps and Raymond loosened the way he was holding her, no longer directing her every movement. The music swayed, the chandeliers above shimmered so that, in moments, the ballroom seemed to be the surface of the ocean itself, ripples of light spreading all around. When the music stopped, the dancers seemed to carry on, filling the brief interludes between music with movements of their own. More than once, Raymond caught Hélène's eye across the floor as her gentleman clasped her too tightly and awkwardly. With a single arched eyebrow, Hélène could tell Raymond everything: the man's hand was too high and too tight, he held her like a mannequin in some expensive Knightsbridge boutique – afraid to drop her, determined to direct her every move, as if it was not Hélène Marchmont who had been crowned Queen of the Ballroom at the Royal Albert Hall two seasons past. But Hélène didn't mind. As they twirled past each other, Raymond even saw the hint of a smile in the corner of her lips. A certain sort of man, she seemed to be saying, just needed . . . indulging. They needed to feel as if they were masters of the dancing arts. Hélène, Raymond knew, loved the evenings with the guests – giving them a glimpse of her and Raymond's world. *She didn't mind if they couldn't dance; just that they loved to dance.* Yet, Hélène lived for the demonstrations they put on each day, when, together with Raymond, they could show the world their talent.

Raymond danced on. At least Mrs Adelman was not trying to prove anything to him. She had no need to. She was here for the thrill of the ballroom itself.

As the hours ticked by, the Grand Ballroom became more crowded still. A little champagne always brought more guests to the dance floor, but so too did the music itself. Somehow, it seemed to infect everyone who heard it with a desire to move . . .

Mrs Adelman rose up on her tiptoes and put her lips to Raymond's ear.

'She's still watching you, you know.'

Raymond furrowed his brows.

'That girl. Your Edgerton girl. Have yourself an admirer, do you, Raymond de Guise?'

Raymond chuckled softly. 'With these looks?' he joked. 'More than one, I shouldn't wonder . . . It is, after all, part of the job . . .'

'Part of your job to let them fall in love with you?'

The music reached a climax, an explosion of trombone and tenor horn.

'Perhaps we might find somewhere a little more private? To . . . talk,' Mrs Adelman said carefully.

Talk, thought Raymond. Mrs Adelman's hand was on his arm. Yes, it would not be the first time one of the ballroom's patrons had asked him to . . . talk. The hotel director almost demanded it: 'Whatever our patrons require, Mr de Guise, you are here to provide.' Perhaps it was the way he held them as they danced, or perhaps it was the way he worked to make them feel that, no matter what else was going on in their lives, in the Grand they could be themselves, just follow the rhythms of their bodies, but people felt . . . safe with Raymond de Guise. He had to admit that he liked that feeling.

'I'm staying in the Trafalgar Suite. It would be a little more private. Shall we?'

The music had died away. Archie Adams was up on his feet, ushering his orchestra off for their well-earned refreshments. In the quiet that followed, Raymond risked a glance over his shoulder. The unblinking eyes of Vivienne Edgerton were still on him. He was not sure whether they were accusing or pleading or worse, but perhaps it would not be a bad thing to escape the ballroom, if only for a time.

He reached out and took Mrs Adelman's hand.

Raymond tried not to catch the eye of Mr Simenon, the slippery head concierge, as he and Mrs Adelman strode, arm in arm, through the doors of the ballroom, past the grill room and cocktail lounge and up into the hotel's lobby – where its celebrated bronze doors stood open to the balmy scents of Mayfair after dark. He did not answer when one of the hotel pages called out his name, nor break his stride when Maynard Charles himself appeared at the reception desk, his spectacles perched haphazardly on his nose as he scrutinised the day reports in preparation for the night manager's arrival. Perhaps they thought less of him, thinking him little better than those 'table dancers' who haunted the booths of the hotel's Candlelight Club, seeking a wealthy patron with whom they might spend the night for a fee. *Let them think what they want*, he thought. *My business is my own.* Not a word was spoken, even as he accompanied Mrs Adelman to the ornate gold cage of the guest lift and she instructed the attendant to take them to the third floor, where her suite awaited.

'Are you staying here long, Mrs Adelman?' he ventured, as they walked together along the burgundy hall.

'Oh,' Mrs Adelman replied, 'it's a one-night thing, Raymond. I'll be gone in the morning.'

A one-night thing, thought Raymond. Yes, he had heard this story before as well: a wealthy dowager, just flitting through, looking for somebody to . . . talk with, for the night.

The Trafalgar Suite. It had been some time since Raymond last ventured in here. Inside, Mrs Adelman took a perch at the end of the great four-poster bed. She had spared no expenses tonight. The room was one of the Buckingham's finest, with a rolling view over Berkeley Square and the great gothic spires of the Church of the Immaculate Conception. Beside an ornate French armoire sat a glass-topped table, upon which a single orchid was presented – and, beside that orchid, a perfect statue of a turtle, cast in ivory and mother-of-pearl. Room service had obviously already been summoned, for a silver bucket was filled with ice and, rising from it, was a bottle of the Buckingham's finest champagne. Mrs Adelman gestured for Raymond and, with his heart beating fast, Raymond popped the cork and poured two glasses. A Moët et Chandon, 1921 vintage.

'Mrs Adelman,' he began, 'I see you are a lady of means.'

'Oh, *means*,' she said, with a wry grin. 'Yes, you're a gentleman dancer, all right. You have the airs and expressions. I suppose you've danced with royalty. There are enough kings and queens and continentals said to stay in the Buckingham Hotel. I can quite imagine you hobnobbing with the gentry, Mr *de*

Guise. But, no, consider this an old lady's way of spending her late husband's inheritance. I can't take it with me, so I'm enjoying myself while I can.' She hesitated. 'You seem a little nervous, Raymond?'

It had been many years since Raymond de Guise was last nervous, even when taking to the dance floor in front of the world's finest ballroom dancers at the Hammersmith Palais the previous season, but yes, he had to admit, he was nervous tonight. There had been patrons like Mrs Adelman before, ladies of an older generation, who came to dance in the ballroom and wanted a little *more* of Raymond's time. Perhaps they were widowed. Perhaps they had been cast off by their philandering husbands, and given an allowance which they sought to fritter away in the ballrooms and drawing-room dances of Mayfair and beyond. Mostly what they wanted was a good-looking younger man from whose arm they could hang, and perhaps speak a little about the gilded Mayfair world. But sometimes – well, sometimes they wanted more.

Raymond caught a fleeting glance of himself in the mirror hanging over the dresser. Thirty years old, but there were still those who would mistake him for twenty. It was only when he laughed that the creases showed about his eyes, revealing his true age. He had curly black hair that was a constant battle to sculpt in time for the afternoon demonstration dances, and eyes that sloped ever so slightly downwards, giving him what a former lover had once called an 'elegantly sad air'. The prominent cheekbones had been inherited from his father, God rest his soul, and his nose had been broken and reset so many times, thanks to the attentions of an unruly brother and events in his previous life, that it made his face appear somewhat crooked. He could see Mrs Adelman appraising him from beyond his reflection.

'Mrs Adelman, I really must . . .' Something stuck in his throat. 'I really must . . . ask . . . why am I here?'

The question hung in the air between them, threatening, as if it shouldn't have been said. He hoped, above all else, that she had not brought him here to proposition him. She would not have been the first – and, if she did, she would not be the first to be told, in the kindest possible terms, that Raymond de Guise was a gentleman, not a gigolo; that, though they might joke about it in the kitchens and the housekeeping lounge, the dancers in the Buckingham Hotel were not the kind to slip out of the ballroom with a beautiful guest and wake beside her the following morning. Mrs Adelman patted the bed beside her and Raymond felt compelled to sit.

Then she looked into his eyes.

'Your mother sent me.'

Of all the things she might have said, this was the least expected and it startled him.

'My . . . mother?'

Raymond's mouth felt suddenly dry. Every other thought that had been in his head was obliterated. An image of his mother hovered into view, and suddenly he felt a thousand miles away from the sights and sounds of the Buckingham Hotel.

'How long has it been, Raymond? Two years?'

A little stab of guilt caught Raymond de Guise in the breast. 'Three,' he whispered, almost contritely.

'Three years, and you her firstborn son.' She said it not with admonishment, but with regret. 'I met her, of course, in the years since you went away. Well, they were hard times for your mother . . . and I know what it's like to lose a son. Mine died at Passchendaele, but how bittersweet to lose your son and yet know he's still out there, and never comes home . . .'

Raymond was not ordinarily unsure of himself, but now he stuttered, 'Mrs Adelman, let me change my question. Why . . . why are *you* here?'

Mrs Adelman lifted a hand and cupped Raymond's own. Though he was anxious, he did not flinch or resist. 'She didn't think you'd listen if she came herself. So, when we got to talking about this runaway son of hers, we hit upon a novel solution: we thought we could kill two birds with one stone. I could take a final turn around the Buckingham Hotel – my husband used to adore this place – and, while I was here, I could ferry a message to her absent son . . .'

'A message?' whispered Raymond.

'It's your brother,' Mrs Adelman said. 'Raymond, he's coming home.'

Chapter Two

'THIS IS IT, YOUNG LADY. Euston station. You'd better get yourself ready. Unless, that is, you *want* to go back the way you came?'

Nancy Nettleton stirred at the rough touch of the train guard shepherding everybody off the train. She had not realised that she'd fallen asleep. She'd had her nose in her *Reader's Digest* magazine and, the last thing she remembered, they were still somewhere in the Derbyshire hills and it was four hours until London. Now she looked through the window and saw the station concourse bustling as travellers stepped out into the hubbub.

'Got someone to meet you, have you, love?'

Nancy's reflection was staring back at her from the fogged window glass. She had thought she looked so smart in her checked overcoat and knitted cap, forest green and embroidered with a single silver star in honour of her mother. Perhaps it was only the hours she'd been asleep, but what London elegance she'd imagined had simply disappeared. The pin in her hair had fallen out, her curls fell, unruly, around her face, and she could even see the indentations the fabric of the seat had made upon her cheek as she slept.

'Not me,' she said. 'I'm here alone.'

The train guard gave her a look that said: *you'll be eaten alive*.

'Perhaps you can point me to the powder room? I have an appointment to keep. I'd like to look . . .' She fumbled for the right word. 'Presentable.'

'You're asking the wrong man there. You'll have to look out on the concourse. Can I help you with that?'

Nancy had begun wrestling with her suitcase. Along with the clutch bag at her side, it contained everything she owned in the world. 'I'm quite all right,' she replied primly, and the train guard was still staring as, three attempts later, she forced it through the doors. He was still staring when, at the end of the concourse, Nancy looked over her shoulder. Her leg was aching, as it had done ever since she was small, but suddenly the awkward way that she limped – so imperceptible, really, such a *tiny thing* – seemed the most obvious thing in the world. But Nancy Nettleton held her head high and heaved her case after her all the same.

She had a Chinese Red lipstick just like Claudette Colbert was said to have worn in *It Happened One Night*, and she'd been saving it for an occasion just like this. First impressions, she had been told, counted for *everything*. She'd put it on, and then she'd be ready.

London. She had been preparing herself for seven months, and now the city – noisy and smoky, full of more movement and life than she had ever known – seemed to dwarf her as she fought her way to the Underground station. If only her father could see her now! Of course, he had had little love for people from the big city. People didn't, when they had lived their entire lives in the same Lancashire town where she was born, surrounded by the same hills and forests and mountain tarns. But London was another world.

Nancy had spent her life imagining its palaces, wondering what it might be like to catch a glimpse of King Edward riding in procession along the Mall, or to witness the excited crowds pouring out of a royal wedding at Westminster Abbey. Yet her first impressions of the city were noise and the fug of sweat and coal dust.

She held the letter carefully. *Nancy Nettleton*, it began. *We are pleased to confirm your appointment to the role of chambermaid at the Buckingham Hotel, Berkeley Square, London, to commence on the first day of August. Immediately upon your arrival . . .*

She had read the letter a hundred times. It was the product of seven months' diligent work – all of those letters of enquiry sent from her cottage home, the dismissive ones she'd received in reply, the correspondence she'd entered into with potential employers that then came to naught, the hours she'd spent canvassing for referees, somebody, *anybody*, who might give her a chance. And all of that done while also putting her late father's affairs in order, making sure her younger brother could finally stand on his own two feet, confronting the solicitor from Morecambe Bay who'd decided, without instruction, that the taxes due on what little her father had left behind demanded further commissions – and all because, as a woman, Nancy supposedly needed extra help in calculating the figures, in managing the accounts. As if she hadn't been looking after the household finances since she was a girl. As if a man could do better, just because he insisted on people calling him *sir*.

She looked up. All of these people crammed around her on the Underground carriage had lives of their own. Some were bankers and some were clerks. Some were, no doubt, chambermaids-in-waiting just like her. Some might be runaway princes, or gentlemen playing at being paupers . . .

A man was staring at her from across the carriage. His face was the colour of pond water, his beard as entangled as briars, and in his bloodshot eyes was a look of quiet desperation. Yes, London was a city for kings and queens, but it was a city for beggars as well, she thought sadly. She pictured the Buckingham Hotel and, kneading some life back into her tired leg, wondered what she might find.

The Buckingham was every bit as opulent as she'd imagined. Where Nancy came from, the local hotel was two rooms above the village inn, or lodgings with old Mrs Gable – who took in miners from out of town, kept them six to a room and fed them on porridge oats at dawn and mutton stew after dark. By contrast, the Buckingham Hotel rose, seven storeys and more, above the resplendent green of Berkeley Square. Its gleaming white facade and the miniature colonnade where hansom carriages and taxicabs awaited each night made it stand out, even on a square where every townhouse was worth as much as every building in Nancy's entire village combined. Marble steps led to the hotel's striking bronze doors, a gold-plated rail sweeping up towards them. The man who attended the door wore a coat of long black velvet, despite the summer warmth, and a top hat that stood out like a shadow against the hotel's bleached brick. Up above, an enormous copper crown stood between the hotel's pavilion roofs, proclaiming it royal by association.

As Nancy watched, a taxicab wheeled around, stopped in front of the hotel and deposited a gentleman with his entourage onto the steps. Moments later, the hotel disgorged concierges and pages to ferry the gentleman's cases inside, while a short, round man that Nancy took for the hotel director came out to welcome the guest with a slight, yet noticeable, bow.

She had been staring too long. It was already creeping towards midday. She was due to meet with Mrs Moffatt, the head of housekeeping, at twelve on the dot. Punctuality mattered.

She steadied herself and set off across the square. This was what she had come here for. Why, then, did she feel such a sudden plunging sensation as she approached the doors?

Pull yourself together, Nancy Nettleton. You're made of sterner stuff than this!

She had not yet reached the bottom of the steps when the doorman barked out in an accent that seemed so unfamiliar, 'Can I help you, miss?'

She stopped dead, aware of how *insignificant* she seemed. The suitcase she was carrying was battered and worn around the edges. It had belonged to her grandfather, who'd bought it at auction when one of his neighbouring villagers died. Even her overcoat, which she'd thought so splendid, seemed, suddenly, to have sprouted holes, the areas where it had been stitched up standing out starkly. Why had she used mismatched thread?

'I'm to . . . start work,' she began. *What's got into you, Nancy? You've never stuttered before!* 'Here, I have my letter . . .'

The doorman's face darkened, so that she thought he was about to let loose a foul tirade – but then he marched down the steps to meet her and whispered, 'You'll have to find the staff entrance, down on Michaelmas Mews. Follow it round, you'll find it easily enough. Want to make a good first impression, don't you? Then don't let Mr Simenon or Mr Charles see you coming through the front doors – least of all, not dressed like that. Lord, they're running around in there like the world's about to end. And all because of some German dignitaries they've got coming in. You'd think the King himself was here for afternoon tea – but no, he's off with that Mrs Simpson of his. Time was he crossed this threshold almost every month. But now . . .'

Nancy stared at him, dumbstruck.

'Well, off with you, then! And make sure you look 'em in the eye when you meet 'em. First impressions count.'

As Nancy took off towards the mews entrance, she glanced again at her wristwatch. Two minutes to midday and counting.

Nancy Nettleton was not usually of a nervous disposition. You did not grow up, the only girl your age in a mining village, without learning to overcome nerves. Even when she was a girl Nancy had given short shrift to the boys who harangued her. She could skim stones and climb trees like the best of them. But running rings around a few miners' sons was one thing. Waiting here in a back corridor of the Buckingham Hotel, moments away from meeting the woman who would be her mentor and supervisor for the next twelve months, was quite another.

One of the hotel pages had brought her here. Along the way, he hadn't stopped nattering on in his lilting Irish brogue – and Nancy had barely been able to make out one word in ten. Now she waited in a hall lined with wainscot panelling, outside a door that read HOUSEKEEPING. Occasionally, she could hear footsteps echoing along the halls around her. One of the concierges strode past the apex of the corridor, peered down towards her, and then strode on, his heels clicking as he went.

Time seemed to have slowed to a halt. Her stomach grumbled and, with relief, she remembered the sandwich and Eccles cake she had wrapped in paper at the bottom of her clutch bag. She had been keeping them for the train – but perhaps it would settle her nerves, if only a little, to take a nibble from them now . . .

She was taking her first bite, her body grateful for the buttery, sugary goodness, when she heard footsteps again. A tall, thin reed of a man was marching purposefully towards her, his grey plaid suit rustling. He had a grave of a face: dark eyes set deep in their sockets, high, pronounced cheekbones and an angular jaw. His eyes, mean and serpentine, narrowed as he approached.

'Young lady, have you no decorum?'

'I'm . . . sorry,' Nancy stuttered. A particularly truculent currant had worked its way into her teeth, gluing them together.

'You might not see guests around you now, madam, but this is not a prohibited area. What if one of our patrons was to see you, flakes of pastry around your face and . . . Really, this is most unsatisfactory – unsatisfactory in the *extreme*! You're—'

A voice echoed along the hallway, cutting him off. 'I'll take it from here, Mr Simenon.'

The man in grey spun on his heel, revealing a lady of not insignificant size bustling along the hall. As she approached, Nancy saw a doughy face framed in white curls. The lady approaching was wearing a house dress of navy blue, with its sleeves rolled up to reveal brawny forearms.

'Mr Simenon,' the newcomer called out, 'to what do we owe the pleasure?'

'This young lady is in breach of staff regulations—'

Barely breaking her stride as she bustled past to reach the office door, Mrs Moffatt remarked, 'Then not a rule has been broken, Mr Simenon. This young lady may be about to join the ranks of this fine establishment, but she isn't a member of staff until I have her signature on my papers. And since those papers are through *that* door –' She lifted a finger to point – 'she can eat as many – what are they, Eccles cakes? – as she wants. Miss Nettleton, do you want to come through? We'll have you sorted in a trice.'

Nancy had no time to reply before Mrs Moffatt took a ring of keys from her house dress, unlocked the HOUSEKEEPING door and stepped through. Mr Simenon's serpentine eyes were still on Nancy as she followed.

Here was a compact room with a desk, a small mahogany cabinet and two velveteen armchairs arranged around a coffee table, on which stood a vase of freshly cut peonies. There was no natural light in here, so Mrs Moffatt turned a dial and the electric lamp dangling from the ceiling hummed into being. To Nancy, whose family home had been lit by paraffin lamps, the light was simply dazzling.

'I've begun on the wrong foot, haven't I, Mrs Moffatt?'

'Think nothing of it. I'm afraid one of the things you'll discover, Miss Nettleton, is that the concierges believe the Buckingham would be little but a crater in the ground if it weren't for them. Mr Simenon's the head of them and, unluckily for you, the worst. If he thought a guest was offended by the blue of his eyes, he'd pluck them out and send them out to be coloured.' Mrs Moffatt must have seen the way Nancy's jaw dropped open, because she threw her head back and laughed. Finding her breath, Nancy dared to smile too.

'Here,' Mrs Moffat said, indicating a clipboard of papers, 'you'll find everything precisely as it says in your letter. Six pounds and two crowns a month, board included. You'll begin on mornings and cycle through until late. I'm afraid you're for Saturdays as well. We've been in need of a Saturday girl for some time. We have eight housekeepers here at the Buckingham. I'm head of those housekeepers, and you'll be with me for your first month. Stay by my side, do exactly as requested, and we'll be the firmest of friends. And at least that way, I can keep Mr Simenon at bay . . .'

Nancy took an inkpot and pen and, mindful that she did not blot the paper, spelled out her name as neatly as she could.

'There.' Mrs Moffatt beamed. 'Now you're *mine* . . . Let's show you to your room, shall we?'

Moments later Mrs Moffatt was leading Nancy onward, pointing out the halls that led to the cocktail lounge, the grill room and the Queen Mary, the first of the Buckingham's six exquisite dining rooms.

As they walked, Nancy saw Mrs Moffatt's eyes dart down to her leg. It was aching more than usual, but that was not unexpected; she had been cramped up on the train for what seemed a lifetime. 'It's a . . . childhood thing, Mrs Moffatt. It won't stop me performing my duties. It hasn't slowed me down yet.'

To Mrs Moffatt, this seemed explanation enough. 'We demand perfection for our guests, Nancy, but Lord knows, none of us are perfect.'

Onward they walked in silence. After a time, Nancy found enough courage to ask, 'Mrs Moffatt, is it true . . . you have royalty to stay? The doorman said that the King himself . . .'

'The good King Edward is a friend of the Buckingham Hotel,' Mrs Moffatt said darkly. 'Something in the Buckingham appealed to the young prince and his associates. But don't go thinking you'll bump into him, young miss. He has matters of state to attend to and, well, that's the business of kings and queens, isn't it, and not for the likes of us.' Mrs Moffatt paused. 'It's true that we'll have royalty here, Nancy. If you're still with us by New Year

– and, Lord willing, I hope you will be – you'll find His Majesty himself here to celebrate with us in our ballroom. Mr Charles is organising a Masquerade Ball – this, of course, being the King's personal request.'

A Masquerade Ball, thought Nancy in awe. The very thought of it filled her with magic. *New Years back home are all about the bonfire . . .*

Mrs Moffatt was still talking. 'Always remember that all of our guests should be treated as if they were royalty . . . don't go thinking you'll be changing the sheets of the high and mighty. We have the King's cousins from Norway staying with us for New Year, but the suites reserved for royalty are attended to by our gentlewoman housekeepers.' She paused. 'That's the way of things here. Some of our more highly prized guests are used to being catered to by ladies of a certain . . . breeding, shall we say. I don't hold with it myself, but there's one thing I want you to understand: when you step through the Buckingham door, Miss Nettleton, you are not from the country any more. You're not from London and you're not from Lancashire. You're not a Scot or a Celt, an Irish woman or a Cornish woman. You're not city or country. You are of the Buckingham. One of us. And that, as far as we who work in the hotel are concerned, is where it ends.'

They had reached the hotel lobby and, for the first time, Nancy saw its opulence first hand. The floor was a chequerboard of black and red squares. The walls were panelled in dark wood with swirling grain and, on a plinth in the heart of the hall, an obelisk of blue and red glass, the donation of some continental artist, was being ogled by a lady guest dressed in fine brown fur. Doors and hallways led in many directions. The golden lift cages were manned by attendants in tall peaked caps, and a porter in blue and gold wheeled past, dragging behind him a trailer full of tortoiseshell cases and black leather bags.

At the back of the reception hall, between two staircases which crossed each other as they rose to the garlanded balconies above, a corridor sloped down, through columns and arches, to two great wooden doors. Above the doors, the legendary 'Grand Ballroom' was spelled out in italicised copper letters. Perhaps she was mistaken, but as Mrs Moffatt led her towards the service lifts Nancy fancied she could hear the sound of a saxophone. It occurred to her how strange it was to hear the instrument without the crackle of the old gramophone her father used to play.

'What's . . . what's down there, Mrs Moffatt?'

The doors at the corridor's end opened up and two guests trotted through. For a fleeting moment, she caught sight of a great cavernous ballroom, lit by sparkling chandeliers. The sound of trumpets and trombones flurried up and, as the doors swung shut, Nancy saw – for the barest moment – two figures turning across the dance floor in long, flowing steps. From where she stood, they seemed to be floating on air.

'That, Miss Nettleton, is the Grand Ballroom. *Pride* of the Buckingham. The demonstration dances are in full flow this afternoon, and every afternoon, for our guests. Don't worry,' she went on, with a wry smile, 'you'll get to experience its glory soon enough. Those chandeliers are due for a thorough clean. It takes a week to haul them down, spruce them up, and have them rehung.'

All through the rest of the day, and long into the night that followed, Nancy heard the music of the saxophone, and saw those two dancers floating across the ballroom, as if nothing else mattered in the world.

Chapter Three

THERE WASN'T A DEPARTMENT in the Buckingham Hotel that didn't believe that, were it not for them, the hotel itself would crumble. Ask the restaurateurs, the concierges, the chief engineer, the bookkeeper, the garage attendants, any one of the hundred pages who scurried through the hotel halls. Even the members of the Archie Adams Band, who were polishing their instruments in the lull before the afternoon demonstration dances began, believed the same. 'We're the heart and soul,' Archie Adams told his orchestra. 'What's a hotel, if it doesn't have a heart? Nothing more than bricks and mortar . . .'

Hélène Marchmont had heard some of the less experienced dancers saying the same thing. It was true that the advent of dancers in the hotel had changed the Buckingham's fortunes – but so too had the wealth of Lord Edgerton, who became majority shareholder and Director of the Board in the same month the Grand Ballroom first opened its doors (so Hélène did not think it wise to draw too many conclusions). Besides, as principal female dancer of the ballroom, it was unbecoming of her to make comment. Right now, with the time for the demonstration dances approaching, she was on her knees in the dressing rooms trying to stop Sofía LaPegna's tears making rivers of mascara down her powdered face. The poor girl was beginning to look like a circus clown, and the dances were only an hour away.

'I'm sorry, Miss Marchmont. You must think me a frightful—'

'I'll hear nothing more,' Hélène said, standing back. 'Sofía, you've every right to be upset, but . . .'

Hélène was a tall woman, a favourite among the hotel's more rarefied guests. She had been tall at thirteen and now, approaching thirty, she stood inches above the rest of the dancers in the troupe. Her striking gold hair was now cut in a fashionable bob to fit beneath her cloche hat, but all that did was accentuate her extraordinary cheekbones and the vivid blues of her eyes. Those eyes had once captured the heart of a photographer, who put her in the pages of *Esquire* and even *Harper's Bazaar*; it was those eyes that had helped to catapult her to the stage and keep her there.

Sofía was starting to calm down. Some of the other girls were squabbling around, helping each other into their gowns or relaxing with the help of the clove cigarettes that Billy Brogan, rising star among the hotel pages, brought from a place in Chinatown. The air in the dressing room was a fug of clove smoke and sweet perfumes: the heady scent of Guerlain's Shalimar, the tropical notes of Je Reviens, all of them provided by a boutique perfumery in one of the Regent Street arcades.

'I'll be fine, Miss Marchmont. I can still dance.'

Hélène admired Sofía's resilience. The fact that English was not her native language, and that she still spoke with the fieriness of San Sebastián, from where she came, made her seem more defiant still. 'Nobody's questioning that, Sofía.'

'It's only . . . I know my brother. It is guns with him. Guns, guns, guns, ever since we were children. Sometimes, all a man needs is an excuse, and . . .'

'San Sebastián is a world away from Madrid. He could be across the border and into France by now.'

'Across the border! Our father would turn in his grave. No, Miss Marchmont, he went south two weeks ago. I am certain of that.' This time Sofía managed to conquer her tears. Hélène saw them welling in her eyes and knelt again, to dab them away with the corner of her chemise.

Two weeks had already passed and what they were calling the Spanish Emergency showed no signs of coming to a close. The BBC had begun to use the word 'war', and the less salubrious news sheets had been using it since the start. Sofía had written immediately to her mother, but as yet there had been no reply. News of atrocity spread so much faster than missives of love. The world would send correspondents to watch the killing, but not to help families.

There was a knock at the dressing room door and Billy Brogan appeared. Brogan was seventeen years old and seemed to have been born in the Buckingham Hotel itself, so well did he know its nooks and crannies. In the last year Hélène had watched him transform from boy to man – but he still kept some of his impishness of old. He had the face of a cherub, even though he now devotedly cultivated the few whiskers he could grow, and even put pomade in his hair (for the benefit, he insisted, of the hotel's finest guests). Billy whistled for her and, leaving Sofía to calm herself, Hélène joined him at the door.

'It's Mr Charles,' Billy said, his voice still rolling with the Dublin brogue, even though Billy had not been back since he was a child. 'He requests the honour of your company.'

Oh he does, does he? She was doing her best to contain her weariness, but the longer she danced at the Buckingham, the more she grew tired of the factions and politicking that went on in the hotel halls. She had come here to dance and, for a time, that had sustained her. Dancing was her life. But now? Now dancing seemed the least of it. *Now there's girls to play mother to, schedules to keep, a hundred different men to keep happy, and all without ever admitting what I really want. When I'm on the ballroom floor, that's when I'm alive. But when I'm not . . .*

Hélène looked back at her girls. Elisabeth was with Sofía and the room was a chaos of ball gowns and cases and missing shoes, but no matter what they looked like now, Hélène knew they would be striding into the ballroom without a hair out of place when the clocks tolled two. She herself would be wearing a floor-length cotton organdie gown with huge frilled sleeves – a perfect imitation of the one Joan Crawford had worn in *Letty Lynton*.

Hélène marched along the hall, up and away from the ballroom as Billy scurried in her wake. 'Billy,' Hélène said when they reached the hotel director's door. 'Is our honoured guest still in the Grand Colonial Suite? You know the man I mean. The Spaniard . . .'

Billy nodded. He was here to star in a picture show they were shooting at the old Heatherdon Hall. He'd brought his leading lady to dine at La Petite Salle, the Buckingham's finest French restaurant (Billy knew she'd stayed the night as well, even though she was not on the hotel manifest).

'Don't suppose he'll be going back to Spain now, will he, miss?'

Hélène tensed. 'He's not to go near Sofía tonight. A glass of champagne and he'll want to dance with her. Do what you can, won't you? A nice little distraction, here and there. Get Sofía partnered up with some other guest for the evening.'

Billy gave Hélène his most ostentatious bow – 'Your wish is my command!' – and then, readying herself for yet another battle, Hélène knocked sharply on the director's door.

Maynard Charles was not what you would call an *insignificant* man – but he did pride himself on being invisible. He knew the names of every guest of note at the Buckingham Hotel. He made it a matter of honour that he could recite them all – and, because the Buckingham comprised two hundred bedrooms and twenty-six suites, this was certainly a Herculean task. And yet very few of those guests would have paid him a second glance had they passed him in the reception hall, or sat beside him in the cocktail lounge as they deliberated over their long Martinis. Invisibility, Maynard Charles had long ago decided, was advantageous.

He was sitting in his office, poring over the manager's report from the night before, when the knock came at the door. The guest in 311, a wealthy Frenchman, had reported a silver pocket watch missing from his bedside table – and though this was not, in itself, an unusual occurrence, it was vexing him today. Monsieur Fortier was worth so much in future profits to the hotel that the situation had to be carefully stage-managed. Things went missing all the time. Only rarely was it theft. And M. Fortier had enjoyed so much of the hotel's finest cognac the night before that Maynard was of the opinion he would later discover his silver pocket watch in the cuff of his trousers, or – more likely yet – the handbag of whomever had shared his bed. Maynard would have to ask Billy Brogan to find out exactly who that was. Even so, it was necessary that this was delicately handled. As a matter of course, he would summon the chambermaids to a conference and ask them to commit to a search of their rooms. Then, when he found nothing, he would make restitution from the hotel's emergency fund to M. Fortier, tell him that the matter had been privately handled, and secure his silence with a complimentary dinner in whichever of the Buckingham's restaurants took his particular fancy. These were the matters in which a hotel director spent his days.

The knocking at the door became more insistent. Maynard Charles called out, 'Enter.'

Hélène Marchmont slipped quietly through the door. Maynard could see that she was flustered; the dancers of the Buckingham Hotel took nothing more seriously than their daily demonstrations. Quite rightly so. Maynard Charles had not been confident that opening a ballroom was the right thing to do when one of the board first suggested it, but the hotel director's job is not to protest at the wishes of the board; it is only to make sure that whatever they desire becomes a resounding success. And so, Maynard Charles had set to work. Reasoning that he was not himself a dancing man – he had been born with two left feet and, regardless, had never been intoxicated by music in the way so many young people were – he had done the only thing he knew of that would guarantee success. He had *spent*. The board had not needed convincing – they were the kind of fellows who understood that the only way to fight your way out of a financial morass of the kind the Buckingham had faced after the Wall Street Crash was to spend. And so the Grand Ballroom had arisen in the place where an ill-attended restaurant used to be. Dancers had been hired from rival establishments, and the Buckingham became the place to be seen. And at least it did not mean stooping as low as the dreadful cabarets that the lesser London hotels had started to open. The dancers and the Archie

Adams Band may cost the Buckingham eleven hundred pounds each month of the year, but what they brought in return was incalculable. Even a man of numbers like Maynard Charles did not attempt to put a value on elegance and class.

'Mr Charles, I was told you needed me.'

'Yes, Miss Marchmont. If, perhaps, you would sit.'

Hélène was reluctant. 'The band is due to begin playing.'

Maynard fixed her with one of his quelling looks. 'This won't take a moment.'

Hélène did as she was told. It was cold in Mr Charles's office – which, as she understood it, was exactly the way he liked it. Opulence for the guests did not, she was often reminded, have to extend as far as those who ran the hotel.

Maynard Charles drew a ledger book from one of the drawers beneath his desk, paged through it until he found the right section, and turned it around for Hélène to see. 'I understand you've reserved the weekend of the fifteenth. Is that correct?'

'I have . . . *family* plans,' she said, stressing the word family as if it were a shameful thing.

'I'm sensitive to my staff, Miss Marchmont. But, plans are written and rewritten. Graf and Gräfin Schecht, the Hamburg Schechts, are flying into London on the twelfth. They've taken the Continental Suite for eight nights.' Maynard was about to close the ledger but, before he did, he took a pencil and ruler and scored a line directly through Hélène's name. 'Graf Schecht has requested you accompany him in the ballroom during his stay. It is, you recall, one of his rare London pleasures, to see you dance.'

How could she forget? Graf Schecht was seventy years old, a whispery man of little grace but fierce determination. His wife, the Gräfin, had stopped dancing with him a generation ago – though she still enjoyed sitting in a ballroom and watching him twirl around someone much younger. Hélène could remember his hands all over her, and shuddered.

'Mr Charles, I reserved those dates for a reason.'

Maynard Charles nodded. 'Be that as it may. Hélène, you won't deny we're always flexible where we can be. Good Lord, the board were flexible enough to grant you an entire year on sabbatical when you wanted to tour California. But now that you're here with us, I really must insist—'

'I can't change things so easily,' Hélène replied, her voice hardening. 'This isn't a—'

Maynard Charles held up a hand and Hélène saw she was in for a lecture. 'Graf and Gräfin Schecht have been patrons of this establishment longer than you or I have graced its halls. They are, as you understand, personal friends of Lord Edgerton. I don't have to remind you of the choppy waters this hotel is sailing, Hélène. We pulled ourselves through the Depression by hook and by crook. With the good King Edward's patronage, our reputation is restored. But that doesn't mean . . . Trust me when I tell you, things can change in a moment. We court the great and the good so that this hotel's reputation soars. Every time the King takes afternoon tea with us, I can tell in the ledgers the way this hotel thrives. Let us pray he sees sense and foregoes his infatuation with Mrs Simpson so that he may be king ever after. The hotel needs a benefactor like this. It is how we present ourselves to the world. That's why we are throwing the New Year ball in his honour. That's why we have the Queen of Norway and her retinue in attendance for the Yuletide season. And that's why we need guests like the Hamburg Schechts. You must give them what they want, Hélène, for if we get a different kind of reputation, a reputation for cutting corners and letting our patrons down, well, worlds have imploded for less. There are twelve hundred members of staff in these halls, and do you know what? Not one of them is bigger than the hotel, Hélène. You do understand?'

He phrased the last as a question, but in truth it was no question at all.

'I understand.' Hélène nodded, defeated, while inside she felt herself erupting.

'Hélène, don't be sore. You are one of this hotel's most *prized* assets. I might even say you are the jewel in the Buckingham's crown. To have you in our ballroom has been an untold delight for our patrons. Hélène Marchmont: the glamorous model who turned down the silver screen for the ballroom. It brings us an air of enchantment. I haven't forgotten the season we opened and were suddenly indulged with guests from the Hollywood Hills, still courting you for their pictures. It means a tremendous amount to this establishment that you chose your love of dance over a shot at stardom. But, when our patrons need you, *I* need you, Hélène. With great beauty like yours, there comes a great responsibility.'

Hélène was not listening. She had stopped listening after Mr Charles had called her a prized asset. *I'm more than an asset, Maynard. I'm a woman. This hotel might be all you have in your life, but I have more in mine. And I needed those days.*

'Mr Charles, may I be excused?'

Maynard nodded. 'The Buckingham is greater for the sacrifices we make, Miss Marchmont,' he said. But, by then, Hélène was already out of the door.

As the dancers prepared to fly out onto the ballroom floor, Raymond de Guise could see Hélène holding herself tensely. His hand was in hers, but it was as if she was in another world.

'Hélène?' he whispered. 'Hélène, what happened?'

'He took my weekend,' she uttered, her voice tight with anger. 'I'm to dance with the Schechts again, when I should be . . .' *No, Hélène,* she told herself. *Not a single tear. Not here. Not in front of my girls.* 'You know where I should be, Raymond. To Mr Charles, I'm just another *prima donna* artiste making demands. He thinks he bought my entire life, and all because of that year I was away. As if all I was doing was sunning myself in Los Angeles . . .'

Raymond squeezed her hand tenderly. 'You're strong, Hélène. You can handle this.'

But as they walked through the doors, Hélène was thinking: *Maybe I can do this. But what if I don't want to? What if there's something more important in the world, some other place I ought to be?*

Later, after the demonstrations were over and the evening dances yet to begin, guests could be heard to remark in the hotel halls how clumsily Hélène Marchmont had danced that day. They wondered if she was tired, or if she was unwell – or if the punishing schedule of dancing at the Buckingham Hotel was finally taking its toll on one of its leading lights. Only Hélène knew why she'd found herself out of rhythm with the music, out of synch with Raymond as they performed their climactic double reverse spin to an expectant crowd.

Secrets were ten a penny in the Buckingham Hotel, but this one she would keep for herself.

September 1936

Chapter Four

NIGHT HAD FALLEN AT THE Buckingham Hotel, and for hotel page Billy Brogan that meant only one thing: *opportunity.*

Billy had been twelve years old when he ferried his first message for a guest at the hotel, and since then he had outlasted one head concierge, three night managers, two grill chefs, one bookkeeper and – as far as he could count – more than three hundred waiting staff, kitchen staff and chambermaids. He had even outlasted Mr Moore, the garage attendant, who had come to the Buckingham as a stable hand and lost no opportunity to talk about how different things used to be in the *good old days.* Five years after running his first errands, Billy considered himself a veteran of the establishment. Why, he was even longer standing than Lord Edgerton himself – and that had to mean something. It would soon be three years since Lord Edgerton had taken majority ownership of the hotel. The days before seemed a bygone age. Billy had often loitered outside the hotel director's door in those months before Lord Edgerton had swept in and made the Buckingham his own – and he fancied he knew more about the financial ruin that had once faced the hotel than anyone but Maynard Charles himself. He'd known about the plans to open a ballroom long before the heads of department; he'd even seen the magazines featuring Hélène Marchmont on Maynard Charles's desk and fancied, before the rumour had even begun, that the hotel board was courting the glamorous star to appear on their dance floor. No, there wasn't a thing that happened in the hotel to which Billy Brogan wasn't privy. And that was exactly the way he wanted it to stay.

Tonight Billy stole across the Grand Ballroom as it filled with guests in black silk velvet and cocoa silk chiffon, and slipped into the musicians' room behind the dance floor. The boys from the band were either lounging around or fastidiously checking their instruments for the performances to come. Behind the practice piano, Louis Kildare, a tall black man, was hunched over his saxophone with Hélène Marchmont at his side.

'You wanted me, Miss Marchmont?'

When Hélène saw that Billy was standing there, she reached into a clutch bag at her side and drew out a manila envelope, inscribed with two words: NOELLE ARCHER. This she handed to Billy, who almost saluted as he took it in his hands. 'Tonight, miss?'

'If you would, Billy,' Hélène said – and Billy recognised a weariness in her tone that she was trying hard not to let show. 'Of course, you have my gratitude.'

For a boy like Billy Brogan, gratitude came in the form of a half-crown pressed firmly into the palm of his hand. 'You have my word, Miss Marchmont.'

The way Billy Brogan said such things, always with an excitable little flourish, made Hélène smile. 'Be off with you,' she said, and Billy was beaming as he disappeared.

Louis Kildare shook his head as he watched the hotel page go. 'You have a soft spot for the boy.'

Kildare was a broad man, with black hair cropped short in the style of all the players in the Archie Adams Band. He was wearing the same white jacket as the saxophonists and trumpet players, though on Kildare the cuffs seemed too short – and he was positively bursting out of the bow tie Archie Adams insisted he wore. When he grinned at Hélène, the smile seemed to dominate his face – but tonight she was not smiling back.

'They'll understand, you know.'

Hélène hardened. 'Who will?'

'I know where that letter was going, and they'll understand. It's hotel business. It isn't your fault Graf and Gräfin Schecht demand the pleasure of your company. Are you hearing me?'

Louis Kildare had a simple way with words, or perhaps it was just his accent that made him seem so blunt. He'd grown up playing trumpets in his native Caribbean, a familiar face in every club from Jamaica to Trinidad and Tobago, but in the end London had offered so much more. He'd come here on the heels of greater musicians than he: Ken Johnson, who made the alto sax feel alive; Ellis Mills, who played the horn but could have shown the dancers in the Grand Ballroom a thing or two if only Maynard Charles might have permitted it; Carl Barriteau – who'd taught Louis to hold his own on the clarinet when they'd bunked together in the bars of Trinidad. All of these people from all over the world, but London was the place they all aspired to be. Here the clubs and hotels were eager for any talented players they could find – and, even though most still resisted having a black musician in a white orchestra, there were other places where it was the music, not the colour of your skin, that mattered. The Nest. The Midnight Rooms. Café de Paris. Louis and his companions had played in all of these clubs until

Archie Adams had chanced upon them and demanded they audition for his own band.

'You ever want to go back to the clubs, Louis?'

Louis smirked. 'Every now and then. They were different to the Buckingham.' He paused, sensing that something was wrong. 'Hélène, has something happened?'

'It's nothing, Louis.' She touched his hand tenderly. 'Don't worry about me.'

'I worry often, Hélène.'

'It's just . . . sometimes I wonder what it's for. Why I'm here. I never danced in the clubs, Louis. I came up through the tea dances, always on the arm of some local lord. But after too long in the Buckingham Hotel, with Mr Charles breathing down your neck, and you start to wonder – maybe there's somewhere freer. Somewhere where you're not being watched every second of every day. You used to love the clubs, Louis. So did . . .'

Hélène's words petered into silence. Behind the area where the musicians gathered, a door led down to the dressing rooms. When she looked up, Raymond de Guise was standing there, looking pristine in his midnight-blue dinner jacket, its rolled collars faced in a shimmering silk. There was something dramatic and sad in the way he gazed out across the musicians. Hélène's eyes lingered on him. Some of the other dancers had been known to swoon when Raymond de Guise sauntered by. They saw in him somebody doomed and romantic, but Hélène knew who he was dancing with tonight – the exiled ballerina Grusinskaya – and that look on his face was only Raymond de Guise, lost in concentration as he prepared to dance with an equal.

'You still feel it, don't you?' Kildare dared to venture. 'You still think about him often.'

'Oh,' Hélène said, her voice more brittle than ever, 'how could I not?'

Raymond de Guise's eyes landed on her. He lifted one eyebrow, as if to ask her if she was ready.

'He would want you to ... be yourself again, Hélène. He'd want you to live a new life. We all do.'

'I know,' whispered Hélène, 'but as opulent and beautiful as this new life is, what if what you really want is the old?'

By the time the Archie Adams Band struck up the first notes of 'No Other Love But You', Billy Brogan was already sailing along the Strand on the top of a double decker bus. London at night was as cold and beautiful as Hélène Marchmont herself. A stiff wind whipped in off the river and, as Billy saw the bright lights of the Savoy Hotel rolling by, he felt a flurry of pride. The Savoy Hotel might have looked grand from the outside, but where was it that Mr Baldwin, Mr Chamberlain and their ministers took private rooms to chair their most important meetings? Where was it that King Edward brought Mrs Simpson for afternoon tea? And where was throwing a New Year's Eve Masquerade Ball in his honour, with royalty from as far away as Norway coming to join in? The thought made Billy Brogan proud beyond measure. To come from a Lambeth terrace and belong to a place like the Buckingham was a very fine thing indeed.

The bus took him over the river, glittering and black, and into the warrens and winding streets of the south. As they went, Billy took the envelope out of the folds of his coat and stared at the name on the front. NOELLE ARCHER. His fingers toyed with the seam, but he had no need to open it. *No,* he thought with a wry smile, *no need to open it at all. I already know what's inside.*

Ordinarily, Billy had no qualms about opening the letters he was asked to ferry around the Buckingham – or, like now, further afield. Jobs had perks. Raymond de Guise got his visits from his own personal tailor, a man by the name of Ernestine who owned one of the most prestigious shops on Savile Row. Hélène Marchmont had access to the safe Mr Charles kept, filled with diamond pins, necklaces encrusted with sapphires, and all manner of other expensive jewellery. Even the bright-eyed new chambermaid – Nancy Nettleton, was that her name? – had her room in the staff quarters and, if she was canny enough, her choice of leftovers from the room service trolleys left sitting untouched in the suites. Billy Brogan's chief perk was *knowledge*. It brought a certain kind of pride to know who was doing what, who'd been disciplined for breaching Buckingham rules, who was meeting whom in the vacant rooms of an evening and taking full advantage of the luxurious satin sheets only the most important guests were allowed.

There was no address on the envelope but, some time later, Billy stood outside one of the old railwayman's terraces on Brixton Hill. There were lights on in the windows of the terrace. He could hear music as well – not music like he was accustomed to, but trumpets and clarinets all the same. Somebody was rehearsing here, but they were putting up a din quite unlike the things Billy had heard in the Buckingham Hotel, faster and looser and more . . . experimental? Was that the word?

There was another sound too. Behind that door, a baby was crying. Somebody cried out in exasperation and, with muttered apologies, the music came to an end.

Billy took it as his cue. He slipped the envelope under the door – and then, rapping on the wood as he turned, took flight up the road.

Chapter Five

On the sixth storey of the Buckingham Hotel, where crown princes and Texan oil barons rubbed shoulders in the burgundy halls, there was one door through which no chambermaid was ever permitted to pass.

At 9 p.m., with the last of the late summer light finally fading across London, the door to the Park Suite opened and Maynard Charles stepped into the corridor. Moments earlier, he had stepped out of his dressing gown and back into the double-breasted grey suit he wore for all formal occasions. With a look over his shoulder, he closed the door behind him, produced a single silver key and made certain that the lock was tight. Then he glided on, until finally he reached the top of the stairs, where he waited as an attendant summoned the lift. In his mind he began listing the tasks he had to complete before the night was through.

Running the Buckingham Hotel was not, as many hoteliers said, like being the captain of a ship. It was more, Maynard Charles mused – as he stepped into the ornate golden cage of the executive lift and allowed the attendant to take him down through the Buckingham's many floors – like being the conductor of an orchestra. All of the musicians had to play in time with one another, or the whole piece would sound discordant and wrong. He allowed himself a thin smile, for he found the idea that he and Archie Adams had anything in common wryly amusing. Maynard Charles was not a man of music, but he could appreciate the value of an orchestra and dance troupe. What he could *not* appreciate was the manner of a man like Archie Adams, and so many among his band, who seemed to live for nothing other than the 'good times' they had with their instruments in hand. *Most of them are too young to have been in Flanders or France,* Maynard thought. *They'd be different men if they had been out there like me and my brothers, if they'd heard the roaring cannonade, sat cramped together in a hole in the earth for days on end while a very different sort of music – the deathly music of mortars, the music of bombs – played all around.* Perhaps that might have drilled some decorum, some sobriety, some *propriety*, into them. Thank the Lord, he found himself thinking, the Buckingham did not host the rhumbas and sambas of which some of his guests had spoken. The world was a licentious place but some bastions of righteousness remained.

The third-floor cocktail lounge was walled in great glass windows that overlooked the treetops of Berkeley Square, with a terrace on which the Buckingham gardeners had reared exotica with such fine fragrances that guests might easily think themselves drinking Martinis on some balmy Mediterranean coast. Regular guests called this place the Garden Lounge, but Maynard insisted upon its proper name: the Candlelight Club. Inside, a harpist was playing on a tiny spotlit stage and the room, bathed in blue light, was alive with guests in lounge suits and bias-cut dresses, while a veritable army of waiters flitted silently between them, keeping glasses full.

The noise of gay chatter increased as Maynard stepped out of the lift and stepped through the doors. The Candlelight Club was suitably busy tonight. The Lebreton-Whites, in from Paris on their monthly sojourn, were being served champagne from a magnum bottle by one of the waiters, dressed head to toe in white. Mr Caponne, from Room 24 – who had made his riches in iron – was perusing a list of wines that the hotel sommeliers had spent years cultivating. Merivale Lloyd, whose librettos were performed on stages from New York to Berlin, had a table to himself in the corner closest to the harpist, until a lady dressed in a scarlet gown presumed upon him to take the neighbouring seat.

As Maynard crossed the club, his eyes took in every last detail. Soon he found himself at the marble bar that skirted the circumference of the room. As he pulled up a stool, the cocktail waiter glided over.

'Your speciality, Mr Charles?'

'Not tonight, Diego. Give me an Angel Face, there's a good man.' It was not his usual drink, but there were some moments when a dry Martini would not do. Tonight demanded something more *decadent*. Something more *indulgent*? Something sugary and sweet, to take the edge off what he was about to do.

He looked over his shoulder. Merivale Lloyd and his new companion had slid closer together.

When Diego returned to present the rich amber cocktail, Maynard asked, 'The lady in red, speaking with Mr Lloyd. Who is she?'

'One of the hotel dancers, sir.'

Maynard nodded. Diego did not mean dancer in the traditional sense. The lady entertaining Merivale Lloyd, and the others like her who flitted through the Candlelight Club tonight, were dancers in spirit only – private dancers, with whom a guest might decide to retire for the night. It was, Maynard Charles had often reflected, one of the more interesting – yet less salubrious – aspects of his role that these workers needed managing, just the same as the cleaners and valets, chambermaids and chefs who made up the rest of the Buckingham army. That these particular hotel dancers were not in the official hotel accounts did not mean he did not keep cards for each of them in his private index. They may not have drawn salaries from the Buckingham books, but they were every bit as important for the health of the hotel. A place like the Buckingham could not expect to exist without attracting some sort of parasites. And better to make sure they were of the correct class and comportment than outlaw them altogether. A lone man, even a man of Maynard Charles's calibre, could not stand up against an unstoppable tide.

'Send for one of the pages, won't you?' he said airily. 'Have someone watch Mr Lloyd's room this evening. I don't recognise our lady friend. If she's above board, then fine. But let's find out first.'

'As you wish, Mr Charles.'

The cocktail waiter disappeared on his errand. After he was gone, Maynard Charles reached into the inner pocket of his dinner jacket and produced one of his White Owl cigars. As he lit it, he turned to the evening edition of *The Times* and scoured its headlines. In Spain the Nationalists had captured San Sebastián. On the second page the editorial led with Mr Hitler's rally. It had only been six months since he'd marched back into the Rhineland and now he was declaring Germany a fully armed nation once again. Maynard Charles had to take deep lungfuls of smoke just to steady his nerves. *My friends died so that there wouldn't be war again. And now look where we're going* . . . It would have made his blood boil, but his blood was already boiling tonight – and not even the drink in his hand was enough to make him relax.

A finger tapped at his shoulder. Instinct told him to turn around – but he was a practised, mannered kind of man, and instead he said, 'Let us find ourselves a table, shall we? Somewhere we can talk.'

Maynard did not look at his guest as he stood up and, summoning a waiter to carry his drink, made haste to a table in a shadowy corner of the lounge. Here the music of the harpist was faint, but the conversations of his fellow drinkers still buzzed around him, so that everything was a single indecipherable noise – which was exactly what he needed.

'Bring my friend a soda and lime, would you, old boy?'

The man named Moorcock removed his Bollman trilby and placed it on the table beside him. In the pale light of the club, Maynard watched as he picked a stray grey hair from the hat and disposed of it under the table.

'I'll take a Martini,' he said.

Maynard simply glared.

'A Martini, Mr Charles. A little hospitality would go a long way between us.'

Maynard Charles bristled, glaring straight through his unwelcome guest. The waiter was despatched to bring back a dry Martini, ice on the side.

'There, that's better, don't you think?' Mr Moorcock took a slow sip. 'I hear things tick along merrily in your fine establishment, Mr Charles. You had the pleasure of Graf and Gräfin Schecht, did you not?'

So, thought Maynard, *he's seen the register.* He made a mental note to speak to whoever had been manning the front reception. All it took was a moment's distraction for somebody to reach over the desk, steal a look at the check-in book, and memorise all its names. Hotel discretion mattered – for *all* their guests, no matter who they were or what they'd done.

'They stayed in the Continental, but I'm quite sure you already know. Listen, Mr Moorcock, the clock above your head is ticking further and further towards ten. The longer I sit here enjoying this scintillating battle of wits with you, the less time I have to attend to my actual duties in this hotel.'

'It is always amusing to see how you try and set the terms of our meetings, Mr Charles. But you and I know that I alone set these terms.'

Maynard Charles glowered. Of course, Moorcock was right. Mr Moorcock was *always* right. And yet . . . there were things he wanted to know too. Things he *needed* to know. 'What word from the Palace, Mr Moorcock? The last time you came, you promised me—'

'I don't make promises, Maynard.'

'The good King was to take afternoon tea here in July. He was to bring Mrs Simpson. When he didn't keep his appointment, the society pages began to say he had, perhaps, moved on. That Mrs Simpson, perhaps, isn't as enamoured by the Buckingham Hotel as the King is. You know how much we rely on the association of His Majesty, Mr Moorcock.'

Mr Moorcock nodded.

'Well?'

'Well, what?'

'We might be in ruder health now, but the winds change so quickly in a hotel like this. The King and his entourage are due to spend New Year's Eve with us here, in our hotel. The Masquerade Ball we are, even now, readying for is a celebration of the fact. It will be *the* event of the season. And yet . . .' Maynard was struggling with what to say next. *I'm twice your age, Mr Moorcock. How can it be that you make me so fearful?* 'We allied ourselves with His Majesty. Our reputations are entwined, one might say. I scarcely think we'd have made it through the Depression if the King hadn't deigned to make us one of his regular haunts. It brought so many new guests. It restored our reputation. It's what brought *you* here too, remember?'

Mr Moorcock remained silent, impassive – but Maynard Charles knew he had struck a blow. When the King had begun coming to the Buckingham, a wealth of new aristocratic patrons had followed.

Of course, it brought unsavoury types too – the type of men Maynard Charles would rather didn't use his hotel. He was staring into the eyes of one of those men right now.

'The King. Is he to . . . ? That is to say, that *The Times* has speculated that . . .' Maynard Charles clenched his fist, found his courage. *Why do I find it so hard to speak to this man, this stranger who comes to my hotel and makes his insidious demands?* 'Is he to *abdicate*, Mr Moorcock?'

For a time, Mr Moorcock said precisely nothing. Then, pointedly ignoring Maynard's nervous request, he said, 'Enough chatter, Mr Charles. Shall we dispense with the pleasantries and exchange gifts?'

'It *matters*, Mr Moorcock. You think a hotel like ours is an ocean of riches? Well, it isn't. The riches it takes to keep our ship afloat are counterweighed almost exactly by the riches we make. Were the King to abdicate and his followers abandon us . . . I don't need to remind you how the shock waves of that might be felt. It takes a thousand people and more to keep our hotel afloat. The good King *is* our reputation, Mr Moorcock. When our reputation suffers, so too does our profit. And if our profits suffer, the members of the board grow agitated. A hotel like ours is a luxury for them, where their money might better be invested in iron and steel – armaments, even, if what is happening in Spain is any indication of our future.' He paused, trembling. 'If you know anything, Mr Moorcock, I implore you to tell. I mustn't let my people down. I cannot send a hundred chambermaids back into poverty. A hundred porters, two hundred kitchen staff and waiters. They are the life's blood of the Buckingham, but they are dependent on . . . our reputation. If our reputation falters, so too do a thousand lives and all the lives that depend on them.'

'Your *gift*, Maynard. Must I ask you a second time?'

Maynard reached into his evening suit and produced an envelope, sealed with the stamp of his private office.

'A little weighty today, Mr Charles. Am I to assume this is a bountiful month?'

'Perhaps.'

'Do you care to elaborate?'

'I do not. You have everything you need, right there in your hands.'

Mr Moorcock smirked. 'All of it verifiable, of course.'

'I trust all of my sources.'

'Then we won't have a problem.'

Maynard stiffened. 'There's no need to belittle me, Mr Moorcock. I know how this works. I've been dealing with men like you almost all of my life. I *know* you, sir.' He paused. Then, he dared to venture, 'You said this was an exchange of gifts?'

'Ah, yes,' replied Mr Moorcock. By now he was on his feet, replacing the Bollman trilby on his head. 'My gift is this, Mr Charles: your secret kept, for your continuing co-operation.'

Maynard Charles quaked in his seat.

'We'll be checking the veracity of these claims, of course, just as we check the veracity of everything you acquire for us. You do know what would happen were we to believe you were lying to us, don't you, Maynard?'

Maynard uttered, 'Yes, Mr Moorcock. We've had the conversation often enough.'

'Good. Because, you know, I could have no greater pleasure than revealing what really happens behind the doors of your beloved Park Suite. All I'm really waiting for is the appropriate moment. But you keep on doing as you're told and your secret's safe with us.'

Maynard found that he was trembling. He gripped his knees beneath the table, gouging the half-moons of his fingertips into them until he found the strength to utter, 'You have my word, Mr Moorcock, as a gentleman.'

'Gentleman?' Mr Moorcock mused – and there seemed to be something particularly amusing in this. 'Oh, Mr Charles, you could hardly be called a *gentleman* now, could you?'

Then he was gone, off into the Candlelight's crowds – while Maynard Charles sat alone, waiting for the shaking to subside.

Chapter Six

FOUR WEEKS HAD PASSED IN a whirlwind of beds changed, floors swept, and one particularly galling occasion in which, quite by accident, Nancy had stumbled in on M. Zweig, the widower in room 114, as he prepared himself for his morning ablutions. Tomorrow was to be her first morning off since she'd arrived in London – and privately Nancy admitted that she could hardly wait. Being a chambermaid was exhausting.

The staff quarters at the Buckingham Hotel were secreted around a corner of the third storey where no guest ever had need to go. Up narrow stairs beyond a locked door, the bed-sitting rooms were arranged in a horseshoe around a kitchen where the chambermaids gathered nightly to drink tea and share meals and trade what gossip they had gleaned from the hotel floors. To Nancy, it felt like the boarding schools she'd read about as a girl – and, indeed, Mrs Whitehead, the housekeeper who lived in the same quarters, played the part of housemistress to perfection. Nancy's mother had had a trunk of books at the bottom of her closet and, if Nancy was good, her father would let her trawl through it, breathing in the scents of the same stories her mother had loved, wondering at the little missives and messages of love inscribed in each one. What it would have been like, Nancy often wondered, to have had a mother!

Tonight, when she climbed the old servant stairs, she could hear Rosa and Ruth already clucking around the kitchen. She paused at the top of the stairs, but did not go in. Nancy had never known that the soles of her feet could hurt as much as they did right now. Looking after her father had been one thing, but six days of waking at dawn to follow Mrs Moffatt and Mrs Whitehead around the hotel was quite another. And Lord, the things she'd seen . . .

It took concentration to steal past the kitchen doorway and reach her own bedroom. If Ruth were to see her, there'd be no escaping; it would be a long night, filled with stories of the time Ruth spied the Dowager Countess of Mazovia in a tryst with a wealthy hotel patron quite evidently not of the same social stratum – or of what Rosa *swore* she saw the Right Honourable Freddie Prince doing with Lord Hoxton's son in the bedroom of the Livingstone Suite. 'Nancy!' they would cry out, and then that was it; the night would be lost.

Weeks had passed but she could still hear the echo of that saxophone playing in her mind. Twice now she had dallied by the doors of the ballroom as the demonstrations went on inside, mindful of the way Mr Simenon glared at her from the reception desk when he happened to look up. The gramophone records she'd play for her father as she sat by his bedside had brought him such comfort in those final months. And yet, to hear it played by real musicians, to catch glimpses of the dancers crossing the ballroom so elegantly – that was something of which she had barely even dreamed! When she had first come here, she had thought of the Buckingham's Art Deco doors, with their bronze revolving frames, as the entrance to another world. Listening to the music she understood there were yet more worlds inside the hotel. The music could carry you there.

Somehow she made it past the staff kitchen. A single bed sat under a window in her room, which looked out only on to other windows across a narrow yard, and beside that was a small wardrobe with space enough to hang her uniform, and a bedside table where three candles had already guttered to stubs. She had a pile of *Harper's Bazaar* magazines she'd taken from the staff kitchen. The girls said that Hélène Marchmont, who danced daily with the debonair Raymond de Guise, was once a regular feature of these types of magazines – draped in the latest ball gowns, adorned with jewellery so fine that only princesses and starlets ever wore it – that, by the time she was Nancy's age, she was being courted to cross the oceans to California, where a dozen different directors said she would become a star. The legend went that Hélène had fallen in love with the ballroom instead, when one of her suitors dragged her along to a tea dance in Kensington. Some of the magazines were snide about that – why forsake the glamour of Hollywood for a ballroom? But Nancy, who had only caught the merest glimpses of the ballroom, believed she could understand.

There was little space to sit down and write, but Nancy cleared an area upon the bedside table and, using her bed as a chair, set herself up with inkpot, pen, and a leaf of paper she'd purchased from the hotel store. She'd been putting it off too long already. So she began:

Dearest Frank,

I hope you know how much I have been thinking about you! I keep thinking of you in front of a roaring fire, with a mug of Cadbury's cocoa, something sweet to send you off to sleep. But I wonder if it is like that, now that I've gone off to London and you are left to fend for yourself? I hope that you're not in the Green Man most nights, and that you haven't forgotten the little pleasures of life. An early bed. Toast and fresh butter for breakfast. The tin bath filled to the brim in front of the fire . . .

I am ashamed that almost a month has passed and I haven't written. But Frank, life at the Buckingham Hotel takes over every inch of you! This is a different world. You couldn't even imagine anything as posh as the grandest Buckingham suites that Mrs Moffatt, our head housekeeper and a lady, has shown me. Can you believe that every Buckingham suite has its own bathroom, its own electric lights, its own telephones? I can't begin to say! Grandest of all is the Atlantic Suite. There's a Russian man, Nikolai Alexeev, so wealthy he's called the suite his own for seven long months! In fact, Mr Alexeev lives his whole life in hotels like the Buckingham, ever since his exile from the revolution in Russia. From one hotel to the next, he crosses the continent and pens his romances from the typewriter he sets up on its stand. Such a life, dear Frank! Here at the Buckingham he lives with Grusinskaya, a ballerina who has become his wife. This morning she caught my eye as Mrs Moffatt and I came to attend to the suite. To be lost and beautiful is such a sad thing.

There are others. One of the girls I work with, Ruth – you would like her, Frank – says she's seen queens in their under-drawers. We are all waiting on King Edward himself. Rosa – she's Ruth's friend – says she passed him once in reception, because he has been bringing his

Mrs Simpson to dine here since before he was King. The hotel is throwing a masquerade ball in his honour for New Year. I hope I get to catch a glimpse . . .

I wonder if Father would have found a way to be proud of me. I think perhaps he wouldn't have believed what his little girl was doing! Do you remember, Frank, his final words? 'It is hard to make your way in the world,' he said, 'but make your way you must'.

Frank, I know by now you will be staying with Mrs Gable and that, perhaps, your new home is not as comfortable as my own, but I hope I have not bored you with my stories. One day, when I can send for you, we can be together again and I will look after you like always.

Your loving sister,

Nancy

Nancy put her ink pen down and read the letter back. In truth, she doubted that Frank would read it. Her brother had never been good with words. She remembered him as a boy, how he'd refuse to hold his pencil, no matter how fiercely she tried to instruct him in his letters; how he wanted nothing more than to run wild with the other miners' sons. Nancy had often wondered how different her brother might have been if he had had a mother, instead of an elder sister just trying to do her best.

Perhaps Frank might have Mrs Gable read the letter to him – but first, of course, he would wait until the other miners he was lodging with were away, or out of earshot, for fear of being called a pansy, a mummy's boy, or worse. Yes, Nancy decided, Frank might have been a mummy's boy – if only he'd got the chance.

Thoughts like this could make her maudlin. She didn't like to think of the old Nettleton cottage with a new family in it, nor of her brother stuck following the same path through life as their father, who had been taken from them far too young when his lungs – diseased after so many years in the mine – could go on no more. One day, she hoped, she would be able to send for Frank and they might have a new kind of life together. But not today. Today was for *her*. Life had been about *them* for so long. She was twenty-four years old and she deserved a little something for herself.

Nancy opened her wardrobe. Her feet were still aching, but what did that matter? *If I don't dare do it, if all I do is curl up and go to sleep, what use is there in living? Nancy, you've got to be brave . . .*

In the wardrobe hung the uniforms Mrs Moffatt had provided. Nancy had had to pay for them, of course, with coupons to be deducted from her future wages, but she didn't mind – for there, nestled among them, was the gown she'd brought, neatly folded up in the bottom of her case. Now that she'd seen the gowns the guests of the Buckingham wore, she was aware of how paltry it seemed. It had been the dress in which her mother was married – but, of course, it had been cut and remade countless times as the years passed by. It would not pass as elegant in these surroundings, but perhaps it did not need to. All she really wanted was to step through the ballroom doors while the evening was in full flow. All she really wanted was to breathe in the music for a few moments, to stand by the balustrade and watch the fabulous Hélène Marchmont turn a two-step across the ballroom on the arm of whichever dignitary she'd been promised to for the evening. Perhaps if she didn't linger . . . she did not have to stand out. Perhaps it would not be such a crime to bring a pinch of magic into her own little life . . .

Chapter Seven

THE BAND STRUCK UP. THE chandeliers were aglow. The smoke of the finest cigars rose up to make great reefs in the barrel-vaulted ceiling of the ballroom. Somewhere, a cork popped, in time with the beating of the drums in the orchestra. And on the edges of the ballroom floor, Raymond de Guise – a vision of elegance in his glistening dinner jacket, his hair newly cropped by Harrison, the hotel barber – approached a lady in a gown of flowing chiffon and lace, her neck adorned with pearls the size of robins' eggs, the tiara in her hair encrusted with diamonds and a single sapphire that glared out like an extra eye, and offered her his hand.

'Shall we?'

'Mr de Guise,' she replied, her voice half a whisper, and passed her cigarette holder, still smoking, to the hotel page at her side. 'You are as handsome as I was told, though you do not look so very French.'

'It is in my blood, Grusinskaya. On my father's side.'

Grusinskaya, the exiled ballerina, spoke with a faraway voice, a voice that told of magnificent Russian palaces, cities frozen for winter, the Imperial court where she had once danced for the last of the Russian Tsars. Grusinskaya was fifty years old, but she looked much younger. Her dark hair flowed around her slender shoulders and her eyes, blue as the sapphire in her tiara, had a bewitched kind of cast. She looked longing. She looked . . . lost.

Raymond took her by the hand to the dance floor and, while the other couples sailed past, he put his right arm around her waist and pressed his left palm against hers. 'In your old world, you needed no man to lead. But perhaps you would do me the honour of allowing me to lead you tonight?'

They were already stepping together onto the dance floor, pivoting once as the rhythm of the music found them.

Grusinskaya smiled. 'The body aches for it sometimes. To be on the stage again. Holding my arabesque. Turning a *grand jeté*. And yet . . . there are other enchantments in dance, are there not, Mr de Guise?'

Archie Adams had upped the tempo and the dancers' bodies responded to the rhythm. Raymond looked into Grusinskaya's eyes, and something in them seemed to thaw as the couple moved effortlessly into a quickstep, making their way in a succession of light hops and skips across the ballroom floor.

'Where did you train, Mr de Guise?'

'If I were to tell you, you would only be disappointed. There is no academy for the ballroom, *madame*. My body is not as trained as yours must have been, dancing ballet for the Bolshoi.'

'And yet you were taught, were you not?'

'I owe my dancing to a master of the arts. Georges de la Motte, a baron of France no less – and the best ballroom dancer I ever observed.'

'You were his apprentice.'

'I was his friend. But apprenticed to him also.'

The music swelled and soared. First the trombones took the lead, then the trumpets, until finally the saxophonist sailed into the song, his instrument filling the cavernous ballroom with its intoxicating sound. Raymond and Grusinskaya turned, crossed the dance floor, turned again – and, as they danced on, the edges of the ballroom seemed to fade away. Soon, though neither said a word, it was as if their bodies were one.

So lost in the dance was he that, at first, Raymond de Guise did not hear the shrieking on the edges of the dance floor. It was only when he turned past Hélène Marchmont and saw her eyes drawn to a place between the ballroom pillars that he looked up. Vivienne Edgerton was looming over a young lady sitting at one of the tables, Vivienne's arm outstretched and her face open in a vulpine howl. '*You!*' she seemed to be shouting. '*You!*'

At that moment, in a clatter of drums and triumphant tenor horn, the band brought its song to a close – and Archie Adams himself was on his feet, taking appreciative bows from the dancers on the ballroom floor. Raymond, his arm still around Grusinskaya, watched Vivienne reach forward, pure hatred in her eyes, and – trying to snatch at the young lady's arm – topple into the table instead. Dazed, she tried to pick herself up. A crystal glass tumbled, shattering onto the floor. More heads turned their way. A waiter, summoned by the disturbance, rushed to clear up the mess, while another disappeared into the shadows on the edges of the ballroom, no doubt searching for someone to come and guide poor Vivienne away.

Vivienne picked herself up. The girl at the table was trying to stand – but the sleeve of her dress was tight in Vivienne's fingers; she was held fast. 'You oughtn't to be in Daddy's ballroom!' Vivienne crowed. 'You've no right! Don't you know your . . .'

Now that Raymond saw her properly, he supposed that the lady *did* look out of place. The gown she was wearing did not seem entirely of a piece; it was as if somebody had taken two gowns and stitched them together. It was pinched at the neckline, and the fabric worn. Even so, it suited her in an unusual way. She had a pretty, round face and big, dark eyes, and in the dark curls of her hair she was wearing a silver pin that dazzled in the chandelier light.

'Mr de Guise, you are a gentleman?'

Raymond was distracted. 'I am, Grusinskaya.'

She leaned forward and whispered, throatily, into his ear. 'Then go to Miss Vivienne, you fool.'

Raymond left Grusinskaya on the dance floor and weaved his way through the other dancers to the table where Vivienne was unsteady on her feet.

'*Mademoiselle*,' Raymond began, 'are you hurt?'

Vivienne turned on Raymond. 'Don't touch me!' she slurred. 'Don't you know what she is? Why, when my father finds out . . .'

Raymond stepped back. The young lady was already on her feet. Eyes followed her as she fled. Somewhere, somebody sneered. Somebody else roared with laughter, for dramas like this were rare in the Buckingham ballroom.

At that moment Mr Simenon, the head concierge, arrived to lift Vivienne back into her seat. She had drunk too much tonight, that was evident. But as she lolled there in her chair, the band sending out the first shrill blasts of a new song, Raymond saw that her eyes were adrift. They had a peculiar, glazed quality. She was having to concentrate to remain upright – and that, thought Raymond, could not merely be the after-effects of the Dom Pérignon she'd been drinking by the glass.

'Mr de Guise,' Mr Simenon began, in his slick, slippery voice, 'I may need some help.'

Vivienne looked up. Her vacant eyes met his. Then she lolled forward and, slumping head first onto the table, fainted clean away.

'Here, take this,' said Mrs Moffatt with an exasperated, yet kindly, stare. 'You'll feel better.'

Miss Vivienne Edgerton sat hunched in a chair in the head concierge's office, while Mr Simenon stood sentry outside and Raymond de Guise dabbed at his evening suit with a damp cloth, eager to be rid of the smears of rouge Vivienne had left on his lapels as he helped carry her through. Mrs Moffatt had wrapped Vivienne in her shawl; the poor girl was shivering, as if finally coming out of her stupor, a wild look in her eyes.

Vivienne took the lemon water Mrs Moffatt had offered and nodded her thanks. She looked chastened, thought Raymond, and so she might. The gossips would be talking. One of these days, word was going to get back to Vivienne's stepfather – and Lord Edgerton was not known as a forgiving man. The rumour was he'd removed his own son from his will over some petty slight; the fact that Vivienne was here at all – instead of left to fend for herself – was only down to the insistence of his current wife, Vivienne's mother. Raymond looked at her. Now that she wasn't screaming, and her lips weren't curling in hate, she was a sorry sight. And he wondered how it must feel to be her. Your own father long gone, your mother married to some strange gentleman from over the oceans who decides he cannot stand the sight of you – because, to him, all you are is a reminder that his new wife used to be in love with another. It had been a year since Vivienne Edgerton was uprooted from her New York home and compelled to cross the oceans, leaving behind all of the friends she used to know – and not to live in the grand west London residence into which her stepfather and mother had moved, but to live here, in the Buckingham Hotel. No matter how grand the Buckingham was, no matter how indulged she was by the management and staff, it was not a *home*. Seeing her now, Raymond thought she looked lonely. Everyone else who lived here had companions. The housekeeping staff. The dancers. Maynard Charles himself. But as for Vivienne . . .

'Get yourself together, dear. When you're ready, I'll take you to your suite. We can use the service lift.'

Vivienne's eyes shot up. 'You won't tell my—'

'Hush, dear. We've been here before, haven't we, you and I? Nobody else needs to know.' Mrs Moffatt's eyes lifted and looked at Raymond de Guise. 'You'd better be back to the ballroom, Mr de Guise, before you're missed.'

He was almost at the door when Vivienne reached for him.

'Mr de Guise . . .'

Her hand was on his elbow. He froze. 'Miss Edgerton, I really must—'

'I want to say I'm sorry. If I . . . ruined the dance for you. And . . . for all those people out there. I didn't mean to. It's not what I wanted. And . . .' She hesitated again, smacking her dry lips. The poor girl was parched again – no doubt the effects of whatever was in her system – and Raymond reached for the glass of water she'd left behind. 'You looked so elegant out there tonight, Mr de Guise. You truly did. With Grusinskaya on your arm and . . . What it must feel like to move like that across the dance floor! But I . . .' And here she found her steel again, her voice regaining its edge. 'I know it isn't for me. I know it wouldn't be becoming for me to be there every night. But I do dream of it, you understand. The life you lead, and Miss Marchmont as well. One day, you know, I'll be a married woman. My stepfather will see to it. I'll be looked after and I'll be kept quiet, and hang all of the dreams I used to have. And then I see you and Miss Marchmont and I wonder . . . what might it be like, to be the person you want to be? To be good at something, to learn something, to always have a partner, to be *admired*.'

Raymond was silent. There was something else Vivienne Edgerton wanted to say, but she couldn't find the words.

'Mr de Guise,' she said at last, 'you said once before that you'd show me a few steps. A little something, just to satisfy my curiosity. It's all I . . .'

Raymond could still feel Mrs Moffatt's eyes on him. He was not sure if that was a sympathetic stare, or if she was warning him. But when he looked down, Vivienne seemed so wretched. 'I'll share some steps with you soon, Miss Edgerton,' he said, 'but on one condition.'

'Anything,' she whispered, and seemed composed for the very first time that night.

'Sober up, *mademoiselle*,' said Raymond, and he slipped out of the office.

Chapter Eight

Dearest Frank,

I have been such a fool. Such a sorry, sorry fool!

Nancy's hand was still shaking as she wrote. She looked up, at the open wardrobe doors, and saw the dress she had worn still hanging there. Only when she'd got up and slammed the doors so she did not have to look at it any more could she bring herself to write again. *How could you be so foolish, Nancy Nettleton? To think that something you patched together with your mother's old needle and thread could ever compare to the silk and chiffon and embroidered lace of the Buckingham's best ball gowns? You're a country mouse, that's all you are, and now . . .* She tried to set it down, explain it to Frank, and this helped a little. On the morning she'd left the village, bound for London and her dream of a better life, Frank had beamed at her and said, 'You'll wind up too big for your boots, Nance, you mark my words. We'll 'ave to start calling you *ma'am*.' It was a thing he did sometimes, poking fun at her because he found it so difficult to say what he actually meant. Frank would have roared with laughter if he'd seen her that night. And, she supposed, it *was* funny – but if it hadn't been for Raymond de Guise stepping in like that, she might have lost her job.

I don't know if I can do this. I thought I could. Oh Frank, I've been so reckless. All I wanted was an adventure. To work hard so that, one day, you can join me here – and maybe, who knows, to have a little fun along the way. We have had precious little fun in our lives, haven't we, Frank? But I wish you were here now. You always keep my feet on the ground. You'd tell me to pull myself together and . . .

She'd been in the Grand Ballroom mere moments. The music and the lights, the dancers as they came together and came apart again – all of it had been everything she'd ever dreamed about. But then everything had changed. She could still feel the sharp tips of Miss Edgerton's fingers as they gouged into her arms. She could still see the look of horror on her face. It was as if, in those moments, the idea she'd had of herself had imploded.

I suppose I ought to be thankful. Miss Edgerton caused such a scene that I am scarcely to be remembered. But even so, when we arrived at Mrs Moffatt's register the next morning to learn our tasks for the week ahead, there were whispers. Chambermaids know everything! Somehow they knew all about Miss Edgerton's disgrace. And somehow they knew about the strange girl in the homespun dress as well.

Nancy looked back at the closed wardrobe door. *You'll have to get rid of it, you silly girl. Or else risk being found out . . .* Her fist closed around her pencil. This was supposed to be the start of a new existence. How could she have risked it all for the merest glimpse of the goings-on in the Grand?

Oh, it's so unlike home here, Frank. In the Buckingham there are people you mustn't look in the eye. There are places you mustn't go and things which, though you see them plainly, you must quickly forget. I don't know if you could survive it, Frank. I don't know that I can! We Nettletons might be made of the same flesh and blood as the Flemish princess whose sheets I change, we might breathe the same air as Miss Edgerton, but we're not the same. In the Buckingham Hotel there are two different worlds. And I must learn to be a town mouse.

I hope you'll write soon, Frank. A friendly word would mean the world to me just now. Are you having trouble writing? Remember that Mrs Gable made a promise: if you tell her what you would like to say, she will put it to paper for you. Tell me about how . . .

Nancy heard knuckles rapping at her door and Ruth's voice called out. 'Nancy Nettleton! What *are* you doing in there? We're supposed to be in the Grand in ten minutes. We're going down in two minutes. If you're not . . .'

Nancy snatched up the letter she had been writing, crammed it beneath the pillow, and in a second was at the door. Rosa and Ruth, along with a gaggle of the other girls, were waiting in the hallway, as if daring her to be late.

Put on a brave face, Nancy. None of them know it was you. How could they? None of them was there – because, you sorry girl, none of them would be so reckless. Chambermaids are invisible! Chambermaids know their place! And what sort of a foolish chambermaid would risk her very position with a misadventure like this? Nancy, it's time to grow up.

Taking a deep breath, Nancy straightened her uniform and forced a smile.

'Shall we?' she ventured, and followed them all down the stairs.

The dressing rooms behind the Grand were eerily silent as the procession of chambermaids – laden with buckets, dusters, mops and brushes – entered by the back doors and walked through. The walls were decorated with great portraits of Hélène Marchmont and Raymond de Guise, photographs taken in black and white of the princes and starlets with whom they danced, right here in the Buckingham Hotel. Hand-painted posters announcing the arrival of the Archie Adams Band stood either side of a bank of great mirrors set into silver frames – and, between the velveteen couches where the dancers and musicians reclined each night, wardrobes stood open, displaying ball gowns of turquoise and coral, robe-de-style gowns of pink peach satin, black evening dresses of soft plush velvet, fitted bodices, ivory corsets and so much more.

The girls were filing through the ballroom doors, out onto the dance floor itself. They must have done this before, because not one of them batted an eyelid as they stepped through the great swinging doors into the cavernous interior. Only Nancy paused as she crossed the threshold. Perhaps this was what it was like to be Hélène Marchmont or Raymond de Guise. *Imagine the music*, she thought. *Imagine the applause*.

But there was no applause today, and no music would be heard in the ballroom all week. As Nancy emerged, she saw Mrs Moffatt holding court over the chambermaids who'd already arrived. Tall scaffolds were being assembled to reach the great chandeliers hanging above. One caretaker, atop one of the precarious-looking constructions, was reaching out with a spanner to ease the chandelier out of the contraption that held it there. Mrs Moffatt had said it took an entire week to bring them down, clean them to perfection, and hoist them back into place – and now that Nancy saw the scale of the endeavour, she could quite believe it.

Other workmen were busying themselves around the corners of the room. The tables and chairs had been stored, and a carpenter and his lads were down on their hands and knees, inspecting the floorboards for the damage caused by gentlemen's brogues and ladies' heels.

The Grand was due to be closed for seven days and seven nights. While Mrs Whitehead stretched the rest of the girls to take care of the rooms and suites, Mrs Moffatt rallied her own housekeeping staff around her. Chandeliers did not polish themselves.

As the girls fanned out, Nancy lingered in the dressing room doorway, breathing it in. She and the chambermaids got to work. Then Nancy heard someone singing quietly to himself – and, when she turned, she saw the figure of Raymond de Guise gliding through the dressing room behind her. His black hair was thick with curls, more unruly than it was on those nights he waltzed so gracefully across the ballroom floor – and it seemed somehow incredible to discover that he did not always wear his evening suit. Today he was wearing strong pleated trousers and a white polo shirt – he seemed completely out of character.

Nancy did not like to think she was spellbound, because she was not that sort of girl, but what else might it have been rooting her to the spot? Raymond de Guise looked as striking off the dance floor as he did on it. He was tall and lithe and . . . Nancy tried to shake the sensation off. She did not believe in fairy tales. You quickly lost your faith in Prince Charming when you lived in a village like hers, with every miner's son in a three-village radius badgering you, at some time or another, for attention. Besides, she had not forgotten what she had written to Frank. There were worlds within worlds in the Buckingham Hotel. Raymond de Guise belonged to another world to Nancy Nettleton.

Pull yourself together, Nancy! There are portraits of him in the ballroom, but he's only a dancer . . .

She slipped into the dressing room.

Raymond de Guise had stepped into one of the wardrobes. It must have been bigger than Nancy realised because, for a moment, he vanished into the dinner jackets hanging there. Then, when he emerged, he was carrying a bulky, green canvas bag.

His eyes met hers. They darted down to the clothes he had collected, and then back up – almost, Nancy fancied, as if they had something to hide.

She was already flushing scarlet, so into the silence she said, 'Thank you . . .'

Raymond de Guise screwed up his eyes.

'That is to say,' Nancy stammered, 'for the other night. For . . . assisting me. If you hadn't –' she looked over her shoulder to make doubly certain none of the other girls were listening in – 'Miss Edgerton would not have let the matter go. I would have been dismissed . . .'

Raymond seemed bewildered, then his eyes lit up in recognition.

'You . . . work here?' Raymond said, glancing over her shoulder, through the great swing doors, to where Mrs Moffatt and the chambermaids were gathered.

'Yes.'

'The ballroom is open to all, of course. It has been ever since the Grand opened its doors. But it draws a . . . certain breed, shall we say? We're about to be full of the season's debutantes. And there you were. I'd thought you were one of our dreamers – they get word that King Edward or one of the princes is going to be in the ballroom and they do everything they can to slip in. I had no idea you *worked* here.'

Nancy was lost for words. Was Raymond de Guise *admonishing* her – or was there, dare she think it, some admiration in his voice? Admiration for her daring? Why would a man as entitled as Raymond de Guise admire something like that?

He smiled. 'You were fortunate that night, Miss . . .'

'Nettleton,' Nancy whispered.

'Miss Edgerton has her virtues, but generosity is not one of them. If she had kept you there, while one of the general managers was summoned – why, we wouldn't be speaking now.'

'I know it,' said Nancy – but, refusing to feel ashamed, she took a deep breath and looked Raymond straight in the eye. 'I'd wanted to see the Grand for myself. I'm not a dancer, Mr de Guise. You won't tell it to look at me, but my leg is . . . not what it might be. And yet – just to *see* it, if only for a few moments. It was worth what Miss Edgerton tried to do to me. I saw you dancing with Grusinskaya. I believe I saw the air between your feet and the ballroom floor.'

Raymond de Guise's lips parted, as if he was going to say something – but it was only the hint of the smile he was trying to suppress. 'You liked what you saw?'

Good Lord, Nancy, why are you blushing?

'I did.'

There was a moment of silence before Raymond finally said, 'It means a lot to hear it, Miss Nettleton. Every night I dance in this hotel, but so many of our visitors are inured to the beauty of it. They've danced in too many glamorous ballrooms to remember what it was first like to step into this world. So thank you, Miss Nettleton. For reminding me how that feels.'

Nancy ventured, 'I'd love to see it again, Mr de Guise. But I think, perhaps, that my ballroom days are over before they've begun. I was foolhardy.'

'I'd say you survived it, Miss Nettleton. If old Mrs Moffatt over there hasn't summoned you to the housekeeping office and given you your marching orders, well, you're probably unscathed.' He grinned, wolfishly. 'Not that I'd recommend you tempt fate twice. You're new here. Am I right?'

Nancy nodded. 'Did my accent give me away? I admit I'm not altogether as polished as some, but Mrs Moffatt said it doesn't matter where you come from, not here. Once you step through the Buckingham doors, once you wear a uniform with the silver crown embroidered on it, you're of the Buckingham Hotel, and that's it.'

A strange look passed across Raymond's face. 'There is some truth in that, Miss Nettleton.' He turned as if to depart through the dressing-room back doors, but at the last moment something stopped him and he looked back. 'Everyone has to know their place in a hotel like this. Not just the chambermaids and the concierges. Not just the pages and the pot boys in the kitchens. Even me. Even Archie Adams has a role to play. Why, even Mr Maynard Charles himself. The point is, if you don't know your place here then Miss Edgerton is the least of the problems, you'll find. I shouldn't say this, Miss Nettleton, and perhaps I'll live to regret it, but – stay away, wherever and however you can, from the Edgerton set. You'll see them in the hotel from time to time. You'll clean up after them and make tidy their beds. The

Hamburg Schechts, or Mr Mosley, any of Lord Edgerton's associates at that Fascist Union of his. They gather, sometimes, in the Grand or the cocktail lounge or the brasserie. If you cross paths with them, make sure you stay downwind, won't you?' He paused. 'I don't know why, but you stick out like a sore thumb, Miss Nettleton.' He looked at her, his sad eyes aglow. 'I mean that as a compliment. But sometimes, just sometimes, you might find that, in the Buckingham Hotel, being invisible is a strength.'

Nancy was about to reply when she heard her name being called out across the ballroom. Raymond nodded at her again, then disappeared back through the dressing-room doors – and she turned to see the rest of the chambermaids gathered around one of the crystal chandeliers, which lay on the ballroom floor like a shimmering giant's crown.

'Miss Nettleton!' Mrs Moffatt barked as Nancy squeezed her way into the fringes of the group. 'Good of you to join us!'

'I'm sorry, Mrs Moffatt. My head was rather in the clouds.' Somewhere beside her she thought she heard one of the girls saying, 'Who on *earth* does she think she is?'

But then Mrs Moffatt was directing them in the ways to unclasp the chandelier's pendants and spurs, how to drain oil from its overflow cups, how to detach each branch from the miniature crown at its end, cupping it against the body to protect the crystals still glittering on its circumference – and, whatever mutterings there were about her were lost as the day's work began.

Chapter Nine

BILLY BROGAN SLID OUT OF the Buckingham's staff entrance and crossed Berkeley Square as the music of the ballroom faded behind him.

Sometimes it pained him to leave the hotel. In there, he felt important, a man who guests and staff relied on to *get things done*. Outside the hotel, he felt smaller somehow, less of a *somebody*. Or at least he felt that way until he hurried past the palace at Westminster and, crossing the old Lambeth Bridge, came to the terrace he had always called home. Billy Brogan might have been seventeen years old, but the pull of his ma's home-cooked dinner still filled him with joy.

He could already hear the sounds of laughter, and his father barracking one of his younger siblings, coming through the walls. These were the beautiful, chaotic sounds of home. It was always quiet when he left of a morning, his father up and out to the fish market long before dawn, the others – his brothers and his sisters – still fast asleep, wrapped around each other in the big double beds. To come home to chaos was one of the most wonderful things of all.

This was an opportunity too good to miss, so Billy crept along the brick archway between his house and the next and, pressing his face against the glass in the back door, waited until one of his siblings cartwheeled by. Here came Patrick and Annie, here came Conor and Daniel, here came Roisin and Holly. Billy's mother, with her flowing auburn hair and round shoulders, was too busy hunched over the cooking pot to notice – but when the smallest of all the Brogans, Gracie May, scurried by, she looked up, saw Billy's face in the glass, and let out such a shriek of delight that it must have been heard from Crystal Palace to Parliament Hill Fields.

'*BILLY!*' she exclaimed – and, moments later, a multitude of hands were clamouring at the door to be the ones to let him in.

By the time Billy crashed through the doors and the children were upon him, his mother had put down her serving spoon, his father had come down the old creaking stairs, and the scenes of jubilation went on and on. Anyone passing by might have thought Billy Brogan had gone away to war and come back a decorated hero, such were the celebrations on South Lambeth Road.

'What have you got for us?' asked little Patrick, seven years old with a mop of unruly red hair.

'Did you bring more pralines?' asked Roisin, beseeching with her big brown eyes.

Billy picked the satchel off his shoulder and spread it open on the floor. 'I got . . .' From the darkness within he pulled out a package. 'A half-rack of lamb! Here, Conor, give this to Ma, she'll have a fit when she sees that. And I got –' from the bag he pulled another package – 'shortbreads, shortbreads for the lot of you. Go on, have your fill! And I got . . .' By now his father was standing over him. William Brogan senior had a curmudgeonly look. His face had once been as cherubic as Billy's, but age had turned it doughy, and where his hair was not thinning it had turned silver as the stars. 'Here, Pa, this is for you and Ma.' Out of the bag came a green glass bottle. William Brogan looked it up and down. 'That's good red wine, that is, Pa. Fit for dukes and duchesses. Taste it. Have yourself a glass. There's more where that come from. And I got . . .' The last package he drew from the bag was what Billy considered the ultimate prize. Half a gateau had been sitting on the side in the hotel kitchen all afternoon, just begging to be taken.

He could see the way his father was looking at the cake. 'Be still my heart,' he said, without taking his eyes off the mountainous crags of whipped cream, meringue and candied lemon.

'You oughtn't be stealing!' his mother called from the same kitchen where, moments ago, she had cooed with delight over the half-rack of lamb.

'I've told you before. It's not theft. It's all piss to them that can afford better. They'd have poured that wine down the drain if I hadn't have helped them out. That gateau was for the bins, or the chambermaids if they were fast enough. All I'm doing is a bit of . . . reorganising. Nobody's any worse off and nobody's any the wiser.'

Begrudgingly, his pa nodded. Then, as he always did, he muttered, 'Mind you don't get caught,' and proceeded to dip his fingers in the fresh cream greedily.

Billy might have spent all day at the Buckingham Hotel, but his work was hardly done. After he had helped clear up dinner, there were seven rowdy youngsters to put to bed. He took it in shifts with his ma and pa – until, at last, not one of them was left awake.

'It'll be off to bed with you too, will it, son?' his father asked finally.

'And you, Pa. You got to be up before dawn, just like me.'

His father's face creased. Almost three decades he'd been up long before dawn and travelling down to the fish market. Sometimes, Billy thought, he seemed to look at the things Billy brought home and wonder: was it all worth it? Surely, *surely*, there must have been a better way to make a living than fish? Billy remembered the first time he'd seen the look ghost across his father's face. It was not envy, as he'd once believed. Nor was it shame – though there was certainly some shame in it, for Billy had sometimes brought home more in a day than his father could in a week. It was, instead, a kind of bewilderment that there were people out there for whom this was nothing: people like Lord Edgerton, like Maynard Charles, people who danced for a living like the debonair Raymond de Guise. There was not one world, Billy's father understood; there were two, one for the rich and one for the poor, and by some strange magic, his son got to flit between the two.

'That reminds me, Pa . . .'

Billy produced a small brown envelope, printed with the emblem of the Buckingham Hotel, and handed it to his father. When his father peered inside, he froze. 'Son, we've spoken about—'

'Pa, I told you. It's because of tips. I get little gifts when I run errands for the guests, or for the concierge, or for almost anybody. You don't get something for nothing. I provide that something. Pa, that's what I'm there for.'

'Yes, son. But . . . *this*?'

He was counting the coins and notes with his fingers, scarcely able to believe. All *this*? It had scarcely been a week since Billy last came home with pockets full and jangling.

'Goodnight, Pa.'

Billy loped up the stairs to the little box room that was his own: an old mattress on the floor, a little tea chest filled with his odds and ends, a rack where his ma had laid out clothes for the morning (because, though he might have been seventeen, she was still his mother). He had already flopped onto the bed, eager for a night's rest, when he realised his pa had followed him.

'You'll be watching yourself, won't you, son?' he said.

'Pa, I've told you. It's just odd errands. You don't understand these folks. There's folks who'd pay you a whole day's rate up at Billingsgate just to get down and shine their shoes. There's some who'll throw you a pound note if you're happy to wipe their arse.'

Billy's father purpled. 'There you go, with that smart tongue o' yours. Just you make sure that Mr Maynard Charles doesn't get wind of it. You lose this job, you'll be hard pressed finding another. We *need* that hotel.'

Only when Billy was certain his father had gone to bed did he lie back on his cot, reach into his back pocket, and draw out the two pound notes he had secreted there. Then, reaching down into his mattress, he dragged out the little tin keepsake box he'd kept since he was young, listened to the rattle of coins and other notes inside, and slipped the new additions within. His father had no need to worry. Billy Brogan knew exactly what he was doing in the Buckingham Hotel.

And if Maynard Charles were to catch wind of it? Well, it would matter not one jot. Those two pound notes now sitting happily in his keepsake tin – they'd come courtesy of Maynard Charles himself.

Chapter Ten

Raymond de Guise was up with the lark, pacing behind the locked doors of the Grand Ballroom. It seemed so much bigger during the day. When it was not thronged with dancers, and the champagne was not in full flow, the ballroom was almost ghostly. To Raymond's mind, there was something sad about it. A ballroom was for living. A ballroom demanded people and laughter and noise. And yet . . .

He did not like the silence. When he was with a guest in the ballroom, or rehearsing the demonstrations with Hélène in the little studio behind the dressing room doors, he was spirited away to some other place, a realm where nothing else mattered but the music and movement. But when he was alone . . .

He had tried to put it out of his mind, but ever since that summer night when Mrs Adelman had whisked him back to her suite, the idea of his brother would not leave him alone. He woke, sometimes, from dreams in which his brother pitched up here, at the doors of the Buckingham Hotel. He imagined the looks on the faces of Maynard Charles and Hélène Marchmont. He wondered what would happen if his brother were to stride into the Grand Ballroom and put his arms around him. He had not appeared yet, but that did nothing to quell Raymond's nerves. *Every day he doesn't appear is just a day closer to it happening*, he thought ruefully. *And then what? How would I explain a man like that to the citizens of the Buckingham Hotel?*

No, there was only so long he could ignore Mrs Adelman's appeal. He looked up at the notice pinned to the wall beside the ballroom bar: 12–19 SEPTEMBER, THE GRAND BALLROOM CLOSED FOR REFURBISHMENT. Every September the ballroom went into a week-long hibernation, reopening as radiant as the day it first opened, the air heavy with the smells of beeswax and varnish. *No dancing for a week*, thought Raymond, *and all of these evenings to myself*. Maynard Charles would make him work for those days off – the autumn season with its new debutantes, the Christmas festivities and New Year Masquerade Ball to come – but that week, Raymond decided, was when he would extinguish the kernel of fear that was taking root in his gut.

This was the week he would go and find his brother for himself.

Raymond heard knocking at the ballroom's door. He crossed the dance floor to unlock it.

Vivienne Edgerton was standing there in her day dress, aquamarine with pleated sleeves and a single felt flower sitting over her heart. Evidently, she had been up early to prepare for her lesson, because she had painted her face as elegantly as if she were stepping out into the Grand for the night. Her lips were striking and red, and her nails were painted crimson. The elegant women of London town scarcely painted their nails, but Vivienne was a New Yorker through and through.

'Miss Edgerton,' he said, 'please come through.'

Vivienne stopped to survey the empty ballroom. Her lips, which had been pursed, parted as she tried to suppress her smile. The whole of the Grand – and all to herself . . .

She turned on the spot to find Raymond closing the doors. When he looked her up and down and noticed the ball gown she had draped over one arm, he said carefully, 'You won't be needing it, Miss Edgerton. It is best if we are free, at least to begin . . .'

For a fleeting second, Vivienne seemed disappointed. Ordinarily she leaped upon any opportunity to wear one of the dresses she acquired in her shopping trips to Knightsbridge and Earl's Court. The gown she had brought was a perfect replica of the one worn by the Hollywood starlet Myrna Loy; she'd appointed a couturier from Bond Street to recreate it herself. Relenting, she draped it over the balustrade and descended the marble steps onto the oak and mahogany chequered floor. 'Shall we?' she began – and stumbled as she attempted a spin.

'First things first, Vivienne.'

Raymond joined her on the dance floor. It had been three nights since he'd had to carry her out of the ballroom. Today she barely seemed the same girl. Her eyes did not have that same glazed, faraway look. She was poised and elegant and, Raymond had to admit, quite beautiful, in her own steely way. She had a dancer's poise, that much was certain. She held herself with a certain confidence, of the kind he'd only really seen in Hélène Marchmont. So much of dance was about confidence and approach. You could learn all of the steps, all of the movements and postures perfectly, but if you didn't have the self-assurance to carry them through, the room would dance on without you, leaving you beached and alone.

'Tell me,' he said, 'have you danced before?'

'A little. There was a club in the East Village, back in New York. Daddy – that's my natural father, you understand – was not eager for me to go there, but Michael knew the doorman and he used to take me for cocktails. Michael O'Hara – he was my . . . close friend.'

A lover, thought Raymond. *But why so surprised? A girl as beautiful and forward as Vivienne Edgerton would never be short of a suitor or two.* Vivienne had a way about her – a way of getting what she wanted, and it seemed to have existed long before Lord Edgerton ever made her his ward.

'There'd be an orchestra and a dance floor, but it wasn't nearly as grand as this, Mr de Guise. When the girls had quaffed too many cocktails, they'd be up on the tables. Nobody seemed to mind. They were jiving or they were Lindy hopping or, you know, just breaking away and moving any which way they liked.'

'We'll be leaving the tables alone today, Miss Edgerton.'

'*Vivienne*. Call me Vivienne.'

It seemed improper somehow, but if that was what she wanted, it was what Raymond would have to do.

'Come then, Vivienne. Show me what you have.'

Just this one time, thought Raymond nervously as Vivienne stepped towards him, closing her body with his and holding out her hand. *All you have to do is dance with her once, satisfy whatever curiosity she has for the ballroom and be done with it. She'll have moved on next week. There'll be some new fascination.*

It felt wrong, sliding his arm around the waist of Lord Edgerton's daughter. Lord Edgerton might not have been the one who hired and fired, but as head of the board, a single withering look or an idle comment could spell the end for anyone in the Buckingham's halls. Raymond had seen it happen. There had once been a porter who brushed Lord Edgerton's case up against a banister rail on his way to the Atlantic Suite – after that incident; never to be seen again. A waiter too slovenly or a concierge too unwilling – Lord Edgerton demanded perfection, and those who could not supply it were suddenly damned. Raymond could only imagine what might happen should rumours of any improper relations with Lord Edgerton's stepdaughter spread around the Buckingham. He already knew how quickly a rumour could spread – particularly among the chambermaids. A rumour about him and Vivienne would be damning, and for a time he held her at a distance – but Vivienne was no timid, meek little thing, and when she sensed his reluctance she straightened up, staring him directly in the eye. She was instructing him, Raymond thought, so he tightened his hold. 'Just mirror me, Miss Edgerton. You've seen it done so much . . .'

First he stepped into her, and then she stepped back. Then he slid sideways, guiding Vivienne as she did the same.

'Look to your left, Miss Edgerton. Try not to look at me.' Raymond allowed himself a fleeting smile. 'Tempting as it might be.'

It was simple, to begin with. Just rhythm dancing, to get them started. Raymond had brought out a gramophone from the dressing room and it crackled with 'The Winter Serenade'. In simple steps, they crossed the ballroom, turned, and came back. He danced her to the heart of the room and held her there. Then he danced her around. He thought: *she can do this. She might not be a natural, but she's studied it, she's seen it, her body's warming up to the music.*

'Miss Edgerton. Let me . . .'

He stepped into her, planting his leg between hers. She was too close – he could feel the touch of her thighs against his – but he directed her all the same. 'I'm going to stay here, on this spot, Miss Edgerton. Use the weight of your body. You're to step around me. Watch, like *this* . . .'

It wasn't the most complicated move in the ballroom repertoire. It took balance and it took commitment and, if you were going to get it right, it took elegance as well. By rights, Vivienne Edgerton ought to have stepped effortlessly around him so that they might dance back across the ballroom floor. And yet, moments later, her foot entangled with his. She tried to right herself, but it was too late; gravity had taken her. Raymond caught her, lifted her back to his side and, once they had found their rhythm again, he urged her into the movement once more.

This time Vivienne concentrated too hard. She'd let the music carry her along, but now she fought against it. So intently was she staring at her feet, trying to make them do everything she instructed, that she didn't think about the rhythm of the music at all. Then, everything happened at once. The music seemed to speed up. Raymond shuffled around. Vivienne's left foot tried to follow, but smashed into her right. Suddenly, all was a chaos of windmilling arms and legs – and Vivienne Edgerton would have crashed into the ballroom floor, if Raymond de Guise hadn't been there to catch her.

Vivienne let out an exasperated howl.

'Try it again, Miss Edgerton. There's no humiliation in not getting it straight away.' Raymond stopped. Her eyes were downcast, looking anywhere but at him. 'Miss Edgerton?'

'For God's sake, Raymond, would you not call me by that name! I'm Vivienne. *Vivienne.* The Edgerton came along and replaced a name I was more than happy with and . . .'

Vivienne ripped herself out of Raymond's hold, clattering across the dance floor to the place where the gramophone sat. In a moment she had silenced it. Then she threw herself, like a toddler in a tantrum, into one of the chairs propped up against the wall. For a moment, she kneaded at her eyes, as if she might cry – but the thought of smearing the Maybelline eyelash darkener she'd painted around her eyes gave her pause. She simply looked up, despairing, at Raymond instead.

'Why can't I *do it*?'

'Vivienne, you're too hard on yourself. A ballroom dancer isn't born overnight – certainly not a great one. And . . . you're not without talent, Vivienne. You have grace and you have poise and . . . what you lack, you don't lack in your body. You lack it up here –' he touched the side of his head – 'in the mind. You need to calm yourself. You need to breathe. You need to know: *it doesn't matter if you go wrong.*'

'I am calm,' Vivienne snapped, with rising resentment. Her New York accent became so much more pronounced when she was angry.

He could see her hands shaking and her eyes darting into every corner of the Grand. He wanted to be delicate with her. He wanted to *help*. It was just that she made it so damn difficult.

'What does it matter anyway?' Vivienne groaned. 'I could be the most talented dancer in the hotel and they wouldn't welcome me here! Not to dance. Not as anything more than a . . . a curiosity! I could surpass Hélène Marchmont. I could go to Paris and eclipse them all in the Parisian tango. I could create new pivots and spins, dances the world has never seen – but I wouldn't be able to do anything with them, and all because of *who* I am. Or who *he* is.' She spat the word as if it was a curse. 'Lord Edgerton. My *stepfather*. I'd bring shame on him, on his whole damn dynasty. Can you imagine – me, Vivienne Edgerton, telling him I'd no interest in inheriting and being married off . . . because all I wanted was to tango?'

Raymond was silent. Then, with a deep breath, he uttered words he hoped he would not regret. 'Miss Edgerton. *Vivienne*,' he corrected himself. 'I've only one thing to say to that.' Then, with a wolfish grin, he added, 'That's absolute rot.'

Her cat-like eyes glared.

'Do you know who taught *me* to dance? Georges de la Motte. Perhaps you've heard the name? I won't bore you with the details. The story is long and I've told it often enough. Georges belonged to a barony, down in the very heart of France. If there were still kings and queens on the continent, why, his father would have been in line – distantly, perhaps, but still with the blood coursing through his veins. Georges might have grown up to inherit one of the barony's estates. But instead I met him at a ballroom in Brighton, where he became champion. He was grander than you or I, grander than anyone in the Buckingham Hotel, and yet he danced among us. And . . .' Raymond was hitting his stride now. He took Vivienne by the hand, raised her back to her feet. 'There is an old friend of mine, from my dance hall days. Mr Warren Sykes. I'm certain you've heard of him! Born in a Bristol slum, and now the reigning champion of England. He's danced with princesses, Miss Edgerton. His father was a fishmonger.'

He could feel Vivienne relenting somehow, softening in his arms. *Yes, this is it,* he thought, *there's a chance she might even understand.* His arm slipped around her waist and his palm pressed against hers, so that they might suddenly be ready to dance again. 'The best dancers come from low and from high. When you dance, the rest of the world can be forgotten. You know how the rest of the world works. The high stay on high and the low get on with things as best they can. But *here*? Here, where there's music and there's dance. Vivienne, don't ever let another soul make you think otherwise. *Here* you get to be what you want to be – no matter what your father might say.'

Slowly, they danced. Raymond stepped forward, so that his leg was between hers again, and she pivoted around him. Perhaps her body and mind were finally aligned, because for the first time she was able to sail around him without stumbling.

'You see,' he whispered, and there was a very real sense of pride flurrying through him, 'you *can* do it.'

Finally, her cheeks flushed red and she whispered, 'It's those chambermaids and concierges and . . . It's all of *them*, looking at me, knowing who I am. I didn't ask to be his daughter. I barely asked to come to the Buckingham Hotel. And . . .' She paused. 'Can't we dance in private, Raymond? I want to dance where no one else can see.' She held him tighter. He was surprised to find her fingers were threaded through his. 'We could dance in my suite. It's big enough, if we clear a space. Would you . . . want to come to my suite, Raymond?'

Her words had begun running together, and now they petered into silence. They stopped mid-pivot and she hung, frozen in time, in front of him. She looked up. Her green eyes were wide and open. Raymond could smell the scent she was wearing. *Chanel*, he thought. Her eyes glittered. Her ruby lips opened . . .

No, thought Raymond. *No.* She was looking at him expectantly, as if a man had never said no to her before.

Raymond stepped back.

The music went on, but the dance was over.

Soon the silence had become uncomfortable. When she was hanging in his arms, Vivienne Edgerton had seemed . . . *human*, he wanted to say. *Fragile. Exposed.* But now her lips had closed, her eyes were sharp, her arms were folded. She looked at him with her jaw clenched and every muscle in her body taut and rigid.

'Perhaps that's enough for today, Miss Edgerton?'

Vivienne swallowed a sob. Then suddenly she was off, marching across the dance floor to snatch up her ball gown from where it was draped on the balustrade.

After she was gone, her footsteps echoing as she clattered up the marble walkway out of the Grand, Raymond sat back and closed his eyes. His heart was beating a panicked rhythm. Surely *that* wasn't what she'd come here for? Giving Vivienne Edgerton what she wanted when she asked for tutoring was one thing; giving her what she wanted when she looked to place her lips over his was quite another. If he had kissed her and the hotel found out, well, there wasn't a chance in hell he'd be dancing with the Crown Princess of Norway on the same dance floor as King Edward himself at the Masquerade Ball this New Year. He'd have been dragged into Maynard Charles's office and summarily dismissed. No, he'd done the right thing, he was certain of that.

The look on her face as she'd fled from the ballroom was emblazoned on his eyes. He hadn't meant to hurt her. He hadn't meant to embarrass or insult. But one thing was certain, when you danced with Vivienne Edgerton, whether you resisted her or did everything that she said, you were dancing with disaster either way.

Chapter Eleven

THE MAN WHO STEPPED INTO the Red Lion Hotel on High Holborn was dressed in the finest bespoke woollen overcoat, with an Austin Reed black bowler hat perched on the top of his head and a walking cane tipped in brass at his side. Minutes after he crossed the threshold, the doors opened again. The man who emerged was dressed in a jacket of brown leather – and, though the cap he wore kept hidden the same unruly black hair, it was crushed and worn and had seen better days. The polished black brogues he had been wearing were stuffed into an army-issue haversack, the same as the rest of his finery, and in their place he wore a pair of tan workman's boots with steel caps in their toes. He kept his head down, fearful that he might be seen.

Then, slinging the uniform of one life over his shoulder, Raymond de Guise stepped aboard the omnibus heading east and watched as the porcelain palaces of Holborn and St Paul's turned into pavements teeming with bankers and clerks – and from there into the tumbledown red terraces of the East End.

The street markets were in full throng along the Whitechapel Road. Market sellers hawked their wares – green apples, ladies' scarves, breads and flowers and rack upon rack of new clothes.

Afternoon was not yet paling to dusk, but the doors were wide open at the Blind Beggar and from inside came the sound of the Irish fiddle. It almost made Raymond want to stop and put on his dancing shoes – but this was not the right part of the world for him to start twirling about a stage, so instead he kept his head down. All of life was here. Irish voices mixed with Polish and Russian and more. The smells, so different from the smells of the Buckingham at night, were intoxicating. Somebody was frying fat sausages on a griddle.

Soon, Raymond left the markets and found himself standing outside one of the noble red terraces. At least, it had once been noble. Now its upper windows were boarded up and the chimney stack was fallen, and the yard out front was a briar patch where nettle and thistle grew wild. Raymond looked up at the sad facade, and felt suddenly conspicuous.

He steeled himself. It was the middle of September, the trees across London were turning to russets and reds, and he had known since Mrs Adelman's visit at the height of summer that he would have to come back here soon. Her message had been stark and simple – *your brother is coming home* – and, after that, she said no more, no matter how much Raymond had asked. *The only way you'll find out anything is if you . . . go back*, she'd said – and with that, Raymond had left.

Now, with a heavy heart, he knocked on the door and waited for it to open.

The woman who presented herself was plump and round, with a face that, though drawn in lines, still radiated kindness. Her fingers were encrusted with a dozen different rings – and her expression, when she considered the man standing on her doorstep, was one of elation mixed with surprise.

'Hello, Ma,' said Raymond.

'Ray Cohen, you layabout! Get yourself through these doors. But give your mother a kiss first, boy!'

Raymond, who towered a foot and more over his mother, had to stoop to get into her arms. He rested his head on her shoulder and smelled the familiar scents of tobacco and carbolic soap.

'May!' his mother called as she dragged him bodily through the door. 'Rebecca! Get yourself into the lounge this *instant*. Our Ray's come back. Won't somebody strangle one o' them chickens?'

An hour later, the chicken – which had spent its day idly pecking at the grit in the scrubland that passed for a garden out back – was broiling in a pot with leeks and carrot from the market, and Alma Cohen was busy kneading dumplings while her son took the last of the evening light.

The garden had gone to seed since Raymond last visited this place – but three years could transform a world many times over. The truth was, it had first fallen on hard times much longer ago. When Raymond was a younger man, this garden had been a highlight of the terrace. His father had green fingers and the sunflowers Raymond himself had helped sow could grow as tall as your head. Raymond still remembered how proud his father had been of those flowers. But then had come that terrible year of 1929 . . .

The Depression might have caused panic for those in their city homes, who went to work in their suits and ties, but it was people like the Cohens who *really* suffered. All across the East End, gardens were upended, new vegetable patches created as people determined to survive. Now, the vegetable patch that had once been his father's pride and joy – and the family's salvation – was a wasteland of fallen masonry, knee-high grass, thistles and the chicken coop, patched up so often to keep the foxes out that it now looked like a fortress. The last of the day's sun was spilling over the chimney stacks of the houses that backed on to this. Somewhere, somebody was bawling at their loved one; the voice flurried up and filled the air between the houses.

'So,' his mother said, calling out through the kitchen window as Raymond knelt down to tempt one of the marauding chickens with a seed, 'you got our message, did you?'

Raymond's eyes darted up at the upper storey of the red brick house. *Is he up there?* he thought. *My brother?* He looked for the net curtains twitching; if he was being watched by that errant brother of his, there was no sign. But then Artie Cohen was a secretive sort. It was secrets that had divided them, in the end. Secrets which had kept Raymond away from home, living a second life, for such a long time.

'You're as crafty as you ever were, Ma. You might have sent a letter.'

'Up to that hotel o' yours? And risk some post boy opening it up and spilling your *precious* secret? No, Ray. You mightn't think much about us these days, but I wouldn't do that to you. I know how ashamed you is . . .'

Raymond tried to ignore the attack. She was goading him to say something, just so she could start a fight, but he was determined to rise above it. 'Who is she, this Mrs Adelman?'

'She's a lady.'

Raymond shook his head. His mother was as vexing as ever. 'This much I understood.'

'I been cleaning for her, if you must know. Scrubbing her carpets and getting elbow deep in her latrine. She has a townhouse down on the river. It was her husband's, but now he's gone. Well, we had that in common, me and Mrs Adelman. I'd been cleaning her *unmentionables* all summer long before we got to nattering one night. It was her that suggested it. That she might go up to the old Buckingham and seek you out. Mrs Adelman had a son too. Lost him in the War – so when she heard about my two boys, neither one of them seen their mother for years, well, she was mortified on my behalf. So I told her – go on up there, but he doesn't call himself Ray Cohen no more. No, he fancies himself *Monsieur* de Guise . . .'

'It's my stage name, Mother.'

Real name too, thought Raymond – though he had long ago decided he would not tell his mother of the day he'd filed the papers with Somerset House and had his new name officially recognised. His ma would think it a slight, an insult to her dearly departed husband – and she did not deserve that. How could she possibly understand a world like the Buckingham Hotel – where, if Maynard Charles were to see a lowly name like 'Ray Cohen' on his accounts each month, questions would be asked? To be taken seriously as a man of consequence, Georges de la Motte had once told him, one needs to inhabit the role – even when one is not in the ballroom. It was advice a younger Ray Cohen had taken to heart.

And besides, he thought, *a Jewish name like mine? In a hotel owned by Lord Edgerton and frequented by all his Union friends? No, that would never work.*

Raymond wandered back into the kitchen. His aunties, May and Rebecca were camped around the tiny table, making a point of pouring tea into dainty china cups. *Only the best for someone as fancy as Raymond de Guise!* When Raymond took one, it tasted bitter and stewed, as only the best Cohen family tea could.

The whole house was a rush of vivid memories. He'd been born here, in these four walls. He'd played in this hall, and, when his brother Artie had come along, it had been Raymond who took him out into the streets and introduced him to the other boys, who looked out for him as he grew up. The house had been so full in those days. As he got older, there were always his father's ne'er-do-well friends turning up, any time of day and night, with mysterious boxes being buried and then unearthed from the yard out back – all of the things they traded down at the market, with never a question about from where they might have come. Artie and Raymond would be out from sun-up to sundown, back for dinner and bathing in front of the fire, while Mrs Cohen kept a pot on the stove almost every hour of the day.

'I've been meaning to come, Ma. I know it's been a time, but you'll have to trust me on that.'

'It's been weeks, Ray. Mrs Adelman sought you out when summer was still high. And besides, when was the last time we saw you?'

'Not since the Christmas after Stanley died,' chipped in Aunt May, who, at a decade older than Raymond's mother, had a smoky, music hall voice. 'December 1933.'

Mrs Cohen wrung her hands on a washcloth. 'We don't think no less of you for it. You do what you got to do, you always did, but . . . it's been a long time, boy. And you know what we've been through here, with your father passing and your brother gone.'

Again, Raymond looked up, as if trying to work out if his brother was *here*, lingering up above, refusing to come down.

'It isn't like you think it is, Ma.'

'What is it like then, *Lord de Guise*?' asked Aunt May sarcastically, fishing tea leaves out of her own cup.

It was like this: a boy who'd grown up off the Whitechapel Road, who'd doted on his father – God rest him – and followed him down to the Brancroft Social Club every Wednesday, Friday and Saturday night. Old Mr Cohen was fond of the dogs, and they took bets in the back room there, but on Saturday nights the place would be cleared, there'd be a pianist, a couple of decent trumpet players, and, if they were lucky, a singer. If the singer didn't show up, they made do with some of the local girls instead – and that was good enough, because, with so many people swarming onto the dance floor, you could hardly hear the music anyway. All that really mattered was that there was enough drink and enough dance. Raymond had seen men who'd brawled with each other in the market one day drinking together the next night, and even stepping out onto the dance floor to waltz with each other's sisters, as if drink and dance could shed all the nastiness of day-to-day life clean away. And his father . . .

His father was the strong man at home. He'd done a stretch in Pentonville for fencing stolen goods – at the trial they said he was the mastermind, that he played father figure to all the young crooks who went out robbing on his account – and this was legend among the family. The bare bones of it were true, but the way they painted him as a dastardly genius, well, that was just rot. When Raymond was small and Stanley Cohen had come back from the War, he'd sold scrap metal to make ends meet. Where the scrap metal came from, nobody asked – nobody but the occasional policeman doing his rounds, who soon got driven out or shut up by the local boys, who always owed Mr Cohen a thing or two. Scrap metal pilfered and scrap metal sold, that was Stanley's line of work – until, one day, the law caught up with him.

But the thing about Stanley Cohen, hard man or not, was that he could *dance*. Didn't care who knew it. Didn't care who saw. Friday and Saturday nights, he'd leave his mates to go to the horses and he'd be in the Brancroft – sometimes somewhere further afield – with his prized dancing shoes on and his hair thick with cream. Once, he'd said to Raymond that he'd watched too many of his friends trot off to Flanders and never come back to worry about what anyone else thought of him, so he was going to spend the rest of his days doing exactly as he pleased. And what pleased him was dancing with whoever would have him, whether they were twice his age or half, box stepping around the Brancroft or foxtrotting up and down the Palais. Raymond was there to watch. And if, on occasion, he noticed his father's hands where they oughtn't be, or got paid a few pennies to tell a little white lie to his mother, he saw nothing untoward in it. He would have done all of it, and more, just to be closer to his father.

'I'm sorry, Ma,' Raymond finally said. 'I've been a lousy son.'

'That you have.' She looked sad. 'But at least you know it.'

Raymond paused. An unspoken question had hung in the air between them, and he readied himself to ask it.

'So . . . is he here then?'

At that moment the front door opened, a broken voice called out, 'Ma!', and into the kitchen bouldered a black-haired rake of a man, with the same sad almond eyes as Raymond, the same unruly dark hair, the same striking cheekbones that gave him the air of some matinee idol.

The figure stopped dead in the kitchen doorway. 'Ray Cohen,' he said, 'as I live and breathe.'

For a moment the two men simply looked at one another, tension crackling in the air.

Then Raymond was lost in a chaos of arms as the new arrival threw himself around him, and his aunties and mother joined in too.

'Welcome home, Artie,' said Raymond, his voice lost in the crush. 'It's good to see you, little brother.'

Later, when the broiled chicken was ready to serve, Mrs Cohen asked Raymond to say some words for Stanley, dearly departed and gone from this world for three long years. Raymond hardly knew what to say, so long had he been away, but as they sat around the table he dredged up the memory of the time their father had taken his two boys down to the canal and they'd sat, together, on the towpath, fishing out old boots and suitcases with a rod Stanley's own father had once owned.

Those are the happy memories, thought Raymond, as he looked at his brother. *The blacker ones come next. What it was like when the coppers trapped Pa and put him in Pentonville. What Artie and I got swept up in while he was gone just to put food on the table . . .*

Artie was not quite as Raymond remembered him. When they had been boys, Artie had always been the rounder one, but now he was rangy and thin. That, Raymond supposed, was what a stretch in Pentonville Prison could do to you. It had been the same for their father.

'You look . . . well, Artie.'

'Ha!' Artie cackled, displaying a mouth in which two teeth had been knocked out in a prison cell brawl. 'I don't, but you're the same old charmer as ever, aren't you, Ray?'

'Is it good to be out, Artie?'

Artie beamed. 'I can't wait to get back inside.'

Aunts May and Rebecca hooted with laughter, but Mrs Cohen was less impressed. She picked up a ladle and made as if to wallop him with it.

'No violence, Ma. They'd put you in solitary for that.' Artie grinned as his mother humbly retreated. 'I'm glad to be out, Ray, but it's not all sweet tea and lemon cake out here. Inside, there was always work for us. Didn't get paid for it, but you got your bed and board, if you see what I mean? Out here . . . Well, who wants to take on an old lag like me?'

'He's been trying for weeks, Ray, but it's not like it used to be, not for the likes of us. There's Mr Goldstein been out of work a year already, and all his sons just scraping by. They think you're Jewish round here, now, and they wouldn't piss on you if you was on fire. Oh, it was always there, that kind of nastiness. But now it's out in the open, and no one pretends it isn't. Your father and me, we had our fair share of it. And you'll remember what the Furness boys was like when you were young – always yapping at you and your brother, on account of what you are. But things have changed, Ray. You won't notice it in that ballroom o' yours, but it's not the same on the streets. There's an . . . atmosphere. Some blackshirt boys turned over the butchers on the Commercial Road. They threw pig's blood all up the steps at the Congregation of Jacob.'

'Pah!' snorted Artie. 'What would Twinkle Toes care about that? He's got more work than he knows what to do with.'

Mrs Cohen continued, 'Most of your father's old crew are back in the old trade, robbing the townhouses on the river. Artie's going to stay out of that this time, ain't he? He's learned his lesson. But proper jobs aren't ten a penny like they was when you boys was just starting out. You got to fight for 'em now. And when you got a history like your brother's—'

'You got to find your own way in this world, Ma. Just like our Ray done.'

Raymond shifted uneasily in his chair, uncertain if Artie was castigating him or not. There was bitterness in the way Artie spoke. *But then, he always blamed me, didn't he? He thought I ought to have been there, on the night they caught him out robbing. That if I hadn't been out dancing . . .*

'It's all right for Ray, see. He's got a *talent*. But when you ain't got a talent, and you been out of work years already, all on account of serving at His Majesty's pleasure, well, you ain't got a hope. It's like it was before I went in. Well, you remember what it was like, don't you, Ray? Back in '32, and all of us Great Unwashed without two pennies to rub together.' Artie paused, shovelling another potato into his mouth. 'Nah, I'm forgettin' myself. You don't remember what it was like back then at all, 'cause you was off dancing up a storm in – where was it that year? Margate? Skegness? Anywhere that'd have you, you rotten sod. And here was the rest of us, on the breadline while you paraded around with that dandy of yours.'

'Now that isn't fair, Artie,' Mrs Cohen interrupted. 'Ray sent us half his winnings, every time he ranked in one of his competitions.'

'Yeah, and the other half he spent on fancy shoes and a nice new evening suit. And all to impress his fancy boy.'

'His name is Georges, Artie. And he's a friend. I owe him a great deal.'

It had been a long, hard road from following his father to the dance halls to waltzing across the Grand Ballroom at the Buckingham Hotel, and Raymond owed it all to Georges de la Motte. In the days after Raymond himself had started dancing in the

Brancroft – the envy even of his father, for all the girls flocked to dance with Ray Cohen – there'd been talk of the ballroom dance festival in faraway Brighton, a place where young and old, high-born and low could pitch themselves against each other for the coveted title Dancer of the Year. Raymond had grown obsessed with going, but it was a fool's dream; Brighton may as well have been over the oceans, an entirely different world. Only . . . Stanley Cohen loved his boy. And when he put his hand in his back pocket and came out with his fist crammed with enough money to get Ray there and back again, it was nothing more or less than an act of love. Raymond had put his arms around the old man then, and even though he had shaken him off – he was a man, after all – he had hesitated just enough that Raymond *knew* how much he was loved.

When he got there, Brighton was a revelation. Not just the seafront and the lights. Not just the girls, who braved the cold and turned Raymond's eye, up and down the pier. The Elysium Hotel was quite unlike any dance hall Raymond had seen before. Opulent glass chandeliers hung down from a barrel-vaulted ceiling, patterned in panels of gold and white. Three walls of the ballroom were lined in boxes for paying customers, each one of them draped in velvet. The dance floor itself was a chequerboard of ten thousand squares of gleaming mahogany, walnut and greenwood – and when Raymond stepped on it for the first time, it seemed to shift with his weight. Waltzing across the hard stone of the Brancroft Social Club could never compare to the sprung dance floor of the Brighton Elysium. Raymond had felt like he was dancing on air.

And then there were the other dancers . . .

The clubs Raymond had been used to were small, dark, underground places where it scarcely mattered whether you danced well or not at all – but here, in the incandescent environs of the Elysium, everything seemed so much *more*. The ballroom itself exuded splendour. The ball gowns and evening suits that the other competitors wore were tailored perfectly to their bodies. Until then, Ray Cohen had thought he was a competent dancer, that he might even have had a *chance*. But now he realised: there was another world out there, a world he hadn't even imagined, a world to which he was desperate to gain access. And right now, as he watched the elegant dancers of high society twirl, standing on the edge of the dance floor in an ill-fitting suit handed down from his father, he felt as if he was on the other side of a glass partition, peering in.

As soon as the heats began, Raymond had known that he couldn't compete. Old men here moved with more elegance than he had ever seen in the Brancroft. Free spins and feather steps, back whisks and telemarks. Raymond had learned much already – but the opportunity to become truly proficient had, he realised with some despair, never been his in the clubs off the Whitechapel Road. However good he thought he was, the most amateur of these dancers was better. He crashed out of the competition in the first round and, chastened, would have fled back to the East End there and then had he not, deep in his cups that night, stumbled into a man by the name of Georges de la Motte. The aristocratic de la Motte, already an international darling of the ballroom, was holding court in the corner of a public house that backed on to the Elysium Hotel when Ray Cohen quite literally fell over his own feet and into him. Some sharp wit in the crowd had cried out, 'That one'll never be a dancer, not with feet like that!', but de la Motte – ever the gentleman – had leaped to his defence, picked him up and made him party to the evening's celebrations.

Georges de la Motte was the youngest son of a youngest son, a French noble by birth – if only there'd been enough estate for him to inherit. While his elder brothers were destined to become masters of country houses and lands with tenant farmers to keep them fat and indolent into their old age, there was very little for the youngest de la Motte to inherit – and instead Georges was expected to join the Legion, or enter industry, or even to dispose of his talents in some charitable endeavour. Destiny, however, had had other plans – for Georges had fallen in love with dance instead. His family, he would later confide in Raymond, had rather disowned him for it. Who, after all, would forsake his fine family for the life of a travelling dancer? But for Georges it was the world. In a ballroom, he was not a noble's forgotten youngest son; he was the noble himself, and the ballroom his inheritance. All of life was in the ballroom.

Raymond had never known why Georges took such a shine to him that night. In the years that followed, he never dreamed to ask, for fear that the spell would be broken and the friendship soured. But de la Motte invited Raymond to the mansion where he was staying and first taught Raymond the true arts of balance and poise. It was de la Motte who had shown him how to weave from a promenade position, how to hold himself in a double reverse spin, or the trick of truly timing the *hover corte*. A year later, when Georges was due in London to accompany some lesser Flemish princess in the ballroom at the Savoy, he had made a personal call to Ray Cohen and – on seeing his down-at-heel East End surroundings – suggested he accompany him on a great adventure.

And that was how Ray Cohen had left the safety of the Whitechapel Road behind, swapping it for the hotels and ballrooms of Paris and Berlin. That was how Ray Cohen had seen corners of the world of which his brother Artie would only ever dream. It was all down to the tutelage and friendship of Georges de la Motte – everything from his closed wing and contra check, to his role at the Buckingham and his new name: Raymond de Guise.

By then, of course, things had been desperate in the Cohen household. It was 1930, a year after the collapse, and there was so little work for Stanley that, most nights, they had little to eat. Stanley was two years out of Pentonville and had no desire to go back in. But how could Ray and Artie see their old man suffer so much? Sometimes Artie found work in the scrapyard. Ray swept floors most mornings at the meat market. But it was not enough. So when one of Stanley's old friends suggested they go out on one of his jobs, standing guard while the old boys robbed one of the townhouses on the river, well, there wasn't really any choice in it. And when, some weeks later, Artie started wondering why all they were good for was waiting outside and taking home a few pennies for the privilege, well, it made perfect sense that he would start casing out houses, warehouses and yards on his own. Even a carriage clock robbed from some old dear's front room could fetch a price. But Artie's speciality became the railway yards. Barely guarded at night, there were railway sleepers and copper and iron, if you knew where to look. And wasn't old Stanley Cohen a dab hand at fencing stolen scrap metal?

So Artie Cohen began a racket of his own, and there was nothing Ray could do to stop him.

'You still see your old boy Georges then, do you?' Artie asked with contempt.

'From time to time. When he's in London for an engagement. I believe he's been in St-Tropez for the summer.'

'St-Tropez! *St-Tropez*, he says, like it's the most ordinary thing! And here's me, banged up in Pentonville for the same summer. It's a mysterious world, Ray, you can't deny that. I never did like the cut of that fella. He *knew* he was better than you, Ray. He lorded it over you.'

'You only met him once, Artie. What impression can you make of a man in thirty seconds?'

'Plenty,' Artie scoffed, while their aunts bickered over who was pouring the gravy at the other end of the table. 'When you spend a stretch inside, you get to trust your judgement – let me tell you that. Not all toffs are like de la Motte, o' course. Some *love* knowing they got one up on you. They bask in it, like a pig in shit. Others, well, they're more . . . sensitive to the matter. They know they're born lucky and they don't rub it in your face. See, this new king they got, this one come up while I was inside. Good King Edward, he's one of *us*. He don't care for all that pomp and circumstance. He doesn't even care for the crown.' At the other end of the table, Aunts May and Rebecca gasped. 'There, I said it!' roared Artie. 'Yeah, he might've been born with a silver spoon in his mouth, same as the lot o' them, but deep down he's one of us really. I seen him, up and down the Mall, when I was up there with Bev – she's my lady friend, Ray, but far too common for *you*. Old kings, now *they* used to wear gowns and furs and ermine and all sorts of that stuff you'll be familiar with down at your hotel. But *this* king – well, it wasn't exactly work boots and coveralls, but he wasn't carrying no sceptre either. See, all that man wants – all any of us really want – is a quiet life, him and his soon-to-be-missus. It's just that most of us don't get the quiet life, because we've got to *graft* . . .'

Raymond's fork clattered to his plate.

'I don't remember you grafting when they caught you ripping up railway sleepers, Arthur.'

'That *was* my graft!' Artie snarled. 'And you'd have known it too, if you hadn't run away like you did that night.'

The night Artie was caught, Raymond thought. *Ripping up railway sleepers for their old man to sell.* Artie had gone out that night in '31, expecting his tight-knit gang to come with him like they always did, thick as thieves they were, and where one went the others always followed. But a vicious fight over the rightful owner of some stolen goods had left Artie on his own. Ray had promised he'd be there that night to help Artie lug the heavy railway sleepers onto the barrow and cart them away. Only, when it came down to it, Ray's conscience got the better of him. This was no life to be proud of. He asked Artie to stop, to leave the sleepers and get out of a life of crime, once and for all. When his brother flatly refused, a bitter argument ensued and Raymond had stormed off to go to meet Georges de la Motte. And that was the same night Georges unexpectedly chartered a boat to take them to Paris and the ballrooms out there. By the time Raymond got word, the trial was over and Artie was already in his prison cell. The guilt stabbed him sharply, even now.

'Didn't even come back, did you?' Artie snapped, jabbing the air with the tip of his knife. 'Just carried on gallivanting around Europe with that ol' lad of yours, while they tossed me in prison and threw away the key. Did you come and visit me once, Ray?'

'I tried to, that month after Pa passed on. You just stayed in your cell like the little boy you've always been.'

'You ain't even said sorry—'

'I'm not your keeper, Artie. What you did that night, it wasn't on me.'

'A promise is a promise, Ray. We're blood. If I'd have had someone looking out for me, I'd have known to scarper long before those coppers come on in . . .' Artie paused. A look of delight had appeared on his face, and he said, 'Pa was disappointed in you, you know. The way you left me hanging like that, the way you sold me down the river. You off forsaking the family while all of the law was ranged up against us.'

Raymond felt his fists clenching. *Don't let him know it,* he said to himself. *He's goading you, that's all. Stanley Cohen wasn't a criminal for the love of it. Artie was always too small-minded to know it – but for Pa, thieving and robbing was just a means to an end. All he wanted was to rise up and out of this poverty. He was proud to see me off to Paris, to Berlin, to Madrid and St-Tropez. I was doing what he wanted all of his life. I was getting out . . .*

'See, me and Stanley Cohen,' Artie went on, 'we weren't like father and son. We was like *brothers.* He did a stretch in Pentonville. I did a stretch in Pentonville. Like I say – *brothers.* Is it perfect? No. But was he proud of it? You can wager your last penny on it, Ray. I shouldn't have got caught that night. I shouldn't have scrapped my way through my sentence, and earned those extra years for it an' all. Hell's teeth, I shouldn't have called the judge what I called him – though he deserved every bit of it, and more. But at least I was honouring the old man. At least he understood.'

But Raymond thought: *I am honouring him. I'm honouring him in my own way. I'm dancing for him, every night I'm out there. Oh, I do it for myself and I do it for them as well – those who'll come to watch me, or dance with my arms around them . . . But I do it for him as well. He's there every time I take a step. But how would they know any of that? They, who only remember him for all the thieving and fencing he did when he wasn't in the dance hall. What he did down the yard, or what he did in the markets after nightfall . . .*

'If you was really honouring him, you wouldn't be dancing in that hotel o' yours. You'd be fleecing them for all they're worth. All them counts and countesses floating through that ballroom while people round here don't have two pennies to rub together. You shouldn't be dancing with them. Leave that to one of the younger fellas, the more dashing fellas, while you're up in their rooms, robbing their jewels. Well, what are they to you, Ray, really? If they *knew* who you were. If they knew *what* you were. There's Jewish boys coming into these streets from Germany almost every week now, runaways with not a thing but what's in the packs on their backs. That's *your* cousins, that is. That's *your* people. And that Buckingham, well, it's home away from home for those sods driving 'em out of their own houses. You ought to have your hands in every strongbox in that hotel.' Artie had thrown his head back with mirth, but now a new look came over his face. 'What do you think, brother? Come back to us Cohens – all this de Guise nonsense can be the perfect cover. You keep 'em busy in the ballroom while I filch through their rooms. All I need's a set of keys. We can spread the good stuff around, help a few folks out down here – and if we keep a little for ourselves, well, that's only right as well. Consider it a commission.'

The fire that had ignited in Raymond's belly wasn't dying down. 'You honour Pa in your own way, Artie. I'll honour him in mine, you hear?'

Then he was on his feet, kicking his chair to one side, and stalking out to the garden, where the light of a silver moon beat down.

Some time later, when the chill was really settling in, Raymond heard the kitchen door open – and out his mother stepped.

For a time she just stood beside him. The chickens set up a racket at her approach. Somewhere, in one of the neighbouring gardens, a fox pricked up its ears.

'I'm sorry, Ma,' Raymond began. 'I didn't come back to cause trouble.'

'It's been the same with you boys since you was small.'

Mrs Cohen folded her arms across her breast. At first Raymond thought it was just so that she could keep in the warmth, but there was a hardness here too. Her expression was as set as granite.

'It isn't that I haven't wanted to come back.' He cautioned himself before continuing, because he was not sure that his mother would understand. 'It isn't that I haven't thought about you all. But ever since Pa died, it's like . . .' *He knew me,* Raymond thought, *but none of you do. He understood that a man can get on in the world, go places, if he's got talent enough. That it doesn't have to be the old ways of doing things. That Artie needn't have gone down the same road as our father. Pa was a crook, but only because he needed to be. And . . .* 'Pa would have been proud of me, Ma.'

'It's easier to leave than to be left behind, Ray. That's the way it's been ever since there's been people.' She paused. 'Artie isn't a bad soul. But to see you, Ray, up there in a different world, different name, forgetting about us all . . . You know what that can do to a soul?'

Raymond snapped, 'You act like it's a betrayal. And all because I'm using what talent I have, using it to make something of myself. What would you rather? That I went the same way as Artie or that I danced?'

'Oh, it isn't the *dancing*,' Mrs Cohen went on – and here her voice became venomous for the very first time. 'Your father liked a dance. There's plenty round here going down to the Social and the rest. Or taking a trip up west to go to one of those clubs down in Soho, where they're dancing all those exotic dances. Bodies rubbing up against each other, hot and sweaty, where everyone can see!'

Raymond pictured those places. It had been so long since he'd danced in a club. Being back here made him long for it. He would have loved to have been able to visit them one more time with old Stanley Cohen.

'No' his mother went on, 'that isn't the betrayal.' She paused. 'But you? Up there, with your Lord Edgertons and the lot of them? Who's been in your ballroom this summer, Ray? Danced with Unity Mitford again, have you? Taken dinner with the Londonderrys, have you? Oh, it isn't that they're rich and it isn't that they're snobs, looking down on all of us. If you wasted time hating because of money, why, you'd hate every bastard out there. No, it's . . .' For a moment, she paused. 'We never took you boys to the synagogue, Ray. Didn't seem the thing for your father and me to do, though we were both of us dragged along when we were small. And I've no love lost for some of my people. But when my own son clasps hands with those who'd wipe us off the face of this earth? When he presses his body up against those who'll be in Germany the very next night, pressing those same bodies up against murderers? That's what breaks a mother's heart, Ray.'

'It's dance, Ma. You leave the rest of the world outside the ballroom. You put your dancing shoes on, and nothing else matters.'

'It matters, boy. It *always* matters.'

Raymond reached out to put a hand on her shoulder. 'Ma . . .'

'Do you know, when you turned up on this doorstep, I thought you might have been coming home to make amends. Dance all you like, Ray. Dance here and dance there. Travel the world going to your competitions. Do whatever makes you happy. But to throw your lot in with the sort of people who'd round your family up and drive them out? To dance with those taking champagne with Oswald Mosley and his union? Those fascist bastards . . .' Mrs Cohen shook off Ray's hand and marched back across the yard. In the light of the doorway, she looked back. 'You know a fancy thing or two, Ray, but you don't know a thing about *family*,' she spat.

Yes I do, thought Raymond as he watched her go. He thought of Hélène Marchmont and Sofía LaPegna, Sebastian Grise and Stefan Sylvester, before they stepped out onto the ballroom floor. Billy Brogan the hotel page, Michel Cotton from the ballroom's bar, Mrs Moffatt. The new girl Nancy Nettleton came into his mind, lingering after the other images had faded behind. *I know the meaning of family. But it isn't here. It hasn't been here ever since my father died . . .*

Chapter Twelve

The housekeeping lounge, tucked behind Mrs Moffatt's office, was already thronged by the time Nancy arrived at dawn. Coming here always made her feel nervous – if you wanted to fit in as a chambermaid at the Buckingham, this was the place to do it – and today her heart was beating like a panicked bird.

Rosa and Ruth had arrived early to lay the long tables, and Nancy joined the girls as they found their places. A big pot on a counter held the morning's porridge, and rack upon rack was filled with bread and toast and yesterday's pastries, no longer fit for the guests of the Buckingham Hotel but more than adequate for those who toiled in its service. What was rubbish to a lord was a delicacy to an underling – *but that,* Nancy silently observed, *is England all over. The Buckingham Hotel just shows England up for what it really is.* She could feel her stomach grumbling. At least this was a good sign. After so many days of not eating because she was so fearful about anybody finding out it was her in the Grand, she was starving. Perhaps the fear was beginning to dissipate.

This morning, Mrs Moffatt kept her girls waiting. Nobody would eat until Mrs Moffatt had delivered her morning address.

Some of the girls were starting to mutter their discontent when the doors opened and Mrs Moffatt stepped through, leading the team of gentlewomen housekeepers behind her. Each one of them looked as imperious as the last.

'Miss Nettleton,' Mrs Moffatt began, in her brusque businesslike voice.

She knows, doesn't she? Somebody told . . . Beneath the table, her knees started knocking. All of her life, every ambition she had, flashed in front of her. All of it squandered, for something as silly as an illicit trip into the ballroom.

'Your turn with the tea. Do the honours, won't you?'

Relief flooded her body. 'Right away, Mrs Moffatt.'

As she got up to begin pouring, she heard Rosa titter behind her, 'Right away, Mrs Moffatt. Two sugars, Mrs Moffatt. How do you take yours, Mrs Moffatt?' The Lancashire accent Rosa was putting on was a knife in Nancy's side, but she was too startled to look around.

Why are they being so snotty, all of a sudden? Because they saw me talking to Raymond de Guise?

Mrs Moffatt began, 'Girls, we have much to do today. Charlotte, Maureen, Flo, Mrs Whitehead is going to take you to fifth to prepare the Atlantic for an honoured guest. Agatha, Edie, Vera – you're on third and fourth. Rosa, Ruth, you'll be in the ballroom with Nancy. The rest of you, listen out for your name. We have much to do . . .'

Nancy found her seat again, but all of a sudden the porridge and toast, honeys and preserves, thick butter, pastries and clotted cream didn't seem so appetising. *But you have to eat,* she told herself. *What would you have said to Frank if he refused to eat before going down to the mine for the day? You'd have caused chaos with him if he'd not finished his plate! 'You need to stay strong, Frank. You need to look after yourself.' Well, listen to your own advice, Nancy Nettleton.*

It was one thing looking after her little brother. When there was Frank to look after – Frank's bed to change, Frank's meals to make, Frank to walk to the end of the lane so that he could join the other children for school – Nancy had barely thought about herself. But this was the new life – and that meant being kind to herself too.

Mrs Moffatt announced the end of breakfast with a simple clap of her hands and the girls cleared the table and hurried off to their stations.

'Nancy. A word, if I may?'

Nancy's heart raced again. *Does she know, or doesn't she?*

Mrs Moffatt bade Nancy to sit beside her and folded a hand over hers. 'You're on edge this morning, Nancy. Is everything—'

Nancy spluttered, 'Everything's fine, Mrs Moffatt. I'm—'

'Tired,' Mrs Moffatt said, nodding her head sagely. 'Yes, it can get you like that, when you're a new girl. It's important you look after yourself – and not just for the hotel. I need my girls fit and healthy, Nancy.' She rummaged in her pocket and produced three barley sugar sweets, wrapped up in wax wrappers. 'Keep them with you,' she said, 'pop one in when you feel like you're starting to flag.' She beamed and, together, they stood back up. 'You'll get through this, Miss Nettleton. I can see it in you. You're smart and willing and, if you're a little rough around the edges, that's nothing as compared to some of the girls I've had with me over the years. You and the Buckingham Hotel, you fit each other like hand and glove.'

It had been two days since the ballroom closed its doors and, since that moment, Nancy, Rosa and Ruth had been dedicated to polishing numerous pieces of chandelier. With tubs of silver polish and diluted cider vinegar, they worked in procession: one vast dust sheet spread out with the pieces of chandelier waiting to be doused in vinegar and wiped clean; another laid out for the pieces to dry, before being gently massaged with polish and reassembled. As the new girl, Nancy was stuck at the front of the production line. She wondered if the smell of cider vinegar would ever be washed out of her nostrils, her fingertips, her hair.

'Look, Rosa,' said Ruth. As Nancy and Rosa looked up, Ruth grabbed a broom from its prop on the wall. Then, holding it as tight as a lover, she twirled across the empty ballroom floor. It was a simple two-step, the sort anyone who'd ever been to a dance hall might dance, but she put her own flourishes in, rocking the broom back and forth as if it was swooning in her arms. 'Madam!' she declared, in a perfect imitation of the King's English.

Rosa spluttered all over the chandelier clasp she had been polishing. 'Give over, would you? If Mrs Moffatt comes back . . .'

But Ruth continued twirling around, dancing some wanton tango up and down the ballroom floor. On the other side, one of the carpenters elbowed his workmate in the side and cried out, 'Here's Hélène Marchmont herself!'

Rosa whispered, 'I'd give anything to be Hélène Marchmont and have Raymond de Guise *all* to myself . . .'

Nancy's eyes shot up. 'Hélène Marchmont . . . and Raymond de Guise?'

'Well, it stands to reason, doesn't it? Two folks as beautiful as them. Bound to happen, isn't it? They hold each other almost every night anyway. And do you think you can dance with someone like that if you're not a little bit in love?'

'I don't know,' chipped in Ruth. 'Raymond de Guise hardly ever leaves the Buckingham. Not unless it's to one of those tea parties, or he's invited to some toff's wedding. But Hélène Marchmont? Now, that's different. She's off, out of here, every chance she gets! Like she's got somewhere better to be.'

'Double life,' said Rosa. 'She's probably lead dancer at the Imperial. Choreographer at the Savoy.'

'Nothing as ordinary!' Ruth crowed. 'She's got a lover somewhere, you mark my words. A lovely doomed affair, like you get in the magazines. Oh, I can just imagine it, can't you? She jumps in a taxicab every second she gets, and then she's up in some Bloomsbury mansion or out at some country estate.'

'Why keep it a secret?'

'Obvious, isn't it? She's somebody's mistress. Somebody who matters. Well, when you're as beautiful as Hélène Marchmont, you get to take your pick.'

'I still say she's with Raymond de Guise. It's just too perfect.'

'Too perfect is right. And, anyway, Lord de Guise hasn't got time for her. He's running himself ragged with all the guests. He goes up to their rooms with them, doesn't he? Not just a dancer, that one . . .'

'Wh-what do you mean?' Nancy stammered.

'Stands to reason, doesn't it? There's lots of wealthy women float through the Buckingham Hotel. Most of them got married out of duty, not out of love. So when a dashing man like Raymond de Guise is around and happy to escort them . . .'

In a fit of mirth, Rosa picked up her broom and mimed kissing it. Then she danced across the ballroom floor until she was looming over Nancy. 'Come on, Nance. You be LaPegna, or one of them Spanish girls. They know how to drive 'em wild, don't they?'

Suddenly, the air was filled with a single sharp word, 'GIRLS!' Nancy looked up to find that Mrs Moffatt had marched through the reception doors. Smirking, the carpenters and painters returned to their toil while the head housekeeper, face purpling with anger, marched onto the dance floor.

'How can you be so reckless, girls? You silly, silly creatures! What if it had been Mr Charles who'd walked in? There are some things I can't protect you from, and what Mr Charles thinks of girls shirking their duties is one of them.' The anger had ebbed out of her as she spoke and, in the corner of her eye, Nancy saw Rosa and Ruth looking strangely chastened. 'Well, if you've got time to dance, you must be near finished, no?' Moments later, Mrs Moffatt was standing over Nancy, appraising their work. She hesitated before saying, 'Get to the fourth floor, girls. Mrs Whitehead can use some help. The floor's filling up today. Mr Chaplin and his entourage are back in town.'

Mrs Moffatt lingered until after they were gone. 'Will you finish up here, Nancy?' Then, in a whisper, she added, 'Time for one of those barley sugars, I should think.'

Soon, she'd forgotten the burning red of her cheeks. She'd *wanted* to dance. Even with a broom. But . . . she reached for her leg. Nobody had noticed, not yet. But they would if she started to dance.

She looked up. The ballroom was empty now the carpenters had disappeared for lunch. She had it all to herself. The brooms were lying where Rosa and Ruth had abandoned them in their haste. Perhaps . . .

Leaving the last pieces of chandelier behind, she ventured onto the dance floor and took one of them in her hands. Then she closed her eyes. If she let herself go, if she let herself *feel* it, she could almost hear the sounds of the Archie Adams Band striking up. It was not easy – more than once she gave up, opening her eyes and ruining the magic – but, with practice, she could hear the other dancers eddying around her. On the edges of her hearing, there was the raucous laughter of ladies and gentlemen at the surrounding tables. Glasses were clinking. Toasts were being made. Somewhere, somebody was tapping their feet in time with the percussion.

She started to move. At first she was only swaying. Then, tentatively, she took one step, then two. Nancy had never learned to dance. There had been a dance hall in the neighbouring village and, once, she had persuaded her father to take her there, just to watch the village ladies coming and going. She tried to remember how they'd danced back then, and then how Raymond de Guise and Grusinskaya had danced, right here. Then, suddenly, she found that her feet *understood*. She stepped forward, then to the side, then back, cradling the broom as she described a simple box step on the floor. She turned – there was a twinge in her leg, but no more serious than any she felt changing beds or sweeping rooms – and began to believe that, when you did not think about it, it was not really so difficult at all. You just let the music in your mind carry you onward.

The music was cut short by a single braying laugh.

Vivienne Edgerton was standing in the arch where the dressing-room doors used to be, before they had been taken from their hinges and carted away to be sanded down and repainted. How long had she been standing there? She was wearing an exquisite gown. Her face was painted, as if she was about to dance for an audience herself. But the look of horror, tinged with delight, that she wore shone through all of the make-up.

'It's . . . *you* again, isn't it? Daddy's dancing *chambermaid*. My Lord, what on *earth* do you think you're doing with that broom?'

Nancy held the broom tighter, her palms sweating. 'I'm sweeping, Miss Edgerton. If you please.'

'Sweeping?' Vivienne strode forward, her head cocked to one side in a way that expressed sincerity, yet her tone of voice made it clear she was anything but sincere. 'Why, I don't believe I've ever seen somebody box stepping as they swept. Show me that again, would you?'

Nancy could sense Vivienne moving closer to her, crossing the dance floor in poised, elegant strides. She was beautiful, Nancy decided. She was austere, but there was something of the look of a Greek goddess about her. She was imperial and proud and . . .

'Can I . . . help you, Miss Edgerton? Forgive me for speaking out of turn, but the ballroom is closed for refurbishing. For cleaning.'

'Well, *you* came here to dance. Maybe I came here to dance myself. And maybe *I* have permission. And, what's more, maybe *I* don't have a . . . Tell me, what exactly *is* wrong with your leg? You carry it an inch behind you, always. What is it . . . *forgetful*? Well, little leg, you won't dance well like that! The body's got to keep perfect time with itself if it's to dance – even with a broom!'

Vivienne's face creased with laughter – but, just as suddenly, it stopped. Her cat's eyes glared threateningly. 'Why don't you take your old lady's leg and get out of here for an hour? Leave the ballroom to me. You can take your broom with you. I wouldn't want you getting lonely.'

Nancy wanted to say something. The words were in her throat – but something, whether it was fear or horror or just the idea that the Buckingham was drumming into her that she should *know her place*, made her choke them back down. *Don't get on her wrong side,* she told herself, *not again.* The broom clattered out of her hand, spinning to a stop on the floor, and she turned on her heel. Then she was off, leaving behind all the half-polished pieces of chandelier.

As she hurried up the slope to the black-and-red tiles of the reception hall, her leg cried out. She stopped to grasp it, stifling a great sob, and was surprised to find Billy Brogan at her side, with his freckled face and his ears sticking out like milk-jug handles.

'Has something happened, miss?'

Nancy shook her head fiercely, and Billy backed away.

'Nothing. It's only . . . my leg.'

'Bad is it, miss?'

Not so very bad, thought Nancy, *and yet bad enough that it doesn't go unnoticed for long.* It pained her, but the pain was not nearly as intense as the spiteful words of Vivienne Edgerton. Those words had cut her like a barb.

'Thanks for your kindness, Billy,' she said, 'but . . .'

'You mustn't let them see you, Miss . . . Nettleton, isn't it?'

'Call me Nancy.'

'Let 'em see you cry, Nancy, and they'll never forget it. And crying in front of guests, it's not the sort of thing that gets forgiven. It can get you pulled into an office for a stern talking-to. I've been on the receiving end of too many, miss, back when I was green.

See, we're meant to be invisible. Listen, there's a washroom in housekeeping. Hardly ever gets used. Shall we . . .'

When Nancy took his hand, Billy felt a surge of such pride as he had rarely felt before.

'We'll have this sorted in a second,' he said, 'get you all cleaned up, and no one will be any the wiser.'

What Billy called the housekeeping washroom was really the site of the old hotel laundry, which had sat silent since the days before the Great Depression. Billy had to kick old packing crates aside to usher Nancy through. Inside, light streamed in from the garages at the hotel's rear entrance. There was a kettle and a hot plate and Billy set to fixing her a brew.

'Officially it's storage, but think of it as the hotel pages' lounge. Take milk, do you?'

Nancy was about to stammer a reply when Billy added, 'Well, we haven't got none, so it'll have to be nice and black.'

After Billy had handed her the hot tea, Nancy began to feel, if not better then at least a little more in control. She looked around, taking in the vast porcelain wash tubs, the great grey flagstones on which they sat, and the abandoned buckets and mops.

'What is this place?' she whispered.

'Now *that's* a story,' grinned Billy. 'See, there was a time when everything got laundered right here, in the hotel. You'd have washerwomen in here, day and night, scrubbing stains out of sheets and hanging them out to dry on those radiators yonder end. Well, things was easy before the Depression, but then it hit. Maynard Charles was like a captain of a sinking ship. Spent day and night baling out water, just to stay afloat. And one night he figures, well, I can save costs on the hotel laundry if I send it all out to one of those industrial laundries south of the river. Forty staff given their marching orders, and all so a few extra shillings could be saved. All you'd have had to do to save them, o' course, would have been to charge a few of the counts and baronesses who stay in this place a little extra every night – but, well, the world doesn't work like that, does it? The rich have got to be looked after, while the rest of us rot. And that . . . that's why I tell you, Nancy, don't let 'em see you cry. Don't let them think you're struggling. Mrs Moffatt won't let on, but things ain't exactly running like clockwork in this hotel even now. The Depression might be gone, but that stuff's like a bad stink. It *lingers*. And now there's the Imperial putting on its cabarets. The Savoy's had its own ballroom refitted. Old Mr Charles, he's more worried than I seen him. He'll be debating more culls, I shouldn't wonder. Wondering where he can start saving costs again. He's staked everything the hotel has on this Christmas and New Year. If we have the best festivities, if all the society pages are talking about is what happened at the Buckingham Hotel, well, we'll get through another year – and another after that . . .'

Billy had been talking for so long and so quickly that he had quite forgotten why he had brought Nancy Nettleton here. Only now did he remember. 'Nance!' he laughed. 'Here am I rabbiting on about lords and ladies and society and . . . there's you, on the wrong end of Miss Edgerton. I . . .'

Nancy was taking small sips of the scalding tea, but at the mention of Miss Edgerton's name, something cracked in her. She started to sob.

Billy Brogan, who spent many a night consoling his crying sisters, knew exactly what to do. He leaped forward and wrapped her in his arms.

'There, there, Miss Nettleton. It can't be that bad. Miss Edgerton's just a—'

'Oh, it isn't just her,' Nancy said, her face pressed up against Billy's shoulder. 'It's . . . everything. It's *me*. I . . . I don't belong, do I, Billy? I thought I could. I thought it would be easy. I been through worse and I thought I could come down here and slide straight in, like nothing was too much for me. But there are different rules. Things I didn't understand . . . It was me in the ballroom the other night. Miss Edgerton saw me and started shrieking and the only thing that saved my job was when Mr de Guise stepped up to stop her so I could slip away. But *she* knows, Billy. And she's making me pay for it.'

Now that Nancy had vented her words, she seemed steadier. Billy was reluctant to let go of her, but he eased her off his shoulder and stepped back. She was very pretty, he decided. Her eyes were red and her hair was out of place but she was the most beautiful thing Billy thought he had ever seen.

'The thing to learn about Miss Edgerton is she isn't here of her own accord. When Lord Edgerton married her American mother, he brought them both over from New York. Only, he didn't want Miss Edgerton in his home. Might be he wanted her mother all to himself. No distractions, see. So Miss Edgerton, she's a permanent guest here at the Buckingham. At first she thought it was a jolly. You'd see her in the ballroom every night, in a new gown she'd bought with that ridiculous allowance of hers. She'd have the concierges hail taxis for her to take her out shopping. She'd sashay through every bar in the hotel and every restaurant in London town. But she is so often alone. The Buckingham might be elegant and grand, but to Vivienne Edgerton it's a cage. And caged animals, well. I sneaked into the zoo up on Regent's Park once. Animals, they don't like to be caged.'

For a moment, there was silence. Billy dared to hope that his story had helped her, if only a little.

'I have to get back, don't I?' Nancy whispered. 'Before I'm missed.'

Billy grinned. 'Go back out there like nothing ever happened.'

Nancy nodded. 'I will. And, Billy . . . thank you.'

'Nancy, if ever you need someone to talk to, somebody who *knows* what it's like to not belong, to have to work it all out for his self, well, you come straight here. You're not alone in the Buckingham Hotel. I came up the same way as you did. I came here to make my own way in the world. So you'll never be alone here. You see, you got me.'

Chapter Thirteen

THE NEXT MORNING, BILLY BROGAN was up before dawn, breakfasted before his brothers and sisters scrambled out of bed, and out of the door even before his father was off to Billingsgate for the day. Crossing London before dawn broke, you could fool yourself into thinking the city was yours alone. A lone street sweeper walked over the bridge at Westminster; Piccadilly seemed eerily silent; even as he walked into Mayfair, the city seemed to sleep. It was only in the Buckingham Hotel itself that time didn't stop. The night managers had worked feverishly through the smallest hours. When Billy crept in through the staff entrance, he heard porters hurrying back and forth across the reception hall. Mr Simenon, the head concierge, was lurking by the guest lifts. He had a vampiric look about him, thought Billy with a sly grin, remembering the posters for a picture show: *VAMPIRES OF PRAGUE!* Mr Simenon looked as if he might have joined the thespians on that billboard very well. He was long and lean, with a nose as hooked as a beak; his face was drawn and the black lines around his eyes were surely the sign of a dark enchantment.

'What have you got for me?' Billy chirruped, delighted at the way the head concierge startled at him coming close.

'Brogan,' Mr Simenon seethed, 'you're late. I was expecting you at dawn.'

'Been up all night, have you, sir?'

Mr Simenon raised a hand and cuffed Billy around the ear. 'That's for your cheek,' he spat, 'and *this* is for your duty.'

Billy found a small roll of pound notes being pressed into his hands. With expert ease, he slipped it into a back pocket.

'On with you, Brogan. Hurry now before Mr Charles realises you're gone.'

The first light of morning was casting its rays across London when Billy emerged from the fine townhouses of Mayfair and made his way across Regent Street in the shadow of the day's first trolleybus. When London awoke, it did so as suddenly as the ogres Billy told his rabble of brothers and sisters about at bedtime each night – but, for now, calmness remained.

Office clerks and workers were streaming up out of the Underground tunnels and the streets were thronged by the time he stood outside the Midnight Rooms. Billy had once passed this way at nightfall, when the music played and you might see girls dancing on the corner. The Midnight Rooms sat off a little alleyway behind the Berwick Street market. The market was already a maelstrom of activity as tinkers and florists and fishmongers and grocers set out their stalls, griping at each other as they staked out their plots. Billy weaved his way through the hubbub and slipped into the open door of the Midnight Rooms itself. At the bottom of a thin, narrow stairwell, some of last night's revellers remained. Billy could hear them bickering, their voices ripe with whisky and gin, but when he reached the bottom of the stairs he could go no further. The darkness had hardened around him. A heavy wooden door, marked with iron rivets, stood in his way.

He knocked and the door drew back.

'You again, Brogan,' came a bass, Irish voice from somewhere down in the dark.

'Aye,' said Billy, 'back again.'

There was silence. Then, the same voice muttered, 'Come through.'

When Billy emerged back into the morning, ten minutes later, he had a small drawstring purse in his hands: a pouch of pink felt stitched with indigo thread and a ribbon to tie it together. Billy weaved through the market's first punters, helping himself to a bright red apple from the grocer's on the way. Sleight of hand was something he'd turned into a high art form in the Buckingham, and the grocer was none the wiser as Billy sank his teeth into the juicy flesh.

By the time he tumbled back through the staff entrance, the hotel was stirring. Maynard Charles always said that there was something dramatic in the way the hotel woke up each morning and today Billy felt it. The lift opened and out stepped the first guests. The kitchens came to life as the dining rooms filled for breakfasts and the flock of waiters marched out to war. If it had all been serenaded by the dramatic trumpet blasts of the Archie Adams Band, it might have seemed something fit for the London Palladium.

Billy kept his head down as he crossed the reception. A short burst up the servants' stairs and into Vivienne Edgerton's suite, and his work for Mr Simenon would be done. Yet, as he barrelled onward, a voice startled him. He looked up. Vivienne Edgerton was standing by the great obelisk, in a pale blue house dress with a cap hiding her auburn hair. By her side stood Maynard Charles himself.

The doors to Berkeley Square opened and Billy saw that a black limousine had drawn up outside. Moments later, the doorman stepped into the reception hall, inclining his head in a deferential bow. The next thing Billy saw, through the open doors, was the rounded peak of a top hat as its owner ascended the marble stairs.

Billy Brogan had only ever seen Lord Edgerton once. The day after he had acquired a majority position on the board, he had descended on the Buckingham Hotel to declare the start of a new era. Everyone here, from the lowliest garage attendant to the hotel director himself, had gathered in the ballroom while Lord Edgerton stood tall on the stage and surveyed them like a general does his army. He was a tall and sinewy man, not given to fat, and his face was dominated by a silver moustache. Beneath the bushy thatch of his eyebrows, his eyes were small and dark, hidden behind spectacles with tortoiseshell frames. There was something imposing about the man. His shoulders were broad, his chest big and round – and, though the way that he dressed was gentlemanly, he carried his cane not as a gentleman would, down at his side to assist in his walking, but in both hands, almost, Billy thought, as if it was a cane meant for thrashing errant children.

Vivienne Edgerton stepped forward, curtseying for her stepfather – who condescended to kiss her once on the cheek. Once Vivienne stepped back, Lord Edgerton shook Maynard Charles's hand and allowed himself to be led into the Queen Mary dining room. Vivienne followed.

Was Billy mistaken, or was the way Maynard Charles had taken a handkerchief from his lapel and dabbed at his forehead a sign of some distress? New figures were streaming through the doors. These gentlemen seemed as estimable as Lord Edgerton himself. Dressed in gaberdine and tweed, they allowed the swarming concierges to take their coats and hats, and soon they too were swept into the Queen Mary.

Maynard Charles returned. His eyes locked with Billy. Billy froze.

'Mr Brogan,' he said, heels clicking across the black and red chequered squares as he reached Billy's side. 'Do you know who those *good* people are, young man?'

Billy nodded. 'It was Lord Edgerton, sir. *The* Lord . . .'

'And the rest?'

Perhaps he ought to have known, but again Billy Brogan froze.

'Those, young man, were confidants of Lord Edgerton. They've chosen our hotel as a forum to discuss the most delicate matters. You know, of course, about the union?'

'The union, sir?'

'Well, of course, there are many unions. Lord Edgerton's friends represent, shall we say, certain interests in this union of theirs. Mr Mosley himself would have attended this morning's meeting, had he not been subsumed in some other business. We're to make them feel . . .' Maynard Charles paused, and Billy wondered if he was himself wrestling with the idea. 'Welcome,' Maynard concluded. 'So I'll be expecting your usual good service. They'll be using the Queen Mary to host various . . . associates over the next weeks and months. Whatever those fellows want, you're to fetch it for them, day or night. We need their custom, and we need Lord Edgerton kept happy. Don't ask questions, Billy. But do, of course, *remember* the things you've heard. You can do that for an old man, can't you?'

'Yes, sir.'

'You're an estimable chap, Billy Brogan.' Maynard Charles extended a hand. 'Off with you now.'

Billy turned as if to take flight deeper into the Buckingham – Vivienne's package still lingered in his back pocket – when Maynard Charles coughed, ostentatiously.

'See if our guests need errands performed first, won't you, boy?'

Inwardly, Billy cringed. 'Right away, sir.'

The Queen Mary was the most ostentatious of the dining rooms in the Buckingham, but it was not ordinarily open for breakfast – and consequently, Lord Edgerton and his guests were alone in the opulent expanse. A single crystal chandelier, all sixteen of its lights aflame, hung above them, so that they appeared to be taking tea beneath an enormous halo. At least this made Billy less conspicuous, he thought. He could linger on the edges of the room and not be seen.

Altogether six men were seated around the table, being waited on by Mr Simenon and a trio of waiters in pure white shirts. Five of them appeared the same age and stature as Lord Edgerton himself, but the sixth was smaller and younger – lithe, thought Billy, with an almost effete look. The youngest man had been fortunate enough to be given a seat beside Vivienne Edgerton, and she too looked relieved to have the company. Whatever the elder men were talking about, at least she had a friend. *Another mouse to toy with*, thought Billy. *Lord help this one if he falls under her spell.*

By increments, Billy came closer, close enough that he could hear Vivienne trying to contain her laughter.

'Vivienne!' Lord Edgerton erupted at the other end of the table. 'Whatever is titillating you, might you keep it to yourself?

You're invited to this breakfast because your mother asked that I involve you. But if you might keep your conversation to a minimum, I should greatly appreciate it. We are men of the world and we have much to discuss.' Billy saw Vivienne flush crimson, but somehow she managed to keep her humiliation hidden. *I've seen this before*, thought Billy, *she bottles it up and bottles it up . . . and the only way to get rid of it is when she's in the ballroom with too many cocktails in her hand, or with the powders Mr Simenon sends me to collect for her.*

At the table, Lord Edgerton gazed imperiously around. 'My stepdaughter,' he explained to his fellows. 'I'm afraid she still has the *American* temperament of her departed father. But you're an English girl now, aren't you, Vivienne? So she's learning English decorum.' He shook his head, resignedly. 'Shall we move on to the matter at hand, gentlemen? The union must be allowed to march freely and unhindered. We'll need to petition Parliament. The demonstration is legal and it must be protected from that East End *filth* . . .'

The lord went on, but Billy's eyes were drawn inexorably back to Vivienne.

'Nathaniel,' she was saying, 'don't pay him any attention. If he speaks to me like that again, then he'll know what a scene I can cause. My mother's in his thrall, but she won't be for ever. She's in love now, but once that wears off . . .'

Her voice had been wavering but, as she spoke, she fought her way back to her usual fieriness.

'I can think of worse places to live than an establishment like this, Miss Edgerton.' The young man named Nathaniel paused. *He's probably only a few years older than I am,* thought Billy, *but when you're born with titles and money, you hold yourself different.*

You're born a gentleman. You're born entitled. 'I'm not like my father,' the young man went on, indicating the most corpulent of Lord Edgerton's guests, a man of ruddy complexion and with a big, porcine snout. 'They wanted me to get a job in the City, like the rest of them. Or in industry. But what's wrong with wanting to *live* a little first? As a matter of fact, I only came at all today because I'd heard such magical things about your ballroom. And here I am, and I haven't even seen it!'

'Tell me,' Vivienne said, '*what* would you have been doing?'

'Oh, some minor adventuring, I should think.' Nathaniel, whose lips barely seemed to part as he spoke, paused. 'Do you think a lady in your position might be able to unlock those ballroom doors, allow a stranger a glimpse of it?'

Vivienne glanced up at her stepfather briefly before she whispered, 'I should think a lady in my position could. Are you a proficient dancer?'

'More so than these fine gents.' Nathaniel's father gave him a look like daggers, but Nathaniel himself seemed undeterred. He straightened himself, brushing his long fringe out of his eyes. 'I demonstrated dances at the Imperial for a summer when I was nineteen. That was until my father over there – Oliver White, he goes to the same club as your father – decided it was too *uncouth*. A dancer in the family he could tolerate – but a dancer at a seedy little place like the Imperial?' Nathaniel threw his head back. 'The shame!'

Billy knew of the Imperial. It wasn't unheard of for him to scurry through there on some errand or other. The pages there thought him an aristocrat himself, and all because he walked the corridors of the Buckingham. The Imperial might not have been as opulent as these surroundings, but it was hardly a hostel for degenerates. The ballroom there had hosted the Tommy Dorsey Orchestra. They had a Friday night cabaret and a continental kitchen where the finest French cuisine was served day and night.

'Do you dance, Miss Edgerton?'

Billy watched Vivienne's eyes light up. The elder men were engrossed in conversation – he heard only snatches, talk of the Mitfords who held society in the palm of their hands, the name of Mr Chamberlain, the Chancellor – but Vivienne sidled closer to Nathaniel.

'I've . . . been known to dance a little. The ballroom after dark, it's like . . . It's positively enchanted.' Vivienne stopped. Her eyes, which had been focused so intently on Nathaniel, flicked up – and, like two stage spotlights, they found Billy Brogan in their glare. 'Billy,' she snapped, 'haven't you a little *something* for me?'

Billy felt as if he was pinned to the glistening floor. The rumbling conversation of Lord Edgerton and his guests petered into silence. Lord Edgerton himself turned to consider him through his spectacles. *Invisible*, he thought. *Pages and porters, chambermaids and valets, we're meant to be invisible.*

Across the Queen Mary, the change in atmosphere must have been noticed, because all of a sudden Mr Simenon and the head waiter reappeared. Abreast, they marched across the restaurant as if they were knights on white chargers rushing to some damsel's defence.

'Can we help you, young man?' Lord Edgerton intoned.

'Brogan, what are you lurking for?' Mr Simenon breathed.

'I . . .'

Mr Simenon threaded his arm through Billy's and, gushing out apologies, swept him aside. He whispered, 'Are you simple, Brogan? Deliver the package to Miss Edgerton's suite, not directly to her. Were you truly thinking to deliver it *here*, in front of her father? You Irish are bog-brained, Brogan, but I expected better of you! Off with you, boy! Don't let me see you here again.'

At the door, Billy looked back. Mr Simenon's words couldn't sting him. He'd heard worse. He'd given out worse, too, because you weren't an Irish lad in London if you hadn't got into some scrap or another. No, what stung him most of all was that Lord Edgerton and his guests were bowed down again, thick in their conversation – and he'd barely heard a single word. There would be no tip from Mr Charles tonight.

On the sixth storey, Billy took out a single silver key and slipped through the doors of Vivienne Edgerton's suite. First time he'd come here, it had been a strange delight to walk among her things, to know he could snoop inside her clutch bag, her wardrobe, the Moroccan manuscript book she kept on the dresser and in which (or so Billy imagined, for in the end he'd been too much of a gentleman to look) she wrote down her darkest secrets. Now, as he looked around, he had another feeling. Was it really sadness? Guilt? The suite had not been cleaned today. Sometimes Vivienne slept so late and dismissed so many chambermaids that it could go days without being swept or the bedsheets being changed. Billy stepped across an open suitcase, through the dresses she'd strewn around, past the unmade bed and to the little chest of drawers. A gramophone record was lying on her pillow but the gramophone itself was nowhere to be seen. On the record's sleeve was a picture of the Dorsey Brothers' Orchestra. It was a copy of 'Tailspin', and scratched so deeply that Vivienne either cared nothing for it, or cared too much.

On the dresser, a bottle of the finest Tabu was knocked over. The perfume had left a stain on the varnish, cutting rivulets down the front of the dresser and to the sheepskin below. Billy followed it with his eyes. He stopped, momentarily, when he saw what he took for a pair of gentleman's drawers lying under the bed – but even this did not make him linger long.

He reached into his back pocket. The little drawstring bag sat in the palm of his hand. He hesitated. Something was making him resist laying the package down on the pillow where it ought to have gone – where it had gone so many times before. He pictured her up here, playing her records, dancing alone, and a part of him wanted to take the drawstring bag and cast it out of the balcony window, or flush it clean away.

Then he remembered Nancy Nettleton. Sweet Nancy Nettleton and her stubborn leg, hurrying away from the ballroom with Vivienne's shrill laughter ringing in his ears.

Billy Brogan laid the package down on Vivienne's pillow and slid quietly out of the room.

Chapter Fourteen

In the bathroom at the Red Lion public house on High Holborn, Ray Cohen looked at himself in the mirror and ran his fingers through his unruly hair. Reaching into the splayed bag at his side, Raymond produced a comb and a little pot of brilliantine. It was not so difficult to effect the transformation into Raymond de Guise in the flesh. He had already shed his brown leather jacket and stepped into his bespoke woollen coat. The chapped leather boots were safely stowed in the bag, and the brogues were waiting to slip onto his feet.

He did not like leaving Whitechapel on such bad terms. Family was family. Blood was blood. But he'd tried so many times to make them see that getting up and getting out didn't *have* to be betrayal, and they never truly understood. So leaving is what he'd done. He was up before dawn that morning, long before his brother would pick himself out of bed, long before his mother was up and about her daily rounds. He left a simple note: *You know where to find me. Don't contact me by name. Take care, Ma. Write to me c/o Billy Brogan.* Then he was gone.

Later, when Raymond de Guise stepped out of the hansom cab on Berkeley Square and looked up at the palatial facade of the Buckingham Hotel, he felt a soaring in his heart that – for the moment, at least – cured all ills. *I prefer this version of me.* The Buckingham, he decided, was a symbol of all he'd accomplished, the troubled life he'd left behind.

He glided across the reception hall, where Mr Simenon was simpering around some new guests – the van der Lindes, newly in from South Africa, where they oversaw a vast estate on the edge of a national park. They'd been photographed, here in the Buckingham, with a baby cheetah they led around Mayfair on a leash. By the guest lifts, two porters were standing to attention in their uniforms of navy and gold, while the obelisk fountain in the reception's centre gurgled.

Yes, thought Raymond, *it's so good to be home. Home is where you hang your hat. And the beauty is that you get to decide what hat you wear. You can change . . . change for the better.*

Raymond was crossing the expansive floor when Billy Brogan appeared alongside him. 'Here you are, Mr de Guise. I been holding it for you.'

The gangly hotel page produced a small white envelope with the name *Raymond* written on the front in cursive script. As Raymond took it, he detected the distinct scent of Chanel.

'Who's this from, Billy?'

Billy held up his hands in mock retreat. 'I just deliver them, Mr de Guise. I don't read 'em.'

Raymond arched an eyebrow. 'A likely story, Mr Brogan,' he said in disbelief – but, by then, the lift doors were opening, so he stepped in.

Raymond's quarters were the grandest of all the demonstration dancers who lived at the hotel. There were six live-in dancers. Their quarters were arranged around a small kitchenette on the hidden seventh storey, above the vaulted ceilings of the hotel's most expensive suites. Raymond's room was not large but its windows opened onto a small terrace overlooking the square, the armoire was of a vintage French design, and the mirror in which he readied himself every morning was so big that it might better have been suited backstage at the Palladium. His bed, a four-poster, dominated the room and he threw himself into it now, barely even bothering to take off his coat. The bag that contained all the vestiges of Ray Cohen's life he dropped at his side.

Even the bed seemed to be welcoming him home. After a night spent tossing and turning, oscillating wildly between pride that he'd escaped Whitechapel and guilt that he hadn't made peace with the family he was once again leaving behind, it was a welcome embrace. He felt he could close his eyes there and then, but the scent of Chanel was still on his fingertips.

Inside the envelope was paper headed with the legend of the Buckingham Hotel. In tiny, precise handwriting, the words read:

Dear Mr de Guise,

I hope you will forgive our moment together in the Grand Ballroom. There is something so powerful in the music, in the movement, in feeling one's body pressed up against another living soul. We forgot ourselves, dear Raymond. We were not in our right minds, and I should hate it if a moment like this might derail our . . . I was going to say 'tuition', but I should rather say 'friendship'. We are friends, are we not, Raymond?

You know me well enough to understand how difficult a letter this has been to write. But I must swallow my pride. Forgive my indiscretion, let us say no more about it, and promise you will dance with me again, when the Grand is ready? I promise you will be rewarded . . .

Yours in anticipation
Vivienne

Raymond let his eyes drift over the letter. He heaved his legs over the edge of the bed and sat hunched there, slumped into a posture that should have shamed him as a dancer. Vivienne Edgerton. *Dancing with disaster*. Even in this letter there were both sides of her: the angel, who wanted only to dance and be admired; and the devil, who knew that, with the right words, she could *make* him do it. He had been foolish to dance with her at all. Whether he said yes or whether he said no, it could only end one way – in humiliation and defeat. She would either loathe him and make it known, or the rumours would begin, rumours of Raymond de Guise and the beautiful Vivienne Edgerton dancing in the ballroom at dawn.

He took the letter between his fingers and, on a whim, tore it in half. Then he tore it again, then again and again, until Vivienne's words were confetti being scattered onto the thick sheepskin rug.

The door opened. Raymond wheeled around, kicking through the falling shreds, and saw a chambermaid – *the* chambermaid – hauling her trolley through the door. In the same moment, she saw him.

Nancy. Nancy Nettleton.

It was Nancy who spoke first. 'Good Lord! I'm so sorry, Mr de Guise. We were told . . .' For a moment, she faltered. 'Mrs Moffatt said we weren't to expect your return for several days. That your rooms were to be in order before you . . .'

Raymond wearily shook his head. 'I came back earlier than I'd intended, Miss Nettleton. I'm sorry. I can . . .'

Nancy brought the trolley into the small suite and closed the door behind her. Then, taking in the room, she said, 'I haven't quite mastered the art of being invisible, have I, Mr de Guise?'

Raymond smiled, remembering his own words. 'You've no need to be invisible here. Please. You'd be surprised, Miss Nettleton.'

'Call me Nancy, please. Should I . . . clean around you, Mr de Guise?'

This gave Raymond pause. 'You'd like me to leave my own rooms?'

Inwardly, Nancy cringed. 'I didn't mean to say . . . I only meant . . .'

'Nancy, I'm jesting.'

'It's only that, when I used to keep our own home, I'd quite happily throw my brother out on his ear if he was lounging around while I was trying to clean. Sometimes I forget – I'm not in Lancashire any more. This is the Buckingham Hotel! There are different rules.'

'Forget about them – for here, at least.'

She had brought out her sweeping brush and, for the first time, her eyes dropped to the scattered corners of paper around Raymond's feet. 'Oh. Should I . . .'

Raymond dropped down and scrambled to get the pieces together himself.

'A love letter, Mr de Guise?' Nancy said, before she could stop herself.

'What makes you say that?' he asked sharply, still down on one knee.

She was speaking too freely – that much she knew. And yet . . . she remembered the fleeting look of admiration on Mr de Guise's face when he realised that she had stepped out of her place and visited the ballroom regardless. Weren't the dancers caught between the two worlds of the Buckingham, belonging to neither, but to one entirely of their own?

'I can smell the perfume, Mr de Guise. Chanel. Once upon a time, my mother had an empty bottle. She bought it at a market in Manchester. I remember her filling it with water. There was still the faint scent, lingering around the rim.'

'Well,' said Raymond, stuffing his pockets full of the scraps of paper, 'it's no love letter, I can assure you of that.'

There was something brusque in his manner so Nancy said no more. Instead, she set about her work. Some time later, she became aware that he was watching her as she moved across the room, straightening the angora blanket upon the chaise longue.

'Your leg, Miss Nettleton. Are they . . . working you too hard? Mrs Moffatt can be a slave driver – no matter how genial she seems.'

The mention of her leg – what had Vivienne Edgerton called it, her *old lady's leg?* – hardened Nancy, and she kept on fussing with the pillows.

'I've said something out of turn, haven't I?' Raymond stopped. 'Your leg – it's an old injury?'

It had seemed as if Nancy was turning into stone but something – perhaps only Raymond's contriteness – broke the spell, and she softened. 'It's only a little stubborn. I had polio when I was a girl. Lots of folks had it in our little village. I was one of the fortunate ones. My leg's a little . . . contrary, Mr de Guise, but nothing more.'

Raymond blurted out, 'Nancy, forgive me.'

She lifted a hand, and busied herself with new bed sheets. 'There's nothing to forgive.'

'I've seen championship dancers with legs weaker than yours.'

Nancy stopped. 'Really?'

'That's why you came to the ballroom that night, isn't it? You wanted to dance?'

'Just to see the place, Mr de Guise. To see Hélène Marchmont and yourself in full flight, and all the patrons, and all the lights, and . . . No, I would never have thought to dance myself. They have nothing more elaborate than the village hall where I come from.'

'Come now! You're not so very far from Blackpool.'

'Not as the crow flies, perhaps, but a world away in real life. We took a day trip once, to look at the pier. But the Winter Gardens? The Empress Ballroom? It may as well have been in the heart of Africa.'

Raymond moved around the edge of the bed, until he stood in front of Nancy. There he opened his arms. 'Would you allow me to show you some steps?'

'Oh, *Mr de Guise,*' Nancy blustered, bustling past him to reach her trolley again. 'The very thought! And . . .'

Something had pained her. Raymond reached out and took hold of her wrist. 'What is it?'

Nancy hesitated. 'It's nothing. I'm speaking too much, aren't I? I always do when I'm nervous.'

'Did you get in trouble, Nancy?' Raymond's voice was hushed.

It was absurd, but the thought that she had been dragged in front of Mrs Moffatt, perhaps even Maynard Charles, while Raymond was out dealing with the ghost of Ray Cohen, made his blood boil.

'No,' Nancy answered, 'nothing like that. But I tried a few steps, just me on my own in the empty ballroom. Only, it wasn't empty. Miss Edgerton was there as well. She . . .'

'She what?'

Nancy whispered, 'She knows it was me. She's not going to let me forget it. And she spotted my leg too.'

So that was it, thought Raymond. Vivienne Edgerton, spreading her maliciousness again. Every time he saw a chink of light in her, every time he spotted a vulnerability, she pulled herself together and returned to her usual business: condescension and cruelty, entitlement and envy. He delved his fingers into his pockets and fished out the crumpled shreds of letter he had crammed there.

'You mustn't listen to her, Nancy,' he said, dropping the pieces into the waste basket dangling from the end of Nancy's trolley. 'She's a bored and entitled little girl. It isn't her fault. She's been in this hotel a year and a day and all she's been is trouble – there, I said it. I'll get hung, drawn and quartered were anyone to find out, so my life is in your hands.' He stopped and smiled, for an idea was forming. 'I could show you some steps, if you liked. Nobody else would have to know. Because nothing – *nothing*, Nancy – should stop you dancing, if that's what you want to do.'

'I'm a chambermaid, Mr de Guise. Have you forgotten?'

'And I'm a dancer.' He pivoted on his heel, spinning on the spot – and was relieved when he saw Nancy's face break into a grin. *If she hadn't smiled, all you'd have been is a twirling fool. Raymond de Guise, what's become of you?*

Nancy was silent. Where her thoughts had taken her, Raymond could not say – but when, at last, she said, 'I should like that very much, Mr de Guise. You have my thanks', he could not mask his smile. There was something about Nancy Nettleton, some indefinable quality that made him wonder what she would really be like on the dance floor. Her eyes were luminous. They looked directly into Raymond's own. It took all sorts of qualities to dance well, thought Raymond. It took rhythm and elegance, poise and self-assurance. But it took intelligence too – the emotion and foresight to understand your partner, to know which way the dance was going. And, stubborn leg or not, Raymond de Guise was certain Nancy Nettleton epitomised this quality most of all.

Chapter Fifteen

PULL YOURSELF TOGETHER, NANCY NETTLETON. After a morning changing bed sheets, sweeping floors, and trying hard not to make eye contact with any one of the hundred guests you've shuffled past, why wouldn't you want to do something for yourself? Isn't this one of the things you came to London for?

There was a studio behind the ballroom at the end of a hallway – the orchestra's practice room and where the demonstration dancers choreographed their afternoon routines. It had no windows, no fixtures – only a single shelf on which sat a gramophone and a selection of recordings from the band itself. The room was laid with mahogany floorboards, though none of them as gleaming as the ones out in the ballroom.

Raymond de Guise was already waiting when Nancy arrived. The afternoon demonstration dances were yet to begin, and Nancy did not have to return to her rounds for another two hours. The other girls had gone off to put their feet up in the housekeeping lounge – there were scones and clotted cream left from yesterday's afternoon tea.

Nancy knocked tentatively as she stepped through the open door.

Raymond de Guise looked up. *He's smiling*, Nancy thought. *Why is he smiling?*

As Raymond placed a record upon the gramophone, he said, 'I wondered whether you'd come . . .'

He turned on his heel and, with the most ostentatious bow – *surely he was teasing?* – he invited her to the centre of the dance floor.

'Shall we?' he asked.

Raymond opened his arms, inviting her into a classic ballroom hold. Nancy took a step towards him, but then she stopped. *I want to*, she told herself. *And yet* . . . Something was holding her back – something that wasn't just nerves.

'No,' she said, and instantly cringed at what she'd done. *Why did you say such a stupid thing?* It had just burst out of her.

Raymond stepped back. 'No?'

'Not until you tell me why. Why *me*. Or do you teach every chambermaid to dance?'

By the way Raymond narrowed his eyes, Nancy could tell he was taken aback. 'You think I'm a cad.'

She really didn't. Rosa and Ruth, they were convinced he was a gigolo – but Nancy could not bring herself to see it. He didn't *seem* a rogue.

But the worst ones don't, do they, Nancy Nettleton? You're not so naïve not to see that . . .

'You don't know me at all,' she whispered. She could see his pained expression and something in that shocked her; it did not feel right to offend him so. 'I'm just a chambermaid. That's all I am.'

Raymond strode towards her, cupped her chin in his hand and tilted her face upward so that he could gaze into her glistening eyes. '*Just* a chambermaid? *Just* a chambermaid? Listen to me,

Nancy Nettleton. Nobody is *just* a chambermaid. We all have stories. Lord knows, I have my own. And a chambermaid who has the courage to dress up and sashay into the ballroom before she's been in the Buckingham a week? A chambermaid who risks *everything*, just for a glimpse of what goes on in there? No,' he said firmly, and Nancy could see the most rapturous smile opening up on his face, 'somebody like that isn't *just* a chambermaid. And you want to know why I'd like to teach you? Why, it's because anyone as brave as that, anyone as foolhardy, must have passion in them. Some sort of fire.' He paused. 'Believe it or not, Nancy, I know a thing or two about having to fit in.' A peculiar look – wistful, perhaps even sad – drifted across Raymond's face. 'And maybe, just maybe, when you approached me in the ballroom that morning, I thought I'd stumbled on a kindred spirit.'

Nancy was used to the boys from the village buttering her up. She was used to deflecting them as well. Ordinarily there was something in the way they stood, some particular tone of voice that set the alarm bells ringing inside her mind. But standing here, gazing at Raymond, there was only silence. There was no other way of putting it: Raymond de Guise meant what he said.

'Shall we?' he ventured again, softly.

You've come this far, Nancy. You're not a girl who runs away. And, besides, you do want to dance, don't you?

She nodded and followed him down to the middle of the dance floor. And that was the first time Nancy Nettleton felt the warmth of Raymond de Guise's arms.

Dear Frank,

It was strange. Unexpected. And dare I say it just a tiny bit wonderful. There was I, Nancy Nettleton – terror of every Lancashire boy – dancing in the arms of Raymond de Guise. I am sure you will think your sister has gone quite mad! But I had the most magical time. I stumbled and I was too tense and I was thinking so much about this leg of mine that Mr de Guise had to stop and remind me – 'you're meant to enjoy this, Nancy!' But do you know what? He was patient and kind and didn't mind at all when I froze or felt so embarrassed I couldn't continue. And by the end, I really did enjoy it after all!

At the end of the week there had been another lesson, and at the start of the following week another one again. Sometimes they could sneak a lesson in before Nancy's duties began at dawn, and sometimes – on Sundays, when the ballroom was closed – they could meet in the studio behind the ballroom after dark, while the rest of the hotel buzzed on around them. Soon, Nancy got to look forward to the hours she would snatch with her dancing partner.

He's never less than a gentleman, she wrote to Frank one night. *And do you know? I think I can do it. Mr de Guise has made me see that, just because my body has let me down in the past, it doesn't mean it has to let me down for ever. It doesn't mean that I should always be 'Nancy with the sickly leg'. Mr de Guise says he can hardly see it any more.*

'It's part of you,' Raymond said one day when, after a hard morning working the fifth floor with Mrs Moffatt, Nancy moved awkwardly across the dance floor – and, angry at the way her leg put up protest, tore herself out of Raymond's hold. 'Don't fight it all the time. Fighting it doesn't make it any better. If you have to . . . why, make it a part of the dance.'

Nancy grinned at the absurdity of the idea. 'I can't imagine Hélène Marchmont or Sofía LaPegna have ever stumbled around and just pretended it's part of the dance.'

'Well,' joked Raymond, 'maybe that's because they don't have the imagination.'

And after that, Nancy wrote later that night, *I hardly think about it at all. Sometimes I'm not as elegant as I might be. Sometimes my leg takes a moment to realise what the rest of our bodies are doing. I used to think about it so much I'd be willing it to happen, Frank. But now? Now we just glide along . . .*

They were gliding along one Sunday evening when the studio door opened and in strode Hélène Marchmont, tall and striking in her coat of sable fur and a red cloche cap. Nancy, who had been learning the rudiments of the tango, felt suddenly exposed. Her legs seemed to dance on, but her body turned around – and only by steadying herself against Raymond's body did she stay upright.

Her cheeks flushed crimson.

'Hélène,' Raymond began, and rushed to meet her at the door. Nancy watched as they whispered together. Once, Hélène looked up, over Raymond's shoulder, and her eyes seemed to take the whole of Nancy in. *I'd never felt so small,* she wrote to Frank. *The Empress of the Ballroom, Hélène Marchmont – and there was me, little Nancy Nettleton. I was having to concentrate just to stay on two feet . . .*

Soon, Raymond stepped back and Hélène, throwing a smile at Nancy – *what does it mean? What's she smiling at me for?* – disappeared from the studio.

'Shall we resume, *mademoiselle*?'

'I don't know,' Nancy said. 'I'm feeling—'

'Whatever it is, feel something else,' declared Raymond. 'No embarrassment! No fear! Listen to the saxophone. That's our own Louis Kildare playing. The greatest saxophonist to ever come up through the clubs.'

The music was extraordinary. Nancy had to admit that. All of the music Raymond had played for her had been extraordinary. The waltzes brought to mind pictures of decadent palaces. The quicksteps, more gay and fancy-free, made her feel like it was the height of summer, even as the nights drew in and October approached. The tango that was playing now was so exotic, it almost made her think she was a different person . . .

'Where's Miss Marchmont going?' she asked, as if to change the subject. 'She was wearing such an elegant fur.'

'Not going,' Raymond said. '*Returning*. The demonstrations begin anew tomorrow. There's no rest for Miss Marchmont and me . . .'

'Some of the girls, they say Hélène has a secret lover. That he charters planes and takes her to Paris and Milan . . .' Nancy saw the way his face twisted as she spoke, as if trying to hide something, and caught herself too late. 'Mr de Guise, have I said something out of turn?'

'No, it's not that. It's just that . . . we all have secrets, Nancy. We all have stories. Even Maynard Charles himself, I shouldn't wonder. Don't you ever think . . . ?' Raymond paused. He had a hand on Nancy's shoulder and he was leading her around, taking classical hold again. This time, Nancy did nothing to resist. Their feet started moving together, a simple waltz around the room. *Sometimes*, she thought, *it's easier to talk when your body is moving. Dancing makes everything so much more . . . comfortable, somehow.* 'We live on top of each other here, don't we? The Buckingham's so big, but it can seem so small. The hotel director and the porters. The orchestra and the dancers.

All you dozens of chambermaids! The garage mechanics and pages. There's not one of them that doesn't have a story – and here we are, all mingling together. The problem is, sometimes you want to keep your story to yourself. You must have a story, Nancy.'

'I do,' she said, 'but there's no secret in it. I'll tell you everything, Raymond, if you like.'

He held her more tightly – then, suddenly loosening his hold, rolled her away from him, held the pose, and rolled her back tight to his body. 'It isn't about what *I'd* like. It's about what *you'd*—'

'My mother died,' Nancy began quietly. After that, the words frothed out of her. They wouldn't stop. 'I was eight and she was frail and the day after she gave birth to my brother she just faded away. I can remember it like it was yesterday. How ghostly she looked in that chair . . .'

Raymond whispered, 'Oh, Nancy . . .'

'I had to play mum to Frank. That's my baby brother. I still think of him as a baby, though he's sixteen years old and six foot tall and as strapping as the rest of them in our village. I cleaned him and cooked for him and taught him his letters. And it was good, for a time, just the two of us with our father in our little cottage. My father got us by, but by the time I was fully grown he couldn't do it any longer. He took a fall at the pit where he worked. Then it was up and in his lungs. They call it pneumoconiosis. By the end, the doctor had him on so much laudanum that he was barely there with us at all.'

For a moment she could not go on. She hadn't spoken of these things since she'd arrived at the Buckingham, but that did not mean she'd forgotten. They were a part of her, imprinted on her heart. Giving voice to them now was a release, but it was a torment too. *I miss him*, she realised. *I miss them both terribly. I want Frank here, with me, not up there – waiting, just waiting, to go the same way as our father. Because that's what will happen. That's what always happens to men like that. They work and they work until, finally, they just drop.*

'I was there with my father on the night that he passed and when he went . . . Well, it was only me and Frank, on the kindness of the parish. I worked hard, Raymond, to lift us up out of it. I stitched and I sewed for any who'd have me. I'm not ashamed to say that I begged. And now my brother's old enough to take work himself, why, I got on a train to London and I came here and I . . . Don't you see? That's *why* I came. To find a new way of living. Not to stay in my little town, marry some miner's son, and have the same thing happen all over again. I want a different life – for me, as well as Frank . . .'

Raymond did not realise, at first, that Nancy had only stopped speaking because she was crying. The music from the gramophone had come to a crescendo – and then, as suddenly as it had started, it was gone, the number coming to an end and the needle just dancing in the groove.

Returning from her memories at last, Nancy tried to step out of Raymond de Guise's arms, but Raymond held on to her. 'Dance on,' he whispered – so, even though there was no music, they danced.

Dear Frank

Sometimes Rosa and Ruth wonder where I go at night. It's no crime not to sit in the kitchenette and play backgammon and gossip like they do, but I know their tongues are wagging! I cannot tell them where I go. Once, I was late for breakfast in the housekeeping lounge and, well, it's fair to say the girls were not happy with me that day! But Raymond is right: everyone has their story. Rosa and Ruth have stories of their own – Rosa comes from sunny Southend, and Ruth? Well, Ruth was orphaned in the Great War and grew up with a grandmother right here in London. I can barely believe it has been two months since I came to the Buckingham Hotel and all of these people, all of these stories, all around me!

In her quarters, Nancy set down her pen. She was, she had to admit, dog tired – and it was getting late. Could it really be the very last day in September? Could it really have been three whole weeks since she first danced with Raymond de Guise?

She picked herself up and, closing her eyes, imagined herself down in the studio behind the ballroom. She could call it to mind in such intimate detail that soon she could hear the music of the gramophone. Though there was nobody to dance with, she lifted her arms until she was in a classical pose. She stepped backwards. She stepped to her left. She came forward and turned, brought her legs together, then parted them again. There was hardly room in this little turret to describe any sort of box step at all, but she went on and on and on . . .

She was so lost in the dance that she did not hear the knocking at her door. Then, suddenly, she heard voices – and opened her eyes to see the bedroom door pushed ajar and, standing in the gap, Rosa and Ruth. The girls were gawping.

'Nancy, you old romantic!' Rosa shrieked. 'What on *earth* are you doing?'

Ruth was beaming. 'Come out in the kitchen, Nance, and show us them moves! It's always the retiring types, isn't it, Rosa? Lord, we could hardly get her to dance down in the ballroom – and here she is, practising her steps in her bedroom at night!'

Nancy hardly had time to put up a protest, for soon Rosa and Ruth were on either side of her, each taking her by the arm and leading her out into the little kitchenette. A couple of the other girls were playing backgammon with their empty tea-cups ranged around, while Frances was half asleep in a chair by the door.

'Go on then, Nance!' Rosa called as Ruth busied herself, clearing away a table to make space. 'Show us your stuff. Girls, Nancy's been teaching herself to dance. *That's* where she's been sneaking off to.'

'Here, she's embarrassed,' said Ruth. 'Let's all give her a hand. Look, I'll be Marchmont – and, Nance, that makes you the dashing Raymond de Guise.' With a shriek, Ruth inveigled her way into Nancy's arms. 'Go on then, show me how it goes. A foxtrot. A Viennese waltz. Nothing too salacious – this is the Buckingham Hotel, after all! Mr Maynard Charles –' and here Ruth adopted an exaggerated aristocratic air '– would not tolerate anything as uncouth in this fine establishment. What would King Edward think if he was to fly through and see a rhumba or a polka –' Ruth let go of Nancy and lifted her skirts and swept them about, while the other girls guffawed '– in this ballroom of ours?'

'Might happen soon,' said Frances as she picked herself out of her chair and headed for bed.

'What's that?' asked Ruth. 'Polkas and rhumbas, in the Buckingham Hotel? Management wouldn't allow it!'

'All I'm saying,' said Frances, 'is it might happen. I happen to know, for a fact, that Miss Marchmont herself is mounting an expedition tonight.'

All of the other girls revolved to face her.

'An expedition?' one of them asked.

At least they've stopped wanting me to perform for them, Nancy thought.

'She's roped in Louis Kildare from the orchestra. And of course Raymond de Guise. They're heading out, as soon as the ballroom closes tonight – down into Soho.'

Rosa erupted in laughter. 'You're pulling our legs. Haughty Miss Marchmont, icy Hélène, wants some action?'

'I'm telling you. I heard them talking about it, right there in the reception hall.'

'And Raymond de Guise going with them?'

'Well, it stands to reason, doesn't it?' Rosa said. 'See, I told you they was lovers. Now it all makes sense. They slope off to Soho for some private dancing, after they've done their duties for all the toffs down here. Goodness, girls, if only Mr Charles knew! They'll be turning his hotel into a house of ill repute next. All those exotic dances!'

All around the kitchenette, the girls were falling around laughing – but, alone among them, Nancy was still. *He didn't tell me*, she thought. *Why didn't he tell me?* While the girls creased up around her, she turned and fled through the kitchenette door, back into her bedroom, and slammed the door.

He doesn't have to tell you everything. Just because you confided in him. He never made a promise. He never . . .

Why was she so angry?

She tried to breathe deeply and, in that way, managed to calm herself down. Raymond de Guise was a man like any other. Of course he had love affairs. His entire life was a love story: the gilded French aristocrat, born to an English mother, who had forsaken his title to dance on a stage. At least, that was what the other chambermaids had told her. She realised, now, that as much as she'd told him of her own life, he'd told her so little of his. Perhaps the real story was even more fanciful. More fanciful, certainly, than her own sorry tale. So of course he had admirers and of course he had lovers – and if that really was Hélène Marchmont, if they really were stepping out to some shadowy Soho club tonight . . .

You can stop this nonsense this minute, Nancy Nettleton, she said to herself, burying her head in her pillow as if it might block out her thoughts. *You didn't act like one of those simpering city girls when you were back home, and you won't do it now. So he asked you to dance with him? So you're taking lessons, now, with the greatest dancer in the Buckingham Hotel? That's something to be proud of! Not something to fret over like some lovelorn schoolgirl. You're twenty-four years old, for heaven's sake. Old enough to know better.*

In moments she was back on her feet. The clock on the wall did not yet read eleven. That meant that the dances in the ballroom were only just coming to an end. Something was compelling her to put back on her house dress, to slip on her shoes. Something else was compelling her to quickly fix her hair in the mirror. For a moment she took in her reflection – her large eyes were shining with anticipation, her dark curls already escaping the pins. She half-heartedly attempted to tuck a wayward strand behind her ear, and then she was scampering out of the room, past the kitchenette where the girls were still rolling around laughing, and down the stairs.

By the time she reached the ballroom the band had finished playing, and a procession of stately guests were leaving for the night. In the chaos, Nancy was relieved to find herself invisible again.

She heard a familiar voice. Her eyes turned back down the marble incline leading to the ballroom and she watched as Raymond de Guise appeared, with the saxophonist from the band. They were so lost in conversation that they sailed past her without even noticing she was there. *They're not wearing their evening suits*, she thought. *They really are leaving the hotel for the night.*

Across the hall, by the grand bronze doors, Hélène Marchmont was waiting. Even dressed down, Miss Marchmont looked as elegant as a Russian princess. Her fair hair was tied up in a bun, and it nestled upon the collar of her rich fur coat. Simple pearl earrings adorned her ears but, on Hélène Marchmont, they looked like exquisite treasures.

Hélène, she thought, remembering the girls in the kitchenette high above and all they had said. *It can't really be true, can it?*

What if it is? she asked herself. *What does it matter to you? You're a chambermaid. He's an aristocrat. A dancer, but still an aristocrat . . .*

It could never be, Nancy Nettleton. You've changed enough sheets to realise that life isn't a fairy tale.

But I have to know, thought Nancy. It was a need, hot and burning in her stomach. She thought of the way he had held her, down there in the studio, when she'd told him about her father. *I deserve to know.*

Louis Kildare, in his brown felt coat and pinstriped hat, was already leading Hélène and Raymond through the revolving brass door. Nancy made as if she might go the same way. Then she remembered who she was. She saw Maynard Charles in deep conversation with a gentleman in a Savile Row evening suit. She heard the hawing of two tipsy guests as they asked Mr Simenon, the head concierge, to summon them a hansom cab for the journey home. Tomorrow morning, she would be changing these peoples' bedsheets. She'd be scrubbing the bowls of their toilets and laying out freshly laundered towels for them to dab dry their delicate skins. Those brass doors were not for her and they never would be. So she made haste for the staff entrance instead.

Moments later, Nancy quickly made her way up Michaelmas Mews. Above her the autumn night was empty and open, the London skyline splattered with stars.

She had almost lost sight of the silhouettes of Hélène Marchmont, Louis Kildare and Raymond de Guise when she heard a shrill whistling behind her. Whoever it was must have been keeping his head down because, rather than squeeze past her and out onto the square, he promptly barrelled into her. When she looked around, to be met with a flurry of apologies, she saw Billy Brogan standing there, mouth wide open.

'Nance! What the devil are you standing there for – and without a coat!'

In a moment, Billy was stepping out of his own coat and putting it around Nancy's shoulders.

'You'll catch your death out here. Look, oughtn't you to be up in your quarters this time o' night? Mrs Moffatt doesn't care for midnight creepers, does she? But if you were to get back up there, well, nobody'd . . .' Billy stopped. Nancy was not paying a blind bit of notice to anything he was saying. She was staring, instead, off across the square, and one of the roads leading east towards Regent Street and Oxford Circus.

'Billy, are you done for the day?'

'I should say so, Nance. I been here since dawn.'

She took his hand.

'Nance?'

'I've got to go that way,' she said. 'Come with me, Billy?'

Billy was bewildered. 'Where to?'

'I don't *know*,' she said, 'but . . .' One more glance across the square told her that it was nearly too late. The silhouettes had disappeared. They were already gone. 'I'm going!' she exclaimed. 'Off into the night. *Me*, a lowly chambermaid with barely any idea how to get around in London town! If you won't chaperone me, Billy, I'll have to chaperone myself.'

She took three great strides out into the square, but soon she heard the clatter of footsteps behind her.

'Changed your mind have you, Billy?' she said, with a sudden spring in her step. There was nothing like the feeling of being spontaneous, not when you'd been buttoned down caring for other people your whole life. To do something frivolous and be free to do it – was there any greater joy?

'It's not that, Nance . . .'

'Well, what is it?' she asked, finally reaching the corner and catching sight of Raymond's silhouette up ahead.

'It's just – you still got my coat, Nancy.'

Nancy stopped. 'Come on, Billy. Haven't you the taste for a little adventure?' She remembered Raymond's words. *Well, it can't be the Buckingham Hotel each and every night now, can it?* 'They're getting away. Where they go, *I* want to go. Isn't that a way to lead your life?'

But as she marched stridently after them, ignoring the protest of her bad leg, Nancy had the distinct feeling that, wherever they were going and whatever they were doing tonight, it was not something a mere chambermaid like her was supposed to see.

Chapter Sixteen

LONG, NARROW BERWICK STREET WAS quiet after dark. All of the market traders had long ago packed up and gone home. But the noises flurrying up from the doorway at the bottom of the market, where the lane narrowed to cobbles and the darker reaches of Soho beyond, were of piano and trumpet, and the raucous cheers of a hundred people dancing. The sign above the door read THE MIDNIGHT ROOMS in florid script.

Louis Kildare was the first through the door and down the uneven stairs – but then, he'd been here before. The Midnight Rooms didn't care whether a musician was white or black, rich or poor – and, in 1929, when Kildare had first sauntered through these Soho streets, fresh off the steamer that had brought him from his West Indies home, the Midnight Rooms had been one of the first to give him a chance. He could still remember sitting on a stool in the cramped basement club, taking his saxophone out of its case and giving them his best rendition of the solo from 'Squeeze Me', the version first performed by Albert Brunies and his Halfway House Orchestra. Kildare had played for the Midnight Rooms crowd that very same night. It was the same night he'd met Gus Black, Fred

Wright, and so many of the others who would one day sign up with the Archie Adams Band.

Halfway down the stairs, he looked back to see Hélène Marchmont and Raymond de Guise still hovering on the threshold, like a married couple uncertain whether they should venture through the bedroom doors. Kildare beamed at them – those two dancers had spent far too long in the cosseted halls of the Buckingham Hotel! – and disappeared into the darkness at the bottom of the stairs.

In the street above, Raymond could tell that Hélène was anxious. A starlet like Hélène had not come up through the dance halls. There was a time when Hélène had been an amateur dancer, the classical beauty waltzing on the arm of whatever gentleman was courting her at the tea dances and private parties of Fitzrovia, Mayfair, and Holland Park. Those were the days when her glacial blue eyes had stared out of the cover of every magazine. But Hélène had wanted more. The world was not kind to the beautiful. It used them and then, when the years took their beauty away, it kicked them aside. What riches she had saved from her days modelling for *Harper's* and *Vogue* had been enough to hire tutors, and it had been one of those tutors who first brought her to the ballroom. Most dancers found their feet in places like this basement club, but Hélène had come through unscathed.

'Aren't *you* nervous, Raymond?'

He didn't tell her that this wasn't his first visit to the Midnight Rooms. He could distinctly remember standing on the cusp of these very same stairs with his father, listening to the wild hubbub below – both of them, simple East End boys, pulsing with nerves at what they would see below.

But that had been the old days. 1925. What new dances, new music, he might find here now, he didn't know.

'It's just dancing,' he said. 'The high-born dance, and so too does the rest of the world.'

The door opened below. Suddenly the music was louder, rampaging up the stairs.

Hélène lifted a single eyebrow. 'It doesn't seem . . . quite the same.'

'Dancing's the same wherever you go. Maybe they drink whisky and rum down here instead of Moët et Chandon, but it's all for the love of the dance.'

Raymond had started to walk down the stairs. Steeling herself, Hélène followed. *This was your idea*, she had to remind herself. And as they reached the bottom of the stairs, she remembered why. The door opened up. Louis Kildare was already standing there, with three tumblers filled with some dark spirit whose taste had never passed Hélène's lips before. Through the reefs of grey cigar and cigarette smoke, a thronged dance floor was surrounded by tables and chairs. In recesses in the walls, gangs of friends were drinking and laughing and watching the dancers. Bodies were clasped tight. One girl was up on the table, head hunched down against the low ceiling arch, kicking her legs wildly. And on a tiny decked stage set into one of the alcoves itself, lit by the light of a hundred guttering candles in braziers on the walls, a six-piece band put up such a sound that Hélène had imagined there must have been a full orchestra hidden in these tiny halls. A saxophone soared. The trumpets were ablaze. A man was singing, his voice half drowned out by the music.

It was paradise – of a sort – thought Hélène as she allowed Louis to take her by the arm.

The only reason Billy Brogan could keep pace with Nancy as she hurried along the now barren market row, past the Blue Posts public house spilling out its drinkers, was because she kept stopping to give her stubborn leg a moment to rest. Up ahead, from a little doorway sandwiched between two closed shop fronts, music spiralled up from a dark basement staircase. She hovered, ten yards away, just . . . thinking.

Billy Brogan had no need to think. The moment they'd come along the open thoroughfare of Carnaby Street, he had known where they were going. By now, the revellers on Carnaby Street had been few – only the after-hours drinkers at the Tatty Bogle had been putting up a racket – but here, off the Berwick Street market, there was no denying the music in the air. It was loud and it was wild and, above all things, it was infectious.

'You don't want to go down there, Nance,' Billy said, catching up with her at the door. 'It's all ruffians. Drinking and dancing and . . . why, intoxicating themselves with whatever they got to hand.' Billy neglected to tell her how he knew this. How on earth did you say 'this is the place I come and collect special packages for Vivienne Edgerton' and still seem the kind of estimable young gentleman Nancy Nettleton might want to be associated with?

'Nance, come on. It's a dance club. That's all . . .'

Nancy had already taken her first step on the stairs. Something was drawing her down. It was not just the need to know what Raymond and Hélène were doing here, together, and if they were lovers. *No*, Nancy thought, it was something more than that.

She wanted to dance.

'Come on, Billy. You're only young once.'

And I'm hardly young any more, she added privately. *Twenty-four years old, and at risk of being either an old maid or a chambermaid for the rest of my life! Better to grab on to life and do things than wither away, follow the rules, and rot.* 'Come on, Billy! Let's live a little!'

By now she was already halfway down the stairs. She had worked herself up so much that she knew she would have gone on alone, but at last she could hear Billy Brogan clattering after her. That stilled her pounding heart a little. She was brave, she thought, but she still wanted him here. He ought to see this too.

In the end, it was only Billy's presence that made the doorman allow them in. When Nancy appeared, he looked her up and down and seemed to find her wanting in some way. Then Billy sloped up behind her and the doorman, his eyes opening in what Nancy thought might even have been recognition, shrugged his enormous shoulders and opened the door.

The sound, the scent, the taste in the air – it came towards Nancy like a tidal wave, almost bowling her over.

She was grateful that Billy was at her side. For the people who spun and jived in front of her, perhaps this was an ordinary night – but to Nancy it was another life entirely. The smoke in the room gave the bustling dance floor a haze. The dance floor, built from sprung wooden floorboards, was the heart of the room. Two girls were kicking their legs in time to the music roaring out of the alcove at the very head of the room. This cacophony must have been what it was like to sit in the very middle of the Archie Adams Band – only these musicians played with so much more urgency, so much less grace. The music was strident and, though Nancy was certain she'd heard this number in the ballroom itself, here it felt different, somehow, newer and more energetic.

She stumbled forward. Somebody was coming through the doors behind them and instinctively she reached out for Billy Brogan's hand. Together, they were swept further into the club.

Billy didn't mind. The chance to wind his fingers into Nancy Nettleton's hand was not likely to come around again, so he made sure he held her tight as he led her into the room.

A young man and his lover had been drinking dark liquor in one of the alcoves on the furthest side of the dance floor, and Billy spied them as they got up and fought their way down to the dance floor itself. 'Come on, quickly!' he said and, still grasping Nancy by the hand, plunged between the dancers. The revellers did not seem to notice. They parted and came together again, and soon Billy and Nancy were safely ensconced in the alcove, the black walls on either side dampening the music and dancers so that they could almost hear each other speak.

'Shall I get us some drinks?'

'What?'

'I said, shall I get us some drinks! Nance?'

Nancy nodded. She was nervous letting Billy go, but she was hypnotised too. The band had moved into a different number. 'Sing, Sing, Sing', the new Louis Prima number. The dance floor, which had momentarily calmed as the band switched songs, came alive again.

She stared.

She found her own feet tapping.

She saw Raymond de Guise.

He was there in the thick of the dance floor, spinning Hélène Marchmont around, catching her and spinning again. Gone was the elegance and grace she had come to know. He still held himself as confidently, he still owned the dance floor in spite of the dozens of others whirling past him, but there was something free – something more fun – about the way he moved too. *Revelling.* Raymond de Guise, star of the ballroom, was a nightclub reveller now. Nancy was captivated. Then she saw the look on Hélène Marchmont's face. Austere, glacial Hélène Marchmont – Ice Queen of the Buckingham herself – was beaming from ear to ear.

It shouldn't have knifed her like it did, but there was no denying the envy Nancy felt at seeing the way they were dancing together. She was certain: the girls were right. What Hélène and Raymond were compelled to hide in the sophisticated surroundings of the ballroom must have felt right, here in the Midnight Rooms. *You've been a foolish girl, Nancy. He was teaching you to dance. That was all. Just look at them! They're perfect together. From the same standing. From the same class in life. They've probably been in love for years and years – and here you are, a little country mouse still, thinking you're something special.* She carried on staring. Even now, their hands were . . .

Billy tumbled back into the alcove, bringing with him two tumblers of an amber liquor that smelled quite vile. Nancy had seen the village boys tramping through the village on a Friday night after drinking too much of their home-brewed beers, and the thought of drinking alcohol at all had always turned her stomach. But she took a sip now. It burned and she recoiled, but she went to take another.

'Take it slow, Nance. This is wicked stuff.'

Wicked was exactly the word. Nancy put the glass down and her eyes were drawn back to Raymond and Hélène. The number was coming to an end and, at last, their bodies came apart. Only then did she find she could relax. *You foolish, foolish girl!* she thought. *You didn't come to London to get yourself in a lather over some man you barely know. You're smarter than this, Nancy Nettleton!*

In the relative quiet between the songs Nancy could hear glasses being smashed in one of the neighbouring alcoves, somebody barking drunken insults at another. The girls on the tables had stopped jiving and looked suddenly stranded, up above all of the rest. Nancy opened her mouth as if to speak – but then the band-leader stood up. 'Now for something completely different!' he announced, into the crowd. The crowd lifted their glasses and cheered, as if in unison.

Then the music began and it was quite unlike anything Nancy had ever heard.

Hélène took Raymond's hand. *This,* she decided, *this is what we came here for!* The atmosphere in the Midnight Rooms was unlike anything she'd ever experienced. The smell of smoke would be in her hair for days; her ears rang already with the racket that the band put up. Their music was trapped and echoed in all of the many vaults around the edge of the stage – it did not soar and glide like it did in somewhere as vast and well designed as the Grand – but somehow that did not seem to matter. It was wild and different. It did not need elegance and grace. And now . . .

The music changed again. There came a time, each evening, when the Archie Adams Band threw in their own version of a Latin number, something to excite the Carmen Miranda enthusiasts in the ballroom. But what Archie and his orchestra played could not hold a candle to this.

The music started slowly but quickly sped up. The Latin rhythm was unmistakable. It infected every movement of the song. On the dance floor, the dancers quickly found their feet. *This is it,* thought Hélène. *The rhumba* . . . The music was bringing more and more dancers onto the floor. She felt hot bodies around her, pressing in ever more closely.

She had seen so much already. The dancers here had been holding each other in classic ballroom poses, and yet they skipped more frenetically across the dance floor than they would ever have done in the ballroom. Now they clasped each other more tightly, shoulder to shoulder, cheek to cheek. If the tighter frames made the girls in the Midnight Rooms nervous, they did nothing to show it. In fact, thought Hélène, they appeared to positively *love* the opportunity to entwine themselves with the gentlemen at their sides.

Hélène and Raymond held on to each other, and launched into the rhumba with glee.

The box stepping was fast, much faster than anything with which they were familiar, but they had no problem keeping up. But the box step was where the similarity to the waltzes of the ballroom ended. The rhythm quickened and slowed. Across the dance floor, hips moved sensually, along with the music. Ankles flashed. Bare arms caught the candle lights. Then, the couple dancing alongside Raymond and Hélène seemed to separate from the rest. The girl threw her head back, and a moment later she had leaped up, locking her legs around her partner's waist as he turned. A rapturous cheer went up from the sides of the room. Then, as they came out of their spin, the girl was set back down again and the dance continued, as seamlessly as if her feet had never left the ground.

Hélène thought she had never seen a more incredible thing. Dancers in the gilded world to which Hélène Marchmont belonged did not do this.

There's a different world down here. It isn't all men in frilly evening shirts holding you stiffly as you let them lead you across the ballroom. It isn't all having to be prim and proper and demure to men who know less than half what you know about dance. Down here, I can be myself.

She looked at Raymond. His eyes had the devil in them. *Temptation . . .*

There was no need for words. Both knew what the other wanted to do. A move like this would have been sacrilegious in the Grand, but after so many years dancing for the rich and the powerful, it was a relief – no, more than that, a *need* – to dance without a care in the world. To remember what had drawn them both to dancing. Hélène nodded. They danced on. And then – without quite knowing she was going to do it – Hélène too was up, with her legs wrapped around Raymond's waist as he turned and turned and turned again.

Some of the other dancers had stopped to watch. The crowd parted around them as they moved together, lost in a world of their own.

But then, suddenly there was the sound of glass smashing and everything changed.

Nancy was the first to see it. A man – six feet tall, with shoulders almost as broad – had leaped out of the alcove next to where she and Billy were sitting. It took him a second to push through the girls swaying to the Latin rhythm on the edge of the dance floor, and another second to paw his way through the dancers turning their hypnotic box steps on the floor itself. By the time Billy had realised what was going on, the first punch had already been thrown. The man, with his shirt sleeves rolled up to reveal dockland tattoos up and down his forearms, was carving Raymond de Guise and Hélène Marchmont apart, bellowing at them.

The band played on.

Through the music, Nancy heard the man screaming: 'Thought we wouldn't recognise you, Ray? Thought we'd have forgotten your face? You've been seen in the neighbourhood, mate. But you're not welcome, you understand? None of *your* lot are welcome.'

A clenched fist connected with Raymond's jaw and he went whirling backwards. The couple who had been dancing behind him were the only thing that stopped him crashing to the floor. By accident they caught him and set him back on his feet – but, by then, the brute had readied himself for another unrelenting strike. He brought the back of his hand across Raymond's jaw, then drove the other clenched fist into his stomach. Raymond doubled over, dropping out of Nancy's sight. In the crowd, Hélène Marchmont screamed.

Only then did the bandleader realise what was going on. The music ended sharply, in a chaotic mess of trombone and dying tenor horn.

In an instant, Nancy was on her feet. Billy cried out – 'Nance, no!' – but, if Nancy heard him, she paid it no mind. She staggered through the dancers flocking away from the dance floor. In their haste to get away from the tumult, they seemed to have formed a cordon blocking her path.

'Raymond!' she screamed, but Raymond was not the one to hear. Hélène Marchmont looked around, saw Nancy, and her face creased in surprise.

Nancy wasted no time. This was not the moment to care about whether Hélène and Raymond were lovers or not. She forced her way through the wall of dancers, just in time to see Raymond fall beneath another clenched fist. Then the huge man was on top of him, pounding at his face. Between each blow he took a breath, as if to ready himself. And all the while he was crying out, spittle flying from his lips.

'You and that brother of yours, the whole goddamn rabble of you. You're up and out of our streets, you understand? You Cohens was always the worst of it. When you weren't out thieving and grifting, you were still taking the work from the rest of us. Well, time's up, *Ray*. Dance yourself out of this one. There's ten thousand of us going to march on Sunday. There's nothing your lot can do to stop it. The Home Secretary his self is sending guards to protect us. You and that thieving, filthy Jewish brother of yours are finished . . .'

The thug had brought his arm back for one final punch. Beneath him, Raymond was lying dazed on the floor. Nancy sprang forward – and, in the same moment she did, Hélène reached out and grappled with the thug's arm. The motion took Raymond's attacker by surprise. He flailed backwards, his fist caught Hélène Marchmont's face, and she too plunged to the floor.

From the crowd, Nancy heard an aghast cry. 'This has gone too far!' somebody growled. Two men – who until now had spent the night ostentatiously dancing, like peacocks trying to attract a mate – waded out of the huddles on the edges of the room. By the time they reached the man, who still straddled Raymond, Louis Kildare too had extricated himself from the crush. He picked Hélène up, wrapped his arms around her.

'Get off him!' one of the men cried out.

The thug just shrugged. 'You friends of his?'

'Not friends. Just good people. This is a dance club. You want to brawl, you—'

'Oh,' the man said, with the barest flicker of a smile, 'a brawl is it?' He stood up, leaving Raymond on the floor, and called out to the alcove where he'd been sitting. 'Boys, we got some heroes sticking up for this sewer rat. This Yid. Want to show 'em a thing or two, or should I have all the fun myself?'

Nancy saw Raymond try and pick himself up. His face was a mask of scarlet and black. He was coughing up blood; one of his teeth had been knocked out. She took a step, as if to go towards him – but, too late, for already more men were kicking their way down to the dance floor. They looked so unmistakably like the brute who had just pulverised Raymond that she could only assume they were his brothers – and every bit as degenerate.

'Stop!' she cried out as they brushed past, trailing the odours of whisky and sweat and smoke. 'Somebody, *stop* them!'

She could see faces in the crowd, looking nervously at one another. Some of the dancers were already crowding the doorway, making haste to get out of the Midnight Rooms altogether. The band remained on the stage, with nowhere else to go – but, as the thug's brothers arrived, the bandleader – a black man with thick coils of hair and an immaculate beard – stepped out in front of his upright piano and ceremoniously removed his smart silk jacket. 'Not here!' he cried out. 'Not in the Midnight Rooms. This is a good place. This is for music. This is for dance!'

The first blows landed. The bandleader vaulted down to join the fray. Soon the rest of the band had ditched their instruments to fight at his side. Seeing what was happening, some of the remaining dancers in the room were emboldened. They charged back to the dance floor – and Raymond was lost behind the new press of bodies.

Nancy felt Billy grappling with her arm. 'Nance,' he said, 'we got to go.'

'But Billy! It's Raymond. What if he—'

'We can't be here, Nance. We can't *help* him.'

'They weren't speaking sense,' Nancy gasped. 'They called him Cohen. His name's de Guise. Billy, they got the wrong man!'

Billy wrenched her around. 'I said I'd get you here safe, and I'll get you out of here safe as well. We've got to get back . . .'

Through the madness of bodies grappling with each other, Nancy caught another glimpse of Raymond lying prostrate on the floor.

As the crowd closed back around him, she saw him mouth one final word.

'Run!'

It was the final encouragement Nancy Nettleton needed. As the fight erupted behind her, she raced after Billy Brogan, back to the barren street market and the moonlit Soho streets above.

Chapter Seventeen

LONG AFTER MIDNIGHT, BERKELEY SQUARE was becalmed. Billy brought Nancy within sight of the hotel's lights and there they said their goodbyes. 'But I'm going to need my coat, Nance. I got to get back to Lambeth and the cold's setting in.'

Billy was helping her out of it when he caught her look. 'Nance, are you—'

Nancy cut him off, 'Was he . . . dead, Billy? Did they . . . ?'

Billy took her by the shoulders. 'Not dead, Nance. Louis Kildare got him out of there. You can stake your last shilling on it.'

The cold of this September night was more bitter than Nancy remembered. A wind curled across Berkeley Square and chilled her to the core.

'But who were they?' she whispered. 'He's mixed up in something, isn't he, Billy? Something bad.'

'You can't think of it, Nance.'

'But he's one of *us*!' She stopped dead. *What did I mean by that?* 'I mean to say . . . one of the Buckingham. He's one of ours, Billy, and they—'

Billy reached up and brushed the hair out of her tear-stained eyes. 'Louis Kildare will get him back here. You can be sure of it. But, Nance, you can't let on where you were. Promise me you won't. Get to your quarters, and get up tomorrow morning as if nothing ever happened.' He paused. 'I'll come and find you tomorrow. See that you're well . . .'

Nancy looked up at the gleaming white facade of the hotel. 'You don't need to do that, Billy.'

'Nance, I *want* to,' Billy said. Then he was gone.

Nancy approached the Buckingham with her heart still pounding, the image of Raymond covered in blood still flashing in front of her eyes. So lost in the images was she that she thought nothing of it as she tramped up the grand marble staircase and pushed through the revolving Art Deco door. She registered nothing wrong as her heels clicked across the red and black chequers of the reception, past the striking obelisk and towards the golden guest lift. The first moment she understood anything was wrong at all was when the hand of Mr Simenon landed on her shoulder and spun her bodily around.

'Nettleton!' he gasped. 'What in the name of all that is holy do you think you're doing?'

As his eyes bored into her, Nancy had the sinking realisation of what she had done. The staff entrance on Michaelmas Mews. She was, she recalled with a terrible finality, supposed to be *invisible*.

'Come with me, Miss Nettleton,' Mr Simenon said. His voice had the sibilance of a snake. It was as if he'd been slithering around reception all evening, just waiting for somebody to pounce upon. 'It's high time we talked about your behaviour at our proud hotel – and, as fortune would have it, your very own Mrs Moffatt is burning the midnight oil this evening. So perhaps it is just and right that you explain yourself to her. *Some* of us work like dogs to ensure the smooth running of this hotel, Miss

Nettleton, while *some* of us think we're better than everyone else, don't we? Now, come this way . . . '

Nancy was shaking as she followed him down the hall, past the hotel director's office, and to the door marked HOUSEKEEPING. She remembered sitting here on her very first day. Barely two months ago and yet how far away it seemed!

Mr Simenon instructed her to stand outside and, with barely a knock, he disappeared through the door. Moments later, he reappeared, leaving the door wide open so that Nancy could see Mrs Moffatt still at her desk, the housekeeping ledger open in front of her and various aborted rotas scribbled on pages strewn around.

'Good night, Miss Nettleton,' Mr Simenon announced with an air of triumph, and marched back along the hall.

Mrs Moffatt did not look up as Nancy lingered in the doorway. Whatever she was concentrating on, it seemed, was much more pressing than the delinquent chambermaid hanging around outside her office, still smelling of the cigarette smoke and cheap rum of the Midnight Rooms. Mrs Moffatt raised her hand and, still not looking up, beckoned her in. With a sinking heart, Nancy stepped through and closed the door behind her.

As she fell into the seat in front of the desk, the image of a bloodied Raymond flashed again across her eyes. *Things like that didn't happen all the time, did they? So what was he mixed up in? Raymond said that everyone had stories, everyone had secrets – but what were his?*

'Mrs Moffatt,' she said, 'I know what I did was wrong. But let me explain. It was a mistake and I made it in the . . .'

Mrs Moffatt lifted a hand and, after spending a moment ordering her papers, looked up. Making a steeple of her fingers, she considered Nancy.

'It was a mistake, Mrs Moffatt. That's all. It hasn't been the most marvellous of nights and I—'

'That's not what you're here for, Nancy.'

Nancy stalled. 'Mrs Moffatt?'

'You know better than to come through the guest doors, Nancy. You're an astute, intelligent girl. It's your rotten luck that Mr Simenon, snake that he is, is working so late this evening – but there are guests coming in on the American Airlines flight. Richard Noble, I understand.' Noble was a filmmaker who courted his stars in the cocktail bar of the Buckingham Hotel. He was known to take great suites and was never a spendthrift with the credit afforded to him by his studio. 'Mr Simenon intends to be here to meet them . . . but that is his business and *this* is ours.' Mrs Moffatt paused. 'We can make allowances, Nancy. It takes time for a new member of staff to find their feet in an enterprise as vast as the Buckingham. But you've been here two months now, and there are *reports*.'

Nancy repeated the word back at her with horror. '*Reports*, Mrs Moffatt?'

Mrs Moffatt seemed to sense something. She wrinkled her nose in distaste. 'It isn't just forgetting your place. The door we might overlook, if that was the only thing. And yet . . . Where have you been tonight, Nancy?'

'I've been . . . out, Mrs Moffatt.' Something hardened in her. *Stand up for yourself, Nancy!* 'Why, I'm not a prisoner here, am I? A girl can still go out, if she wants to. I'm not at work until six. I can—'

'It's things like this, Nancy. This answering back. Do you know what not knowing your place could cost you, Nancy?' There had seemed such fury in Mrs Moffatt's voice, but now she softened. 'I'm saying this because I like you. I'll talk to Mr Simenon. I'll smooth it out. But that man, his mother didn't love him hard enough, or his father was too free with his cane, and he's a difficult man to convince . . . If one more complaint was to be lodged with Mr Charles—'

'One *more*, Mrs Moffatt? Who's . . . ?' Nancy was about to ask who on earth could have complained about her before, when realisation hit her like a freight train between the eyes. 'Miss Edgerton,' she breathed.

'Miss Edgerton is the daughter of the head of the hotel board.'

Better than me, thought Nancy. *Better, and all because of who she was born to, or which family her mother married into. And isn't that what this hotel is, through and through? One door for the likes of me, one door for the likes of them. One of us to clean their bedsheets; them to sleep, safe and sound.*

'You were seen in the *ballroom*, Nancy. By the look of you, I'm given to understanding that you thought it had not been noticed. Well, I'm afraid that was never the case. Nancy, I'd do anything for my girls. I've managed to keep it from Mr Charles, but that was only because Miss Edgerton was so indisposed that evening. Is it illegal? No. Is it against hotel rules? Well, nobody told you not to. There is that in your defence. But some rules don't need to be written down.'

Nancy bristled. Beneath her breath, she whispered, 'Rules like, know your place.'

'It isn't just Miss Edgerton. The other girls have noticed it, Nancy. Rosa and Ruth, and even Mrs Whitehead. We all think we're different from the rest, Nancy, when we're young. It's as you get older that you start realising: we're all just the same as everyone else. Isn't it time, Nancy, to do some growing up?' Mrs Moffatt leaned across the table to take Nancy's hand – and, because Nancy had so little alternative, she let her. Mrs Moffatt's hands were leathery, but the touch was gentle. 'I'm not trying to be cruel, Nancy. Of all the things I am – old and senile to boot – I am not cruel. As I've said, and you can believe this or not, I *like* you. I may even see a little of myself in the pluck you've shown coming down here to our hotel. If you want it, I believe there's a bright future for you at the Buckingham. There'll come a day when I won't be here. Somebody will be needed to fill these shoes. Do you think a girl like Rosa or Ruth, good chambermaids but without a single original thought between them, could do this? No, dear. Housekeeping isn't just housekeeping. It's numbers and it's writing, and it's confidence and verve. Those things *you've* got, Nancy. But you know what else it takes? Patience. Knowing how to speak to your superiors. Knowing when to speak your mind and knowing when to hold your tongue. Do you understand?'

Nancy thought that she did, but Mrs Moffatt's words were not having the effect they might. All she could think about was whether Raymond was still alive. He had looked so beaten . . . there had been so many punches thrown . . .

'Let this be the last mistake. Off you go, then, Nancy, and I'll put a stop to Mr Simenon. I don't want you leaving the Buckingham Hotel without a reference. Please, Nancy. Think about it, won't you?'

Nancy could not have thought about it, even if she'd wanted to. All she was thinking about as she stepped out of the guest lift and marched to the staff quarters was what had happened to Raymond. At least Rosa and Ruth were already in bed. At least she would not have to face them. With her bedroom door firmly closed behind her, Nancy fell onto the bed. It was only as she lay there that the tears flowed out of her, hot, hard and fast.

What am I even doing here? she trembled. *All those weeks and months of saving and planning. Get a job in London, Nancy. Work hard. Live frugally. Save what pennies you get – and, when you can, send for Frank to come and join you. What was it all for, if it can all be obliterated on a whim?*

After a while, she was able to fight the tears down. Spent, she picked herself up, sat on the end of the bed, and dried her red, raw cheeks. Feeling sorry for herself would get her nowhere. She was tougher than that.

But the image of her dear Raymond de Guise, lying bloodied and broken on the floor, would not leave her alone.

Moments later, Nancy was back on her feet. This, she supposed, was what Mrs Moffatt was talking about – how she couldn't just meekly sit by, how she couldn't keep herself to herself, how she couldn't stop *caring*.

She had to know if he was all right.

If she took the staff entrance, Mr Simenon need never know. Despite Mrs Moffatt's words, she had to see for herself. She had to do *something*. So, in her black felt coat and embroidered cap, she marched straight back to the service lift and down to the ground floor.

She got to the staff exit without being seen. Then she was out, back into the chill darkness of Michaelmas Mews.

As she reached the end of the mews and slipped out into Berkeley Square, she saw the headlamps of an approaching cab. Nancy stopped dead. The cab had screeched to a stop directly in front of the Buckingham Hotel and, as its doors opened, she saw Louis Kildare and Hélène Marchmont scrambling out. It was

Louis who heaved the limp form of Raymond out of the back seat. He was bloody and bedraggled and, as Louis tried to hoist him up, he plummeted to the first of the hotel's marble steps.

'Go!' Louis said urgently. 'Hélène, get help!'

Hélène Marchmont disappeared through the revolving bronze doors. When she returned, dragging Mr Simenon with her, the concierge's face was a rictus of pure horror.

'What in the Lord's name happened to him?'

'Help me with him, Albert. We'll explain later . . .'

'And get blood on this suit?' Mr Simenon recoiled. 'Wait here. I'll fetch . . .'

Mr Simenon made as if to retreat through the revolving door, but Hélène grappled with his arm. 'Help him, you fool.'

'Get him to the staff entrance,' Mr Simenon hissed. 'If the guests are to see—'

'*No!*' Hélène cried. 'He needs—'

Mr Simenon seemed animated, hopping from foot to foot with irritation. 'If you people won't listen, I'll simply fetch Mr Charles. I'm waking Mr Charles this instant!'

As Mr Simenon vanished back through the doors, Hélène clearly decided enough was enough. Dropping down, she inveigled herself under one of Raymond's shoulders. Raymond dangled between Hélène and Louis heavily as they heaved him up the marble stairs – and the last thing Nancy saw, as the cab took off again with a screech of tyres and a spluttering of exhaust, was Raymond lolling between them as they disappeared through the revolving door.

He was alive – and, even in spite of how battered and bloody he was, it made Nancy Nettleton's heart soar.

Chapter Eighteen

THE SUN HAD NOT YET cast its first glorious light on the trees and rooftops of Berkeley Square, but Mrs Moffatt moved hurriedly through the hallways of the Buckingham Hotel, riding the service lift to the staff quarters, then backtracking down the service stairs until she came to the secluded area where the managers' residences lay. Behind the first door the night manager, a shadowy fellow who went by the name of Victor Garlick, was fast asleep; Mrs Moffatt fancied she could hear his snoring reverberating along the hall. She hurried past, to the door at the very end of the hall and knocked sharply. When no answer came, she knocked sharper still – and when no answer came again, she did something she had not expected to do. She reached into her pocket, produced a ring of keys as impressive as those of a medieval gaoler, and opened the door herself.

The suite was empty. Mr Charles was nowhere to be seen. The four-poster bed in which he slept appeared untouched. His desk was neatly organised, with the Monarch typewriter sitting patiently and the ink pot, pencils and ruler arranged at perfect right angles. His evening suit was still hanging on the hanger in the open wardrobe. On the other side of the room, the curtains remained drawn – and it was this, more than any other thing, that convinced Mrs Moffatt that she was right; Maynard Charles had not awoken here in his official quarters, not this morning.

But there is another place, she thought. *Not that anyone knows about it but me . . .*

Locking the door behind her, she marched back to the lift and rode it down a further storey – where, by accessing another locked door, she slipped unnoticed among the guest suites. There was no time to apologise to Mr Levant, the ageing star of the Parisian music halls, as he stepped out of the Pacific Suite with his paramour, a young lady forty years his junior. Mrs Moffatt bustled past and turned the corner, where at last she stood in front of the unassuming door of the Park Suite.

She knocked.

She waited.

She knocked again, more urgently this time, and relented only when she could hear the footsteps approaching on the other side.

The door opened a crack and Maynard Charles appeared, his jowly face screwed up in consternation. 'Emmeline,' he ventured. 'Something's happened, hasn't it?'

There was no other reason that Mrs Moffatt might disturb him so. She knew better than to come to the Park Suite on a whim.

'They've been looking for you all night, Maynard. Mr Simenon's been high and low trying to track you down.' Maynard Charles's face curdled, but he gave Mrs Moffatt the nod, as if instructing her to go on. 'You better see it for yourself, Maynard. It's Raymond de Guise. Something terrible has happened.'

By the time Maynard Charles got to Raymond's quarters, one of the hotel doctors – summoned at dawn from his Harley Street practice – was already in attendance. He sat at his bedside, and de Guise himself was trussed up like a hog. His face, a purpling mess of bruises and abrasions, was patched up in places, and his hair was smeared back to reveal where his scalp had been opened up in what Maynard Charles could only take for a public brawl. One of his arms was hanging in a sling, and he sat on the edge of his bed, stripped to the waist while the doctor – whom Maynard Charles recognised as Evelyn Moore, greying and distinguished after serving admirably in France during the Great War – ran fingers along his ribs and listened to the rattle in his breast.

Raymond winced as Maynard Charles appeared, with Mrs Moffatt trailing behind. On another day he might have leaped to attention, but Doctor Moore had already told him that at least three of his ribs were fractured. The wrist in the sling was only a sprain, but that was little consolation, for he had already tried to hold a classic ballroom pose with the good doctor and the pain had been excruciating. The reason he did not smile at Mr Charles's appearance was less to do with the solemnity of the occasion than it was the fact that one of his front teeth had been sheared off at the root, and – no matter how many times he swilled his mouth out – the rest of it was still rimmed in scarlet.

'Raymond,' Mr Charles began. 'You're . . . alive, at least.'

'Alive he might be,' the doctor said, 'but it isn't good news, Maynard. His arm will take a week to stop feeling as sore. Another blow or two might have seen one of those ribs break fully. I've seen lungs punctured by little worse than this. But it's his foot, Maynard.' Doctor Evelyn Moore moved aside, to reveal the swollen horror of Raymond's right foot. 'I can't be certain here, but I'd hazard it's fractured *here* and *here*. We'll have to use a compression dressing. Plenty of ice. Keep it elevated. He can try putting weight on it in a couple of weeks. But as for dancing? Well, if you're lucky, you can have him at Christmas. If not—'

'Christmas? That's ten weeks and more . . .'

Only now did he realise his mistake. When he'd opened his mouth in disbelief, he'd revealed the devastation of his smile. He breathed deeply, but his sinuses were swollen where his nose had been broken and reset – and the thought dawned on him that the handsome, debonair Raymond de Guise of old was gone. It was more like Ray Cohen to get caught in the middle of a public brawl than Raymond de Guise. The thought unnerved him.

'Raymond, you *bloody fool*!' Maynard Charles could barely control his fury. It erupted out of the corners of his mouth in a spray of spittle, before he swallowed it back down. 'What in God's name have you done to yourself?'

Raymond uttered, 'You should have seen the rest of them.'

If Raymond had thought it might defuse the tension, he was wrong. Maynard Charles balled his fists and, this time, he could not control his explosion. 'I *pay* you to be handsome, de Guise. I pay you for your elegance. Any damn fool can put on a show in that ballroom! What did you think it was that set you apart? Your dancing *shoes*? No, de Guise. *Your face*. Your beautiful, boyish face. Good Lord, man, was it worth it? Whoever's wife you touched? Whoever's sister you were romancing in one of your gentleman's clubs?'

Raymond thought: *I could tell him that it wasn't nearly as sleazy as he thinks. That they jumped on me because of what I am, what my real family are. But that would mean telling him that all of the magic we've been spinning in the Grand, it's all been horse shit. It would almost be worth it, to see the look on this face. But . . .*

I don't want to be Ray Cohen, Raymond thought. *Ray Cohen's gone. I buried him, didn't I? Why can't he just stay six feet under?*

Maynard Charles continued. 'You understand what you've done here, don't you? The ballroom – *my* ballroom, lest you forget – demands you down there. Christmas is coming, not to mention New Year. You *know* what this season means to us, Raymond. You *know* the peril we're in! Put the Buckingham on the society pages for the spring and we may yet survive. But to do that we *need* this Christmas. We need the Masquerade Ball at New Year to leave whatever they have planned over at the Imperial and the Savoy and the Ritz in the shade. I've been planning this season since the last one ended – and now it's to go to waste, because of one drunken night by my principal dancer? They're coming to see *you*, Raymond. The King himself is gracing us with his royal presence. You're to dance with the Queen of Norway, with Märtha, her crown princess. Lord Edgerton will be in attendance. All of the board.' Maynard Charles's face was purpling with rage. He looked like an incandescent beetroot. 'Your responsibility here extends much further than your own little world, Raymond. *You* are part of a much bigger whole. Raymond de Guise, the lovelorn aristocrat dancer and his glacial beauty of a partner, Hélène Marchmont. You remember what happened when Hélène took her leave of us for a year? Finding a replacement for somebody as popular and loved was near impossible. And now I have to do that for *you* with only weeks before the Christmas season begins.'

'Mr Charles, if you'll let me speak—'

'I don't want to hear another word!' Maynard Charles thundered. 'When this gets out, what do you think is going to happen to our ballroom? They'll be laughing at us, Raymond. Laughing all over London! At the Savoy and the Imperial and all those other *parochial* little palaces. The King coming to a ballroom where the principal dancer is a bloody mess. *A bloody fool!*' Maynard Charles stopped to catch his breath and, the moment he did so, another thought, even worse than all these, occurred. 'I'll have to explain this to Lord Edgerton. There'll be questions from the board. Why the gentleman dancer I insisted we pay for is spending the Christmas season lounging in bed. What these mysterious bills are. Doctors and *dentists*.' He spat the word with such opprobrium it might have been the most unutterable curse under the sun.

Instinctively, Raymond tensed. Perhaps the adrenaline was still coursing through his body, but for a passing moment he wanted nothing more than to drive his fist into Maynard Charles's angry face. *But no,* he told himself. *That's Ray Cohen talking. Not the debonair gentleman Raymond de Guise.*

He composed himself. 'I can still go to the ballroom. I can still fraternise with our guests—'

'I don't care if you can fly. I don't care if you can foxtrot on air. I don't care if you move like a Greek goddess. Not when you have a face like *that*. Raymond, it's time you understood your worth. It's beauty I want in that ballroom.' He turned on his heel, pointedly ignoring Raymond and turning to Doctor Moore. 'Patch him up. Send for your orthodontist. Fill him full of whatever potions you have. Just get him ready for the battle.' Maynard marched to the door, and there he stopped. 'Raymond, you're to rest. I'll have one of the chambermaids come and turn this room over. We'll send up food – soups, I should think, looking at the state of you. But, heaven forfend, if I see you out of this room looking like that, there'll be no place for you at the Buckingham Hotel. I want to contain the rumours. Do you understand?'

Raymond nodded. 'I understand, sir.'

Then Maynard Charles was gone, leaving a fuming Raymond de Guise behind.

On the ground floor, as the day manager welcomed a party of guests up from the Côte d'Azur, Maynard Charles slammed the director's office door and threw a wild kick at his leather chair. Then, still purple with fury, he opened his cabinet and drew out one of the many card indexes inside. To a man in charge of so many different departments, so many moving pieces, a card index was a priceless resource. Maynard Charles sometimes thought that his card indexes were like little pieces of his brain carved out and filed away – and, ordinarily, the thought gave him enormous pleasure.

Not now. Now, there was too much anger pumping through him to make room for any pleasure at all. This particular card index categorised all the many dancers who had auditioned for a place in the Grand's demonstrations over the years. But, more than that, it detailed all of the dancers at the Savoy, the Imperial, all of the other ballrooms across London where dancers were perfecting their art – and drawing in business for their establishments. Maynard Charles was a man of many talents, and the most important talent of all was self-preservation. The indexes in this office afforded him recourse in almost any situation. He had always known he would need to replace Raymond de Guise sooner or later. Gentlemen dancers got bored. They disappeared on midnight trains across Europe, or fell in love with an aristocrat who'd partnered with them on the ballroom for the night – or they got themselves embroiled in some scandal involving a minor royal, or a notable member of society. When that happened, Maynard Charles would need to know who the best dancers were in the other ballrooms across London. It would not do to merely promote somebody from the ranks. No. He needed to make a statement – and he needed to make it fast.

He had barely begun to consult the oracle that was his index when there came a knocking at the door. Scrabbling to put it away, he barked, 'Enter!', and looked up to see Mr Simenon guiding Vivienne Edgerton through the doors. This morning Vivienne was dressed in a burgundy house dress, with a single pin in her hair. Her lips were painted with a striking lipstick and there seemed something strange about her eyes; she had the look of a lady who had spent all night in the cocktail lounge, being indulged by her various suitors. Her pupils were big and round and she seemed to glare.

'I'm in the middle of something quite important, Miss Edgerton. Might this wait?'

'Mr Charles, I believe I know your predicament. And I believe I may have a solution.'

'My . . . predicament?' So, thought Maynard Charles. The manic look in her eyes was evidently not because she was still riding the waves of last night's Cointreau and vermouth. 'Tell me, Miss Edgerton, what do you know of my predicament, and how do you know it?'

Maynard Charles hardly needed an answer to that question. Mr Simenon was, even now, bowing his head and sloping backwards through the door, off to offer his services to the party from the Côte d'Azur. He was indispensable with his knowledge of London, its theatres and galleries, its private parties and invitation-only boutiques, but his thirst for all knowledge extended too far in this hotel. One day soon Maynard would have to put a stop to that wagging tongue of his.

'I have a suggestion, Mr Charles. You might laugh, and you might think it not my place, but . . . When my stepfather was here, he had in his company a dancer of the most superlative talent.'

Maynard Charles sank back into his seat. Why did he feel, suddenly, like a fly caught in a spider's trap? It was not only in the words Vivienne was speaking. There was something about the confidence with which she said it. One might almost think it was Vivienne herself who had laid waste to Raymond de Guise.

'Miss Edgerton, there are a hundred talented ballroom dancers across this city, and every last one of them is champing at the bit to come and dance for me in my ballroom. I'll consider your suggestion, but perhaps you might leave this matter to those of us more . . . capable?'

He ought not to have said it. Immediately, and in spite of the petty thrill it gave him, he regretted it. Seeing Raymond this morning had inflamed him. It had addled his mind. He knew better than to speak to Lord Edgerton's stepdaughter like that. He watched as the anger that erupted on her features settled into a kind of knowing glee. For Vivienne was certain, now, that she would get what she wanted.

'Nathaniel is everything Raymond de Guise is and more.' Was Maynard Charles mistaken, or did he detect some bitterness in Vivienne's voice as she said Raymond's name? 'He has demonstrated at the Imperial, but I know for a fact he'd drop everything in a second if the Grand opened its doors to him. You said you wanted something special, Mr Charles. Well, believe me – Nathaniel is special. He is –' she hesitated before using the word – 'beautiful, Mr Charles. And, you must understand, he *is* the son of one of Daddy's colleagues . . .'

Daddy, thought Maynard. She uses it so easily when she wants something – and yet, in private, she seethes at even calling him her stepfather.

'He would be an excellent replacement for Mr de Guise. Dare I say it . . . but I believe he might even surpass him for elegance on the dance floor.'

'You've been to the Imperial, have you, and seen his work?'

Vivienne's eyes flickered at him. 'I've seen *all* of his work,' she said with a vaguely licentious air. 'He moves like an angel.'

Every muscle in Maynard Charles's body was suddenly rigid. 'I'll consider it, Miss Edgerton.'

After she was gone, Maynard returned to his cabinet and reached for his index. Flicking forward to the cards that were marked IMPERIAL HOTEL, he picked out the one for NATHANIEL WHITE. Twenty-three years old. Champion of Blackpool and Edinburgh. He'd danced a season at the Café de Paris, then taken himself to Europe for a tour of the palaces. Yes, Maynard thought, perhaps a boy like this might be a draw. Something to bring extra magic to the world of their beautiful ballroom. But he was also one of . . . *them*. There was nothing here to indicate that Nathaniel White belonged to the British Union of Fascists like the other men who'd come to meet with Lord Edgerton – but he was a blood relation, and blood did flow thicker than water.

When you ran an enterprise as vast as the Buckingham, you had to be willing to make sacrifices to your honour. The gold coins of a fascist were worth every bit as much as the gold coins of a man of absolute morality. You could not deny any man a bed for the night, not if he had the means to pay for it. But the thought of *inviting* somebody like that backstage at the Grand? Maynard Charles had spent the best years of his youth on the battlefields in France. To court men who would make war again was one of the bitterest pills he had ever been asked to swallow.

Maynard Charles turned the card over and over again. The simple truth was that the decision had already been made. He fancied he could still smell Vivienne Edgerton's perfume lingering in the air – and he wondered, not for the first time, how much of this hotel he really ran at all.

October 1936

Chapter Nineteen

THIS MORNING, AS BILLY SIDLED in along Michaelmas Mews and through the passageway behind the reception hall, where the deputy night manager was compiling his list of the evening's occurrences, he kept his head bowed down and scurried onward. He'd heard the concierges talking about Mr Simenon, and what he'd done to the poor girl caught sneaking in after hours, and in the week that had passed since then a kernel of guilt had been hardening in his breast. He'd brought Nancy Nettleton back to the doors of the Buckingham, ensured her safe passage across Soho after dark, and the moment he'd let her go (taking her coat no less!), she'd walked straight into the oldest trap of them all.

In the reception hall, Maynard Charles was attending to a new guest. Cormac E. Colby was fresh off the plane out of New York, but had arrived on the Buckingham steps with not a hair out of place. Billy stopped as he sidled by. Ordinarily, guests arrived at the Buckingham trailing enough suitcases and trunks to make a boy like Billy believe they were transporting a small country behind them. Rupprecht, the Crown Prince of Bavaria, had been just like that – last week he'd appeared, a vision of old-world elegance, through the revolving doors and waited as a procession of servants and hangers-on brought through so many trunks, cases and smaller valises that the other guests must have thought he was here to fortify a castle. But Cormac E. Colby, with his slicked-back hair and pinstriped suit, arrived with only a small black leather bag and the golden pen with which he was now signing his name on the hotel manifest.

In his hands Billy held a brown paper envelope, brought to the staff door and delivered to him by name. The name on the front of the letter said RAYMOND in big black letters. That was all. There was no address, no surname, nothing else to indicate who it was for. But Billy knew only two Raymonds at the Buckingham Hotel – and Raymond Owen, the garage mechanic, was not the sort to receive mysterious letters before break of day. Besides, the first thing Billy had done upon receiving this letter was sneak into the kitchen behind the Queen Mary and steam the envelope open. It was there, lurking between the industrial pot wash and the roasting oven, that he first knew for certain this letter was for Raymond de Guise.

Raymond had not been seen in the ballroom for seven days and seven nights. The rumour circulating around the hotel was that he'd been laid low with a particularly virulent strain of measles. In a place like the Buckingham, this was the sort of news that the management would keep hidden by any means necessary – for any inkling of pestilence in the hotel, and the veneer of glamour they worked hard to cultivate would vanish in an instant. Billy had heard Rosa and Ruth tittering that it was, inevitably, some other kind of pox that Raymond de Guise had fallen ill with – for wasn't Raymond known to be a gigolo as well as a dancer? One of the concierges had posited that de Guise was actually holding Maynard Charles and the hotel board to ransom, refusing to come out of his chambers until a new, elevated contract was signed. This was the sort of thing that fallen gentlemen like Raymond de Guise did.

Alone among them, only Billy knew the real reason Raymond was confined to his chambers. The memory of him, spread-eagled on the floor of the Midnight Rooms as the mob surged, remained vivid in Billy's mind.

Billy rode the service lift up to the staff chambers and knocked on Raymond's door. When no answer was forthcoming, he knocked again. 'Raymond!' he called out. 'Raymond, open up. It's Billy.'

When the silence lingered, Billy lit upon a brilliant idea. He was proud of this; it would get him a reaction for sure. 'I got a letter for you, Raymond. Courtesy of your . . . mother. But if you're not here to take it, well, I s'pose I can always leave it with Mr Charles and you can collect it later—'

The door was wrenched open. There he stood, his face still swollen and marked with bruises, which had once been purple, but were now fading to yellows and tan browns. He was holding himself awkwardly, one hand braced against the door jamb, the other gripping the cane on which he held himself aloft. At the end of his right leg, his foot was encased in a thick bandage.

'Get in here, Brogan,' he snapped, and Billy was happy to oblige.

On the edge of the bed, Raymond's eyes scanned over the letter: three-and-a-half pages of words scribbled in fury and haste.

'You've already read this, I presume?'

Billy's face opened in horror. 'The thought of such a thing! Mr de Guise, what do you take me for?'

'Maynard Charles has his fingers in every letter and package that goes out through the hotel post room. Don't deny it for a second, Billy. You know it's true. So why on earth would a letter enter this hotel that didn't have his eyes on it?'

Billy paused as if to concoct some elaborate lie, thought better of it, and finally said, 'I know better than to show something like that to Mr Charles. It's worth more as a secret than it is shared.'

Raymond shook his head wearily. Then he stood up, ferreted in a drawer for a single pound note and pushed this into Billy's hand. 'There's a couple of crowns on the dresser. Take them, Billy. They're yours.' Raymond sank back to the bed. 'You're the only one who's read this?'

'I am.'

'Then, anyone else hears about this, I'll know it comes from you. Understand?'

'I understand, Mr de Guise. You have been very charitable.'

Charity, thought Raymond. *Charity and blackmail, they're all the same to lads like Billy Brogan. But I'd be doing the same in his shoes. Getting something out of nothing, that was always my father's way too. And the boy's got family to take care of. Billy Brogan's doing nothing that the Ray Cohen of old wouldn't do.*

His eyes scanned over the letter:

Dear Ray,

I know you said not to contact you, but you left us the name of your boy, so perhaps you did not mean it. In any event, there are things you should know. No doubt you've been too caught up in your palaces with your princesses to know what happened on these streets. But 4 October 1936 is a date that will echo loud through the years.

As Raymond read on, a sick feeling curdled in his stomach.

They were calling it a battle. Oswald Mosley and his British Union of Fascists had marched into Whitechapel and Stepney Green. They called themselves patriots, but that wasn't what they were: they were just common thugs, Blackshirts every last one of them. They'd been marching east. It was all over the daily news sheets – and at least Raymond had been able to read these, while locked away in his tower all day and night. It was just like that man in the Midnight Rooms had said. Even now, Raymond could hardly remember who he was. Just another one of those thugs from the streets where he grew up, just another man full of hate. Raymond was probably not the last person who'd felt the fire of his fists.

They'd come to – what? Demand a cleansing of the streets? Show their allegiance with the National Socialists in Germany, who were putting bricks through Jewish shop fronts at night and daubing crude yellow Stars of David over every Jewish door? Or just to lash out, at something they didn't understand?

But we weren't going to let them, Raymond's mother wrote. *Your father would have been out there with the best of 'em, and so was we. Hundreds and thousands of us turned out to see it done. Even when the police showed themselves, we was there.*

She wrote about upturned buses. She wrote about little old ladies casting their chamber pots out of their windows. Pots and pans. Skillets and stones. Anything that came to hand – and all to drive the police and the fascists they were protecting out. Cable Street, which Ray knew so well from the days dancing with his father – that long, bustling row of drinking dens and opium houses, of places where gentlemen could go to find a woman – had been consumed. What had happened in the Midnight Rooms was like two children playing rough-and-tumble in the park when set against the violence of Cable Street.

And who was there, with the best of 'em? Raymond de Guise? Was it Raymond, in his evening suit and dancing shoes, holding the line when the police tried to drive us out? Or was it his brother, Artie? Poor, destitute Artie – not a penny to his name, not a hope in the world of making a living for his self, but proud and determined to stand up for what's right.

But I am not writing to scold you, Ray. You know what we think, and we got hope in our hearts that you see the light. No. I am writing for Artie's sake. There was many fallen that day. And Artie among them. Some Metropolitan cantered by on his horse and brained him with his truncheon as he went into the crowds. His shoulder is broken and the doctor says he might never work again. You won't remember, Ray, what being out of work and with no hope of getting it can do to a man. He can't eat. He can't sleep. But he has asked after you. You might not think it after last time you was here, but he still has faith in you, son.

We wait, in hope and in hunger. And I remain,
Your loving mother
Alma Cohen

Raymond stared at the letter for a long time. He tried to picture Artie, as battered and bruised and broken as Raymond himself. *That was what it was like when you were little, wasn't it, Ray? The two of you, tearaways together, and when one got beaten up, so did the other. There's a nice irony in that.* He lifted one of the fingers of his good hand and traced the black bruise around his eye. *Maybe she's right. Maybe I ought to have been there. I'm safe here in the Buckingham Hotel, safe where nobody knows my name. But step outside the ballroom, step outside the hotel grounds, and a fancy new name and a pair of dancing shoes doesn't keep you safe for very long.*

Artie, he thought, *I'm sorry.*

Starkly aware of Billy Brogan still lurking behind him, he screwed the letter up and cast it to the floor.

'What is it, Mr de Guise? You upset on account of your brother?'

That and everything else, thought Raymond. *You've gone soft, Ray. You're living in a false world and it's turned you soft. The real world is brittle and nasty and full of inhumane sorts. You might have escaped from it yourself, but not everyone can run.* He thought back to the stories he'd seen coming out of Germany. Hadn't Artie himself said that Jewish runaways were already turning up in the East End, on the run from the National Socialists in Germany? Well, if Cable Street was any indication – if the fracas in the Midnight Rooms was any sign – they were running from one fire straight into the next. A few short years ago there had been singing and dancing and prosperity, of a sort, in Germany too. *Now look at them. How long until it happens here as well?*

Stop kidding yourself, Ray. It's already happening.

Perhaps it was suspicion that was putting down roots in his head, growing stronger and sturdier with every day that passed. Suspicion that his father, who would have been so proud of how elegantly Ray Cohen could dance, would never have countenanced him dancing here, in the Buckingham Hotel. A place whose lord was a close compatriot of the type of men who marched through their home streets, meaning to drive them out – and all because of who their fathers were, and their fathers' fathers before them. A place where the Londonderrys came to dine, and spoke so eloquently about their noble German friends. A place where he, Ray Cohen, had danced with Unity Mitford from the richest family in the land, kissed her once on each cheek and watched as she was chauffeured off to meet her plane and – at the other end – the hateful Führer Hitler to whom she was so devoted.

Maybe it was the realisation that, bitter and angry and playing him for money as they were, his family might just have been *right*.

He came out of his agony and fixed Billy with a glare. 'You'd do me a favour, wouldn't you, Billy?'

'That's what I'm here for, Mr de Guise.'

'There's a girl here. She works under Mrs Moffatt, in housekeeping. Her name's Nettleton. Nancy Nettleton. Find her and bring her to me, would you, Billy? I have some . . . explaining to do.'

Nancy Nettleton was in the housekeeping kitchenette when Billy Brogan appeared at the doors. In the week since Mr Simenon had delivered her so joyously into Mrs Moffatt's hands, she had tried her best to remain invisible.

It was hard not to think about Raymond. Once, she dallied by the ballroom, hopeful of hearing something – but Mr Simenon was prowling the reception hall and she dared not wait long. Another time, Hélène Marchmont floated past on the way to the Queen Mary and Nancy was a moment away from calling out and asking her for news. Every time she had heard a rumour about the absent Raymond de Guise, she had breathed not a word – and this was the hardest thing of all.

Nancy was sitting over the backgammon board, being roundly trounced by Rosa – who treated the game as if it was her moral duty to win – when Billy Brogan rapped his fingers on the door. 'Nance,' he said, when the girls looked up, 'you'd better come.'

Nancy could sense the suspicion in Rosa and Ruth. She had not forgotten what Mrs Moffatt said: that the other girls had *noticed*. 'Can it wait, Billy?'

'I'm afraid it can't, Nance.'

Rosa lifted her eyebrows and smirked. 'Got yourself an admirer there, Nance.'

In the doorway, Billy Brogan blushed scarlet. 'It isn't that, Nance. But . . .'

Nancy did not know whether to stay or go. The dice were in her hands. She cast them. 'Well, what is it, Billy?'

Billy was coiled. He tried to keep it in. He did not want to embarrass Nancy. She'd already suffered enough, after what Mr Simenon had done. And yet the eyes of the other girls were boring into him. They were laughing . . .

'It's Mr de Guise,' he said, forthright. 'He wants to see you.'

The dice clattered out of Nancy's hands. The eyes of the other girls had turned to her, now. They were considering her closely, demanding whether she was going to go – or whether she was going to stay here with the rest of them, where she belonged.

'I'll be there directly, Billy,' she said – and, hoisting her skirts, hurried out of the room.

Nancy knocked on the door, and had no idea what she was supposed to think as she slipped through and into his suite.

He was dressed in his full evening wear, as if he was ready to take to the floor, but the face above his collar was hardly his own. It was still yellow and distended where the thugs had laid into him; one of his eyes was swollen shut, but starting to reveal itself again – like a ripening fruit ready to burst open. His suit had been ironed and pressed, but he was not wearing his dancing shoes, and nor could he – for one of his feet was bound up so tightly in bandage it looked twice the other's size.

You still look like an angel, she thought, *but . . .* She thought she could see the lines of pain on his face – and all she wanted was to go to him, to tell him he was going to get better, to look after him until he was himself again.

'Oh, Raymond,' she breathed with a tremble in her voice, 'what did they do to you?'

She came forward in stuttering steps, as if she might nurse him as she had once nursed her father – but then she stopped. She had forgotten herself, again.

'Nancy, I'm sorry,' he whispered. His voice was frail too. His one good eye had a faraway look. 'I meant to send for you before but I've been . . .' He shrugged, and when he smiled she could see his new crooked smile. 'Indisposed.'

Indisposed, thought Nancy. At least he had his sense of humour then. At least he had his charm.

'Nancy,' he went on, 'I owe you an explanation.'

'You don't owe me anything. I'm only glad you're—'

'Alive?' he joked.

'Alive,' said Nancy. 'Raymond, I—'

'I know you were there, Nancy. I saw you across the dance floor. You followed us, didn't you?'

Nancy was not sure what to say. The truth was too foolish. 'I'm not proud of it, Raymond. I'm sorry. But I wanted to see it for myself. Can you understand that?'

'You saw more than you, perhaps, had thought you would.'

There was a question waiting to be asked. At first Nancy thought better of it. Then she blurted out, 'Why did those men attack you, Raymond?'

It was what he had asked Billy to bring her here for. He readied himself by taking deep breaths.

'I want you to listen to me, Nancy. Listen and, after I've spilled it all, if you want to leave this room and tell everyone in the hotel, then I'll understand. But I had to tell it . . . to you. You told me everything about yourself. You should know the real me. I . . .' He was nervous, but he pulled himself together and said, 'I want you to know who I am.'

Nancy waited.

'My name,' he went on, 'was not always Raymond de Guise. The name I was born with is . . .' It felt like stripping out of his evening suit and standing naked in front of her. 'Raymond Cohen. My family call me Ray. I was born in Whitechapel. My family are tinkers and tradesmen. No, hang that. They're thieves and con men, pure and simple. And there was a time that I almost went that way too. It doesn't mean there isn't good in them. It's just the way things were. In another world, I'd have been out there still. But I had something my brother didn't. I could *dance*. I got up and I got out and . . . I thought I'd left it all behind. But you can't, can you? You can't outrun your past. All these years, I've just been dancing while the world staggers from one disaster to the next . . .' He paused. 'In here isn't like it is out there. There's order in here. You're upstairs or you're downstairs and you know your place. But out there it's messy and ugly and . . . Those men who mobbed me in the Midnight Rooms, they came from the same streets where me and my brother were raised. They recognised me from the old times. They hated us then for what we are, though they didn't show it. Only now . . .'

Nancy had listened to it all with a blank expression. Now her face developed creases and lines. 'You lied to me,' she whispered, in disbelief. 'You lied to us all, to everyone here . . .'

'Little lies,' Raymond ventured. 'Here and there, daily little lies. But they all add up. I'm sorry, Nancy. It's my own fault. I've been a fool. I should have stayed here, in the Buckingham, in my ballroom, where everything is crystal clear. I should have known that, the moment I stepped out there, the old world was waiting.'

Nancy was uncertain what to say. She had, she decided, no *right* to feel aggrieved. What was Raymond de Guise to her? What was Ray Cohen? A man she'd known for scant weeks. A man who'd shown her a little quickstep, the art of box stepping, a little rhythm and poise. *That's all. Well, isn't it?*

Why, then, did it feel like so much more?

Because I told you my life, Raymond – and all the while you were lying about yours . . .

'That life isn't mine any more. I feel the pull of it sometimes. But it isn't mine. *This* is mine. But if Maynard Charles were to find out. If—'

'They'd cast you out.'

'It isn't that. They'd think me a liar, but they'd cast me out for the very same reason those men mobbed me. Because my family are Jewish.' He stopped, momentarily unable to go on. 'You know the circles our Lord Edgerton moves in. You've seen the sort of men he entertains here at our hotel. Damn my eyes, I entertain them too. I danced with Unity Mitford. I clasped hands with Gräfin Schecht and twirled her around *my* dance floor. And all the while their friends and colleagues in that union of theirs are marching against people like me, people like my brother. And that's why, Nancy. That's why they must never know who I really am. I've been lying to myself all along. I tell everyone who'll listen that, once you're inside the Grand, it doesn't matter who you are or where you were born. All that matters is the dance. But it's wrong, isn't it? They marched through my old neighbourhood this week. My brother was up on the barricades, brawling with the Metropolitan Police and those fascists they came to protect – and all the while here I am, dressed up to the nines and dancing with the very same people . . .'

Nancy could see the way the idea was tearing him apart. She went to sit beside him, on the edge of the bed. She took his hand. It was a revelation to see him so shaken. *Maybe you're not the man you said you were, but maybe you're no worse for it.* Suddenly it made sense: why he had so admired the way she'd dressed up and entered the ballroom, even though it was no place for a working-class girl like her. All of his talk about secrets and stories, right here in the Buckingham Hotel.

'You can't hate yourself for it, Raymond. You . . . you got out of there, the only way you knew how. What if you hadn't been able to dance? Is it more honourable to steal and fight than it is to, what, foxtrot and waltz with people you find distasteful? I want to tell you something, Raymond. I know what hard work is. I've done it all of my life. You have a talent. You're allowed to use it. And you're allowed not to feel guilty about it as well. We all have to get on the best we can.'

Raymond was still.

'You've been strong, Nancy Nettleton.'

Nancy smiled. 'And then I come here and being strong isn't what they want. You have to learn to be meek and quiet. You have to learn not to be noticed. You have to be something other than yourself.'

Her hand was still in his. By instinct, Raymond tightened his hold on it. 'You never have to be that, Nancy. Let them *think* you're invisible. Let them *think* you're somebody else, if that's what it takes. But always stay *you* where it matters.' He lifted his other hand and hovered it over her heart. 'In *here*.'

Raymond had not been planning it, but now that Nancy was this close he could smell her scent: sweet and simple, nothing like the ostentatious scents of Paris and Milan that mixed with the cigarillo smoke in the Grand every night. He inched closer. Then, when he felt her finger tracing tiny circles on his palm, he inched closer still. His lips were still sore, but he inclined his head to brush her lips with his.

Nancy's lips opened. He felt their warmth as he touched them for the first time. He kissed her gently. Then he kissed her harder. Then, just as she began to kiss back, something made her stop.

'What is it?' he asked gently.

'It's . . .' She stopped, telling herself she was a silly girl. 'I thought you . . . and Hélène.'

Raymond's face creased with a smile. 'No,' he said. 'Nothing of the kind. Poor Hélène has problems of her own, without getting embroiled with a ruffian like me. And anyway . . .'

Nancy wanted to ask more – but every question she had simply melted away, for suddenly she was kissing him back, tasting the salt on his swollen lip, the ridges where he'd been battered and bruised. But none of it mattered. *She was finally kissing Raymond de Guise.*

Outside the chamber, in the hallway where the door remained open the merest sliver, Billy Brogan watched as Nancy's lips locked with Raymond's. He watched as she lifted a hand and cupped it around Raymond's swollen, discoloured face. He was watching still as Raymond wrapped his arms around her and ran his fingers around the collar of her dress. Only later, as Raymond ran his hands through Nancy's hair and they laughed together, pure and simple and *honest*, did he stumble back along the passageway. Unable to watch any more, he made a hasty retreat to the service lift, rode it down to the ground floor with his heart beating wild. Nancy Nettleton. *His* Nancy Nettleton. He'd been foolish. He was a little brother to her. That was all. She was with Raymond de Guise now.

No, Billy thought, and remembered all he had heard. *She was with Ray Cohen.*

Chapter Twenty

VIVIENNE EDGERTON OPENED HER EYES.

Her recollection of the night before was not what it ought to have been – but then, these days it never was. Dimly, she remembered being in the ballroom for the afternoon demonstrations. They were nothing without Raymond de Guise, of course, and the guests in attendance knew it. Vivienne had heard one of them, a handsome dowager wearing priceless pearls around her neck, scoffing at Frederic, one of the porters-turned-dancer who was now stepping out onto the dance floor with his arm around Hélène Marchmont. A dull porter's boy could never compare to the refinement of a man like Raymond de Guise. But Raymond had been gone for ten nights now, and everyone in the hotel knew that the ballroom was poorer because of it.

After that, Vivienne's recollections were hazy. She recalled a visit to Mr Simenon, who in turn had sent his errand boy Brogan out into Soho to procure some of her special powders. After that, there had been at least one cocktail in the third-floor lounge – and evidently she had made significant demands of the room service too, because a trolley laden with silver platters had been left in her suite. She was still wearing the gown of last night, one of her *Vogue* numbers, black satin tied with great bows at each shoulder.

Somewhere along the way she'd shed the shimmering emerald capelet that ordinarily went with it – but what did that matter? Her stepfather would send her monthly allowance soon. There were always more gowns to wear.

She went to the dresser to powder her nose. Underneath the spilled Chanel and champagne flutes – *two*, she noticed, so perhaps she had not been alone last night – were the scrawled attempts of another letter addressed to Raymond. It was only as she stared at them that fragments of the night before finally came back to her. There was, she had decided, the faintest of chances that the reason he'd never responded to that first missive (over which she'd so delicately slaved) was because of his indisposition. So she had decided to write to him again. Evidently she had not got very far, for every letter petered into meaningless scribble and half-finished words. Now, in the cold light of day, she was happy she hadn't had the faculties to compose a full missive and have it delivered. Until three days ago, Raymond had been locked up in his tower, Maynard Charles the turnkey who refused to let him out – but since then she had caught sight of him hobbling along the hotel halls, sneaking down to the studio behind the ballroom as if he might discipline his body to ignore swellings and broken bones and begin dancing again. He had even found himself a partner to practise with. The memory of it stuck in Vivienne's throat, so she swallowed it down like a lump of particularly difficult gristle.

The chambermaid. That *chambermaid . . .*

She used a ball of cotton wool to clear the make-up from her face, revealing the real Vivienne piece by piece. There was something special about today, she thought. Something she wasn't properly putting her finger on.

Her eyes drifted back to the letters. *Dear Raymond,* read one. *I told you, you would be sorry you made a fool out of me, and the day has finally come.* Well, *that* was different. She peeled it off the page underneath, and here the letters – blurred by the spilled perfume – were harder to decipher. *You think you're a king, but the Grand is hardly a kingdom.* The third page was even more smudged and difficult to make out, but the one under that was clearer. *Tomorrow, when he comes, we will see how quickly the Buckingham guests forget the name 'de Guise'* . . .

Oh, she thought. *That's what's happening today*. She watched herself in the mirror as her face opened up in a smile.

The car that delivered Nathaniel White to the Buckingham Hotel was a glistening Rolls Royce with cream paintwork and a square roof, open up to the clear blue skies above Berkeley Square. As it pulled to a halt, its horn tooted proudly and the doorman cantered down the stairs to open its door, revealing Nathaniel White to the world. He had arrived wearing grey checked slacks, and a sports jacket decorated with the crest of Gonville and Caius, his Cambridge *alma mater*. The doorman busied himself collecting cases from the trunk of the Rolls Royce and, as he accompanied Nathaniel up the stairs, Maynard Charles himself appeared from the revolving bronze door. Nathaniel almost breezed past him as he approached. It was only as the curmudgeonly hotel director extended his hand that he stopped and recognised him.

'Mr Charles. May I say what an honour it is to be invited to dance at your fine hotel.'

Maynard Charles returned the greeting with a simple nod of the head. 'If you'll follow me, Mr White.' The reception hall was buzzing this morning. A party of guests from Tanganyika – they oversaw one of the great national parks, where Mr Churchill himself was fond of going big game hunting – were checking out and the hall was piled high with their cases. Nathaniel stopped to take it all in. There was the striking obelisk, with the water coursing down its points and curves; the sweeping mahogany check-in desk, the golden cage of the guest lifts; and there, to his left, the marble arch that sloped down towards the doors of the ballroom itself. *His ballroom*, he had to remind himself.

It didn't matter how you made it here. What mattered was what you did once you arrived.

Maynard Charles summoned Mr Simenon. Permitted to travel in the guest lift (with only a subdued hint that, even though he was a personal acquaintance of Lord Edgerton, the guest lift was for the use of *genuine* guests only), Mr Simenon opened one of the empty rooms in the staff quarters and allowed Nathaniel inside.

'I presume it meets your satisfaction, sir.'

Sir, thought Nathaniel. Yes, he could get used to this kind of service. They had looked on him admiringly in the Imperial, but none of them had bowed their head in deference as the concierge did here. That, he supposed, was because of his connection to Lord Edgerton, but it buoyed him all the same.

He looked around the room. It was simple, rather than sublime. On the journey here – his father had sent one of his fleet to pick him up from his Holland Park residence and convey him in style to the scene of his future glories – he had imagined it as vast and ostentatious as one of the Buckingham's finest suites. By comparison this was much smaller, but he had already caught sight of himself in the mirror that hung at the foot of the bed, and he liked the look of what he saw: Nathaniel White, principal dancer at the Buckingham Hotel. There were two months until Christmas. Maynard Charles had already impressed upon him the importance of the event, but he had no need; the King and his Norwegian cousins might have been in attendance, but Nathaniel intended to be king of the ballroom by then.

'If there is anything you need, Mr White, don't hesitate to contact me personally,' Mr Simenon ventured.

'There is one thing, Mr . . .'

'Simenon,' the head concierge replied, though he was quite certain he'd said it several times already.

'I'd like cut flowers. Dahlias and chrysanthemums. Arranged in a magnificent bouquet. Separate the stalks with some of those ornamental grasses, would you? I'm sure you know the sort. Then bind them in scarlet ribbon with a simple white card inscribed with only my name. They'll need to be lilac and pink and the card must be perfumed with a certain scent. A Guerlain or a Caron. And, Mr Simenon?'

Any of the other concierges might have bristled at such a specific and exacting request. But for Mr Simenon, this was a joyful thing. He would prevail where lesser concierges fell.

'Yes, sir?'

'Have them delivered to Miss Vivienne Edgerton immediately, with my eternal thanks.'

With a vermouth cocktail in hand, Nathaniel White stood on the cusp of the Grand, preparing to take his first breaths of ballroom air. Tonight he would dance with whosoever desired him, but it was not until tomorrow that he would take his place in the demonstrations. Today he could watch and . . . he wanted to say 'admire', but admiration was not it. He needed to calculate. Calculate the strengths and weaknesses of the other dancers in the troupe. Watch Hélène Marchmont for her tiny imperfections. Because Nathaniel White intended to look *good* on his first day in the ballroom – and in that quest he would leave nothing to chance.

Nathaniel spotted Vivienne Edgerton alone at a table beside the dance floor.

Fortune favoured the bold. It had carried him thus far. So Nathaniel sashayed across the ballroom floor – that would soon be his – and, not caring to ask her permission, slipped into the seat alongside her.

'Nathaniel White,' she remarked at last, 'you might have startled me.'

'I announced my approach with a bouquet,' Nathaniel replied. 'I trust they were to your satisfaction?'

Vivienne shrugged. One bouquet of flowers was as good as another, but she didn't have to tell him that. He would learn – if he didn't know already – that spending money on a person meant nothing, not when one's pockets were infinitely deep.

'You aren't to dance this afternoon?'

'I'll need to instruct Hélène in one of my routines first. The dances she performed with de Guise are not to my taste. They're too stiff by far. They lack daring. They lack a certain *passion*. Well, I'm right, aren't I? And I'm here to replace him, not to slip into his shoes.' Nathaniel paused. 'I understand I have *you* to thank for that.'

Vivienne remained impassive, though a slight smile twitched in the corners of her lips.

'Of course, it begs the question . . . *why*,' he continued.

'*Why?*' asked Vivienne – and for the first time she shifted so that she was looking at Nathaniel. He had a boyish face, more boyish than Vivienne remembered. Ordinarily she *despised* boyish men. There had been too many men like that in New York, chasing after her, trying to buy her cocktails in every speakeasy they could find. Vivienne was barely a woman herself and yet there was something odious about men who looked as if they had only just stopped nursing at their wet nurse's breast. Nathaniel White kept swiping his shockingly blond hair out of his eyes, and fluttering his long dark eyelashes as he spoke. *Impish.* Yes, that was the word. And yet there was something about this particular imp that delighted her.

Perhaps it was only what he was here to do. Ousting Raymond de Guise from his position in the Grand had not been in Vivienne's plans – but this was not to say that it did not entertain her. She had sent him that letter as a token of her affection, but as an apology too. The fact that he had not replied was a constant reminder of how he had spurned her.

But I won't be spurned for ever. I'm going to show them – show my mother, show my stepfather – that I'm not a girl to be forgotten. Not somebody to be shut away and ignored. You can't just drag a girl from her home and her society and deposit her here and expect her to be quiet.

Suddenly, she stood. 'Nathaniel, I'll show you *why*.'

Vivienne opened the door to the shadowy studio behind the ballroom but hovered in the doorway before permitting Nathaniel through. 'You'll be here with Miss Marchmont soon, I shouldn't wonder. To show her how it ought to be done,' said Vivienne. 'Well, don't you want to see it for yourself?'

Nathaniel knew he was being baited. There was a temptress's look in Vivienne's eyes, but she took him by the fingers and placed them on the door – and Nathaniel did not want to resist.

He stepped through and stopped short in surprise.

At this time of day, with the dancers preparing to step out into the ballroom, the practice studio ought to have been empty. And yet there he was: Raymond de Guise, still battered and bruised, still holding his body more rigidly than any natural dancer, slowly waltzing around the room with a girl in his arms. He did not look so mighty, thought Nathaniel. In a certain light, he barely even looked noble. Certainly not as noble as Vivienne's father or Nathaniel's, or any of the rest of their set. Yes, he thought, Raymond looked . . . like a *common* barrow boy. His nose had been ill-set and one of his eyes was barely showing through the swelling of his face. His broken foot was in an open boot but he barely put any weight on it as he moved. The girl was practically holding him up. Whoever had ambushed this man seemed to have taken all his dignity and bearing.

Nathaniel noticed the girl in his arms almost as soon as he noticed Raymond de Guise. She was petite, with dark hair and a delicate heart-shaped face, her expression alive with the enjoyment of the moment. But she moved awkwardly too. One of her legs hardly seemed to obey instructions; it lagged, a fraction of each second, behind the rest of her body.

'Two cripples,' Vivienne whispered cruelly, 'fit only for each other.'

As Raymond turned he caught sight of them. He released Nancy from his arms, reached for the silver-topped cane propped on the wall, and put himself between Nancy and the intruders, as if to spare her embarrassment. Framed by the light of the hall outside, Nathaniel White looked almost angelic. He nodded knowingly, then slipped back out, the door closing behind them.

'Maynard Charles had him locked away, but he's been bringing her here for the last three days, ever since the doctors told him he could try putting weight on his foot again. She's a . . .' Vivienne could hardly say the word. She clenched her fists, and Nathaniel noticed for the first time that she was trembling. She was perspiring too. A droplet appeared on her forehead and trickled unnoticed down her cheek. 'She's a chambermaid,' she finally spat. 'He's tutoring her. Or she's *helping* him recover. And . . .'

That's why, she wanted to say. *That's why you're here, and that's why you'll be the star of the Grand. Raymond de Guise needs to learn you don't reject a lady*. But something stopped her. She did not know how he would react. Men were such vain and foolish creatures. If you damaged their pride once, they too often took a lifetime to recover. They needed handling carefully. She'd learned that in New York – all of those sons of bankers who'd come after her at her mother's tea parties, or picked her up at the private college gates so that they might take her out on a drive after her schooling was finished. They'd all needed winding up and pointing in the right direction. Nathaniel would not want to know he was here as her tool. He wanted to believe . . .

And, besides, boyish as he was, there remained something striking about him. The way he was looking at her now, for instance. His eyes were devouring her. Possibly he thought she was crazy. Most of them did. But Vivienne knew when a man wanted her.

'I should like to dance, Nathaniel,' she declared, the words exploding out of her in a frenzy that took Nathaniel quite by surprise. 'I should like, this New Year, to be in the ballroom with everyone else, to take the floor alongside the King and tango and waltz and quickstep with the rest of them. My mother is going to be there and I would have her know I am not a pet dog, to be forgotten when the mood suits her. I would have her know I am my own person, with my own passions and prides and my own life to lead. That it takes more than *money* to get rid of me. And yet . . . I would not make a fool of myself. If I am to dance at the New Year's ball, I should like to know I am befitting of the ballroom. Would you . . .' The fire with which she'd been speaking was guttering out. The words began to run together, merging into a monotonous mess. '. . . tutor me? Just as de Guise is tutoring that simpering wretch in there?'

Nathaniel paused. The door to the dance studio was still open a fraction and, by the light of a dozen lamps, he saw Raymond and the girl stumbling across the room. Their silhouettes made a strange shadow dance across the walls. Then his gaze drifted back to Vivienne Edgerton. She was curious, this creature. She was driven and bold . . . and yet the fire she had was concealing something else. Something half-broken, something that was crying out for someone to piece it back together.

'Meet me in the ballroom at dawn. We shall begin at once.'

Chapter Twenty-one

On the upper deck of the number 6 omnibus Hélène Marchmont pulled her burgundy cloche down low. Few of the office clerks and day-trippers around her would ever have set foot inside the Buckingham Hotel, but there had been a time when Hélène's face had gazed out from the billboards at Piccadilly Circus, or graced the covers of the magazines in the roadside stands, and Hélène was not in the mood to be recognised.

By the time she stepped off the bus, she felt freer. Brixton Road was a rush of office clerks and railway workers coming home for the night. The crowds outside Marks and Spencer on the corner of Atlantic Road were deepening and, further up the high street, shoppers streamed out of Morley's department store. The lights in the music hall gazing down the hill were just flickering to life, drawing people to them like moths to a flame.

It began to rain as Hélène marched into the still bustling markets of Electric Avenue. Half an hour later, she emerged back onto the high street, where one of the last remaining horse carriages was disgorging its passengers, with a bunch of daisies in one hand and a small rag doll in the other.

It was getting dark. She was late.

The houses along Brixton Hill had once been grand residences, the perfect imitation of the bigger townhouses that Hélène looked out on from her Buckingham quarters each day. But it had been a generation and more since the railways came and the once desirable residences had been partitioned, partitioned again, leased and sold off to whoever could afford them. Now some of the facades looked ancient, and black with smoke.

Sudbourne Road was one of the lesser terraces, but even here the buildings had been carved up and carved up again. Hélène stood outside one and felt a rush of warmth. The lights were on in the basement flat. Through the walls, she could hear the sound of somebody playing a trumpet – not as expertly, perhaps, as Louis Kildare and the rest of the Archie Adams Band, but with a certain kind of amateur flair that, nevertheless, made her heart soar.

If only Maynard Charles could see me now, Hélène thought, with a wry smile. *If only he knew what I was really doing in that year I was away from the Buckingham Hotel! He'd have one of his fits . . .*

She gently knocked on the door.

The lady who answered was diminutive in stature. She was wrapped in a cream shawl, and underneath that a simple house dress and apron. The slippers on her feet were evidently her husband's, for they were far too big. Upon seeing Hélène, her face broke into an irrepressible grin and she opened up her arms to take her in. Hélène bent down, so that the elder lady could press her wrinkled black cheek against Hélène's own.

'Noelle,' Hélène whispered.

'We've missed you, girl.'

'I know. I know, Auntie.'

Then Hélène was through the doors, the sound of the trumpet playing stopped, and on Sudbourne Road a miniature celebration began.

Maurice and Noelle Archer had lived in this same basement flat for fifteen years. Twenty years as a merchant seaman, plying British waters even when the whole world was at war, had left Maurice Archer with a payout to be proud of and an invitation from His Majesty to settle in the home of the Commonwealth, to take work as a office clerk or railway worker, whatever his skills and situations allowed. It was an opportunity that Maurice had grasped with both hands (though it had taken his sweet wife, Noelle, a little longer to start believing). London, so different from the sun-kissed Caribbean island they called home, had not welcomed them with street parades and notices in *The Times*, but in 1921 it had become a new home – a new start in a bolder, more prosperous land.

Or, at least, that was what had been promised. Maurice Archer had heard his fellow seamen talk about the bite of a London winter, the taste of tap water, the way the English deep-fried their fish until it had been sapped of every ounce of flavour, but in his mind London was a city of golden boulevards and royal parks, where his darling Noelle might take tea with the Duchess of Kent, or be invited to the weddings at Westminster Cathedral – or where, when he wasn't being fanciful, his sons and daughter might work hard and grow up to be wealthy, secure individuals, with houses and families and prospects of their own.

Living in London day in and day out was a different matter. That first winter, when he was working on the railway and the Spanish flu – which had already laid waste to so many – returned for a valedictory tour of the city, first Noelle, and then all three of their children, were taken to their beds. Maurice looked in on them after his shifts had ended each night and the thought preyed on him: is this *it*? Is this what I brought my children to England for?

Even after they were recovered, the fear that this had all been a dreadful mistake remained. He might have returned, then. There were ships taking families like his back to the islands from which they came. People couldn't stand the weather, or they couldn't stand the dreary, smog-soaked city – or they couldn't stand the way some Englishmen crossed the road so they wouldn't have to brush shoulders as they passed, asked for their glasses to be changed at the free house on Brixton Hill, in case a black man had touched it. But his youngest son, Joseph, had barely been three when they took to the oceans together; was it right to uproot him again? And his daughter, Samantha, beautiful Samantha . . . At nine years old, she was his princess. She'd seen snow for the first time that winter and never was there a more magical thing.

And then there was Sidney. Sidney who, thirteen years old in the year they set sail, had taught them that the cold and dark did not matter, that there were things to love about this new world of theirs. Sidney who, in spite of the scornful looks from some of the other boys along Brixton Hill, had woken every morning with a grin on his face, dressed eagerly for school and made friends. And all because of that battered old trumpet of his . . .

Maurice Archer was laying the trumpet back in its case, the same case with which Sidney had trotted off to lessons every Saturday morning, when Noelle brought Hélène into the room.

Sternly, he wagged his finger. 'Hélène Marchmont, I thought you'd vanished off the face of this planet.'

Hélène presented him with the flowers, but kept the rag doll to herself. As he accepted them, he grinned and took her by the hand. 'You're still a picture. Isn't she a picture, Noelle?'

Noelle was busy arranging a tray with a teapot and saucers, all the best china brought out for their visitor, so she only rolled her eyes at her husband and grinned, 'You always say it and you're always right', before shuffling out of the room.

Maurice was a big man, in height as well as girth. To see him alongside Noelle was to imagine that a pixie had married a giant. He had big, brawny forearms and hands that made the cups and saucers his wife had laid out look like toys. His whiskers were tufts of white and he kept them solely because his wife told him not to, because it entertained him to see her cringe away when he went to kiss her goodnight.

'It's good to have you, girl. Here, get off those feet. You've come a long way.'

There was not a place in the world that felt more like home to Hélène. Her own parents might have had that palatial house off the seafront in Rye, but this basement flat in Brixton seemed, to her, the world entire. The photographs on the wall, the mirror bought at the second-hand market, the towers of beer mats Maurice and his sons had collected from their visits to the local free houses. All of these were like holy relics to Hélène. Never mind the four-poster bed in the room at Rye. She wasn't welcome there any longer – and, even if one day they condescended to take her back, she wouldn't give them the time of day. *Here,* Hélène thought. *Here is home.*

Maurice was clearing a place for her on the sofa, when Hélène spoke. 'Can I see her?'

'Samantha has her. They're in the back bedroom. Don't think you need to ask, Hélène. This is your house too. We've said that from the start.' Maurice paused and smiled gently. 'Well, what are you waiting for? Be on with you!'

Hélène held onto the rag doll and turned sideways to squeeze along the cluttered hallway, past the kitchen and 'master bedroom' and to the little box room at the end.

Samantha, tall and slender and wearing a dress that Hélène recognised well – it had been a cast-off from the Buckingham wardrobes, dutifully re-stitched – was standing with her back to the door, looking down into a simple wooden crib. Baby Sybil must have been awake, for Hélène could hear her cooing with delight when Samantha's finger darted in to tickle her beneath the chin. For an age, Hélène hung in the doorway, just listening to those sounds. Soon, Samantha leaned in to take hold of the baby.

'May I?' asked Hélène, and the voice of Samantha's father came echoing down the hall: 'Tell her she doesn't need to ask!'

Samantha stepped aside. Sybil was fourteen months old already – and, goodness, how she'd grown! Hélène felt her heart break a little at that. How long had it been since she'd seen her? A whole month? But that was an aeon to a baby. The hair that had once been wisps on top of her head had turned into black waves, and when she saw Hélène she hoisted herself onto her feet at the bars of her crib. Her cheeks still had the roundedness of the baby she'd been, and yet her face was changing. She looked half a little girl, half a babe in arms.

'Hello, little one,' said Hélène, lifting her. 'Remember me?'

She did. Or perhaps it was the rag doll with which she was presented, making her eyes light up.

'How's she been?'

'Lord, she's kept me up nights and nights. Sleeps in the day and wants to get up and dance *all night long*. It's lucky I'm not cleaning down at the cinema any more. They let me go. Seems I clean too good. We were finishing so early they decided to let one of us go!' Samantha's laughter was the best thing about her. They didn't laugh like this in the Buckingham. There they just opened their lips and tittered, or raised a glass in an appreciative smile. 'Hélène?'

Hélène had been lost, cradling Sybil. 'She's beautiful . . . as ever.'

'She has her father's eyes,' said Samantha.

She did. They were eyes of the darkest brown, and yet they still seemed bright and alive.

'I was trying to settle her when you walked in. Her grandpa out there decided he'd entertain her with the bloomin' trumpet, and right before bedtime too. She loves it of course. Just like her father!'

Hélène nuzzled the baby's neck. Babies – they always had the most wonderful smell. Somewhere beneath the coal tar and talcum powder there was the smell of innocence. Hélène loved that. She thought it didn't matter what happened out there in the world, not when you held a baby and breathed in all of that beautiful, unspent life. The newsreels were full of the Germans overturning old treaties. Nights of violence in Hamburg and Berlin. The war intensifying in Spain, and none of it with an end in sight. But here, with Sybil, all of the madness melted away.

'Do you want to take her?' Hélène asked.

'You bring her,' said Samantha. 'She wants you, Hélène! I can see it in her eyes. She wants her mama.'

Noelle had not been planning a great feast, but she was the sort of woman who could make a family banquet out of tinned fish, pickled eggs, and whatever other odds and ends she found in the larder. The things this woman could do with spices were incredible, unknown to even the most daring of the Buckingham chefs. They had brought such otherworldly flavours with them from the Caribbean; the thought of Lord Edgerton, or Graf Schecht, or any of the rest tasting Noelle Archer's rice and peas brought Hélène untold delight.

Before they ate, they clasped their hands so that Maurice could say grace. 'For what we are about to receive,' he whispered, 'may the Lord make us eternally grateful.' Then, as he did every night, he raised a glass. 'To Sidney!' he declared. 'Gone, but not forgotten.'

'To Sidney!' they all agreed – and, as glasses were raised, Hélène pressed her lips to Sybil's brow and repeated the words gently in her ear. 'To your daddy . . .'

It was still strange to hold her. Hélène felt stabs of guilt whenever she admitted it to herself, but every time she came to the Archers' home it took her an hour, two, sometimes a whole day to start *feeling* like a mother again. *It isn't that I don't want to be here, little girl. You must know that. One day, I'll tell you it all. How I fell in love with your father. How he fell in love with me. About the day I realised I was pregnant and how panicked and elated we were, all at once. Well, we had to concoct a plan, didn't we, Sybil? I told my own parents but they near disowned me . . . and all because your papa was black. And a black musician no less! Could anything be any more disgraceful? Well, what other plan was there? I tricked Maynard Charles into resting me from the Buckingham – I told him I was headed to California, to finally try my hand at the silver screen. He took some convincing . . . but the idea of an actual movie star gracing his ballroom and all it might do for the Buckingham's reputation finally swayed him. And I came here and I had you, my baby girl, the only thing that matters in all of the world, and . . . if it hadn't been for what happened to your father, well, I'd have lived out my days here, as a mother.*

But life has a funny way of destroying the best-laid plans, doesn't it, Sybil?

Dinner had been served around a little wooden table in the living room. Hélène held Sybil, who reached out eagerly for whatever was on the plate, while Maurice regaled them with the stories his fellow railwaymen had told him – the drunk city barrister found asleep on the platform at Euston, who'd woken and thought himself on trial – and Samantha told Hélène every last detail of Sybil's past weeks: the babbling sounds she made every morning; how she pointed bossily at whatever toy she wanted; which lullabies were her favourite this month, and which would prompt a maelstrom of tears.

As if on cue, Sybil starting babbling now. 'Dadadadadadadadadaaaa!' she chanted. *Every bit as musical as your father.*

It doesn't feel right, does it? Not to know these things myself. Not to have lived and breathed every second of it. Thoughts like these could drive Hélène to madness, but all it took was for Sybil to reach up and play with her hair, and all those worries faded away. Love did not fade. Love had crossed vaster distances than these before. *And it isn't for ever, Sybil. I'm going to find a way that it doesn't have to be for ever. But what would Maynard Charles say if he knew the truth? A child born out of wedlock . . . and of mixed heritage at that? Maynard Charles might countenance black musicians in his orchestra, but if he knew one of them had fathered the secret child of his star dancer? Well, the Buckingham is only the Buckingham because of what people think of it. He'd protect that reputation at any cost, even if it meant getting rid of me – and then where would we be? If I couldn't send money back here every month, what would become of us all?*

Baked apples and cinnamon were already being served by the time the front door opened and in bouldered the Archers' youngest son, Joseph. Not yet twenty years old, Joseph was small and slender, with the same tight curls of hair as his mother. As he crashed through the door, he was singing to himself, a song Hélène did not know.

'Hélène!'

He was barrelling over to plant a kiss on Hélène's cheek when Noelle slapped his hand away. 'Wash first, young man! Hélène, you don't know where he's been . . . but I do. You been hanging round those clubs again, boy?'

'Ma, I'm telling you, there's *work* there.'

'Work!' Noelle muttered darkly, as Joseph strode off to wash the grime from his hands. 'That boy's been laid off more times than I've had hot dinners.'

Joseph reappeared, dragging a chair behind him to join them at the table. Soon his plate was being piled high with rice and peas, salted fish, little potatoes rolled in butter and a single pickled egg. 'They got me relaying a floor.'

'You don't know how to lay a floor.'

Joseph shrugged, his mouth already full. 'I know how to do what I'm told.'

Hélène grinned. 'Where are you working, Joseph?'

'They call it –' his eyes sparkled – 'the Midnight Rooms.'

Hélène's eyes darted up.

'Our Joseph finds himself a citizen of Soho,' Maurice chipped in, with more than a smirk. 'Been out dancing, have you, boy?'

'I got a good pair of dancing feet.'

'And they let you dance in there, do they?'

'Pa, you don't know a thing. A place like the Midnight Rooms doesn't care where you come from. As long as you got the love for the music. That's right, isn't it, Hélène?'

'You want to stay away from the Midnight Rooms, Joseph,' Hélène said. 'Mark my words, it isn't the place Sidney used to speak of . . .'

She hadn't told Raymond as much, but it had been one of the reasons she was so eager to go. Louis and Sidney had played in the Midnight Rooms more times than either could remember. Even years after he'd left the clubs behind and devoted himself to Archie Adams and the band, Sidney had spoken of the club as a wild little paradise where music and dance ruled the roost.

'It's the *place*, Hélène. The *place*! There's girls there dancing the rhumba. They're on the tables dancing the cha-cha. Have you ever cha-cha'd, Hélène? They have contests, every Saturday night. Finest dancers. There's champagne. They treat you like *royalty*. I'm going there tonight, Hélène, if you—'

Noelle smiled indulgently. 'That's enough of that. Hélène's got other things to do tonight, haven't you, love?'

In her lap, Sybil started to babble again. 'Dadadadadadada-dadaaaa!'

'You can keep your Midnight Rooms.' Hélène grinned. 'There's only one place for me. But Joseph . . . be careful there, won't you? We . . .' *How much to tell them?* she thought. But then she decided: *they're my family. I should tell them it all.* 'We went there, me and Louis and Raymond, my partner in the ballroom. I guess we wanted to see what it was like. The rhumbas and the cha-chas, everything Sidney had loved. I wanted to see it for myself. To see where Sidney started out. And, well, for a time it was everything I hoped.' She paused. 'Then everything went wrong, Joseph. Some men charged in and mobbed Raymond. They wouldn't stop. He's back at the hotel, broken and trussed up. They're making me dance with some . . . juvenile they've brought in from the Imperial.' Hélène could hardly keep the disgust from her voice – but here, surrounded by people she loved, she had no need to. 'So watch yourself, won't you?'

Joseph beamed. Picking himself up, he planted a single kiss on Hélène's brow, then leaned down to tickle Sybil's chin. 'See how good a mother you are, Hélène? You worry about me like I'm your own son!' He laughed. 'I'll be careful, Hélène.'

'It isn't just the club though, is it, Joseph? It's . . . the whole world. One of my dancers at the hotel, her brother has vanished in the horrors in Spain. There still isn't any word of him. And now the riot in the East End? It doesn't feel . . . right out there.'

'Still no word from the King either,' chipped in Joseph's father. 'Will he give up Mrs Simpson or give up the throne?' He paused. 'The world has always been full of uncertainty, Hélène. It will never be any other way. But keep your focus, keep thinking on what matters most – that baby, right there in front of you – and you'll be all right.'

Soon it was time for dinner to end. Hélène lifted Sybil and tidied her up; Joseph reappeared in a green checked jacket, with peaked lapels and only two buttons on its breast and – despite the hoots of embarrassment from his father – disappeared out the front door with a flourish. Noelle worked her magic in the kitchen, while Maurice swept the rug. And, through it all, Hélène felt as if she was a world away from the Buckingham, the trials and tribulations of guests and concierges and hotel management.

'Time for me to get some sleep,' announced Samantha. 'Richard will be back from shift soon enough. Ma, Pa, goodnight. Lovely to see you, Hélène. And –' her eyes dropped down to the baby Hélène was still holding – 'night night, Sybil.'

Hélène took Samantha's hand. 'Thank you,' she whispered, and Samantha looked at her and replied gently. 'Never say that again, Hélène. You're family. You *both* are.'

At last, it was only Hélène and Noelle still up. In Hélène's arms, Sybil looked forlornly around, as if searching out Samantha. *But I'm here, Sybil. Your mama is here.* Then her face opened in an enormous yawn, revealing a mouth full of tiny white teeth.

'Well, somebody's sleepy. Do you want to put her down, dear?'

Hélène was hesitant. 'Isn't it silly,' she said, 'how nervous one can get?'

'You dance for princes every night. How could a little thing like this make you nervous?'

Because, Hélène thought, *she matters so much more.*

With Sybil still lolling in her arms, Hélène squeezed down the hallway to the little nursery at the end. Behind her, Noelle sang a ditty to herself as she tidied everything away. In one of the flats above, a pair of young lovers were arguing. Through the walls, Hélène could hear the sound of the BBC news buzzing out of the wireless, news of Germany and Spain – and, of course, the daily bulletin about King Edward and the glamorous Mrs Simpson. But here, safe in the nursery, everything was still.

Hélène did not want to put Sybil down. She clung on to her until her own feet were tired, simply breathing in her scent. Then, at last, she bent over the rail and laid her down in the crib. After that, she gazed over her for the longest time, humming a lullaby whose words she felt certain she'd forgotten. But the melody came naturally – and so too, Hélène remembered, did motherhood. It was a wonderful feeling. Each time she came back, she was afraid it had slipped through her fingers – but life was lived for stolen moments like these.

'Sleep tight, little princess,' she said as she left a kiss on the baby's head. 'Mama's with you now. Mama's here.'

November 1936

Chapter Twenty-two

THE LAST LINGERING GUESTS OF the season had vacated the suites of the Buckingham Hotel. Nikolai Alexeev and Grusinskaya had departed to over-winter in the sunnier climes of some Moorish castle on the north Moroccan coast; Cormac E. Colby had returned to the promise of snow in New York City; the Schechts, the van der Lindes, the Townsend-Stuarts, all had returned to their mansion houses and Continental estates. Of all the suites, only the Park Suite remained occupied – and, as any senior member of staff at the Buckingham Hotel would have told you, this too was the only suite not mentioned in the hotel's glamorous brochures. Soon, the suites would have new guests to inhabit them; some would come for days and some would stay for weeks – for, with the nights drawing in, talk of Christmas and New Year was suddenly on the tongues of everyone at the Buckingham, from the lowliest hotel page to the hotel director himself.

As the eleventh hour drew near on a cold November night, two figures strolled arm-in-arm across the green expanse of Berkeley Square. The gleaming white facade of the Buckingham loomed above them, imperious in the winter dark. The lights in its windows were like a thousand glowing eyes, each staring out across the London sky.

Raymond de Guise took his arm out of Nancy's and rested on his cane. It had, he decided, been the perfect evening: an evening to escape his confinement to quarters in the Buckingham Hotel; an evening to test his broken foot – which still throbbed, but had borne his weight well tonight; an evening to be free with her, with Nancy Nettleton, out in London town. The fireworks had rained over the river in beautiful arrays of oranges, reds and white. In Hyde Park the bonfire still burned, though it had long ago devoured the great effigy of Guy Fawkes that had been cast into it. The smell of woodsmoke was still in his hair, where it mingled with the scent of Nancy's perfume: not the Chanel or Caron of Vivienne Edgerton, but the much subtler scent she'd picked up from the John Lewis department store two Saturdays before.

'In through the guest door, perhaps?' said Raymond, with the hint of a smile.

He was teasing her. Nancy rolled her eyes. 'I think not. Unless, that is, you were planning on getting me thrown out? So you can finally start romancing Miss Edgerton?'

Raymond's braying laugh echoed across Berkeley Square. 'The tradesman's door it is.'

They stole through together. Then, in the shadowed hall, before they approached the housekeeping lounge and chequered reception hall, Raymond stopped her. A stolen kiss later, they were crossing the hall and nearly at the Grand.

Her head down, Nancy clung to the walls as she made for the service lift – but she didn't get far. Raymond's hand was on her shoulder. 'Just one peep,' he said.

'I can't. You know what will happen if they see us.' She thought about Rosa and Ruth, and all their bitter comments; Mrs Moffatt, telling her to remain unseen.

She squeezed his hand and slipped away.

Head down, Raymond positioned himself just outside the ballroom doors. The Archie Adams Band was playing a slow foxtrot, 'On the Air', as the evening came to its end. From the edge of the dance floor, the dancers looked divine, each couple turning against the other in perfect synchrony. Raymond felt a strange longing tug at his breast, where his fractured ribs had finally knitted themselves together and stopped stinging every time that he breathed. He caught sight of Hélène Marchmont in the arms of some socialite come to London from his country estate. Fleetingly, she caught his eye and raised her eyebrows in acknowledgement. That look told Raymond everything: *Get back in here, Raymond. We need you.* Well, it wouldn't be long. He'd been working hard – harder than the doctors said he must. Every moment he could, he spent walking. He stretched three times a day, desperate to keep his body as supple as it ever was.

As Hélène danced on, she turned past Nathaniel White – that cherubic snake-charmer who'd managed, Raymond had no idea how, to take his place in the ballroom. Well, Raymond could feel his body healing. *And it can't come soon enough. What right has he to be here in our ballroom? He dances no better than a guest . . . It's because of who he is. Who his family are.* Raymond hadn't forgotten those men, what they had done out on Cable Street, what they had done to his brother. It wasn't long ago that Raymond thought he wouldn't mind never seeing his brother again. But somehow all of that had changed.

His eyes took in the room, the starlets and gentlemen dancers – and then they landed on Vivienne Edgerton. He had not seen it at first but, as they danced back across the ballroom, he realised it was Vivienne in the arms of Nathaniel. Well, he supposed, she *was* a guest, after all – and that was what Nathaniel was here for, to dance with guests while Raymond was indisposed. But the way Vivienne was moving? The confidence with which she stepped and turned? The way she threw herself into a spin and laughed joyfully as Nathaniel caught her? Raymond felt a plunging sensation in his stomach. She had not been capable of this that morning he tried to tutor her here in the ballroom.

No, he thought. Things had changed in his ballroom while he was away.

At the end of the evening, Hélène walked back through the dressing-room doors, with the band and the rest of the hotel dancers. Only Nathaniel strutted in behind her – he, the showman of the ballroom, always the last to leave, to the applause of the guests who remained.

The band were tearing off their bow ties. Evening jackets were strewn around, dancing shoes kicked off, and the other girls were tumbling through to their own dressing room ready to hit the town. Hélène followed after them, catching Louis Kildare's eye. Kildare still wore his white jacket and waistcoat while he took the mouthpiece out of his saxophone, inspected the reed, cleaned it and stowed it away again. Then he worked at the instrument's shine with his cuff, flashing her a toothy grin. He mouthed four words – *Be patient, Miss Marchmont!* – and thank goodness he did, for they had a restorative effect on Hélène. The anxiety that had been tightening every muscle in her body began to seep away. Louis could have that effect on her. It was something that he and Sidney had both shared, that simple way of shrugging off the worst of things and getting on with the business of music and dance.

It was times like this that she missed Sidney the most. Louis did what he could – he had been a good friend to them both – but it was not the same. In an age gone by, she might have stalked off the dance floor, spent and exhausted, and Sidney would have been there, already practising some new trill on his trumpet. He'd have dropped it (or stowed it safely away – Sidney Archer had been as in love with his trumpet as he was with Hélène) and come to her side. They'd have made some pretence, and then they'd have slipped away together. The band might have known, but not one of them mentioned it, for they all knew what Maynard Charles would make of a union like theirs. But none of it – the secrecy, the lies, even the panicked moment when Hélène first understood she was pregnant with Sidney's child – mattered, because Sidney was there to help her shrug it all away.

Now, with Sidney long in the ground and Raymond yet to return to the ballroom, Hélène would have to shoulder it herself. She steadied herself with deep breaths and followed Sofía LaPegna into the dancing girls' dressing room. Sofía was already stripped out of her ball gown. Hélène paused. She had to remember: it had been tough for Sofía too. Over the weeks her despair had slowly turned to hope, and that hope had itself solidified into a devout belief that somewhere, out there, her brother not only survived – but was thriving.

Sofía scurried over and helped Hélène out of her high-backed gown. 'Were his hands all over you again, Hélène?'

Hélène shook her head. The other dancers made a joke out of it – but Nathaniel's were not wandering hands, not in the way Sofía meant. Nevertheless, she felt as if she could feel them on her, even now. When she danced with Raymond, it was with the lightest of touches. He led the dance only because somebody had to lead the dance – yet, when Nathaniel put his arm around the small of her back, and pressed his other palm to hers, it was as if she was a puppet and he her puppeteer. They did not dance *together*. No, Nathaniel White was the one dancing – and she, Hélène Marchmont, starlet of the Buckingham Hotel, was something closer to a doll. The way he folded around her made her feel constricted, confined. It was, she had thought after that first demonstration they danced together, as if she was one of those dancing figurines fixed to the top of a music box, unable to move of their own volition, pirouetting only at somebody else's command.

She'd walked out of that first demonstration humiliated and ashamed. That night, as she'd prepared to dance with the hotel guests, Louis Kildare had caught her seething at the dressing-room doors. Some of the other girls had been whispering: White's only here, they said, because of who his father is. One of Lord Edgerton's set. Only Louis Kildare preached calm. 'He's just a boy,' he said. 'Nathaniel can't help who he was born to any more than you or I. This is the Grand Ballroom, remember? Young or old, rich or poor, black or white . . .'

Well, Hélène thought, as she fastened the brooch on her evening blouse and made sure her floor-length skirts were fastened, he'd had time. And the way he'd ignored every other guest this evening, while twirling Vivienne Edgerton around like another of his playthings, was distasteful at best. Somebody ought to tell Maynard Charles – paying guests are being overlooked while Nathaniel indulges Miss Edgerton – but of course nobody would.

At that moment, Billy Brogan appeared in the dressing room, to the shrieking of Sofía and the other girls. Billy rolled his eyes, as he did every time.

'Miss Marchmont.'

Billy was holding an envelope in his hands, with only her name written on the front. Hélène took it off him with eyes like daggers – a scathing look that said, *'Never in front of the girls, Billy!'* – and turned it over.

The envelope was folded rather than sealed, but Hélène believed she could feel a faint moisture, as if some keen observer had been steaming it open. She had heard a number of times the secret policy of the hotel post room, that no letter could come in or out without the prying eyes of Maynard Charles first knowing what it said. It wasn't beyond a boy like Billy to pick up some of those tricks. But she'd been using Billy to ferry messages back and forth to the Archers ever since she came back to the Buckingham Hotel. She had to trust *somebody*.

'It came that way, Miss Marchmont. There's no one had it but me. It was dropped down in Lambeth, just like always.'

Hélène nodded, dismissing Billy – who left to mock declarations of love from some of the girls. It would take more than that to make Billy Brogan blush, thought Hélène. He must have seen it all, sneaking in and out of the hotel suites as he did. Then she opened the letter.

Dearest Hélène,

She walks! At eight this morning (10th November), Sybil picked herself up without first reaching for Maurice and tottered five whole steps to reach me in my chair. The delight on her face was plain. The delight on ours will continue to Christmas and beyond. Next time you come, she will be running and jumping!

We enclose an artistic rendition in Sybil's own hand in celebration of this grand occasion.

More news soon, our precious Hélène,

Noelle xxx

Hélène took the last page out of the envelope. On it were the quick, urgent scribbles of a fifteen-month-old's hand. The paper had torn where Sybil's chubby fist had clutched the pencil, then worked ferociously to make marks across the page.

Hélène's heart was pounding. She should have been feeling delight – and she was; somewhere deep in the furthest recesses of her heart, she was cheering – but, eclipsing all else, was a kind of . . . grief. Sybil, up on her feet, staggering around the old house in Brixton, cheered on by her grandparents – and all while her mother was beached here in the Buckingham, earning their keep.

I have to do it for you, Sybil. I have to. If there were any other way . . .

The paper strained between her fingers. She was not aware she was crying until two fat teardrops landed on the page, smudging the marks Sybil had made. This seemed the most terrible thing in the world, and Hélène was busy dabbing them dry, trying to preserve this memento of her daughter, when another knock at the dressing-room door announced the appearance of Nathaniel.

Hélène scrabbled to hide the letter and drawing.

Nathaniel was dressed down, but he still held himself with the same imperious air that he did in the ballroom. 'Hélène,' he said, 'I came to tell you: we'll meet in the studio behind the ballroom before dawn. New Year is coming. We need to change the demonstrations or . . . Well, the guests deserve a little something extra, don't you think? Something a little more *special* for the King? I have something in mind, Hélène. I'm sure Mr Charles has already impressed upon you how important these festivities are. Well, I have something that can blow the Imperial away. Follow me and we can give them a New Year to remember.'

Hélène stiffened. *Follow you?* If he'd caught her a few moments ago, before Billy delivered that letter, she might have resisted. She might have looked him straight in the eye and told him that her choreography had served her and Raymond de Guise well for seasons – that, when they charted new demonstrations, it was for her to decide, not for the upstart new blood in the ballroom, no matter what connections his father might have had. But her mind was still on the letter – so instead she remained silent as she walked past him, up and out of the dressing room, wrapping her arms around herself.

Nathaniel only stared after her. 'Six o' clock!' he called out. 'Before the breakfast services begin. Be there, Hélène – we're dancing the new routines in the afternoon demonstrations.'

But by then, she was already gone, marching across the reception hall as if she would rather be anywhere else in the world.

December 1936

Chapter Twenty-three

THE LESS HÉLÈNE DWELLED UPON these last few weeks, the better. The mornings in the studio, taking Nathaniel White's direction as he showed her his new take on Maxwell Stuart's classic double reverse spin (a lumpen mess which ended in Hélène standing woodenly while Nathaniel pirouetted ostentatiously around her); the afternoon demonstrations, in which it was only Nathaniel's ego being exhibited to the crowds; the evenings in the arms of men she would have crossed the street to avoid – and all while Sybil, *her Sybil*, was growing and changing at Noelle Archer's home. Perhaps it was the dark skies over London that were hardening her mood, for by mid-November the first flurries of the winter's snow had brought the trams and omnibuses of London town to a standstill. Or perhaps it was the ballroom itself. It too was changing. She remembered the long hot days of summer, when the dressing rooms were filled with laughter and cheer: she and Raymond in the studio every morning, limbering up for the demonstration dances, daring each other to perform ever more exacting stunts that might dazzle the crowds. She remembered the way they'd collapse together, the dancers and musicians, at the end of a long night in the ballroom – how it was always Louis Kildare who produced the magnum of champagne and shared it around.

And most of all she remembered the sense that, no matter how tough life outside was, theirs was a precious, gilded world: their own little bubble inside the Buckingham Hotel.

She missed Raymond. This morning Nathaniel had taken her to the studio and made her dance alone for a whole hour performing his choreography, demanding she follow his every instruction. Hélène had stood there and seethed. *I've been dancing since you were a choirboy*, she thought, *and yet you stand there, telling me how to move in my own ballroom. Every time I make a suggestion. Every time I have an idea . . .*

Tonight, after the final dance, Hélène didn't linger with Louis and the others in the dressing rooms. She marched, instead, to the upper storeys, knocked directly on Raymond's door and collapsed in the chair at the side of his dresser.

'You *need* to get better,' she said. 'You need to get better *now*. He has me standing there while he cavorts around me. Like I'm a . . . maypole!'

Then, together, they exploded with laughter.

Raymond gathered himself. 'You shouldn't make me laugh like that, Hélène. If I break more ribs . . .'

'Don't you dare,' she said, and produced a half-bottle of champagne she'd been hiding behind her back. 'There isn't enough champagne in the world. If I have to dance with him at the New Year Masquerade Ball . . .'

Raymond poured the champagne and clinked his glass with hers. 'I'll be ready,' he said – and Hélène was convinced, because how could she not be? Raymond could convince anyone of anything when he had that devilish twinkle in his eyes. 'I swear it, Hélène. I'll *be* there.'

'Heave!'

The service lift opened, depositing Nancy, Rosa, Ruth and a host of other chambermaids, into the housekeeping hall – and the first thing they heard was the cry of Ralph North, the porter, echoing along the corridor from reception.

I can smell it, thought Nancy with glee. *A smell like this, it takes you right back to being a little girl . . .*

It was before dawn, and two weeks until Christmas. In an hour, the Buckingham would awake. These were the hours the guests never saw. These were the hours when the magic would be performed.

In the reception hall, a group of porters were ranged around a fir tree taller than the little cottage that Nancy used to call home. Ropes had been tethered to its highest point and, under the direction of Ralph, the porters were hoisting it into place.

The chambermaids now watched, excited enough that not one of them spoke. Three great heaves later, the tree stood proud and tall. As the porters balanced it there, others rushed in to anchor its stump, and yet more emerged with the stepladder that had been used to dangle tinsel from every rafter in the ballroom.

'Oh, Nancy,' Rosa thrilled, 'isn't it beautiful?'

It's more than that, thought Nancy, marvelling as the ropes were unbuckled and the tree stood alone for the first time. *It looks so real. Like it's back in the forest.*

The lower boughs, which reached almost to the ground, rustled, and from behind the tree stepped Mrs Moffatt. 'Girls,' she said, 'it's time we had some fun!' She gestured for the girls to follow her around the tree and, when they did, it was to discover great boxes and crates – and in them, glittering like treasure, baubles of silver and gold, miniature bells, snowflakes carved in ivory and glass, and mountains of tinsel that shimmered in the electric light.

'When the guests awake this morning, let them discover a Buckingham transformed.'

The girls rushed forward, delved deep into the boxes excitedly, and hurried about their task.

The upper echelons of the Buckingham Hotel had been contemplating Christmas since long before the first snows. In an enterprise as vast and interconnected as the Buckingham, Christmas was an affair not for the cold winter months, but for the final days of summer. Maynard Charles had directed his subordinates to source the great Norwegian fir that was now being hoisted into pride of place in the hotel reception. Mr Simenon had been tasked with procuring the very best in crystal baubles and stars, and all of the other candles and crosses, tinsel and trinkets, which – by the time the guests awoke – would adorn the halls and lounges of the hotel. Maynard Charles had but one directive: if our hotel is to become a grotto, then let it be the most elegant and lavish grotto in London.

An army had been enlisted now. Nancy and Rosa and Ruth busied themselves draping tinsel and scattering stars, all under Mrs Moffatt's watchful eye – 'this is my twenty-first Christmas at the Buckingham Hotel, and I've never seen a finer tree! Great job, girls! Keep it up!' – but they weren't the only ones. A flurry of hotel pages skittered through reception, carrying the glass stars that would adorn the guest lounges. Kitchen hands, waiting staff and concierges passed, on their way to decorate the Queen Mary, the Candlelight Club, the brasserie and the ballroom. To Nancy, it seemed the most incredible thing in the world. The Buckingham was transforming in front of her eyes. One season was changing into the next – to the guests it would surely seem like magic.

In an hour, the tree was bedecked in glass angels and snowflakes, tinsel arranged so splendidly it constantly caught the light – and all that was left was for Maynard Charles himself to huff and puff his way to the top of the ladder and, watched by the assembled throng, place a single silver star at the top of the tree. Later that day, Billy Brogan would be dispatched to take careful note of the decorations on display at hotels such as the Savoy and the Ritz – and come back reporting that no tree was larger, no star brighter than that which shone at the Buckingham Hotel.

I wonder what it's like at home, Nancy thought as she gazed up. *Not that it's really home any more. But . . . I wonder if there's a tree for Frank this year. I wonder if Mrs Gable will wrap him a present.* Raymond had taken her to Fortum and Mason, and there she had bought a little Christmas cake to send to him. *Because you might be sixteen, Frank, but you're still my baby brother. I'm going to make a home for you – for us both – down here. I just need a little more time . . .*

'You can be very proud of your work here, girls!' Mrs Moffatt announced. 'I wouldn't have done it finer if I'd done every bit myself.'

'It feels like Christmas now, doesn't it?' Rosa chirped gleefully. 'Everything feels so much more—'

'Festive!' Ruth announced.

'It makes you want to sing.'

'Well, we should,' one of the other girls chipped in. 'We could go carolling. Sunday night's off night. We can take some carols out there. Go a-wassailing, like when we was girls . . .'

'What do you say, Nance? Carolling this Sunday. We can get all the girls up in the kitchenette tonight, practise some numbers. You'll come too, won't you, Mrs Moffatt?'

Mrs Moffatt smiled as she shook her head. 'My carolling days are behind me. Don't you girls go thinking that, just because it's Christmas, there'll be any less work in this hotel. Do you want to know a little secret?' She leaned in and, grinning, whispered, 'There'll be *more*. But, I suppose, one night of carolling wouldn't hurt.' Dusting her hands off, she marched away, bound for the housekeeping lounge. 'Breakfast in ten minutes. We still have rooms and suites to take care of.'

'Well, Nance?' Rosa went on, after Mrs Moffatt was gone. 'Come practise some carols with us tonight?'

Nancy froze. 'I'll be there,' she finally said – but inwardly she felt bereft. The girls would be disappointed in her – there'd be gossip again, she was certain of that – because if she joined them at all, it would be after the carolling was over.

Tonight, there was some place else she had to be.

The decorations extended even as far as the little windowless studio behind the ballroom. Here sprigs of last year's holly, preserved all summer long, were entwined around the braziers in which a myriad of candles flickered – and the baubles hanging from the rafters, though faded from years of use, were no less brilliant. An hour before the ballroom was due to open its doors that night, Nathaniel opened the studio door and stopped dead.

The wireless in the corner was buzzing out George Hall and his orchestra, 'Santa Bring My Mommy Back to Me', while across the studio Raymond de Guise and his chamber girl danced a simple two-step.

Hélène stumbled into the studio alongside Nathaniel. Nancy must have finished her duties for the day, for surely she would not have absconded to come here and dance. A few weeks of dedicated dancing had not turned Nancy into a professional, but there was more elegance, more grace to the way she pivoted and turned. Some of the art was radiating out, from Raymond into her.

I've never seen Raymond in love before, thought Hélène. *Love?* The word had caught her by surprise. *Is that what this is? The way he holds her, it seems so much more natural than the way he held Grusinskaya, or Philomena, or any of the other guests he's danced with in the ballroom.* Hélène had forgotten how technically brilliant Raymond could be, but he wasn't technically brilliant tonight. *You can see how he doesn't dare put his whole body's weight onto the foot he's stepping with. You can see he's holding back. But none of that matters, does it? What's technical brilliance when set against real connection?* Hélène was almost envious. *In all the years we've danced together, not once has he looked at me like this . . .*

Nathaniel clapped his hands, slow and deliberate, and suddenly Hélène was pulled out of her thoughts.

On the studio floor, Raymond was so lost in the music – *lost in his love,* thought Hélène – that it was Nancy who noticed first. She pulled out of his arms and came to a stop, revealing her lazy leg for the first time.

'Time's up, de Guise,' said Nathaniel flatly, striding down the step to the centre of the studio floor. 'Hélène and I have real work to do, there's a good fellow.'

Raymond's withering eye flickered from Nathaniel to Hélène – who merely raised an eyebrow – and then back to the boy. Silently, he picked up his jacket, extended an arm to show Nancy the way, and walked with her past the spot where Nathaniel stood, glowering.

'Raymond, I'm sorry . . .'

Raymond whispered to Hélène out of the side of his mouth, 'Don't worry, Hélène. It's not your doing.' Then something emboldened him and he spoke louder. 'When the lord clicks his fingers, we all have to dance. Even when it's with a *fascist dog* . . .'

Nathaniel tautened. 'You'd be advised to mind your manners, de Guise. You're confusing your master for your dog.'

Nancy took Raymond's hand, as if to heave him out of the room. 'Raymond, leave him. He's not worth—'

'Oh, he's not worth a *thing*. Imagine a man, Nancy, who didn't get where he is today by the talent in his feet, nor even the courage in his heart. Imagine a man who got where he is today by a pat on the back from Daddy. A man who thinks he owns somewhere as grand as the Buckingham because his father went to school with somebody who went to school with somebody who once held Lord Edgerton's valise. And imagine – just for a second, *imagine* – a man who thinks that he can *dance*, when really, he's just tumbling around the room like a circus clown.'

'ENOUGH, de Guise!'

Nathaniel's voice took on the shrillest of airs when he shouted. His cheeks were bunched and the creases that appeared between his eyes gave his face a nasty, pinched look – precisely befitting the man, thought Raymond.

'You can't deny it, boy,' Raymond spat. 'You dance *half* as well as some of the porters here in the Buckingham. You're here because of *who* you are, and who you are is the worst of the world. Your father and Edgerton and all their hired thugs. Well, they turfed you out of Cable Street –' at the mention of the place, Hélène looked perplexed, unable to make the connection, and yet Raymond carried on – 'and I'll be the one ejecting you from our hotel. You see these feet, Nathaniel? You see these shoes? They're the ones that will be dancing in the Grand on New Year's Eve. They're the ones that will be dancing up a storm when your papa sends a gleaming Bentley to take you back to mama.'

'You go too far, de Guise. One word to Lord Edgerton and . . .'

'Oh, *please*. Whatever else Lord Edgerton is, he's a businessman first. What matters to a man like him is the money. You must know how much our ballroom means to this hotel. And who do you think's worth more in the ballroom, boy? You, indulging only his wayward stepdaughter night after night in a crass attempt to bed or even marry her . . . or me, indulging his guests, giving them some glamour, giving them the confidence to move and turn and spin, and come back for more?'

There was momentary silence in the studio.

'I thought as much,' said Raymond. 'You're a disgrace. You and all your kind. But your days are numbered in this hotel. Mark my words.'

Moments later, Nancy – the poor girl's face aghast – was following Raymond out through the studio doors.

Hélène looked at Nathaniel, his face twisted with rage. She moved towards him – to placate, not to console – but before she could say a word, there came a deep, bass voice from the wireless. 'You are listening to the words of Sir John Reith, Director General of the BBC. We take an intermission now from this evening's broadcast to bring our listeners an announcement. This is Windsor Castle, His Royal Highness Prince Edward . . .'

Nathaniel's face creased. '*Prince* Edward?' he whispered.

On the radio the voice continued: 'At long last I am able to say a few words of my own. I have never wanted to withhold anything. But until now it has not been constitutionally possible for me to speak. A few hours ago I discharged my last duty as King and Emperor . . .'

Hélène was still staring after Raymond – but these words grabbed her and turned her around. By now, Nathaniel had crept close to the wireless. And the voice rumbled on . . .

All across the Buckingham Hotel, in bedrooms and suites, in the housekeeping office and staff kitchenettes, people gathered. In the Candlelight Club, the head barman and his crew hunched over the wireless. In the staff kitchenette on the hotel's uppermost storey, Rosa, Ruth, Mrs Whitehead and an assortment of other chambermaids listened as the prince – no longer their king – intoned, 'My first words must be to declare my allegiance to him, our new king. This I do with all my heart.' In the kitchens, chefs put down their knives. In the cocktail lounge, drinks went untended. In the reception hall, in the shadow of the great Norwegian fir, Mr Simenon grabbed Billy Brogan by the collar and wrenched him into the head concierge's office, where another radio crackled. 'You must believe me when I tell you that I have found it impossible to carry the heavy burden of responsibility and to discharge my duties as King as I would wish to do, without the help and support of the woman I love . . .' For seven long minutes, as long as the prince spoke, the great engine of the Buckingham Hotel came to a standstill. Time was out of joint.

And then the whispers began.

'He was going to be here for New Year, wasn't he?' Rosa said in a low voice.

'Wasn't that why there's a masquerade ball at all? At the behest of the King . . .'

'They'll all turn away,' Mr Simenon seethed, as Billy Brogan pressed his ear to the buzzing wireless. 'If the King isn't in attendance, what of the Norwegians? There'll be panic in the board. We've spent so much already to make this New Year an extravaganza . . . Mr Charles,' he gasped. 'I have to find Mr Charles.'

In the Queen Mary and Candlelight Club, in the French brasserie and cocktail bar, guests turned to one another in quiet reverence, unable to believe the whispers spreading among them. But it was the staff of the Buckingham Hotel who felt the blow most keenly. In the Queen Mary kitchens, the head chef sized up the menu he'd composed for New Year. The bookkeeper's thoughts turned, inevitably, to the money squandered on reserving King Edward's chosen suite. And, alone in his office, Maynard Charles hung his head and quaked. *The whole spectacle*, he thought. *The whole extravaganza. The Buckingham's reputation itself. All of it staked on a New Year masquerade ball thrown in honour of the new king. And now he's fallen . . .*

The voice on the wireless crackled on until, at last, the former king was finished. 'The decision I have made has been mine and mine alone.' Then, as one, the hotel inhabitants let out the breath they had been holding. The clocks started ticking once more. Porters re-emerged into the halls. Maynard Charles opened his office door, and Billy Brogan darted off on some new errand. The world would carry on turning, but its old king was gone and a new one was being elevated in his place.

Alone among the denizens of the Buckingham Hotel, only Raymond and Nancy did not gather to hear the news of the king's abdication. As the old king was making his proclamation, they rode the lift and emerged onto the hotel's uppermost storey. The rage had hardly left Raymond by the time they had reached his room. Nancy caught hold of his arm as he forced his way through the door, the key half-jamming in the lock.

'Raymond!' She'd been imploring him all the way across the hotel. This time, when he did not look back, she snapped, '*Ray!*'

That single syllable brought him to his senses. By now the door had flown open and Nancy followed him inside.

It did not feel right, to march so brazenly into his room. *If Ruth and Rosa were to know . . .* Courting Raymond was difficult enough to keep quiet in the hotel. *But if Mrs Moffatt were to think I was coming up here, to Raymond's room. If Mr Charles were to find out . . .*

Now, seeing the hard set to Raymond's face, how he carried himself not as lightly as a dancer but as forcefully as those thugs who'd broken him in the Midnight Rooms, she wondered if she had been foolish to follow him here. The anger still rippled up and down his arms. He prowled, back and forth, back and forth, like a man in a cage. Was it right that the same arms that had enfolded her and made her feel so safe could also be so ready to lash out?

'Ray!'

'Don't call me *that*, Nancy.'

He had spoken with such venom. 'But that's who you're being, isn't it? Ray Cohen, not Raymond de Guise. I never heard Raymond de Guise speak to a man like you spoke to Nathaniel. I never saw Raymond de Guise with that kind of hatred in his eyes . . .'

Hatred? thought Raymond. *Was that it? Well, why not?* They hated him. *They* were the ones who'd torn up the streets where he lived, put his brother in the infirmary. *They* were the ones fomenting hate and unrest on the streets of London town.

'How dare he come into the ballroom? How dare *we* all let him? And how dare you *defend—*'

Nancy felt hot anger of her own now. 'Defend him? For what? For being an obnoxious fool? For being one of those rich boys who think they own the world, and all because of the money in their back pockets? You've been in the Buckingham longer than I. You *know* the way of this world. But defend him as a . . . a fascist? You've danced with them before, Raymond. You said it yourself: the Grand is the Grand, and what happens inside—'

Raymond was quelled. 'I was wrong—'

'What changed?' Nancy whispered. 'What changed in *you*?'

The thought of them, men like Nathaniel, all his union friends, tearing his brother down from the barricades and trampling him into the earth. It was . . . the guilt. At last he admitted it. The guilt that he hadn't been there. That he'd forsaken them all. That he danced for his supper for the very same men who would have seen his family driven out of their homes.

'It's our ballroom,' Raymond stated. 'I'm taking it back.'

Maynard Charles dialled the number furiously, so furiously that the telephone on his desk skittered off the edge and he had to pick it up from the floor and start all over again. Since the king – he would have to stop calling him the king – had stopped speaking, the radio had maintained a dignified silence. Now, as the voice of the BBC newsreader returned, he pulled the electric cord from the wall and waited for the voice on the other end of the line.

'Yes,' he began, when a lady finally answered, 'I'm seeking Lord Edgerton. Yes, I need to speak to him immediately. Tell him . . . tell him it's Maynard Charles. Tell him we must speak at once.'

The timid voice on the end of the line, no doubt Lord Edgerton's housekeeper, did not get a chance to reply – for at that moment fists hammered at the office door and, even though Maynard barked out an order to wait, the door drew back to reveal Raymond de Guise. Maynard gave him a sharp look but the broken dancer closed the door behind him.

'Raymond, this is going to have to wait. You'll understand, this is a sensitive moment—'

'And for me, sir, but I have to speak with you.'

'Raymond, by God! I'm wrestling with something of far greater significance than—'

'No,' declared Raymond. 'I insist. This can't go on a moment longer.'

There was something so severe in Raymond's tone that Maynard slowly replaced the telephone on its receiver. The housekeeper would, no doubt, be the recipient of Lord Edgerton's ire, but that was somebody else's problem.

He looked over his pince-nez at Raymond. 'What's happening, Mr de Guise?'

Raymond's eyes were temporarily gazing beyond Maynard Charles, to the little safe in the wall behind him – containing the jewellery Hélène Marchmont wore on each celebration in the ballroom, but no doubt full of cheques from Lord Edgerton's union friends, bankers' drafts from whichever princely guests had called the Buckingham home in this last month as well. *Keep it all in there, don't you? All your ill-gotten gains. Taking money from the scum of the earth.*

'I'm going to dance tomorrow,' he declared, with barely a tremble in his voice. 'In the demonstrations, as well as the ballroom at night. I'm going to take my place.'

Maynard removed his glasses from across the bridge of his nose and took a long, wearied breath. 'Tonight, Raymond? You want to discuss this . . . tonight?'

'It's been too long, Mr Charles. The ballroom needs me.'

Maynard's eyes returned to the telephone receiver, sitting in its cradle. The words of the king of old were still resounding in his ears. He could recall every tremble in that proud and dignified voice. There was something to admire in a man who would give up his ancestry for love. Maynard was certain others of his rank would not see it as such. There were more men in the world who would give up love for rank and idolatry than the rest. It was going to cause untold problems for the Buckingham – what would happen to their reputation without a prince or a king to grace their halls? And yet he found his heart soaring at the idea. He was, he decided, a sentimental old fool.

'I'm sorry, Raymond,' he said, diverting his attention back to his desk. 'Doctor Moore instructed bed rest until Christmas. I've been lenient enough with that prescription. Yes, I know you've been sneaking about the ballroom with a chambermaid. I haven't caused a fuss. We are in the business, here, of managing risks. But I won't risk you in the ballroom, Raymond, not until

Doctor Moore has attended you and declared you fit. You're an asset to this hotel, Mr de Guise. We look after our assets.'

'I can dance, Maynard.' Raymond caught himself. 'I can dance, Mr Charles. I've proven it to myself. I don't need a doctor to declare me—'

'No,' said Maynard, with an air of finality. '*I* do. I have your body insured, Mr de Guise. Your feet are worth two thousand pounds each. What would my brokers say were I to throw you back to the lions without a doctor having signed you off? No, you'll wait it out, and we'll talk about it when the hour is right. Nathaniel is keeping your seat warm, Raymond. The ballroom is in safe hands.'

'That dog is to leave, Mr Charles. I'll drive him out if I have to. I'll put him down.'

Maynard Charles stood. Though he was not a tall man, something in his girth was nevertheless imposing.

'I beg your pardon, Raymond?' he said through gritted teeth.

'The Grand deserves better.'

'The crowd enjoy his spectacle. The boy has received rave notices from some of our most valuable clientele.'

'His father's friends, perhaps. Lord Edgerton and the rest. White was their lapdog before he set a foot in our ballroom, and you know it. The boy has no elegance. He's here for them – part of their entertainment after their supposedly secret meetings, not for us.'

Maynard Charles shook his head. There was so little time to argue, on this of all nights. Good Lord, it wasn't as if having Nathaniel White in the ballroom was his idea. Vivienne Edgerton had been cunning, and that was that. But there was something in Raymond's tone that he would not tolerate.

'Your critique of Nathaniel's dancing prowess is duly noted, Raymond, and duly dismissed. The guests of our hotel expect a certain something. Nathaniel has it. You might be the better dancer, Raymond. But who would a lady of grand esteem rather have hold her – a boy of breeding like Nathaniel White, or a common street thug who thinks a little make-up across his face will elevate him a social standing or two?'

Raymond stammered, 'I beg your pardon, sir?' while, inside, his mind whirred. How did he know? *Did* he know? *What* did he know? There wasn't a soul in this hotel who knew his story – not a soul . . . except Nancy.

'You'll have a place in the ballroom when you're healed,' said Maynard, returning calmly to his seat. 'We'll discuss who remains principal when the time is right. But Nathaniel is to maintain his duties until the New Year is done. Isn't New Year a mess already without us arguing over who takes the hand of the crown princess? That's if we have any royalty left . . .'

Raymond's mind was still in disarray. *A common street thug.* That's what Maynard Charles had called him. Images of Cable Street arced across his eyes. His brother, under a barrage of boots. His mother and aunts, out with their skillets to defend the barricades, the upturned bus . . .

I should have been there. It was my duty to be there.

Somebody was speaking. He did not know until he was already in full flow that it was his own words streaming out. 'You're one of *them*, Maynard. I don't know why I didn't see it before. You and Lord Edgerton, all those fascist pigs who come and fraternise in our hotel. You serve them up whatever they desire. You crawl around and you beg at their heels. You're a pig yourself, Maynard. Good God, this hotel was a grand place before his lordship came. *You* yourself were a noble man. But now? Now the Edgertons are here, with the Astors and the Schechts and the Whites and the Mosleys. Stirring up hatred, jetting off to meet their Nazi cousins, petitioning Parliament to turn a blind eye, to make a dirty deal, to go along with whatever their Führer wants. Well, out there – there in the real world – they might think the Buckingham is high and mighty, but it's not, is it? We might have queens and princesses here. Mr Baldwin and his ministers might come to entertain. There might be the stars of stage and screen. But we're gone, Maynard. Our soul is gone. You *sold* it. You sold it to the same kind of bastards who're making war in Spain. You sold it to the same kind of bastard who turned London streets to pitched battle. You sold it to those society fools in bed with Nazis. And you turned *me* into a part of it too. I danced with a Mitford for you, you dog. I let you sell a piece of me. Well, I won't sell it any longer. You don't *own* me, Maynard. The Buckingham doesn't—'

'Well then,' interjected Maynard, maintaining the repressed calm in which he'd endured Raymond's assault, 'it seems your mind is made up.' He stopped. His eyes had returned to the telephone, and it was only now that he realised it was not sitting correctly on its cradle. The call he had placed to Lord Edgerton's residence had not ended. He lifted the receiver, put it to his ear – but all he could hear on the other end was silence. *Had somebody heard?* he wondered. Had they listened to all the foulness Raymond de Guise had spewed out, here in his office? His heart was beating a new kind of rhythm now. He had kept his anger in too long.

'Get out, Raymond,' he uttered. 'Or should I say *Ray*?'

That single syllable felled Raymond de Guise. Something changed in his eyes. His hands curled into fists and his eyes darted into every corner of the room. *How?* he gasped, inwardly. *How does he know?*

Maynard Charles paused, evidently taking delight in the way the word transformed Raymond's face. 'Call me a fascist, would you? Tell me I sold my soul, when I freely gave it away fighting in Flanders for the freedom of people like you – so you could grow up and do the things you loved to do. The music. The song. The dance. You don't know the cost of a thing, *Ray Cohen*. So no, you're not dancing in the ballroom this Christmas. You're not stepping out with the crown princess this New Year. The fact of the matter is, you're not dancing in the Buckingham Hotel *ever* again.' He paused, allowing himself one last breath. 'Your contract with us is terminated. As of this instant, you are no longer welcome in the Buckingham Hotel.' Maynard Charles picked up the receiver, prepared to dial a number again. 'You have half an hour, Mr Cohen. Collect your things. If I see you here in the Buckingham again, it will be the end of every secret you have.'

Chapter Twenty-four

LONG PAST THE MIDNIGHT HOUR, Nancy Nettleton sat awake in her quarters, watching the fat flakes of snow drift down across Berkeley Square. The snow had been tumbling down since darkness first fell, transforming the rooftops of the city to a crystalline wonderland of white. Even the tracks Raymond had left in the snow as he'd stalked out of the Buckingham had vanished. Now that he was gone, there was hardly any trace of him at all.

The letter was half finished in her lap.

Dear Frank,

It's gone. All gone. Three hours ago, I watched Raymond leaving the hotel. I couldn't get near him. He was throwing his things into his pack, and then he was being marched out by Mr Simenon and Diego from the Candlelight Club. I'm quite sure I saw Mr Simenon smile. Raymond wouldn't even look at me. What if it was all just rot, every last moment of it? What if I never see him again?

The tears fell hard and fast, blotting the ink on the page. She had been there when Raymond stormed back into his quarters and began collecting his things. She'd pleaded with him, demanded he tell her exactly what was going on – but the look he gave her was one filled with venom, almost as if he was *accusing* her – though of what, Nancy could not say. She had tried to take his arm so that he might be forced to talk to her – and that was when Mr Simenon had appeared at the door, flanked by the head barman from the Candlelight Club. That Nancy was there at all was an affront to them, so she quickly exited and left them to it. Minutes later, when Raymond shoulder-barged them out of the way to march down the hallway of his own accord, she called out his name – but he didn't break his stride, didn't even look her way.

Oh, Frank, I wish you were here. How can a day that began so brightly end like this? If you were here I would make us cocoa and drop so many sugar cubes in it that it would turn sickly sweet. I would get out mother's old blanket and we could wrap up in it together, to listen to the wireless or read our books.

Frank, I miss you. I haven't said it enough. I miss you, little brother.

I have been a fool. A romantic fool! I came here to find a way to build a new life for us. I wasn't supposed to fall in love and make a nonsense of myself in the process. But that's, precisely what I have done.

Nancy

In the Candlelight Club, all talk was of the new king and the old. In the Queen Mary, where the cast of the Ziegfeld Follies were being hosted by Maxwell Lloyd – the West End impresario intending to bring them to London from their native New York – they whispered of the coronation to come. In the cocktail lounge and French brasserie, they talked about the sweet release that must have come for the prince, knowing, at last, that he could be with the woman he loved. But in the Grand, where Nathaniel put his arm around Hélène and tangoed in the centre of the ballroom, the whispers were different. The guests might have bemoaned the loss of a sovereign sympathetic to their cause, but in the dressing rooms the talk was of another fallen king.

Raymond de Guise was gone.

Late that night, after the revelries had finished and the last notes of the Archie Adams Band had died away, Vivienne Edgerton stole across the upper storeys of the Buckingham Hotel and gently tapped at a narrow mahogany door. Inside, by the light of a dozen candles, Nathaniel was admiring himself in the mirror above his armoire. He turned to greet Vivienne. She had looked ravishing in the ballroom tonight, her lips plump and red, her hair sculpted so that she seemed a style icon out of the pages of *Vanity Fair*, her black velvet gown with its striking silver sash procured from a Knightsbridge tailor who had made pieces for Greta Garbo. She stepped through and closed the door softly behind her. Then she opened up in the most radiant smile Nathaniel had ever seen grace her face. He had thought he had seen her in the throes of ecstasy before – but this simple, childish joy was something else altogether.

He stood and embraced her.

'Oh, Nathaniel, it couldn't have happened better if I'd planned it myself!' She lay her head on his shoulder, then drew back so that she could plant her lips on his. They hovered there for a moment, enticing, before she kissed him. 'All that fool had to do was bide his time. Broken bones heal. Bruises fade away. They'd have had to put him back in the ballroom eventually. The guests would have demanded it. Where's Raymond de Guise, they'd all say. But now . . .'

Nathaniel kissed her again. They slid, together, onto the foot of his bed.

'Do we know what de Guise did?'

'Mr Simenon spilled it all. He always does. Raymond hanged himself. He went down there meaning to lash Mr Charles and force you out of the ballroom, but he wound up flogging himself. Isn't it the most *delicious* irony?'

Nathaniel beamed. Sometimes, the stars really did align. Two weeks until Christmas – and the only thing standing between him and dancing with the Queen of Norway on his arm when the New Year bells tolled was suddenly gone, cast out into the snow. *My ticket to greater glories yet. My ticket to the palaces and boudoirs of the continent. To becoming a star for the ages* . . . Surely there had not been a more satisfying Christmas story in the history of the world.

'I saw the way they looked at me in the ballroom tonight. Not the guests. The dancers. Those ingrates in the Archie Adams Band. Kildare, that swaggering saxophonist who's always creeping around Hélène – as if *she'd* ever stoop so low as to dance privately with one of *them*. They think I'm the reason de Guise is banished. As if I pushed him to it . . .'

Nathaniel had started to grow tense at the memory of those eyes burning into him, but Vivienne drew him nearer. 'Let them think what they like. They can follow de Guise, if that's what they want. They've been lording it over the ballroom for too long. New Year's coming. The Masquerade Ball. You're the star, now that de Guise is gone.'

'It's Hélène that's the problem now. It's like she . . . resists me. Every time I show her how I want her to dance, a blank look comes across her face. And where does she go to, anyway? It feels like it's every week. Whenever the ballroom's closed. She *evaporates*. Leaves the hotel, when what she ought to be doing is *rehearsing* everything I'm teaching her.'

'Off with some lover, no doubt. She keeps her secrets. She left for an entire year, not long ago. Some rich paramour was jetting her all over the world—'

'She can have as many paramours as she wants. But she has a job to do. And that job is making me look *magnificent*.'

Vivienne bristled. *Must we talk about Hélène Marchmont, even now?*

'You don't need to think about her, Nathaniel. Think about *us*. That's what this New Year could be, isn't it? A chance to show the world, not just the Buckingham, exactly who you are, exactly what you can do. There's more than just glory in it, isn't there? There's riches as well . . . You can tour the continent, on a reputation like that. You can see the world. And me? I can finally show my mother that I'm not someone to be cast aside like an unwanted dog. *Just think* . . .'

Nathaniel did. New Year: the night of the Grand masquerade. When the clocks struck seven, the doors of the Grand would open, the Archie Adams Band – and whatever guest singers they'd drawn in – would strike up, and the dancers would stream out for the Grand demonstration. Then, the lords and ladies in attendance would choose their partners for the night. Nathaniel pictured himself, sweeping the crown princess across the dance floor one moment; holding the warm body of her mother the queen the next. The King may no longer be in attendance, but that did not mean there was not a reputation to be made.

'And a little space, perhaps, for me, Nathaniel? After all I've done . . .'

Nathaniel beamed. 'Always,' he said – and, as they slid together upon the bed, he kissed her again.

Chapter Twenty-five

SNOW EDDIED AND WHIRLED IN the mews as Raymond de Guise rapped his knuckles urgently on a nondescript door. The Académie des Artistes sat on one of the cobbled rows snaking away from Covent Garden, the only thing to announce it a simple silver plaque on the wall between the French restaurant La Folie and an antique bookseller of high renown. The door itself was unremarkable – the Académie did not have to announce itself to the world. Those who knew of it, knew where to find it.

The doorman, when he appeared, was a man who had been born in the heart of the last century; his wrinkled skin hung loose around what had once been his significant jowls, and the suit he was wearing seemed to come from another century as well. He considered the man standing on the cobbles coldly. Then, recognising him, he stepped aside and admitted Raymond within.

Raymond was thankful for the heat emanating from the flickering fires. A narrow set of stairs led to the gentleman's club on the building's uppermost storey. The Académie des Artistes had a long and noble tradition. A small club with private smoking chambers and a staircase leading down to a secret back room and the restaurant below. The great Russian ballerina Anna Pavlova had made the Académie her home when she came to London with her rendition of the Dying Swan in the years before the Great War. Dancers and choreographers as feted as Jules-Joseph Perrot, the balletmaster of the Imperial Ballet in St Petersburg, had come to this place and dined among stars. Marie Taglioni, who first pioneered *La Esmeralda*. Enrico Cecchetti, the virtuoso from Milan, who had hidden from the world that he could only turn in one direction across his entire career. Eduardo Corrochio had celebrated here the night after he became the world's first Tap Dancing Champion in 1890. Joe Frisco, the American vaudeville performer who took Broadway by storm with his Jewish Charleston, was known to frequent the Académie every time his shows brought him to London. There was even one night, which horrified the Imperial ballet artistes dining in the secret restaurant room, when Mata Hari herself was said to have draped herself across one of her paramours here, in this same smoky room.

And now came Raymond de Guise.

If they knew what kind of ruffian I really am, they'd turf me out on my ear. Even so, the wonder of climbing these stairs, where dancers so much greater than he had once trod, was exhilarating. No matter how many ballrooms and palaces he visited, the wonder of it still touched Raymond. *That's how I know I've never really belonged,* he thought. *Somewhere inside, I'm still Ray Cohen, standing on a street corner at night on lookout while his brother and friends clamber through some broken window . . .*

The club was serene this afternoon, though two men in velveteen waistcoats were seated by the small corner bar, locked in conversation with Almira – the manageress who, if history had followed a different path, might now have been sunning herself on the ramparts of some palace in Persia. Almira recognised Raymond almost as soon as he stepped through the doors. Her black eyes gleamed at him and she directed him to a table in the corner, where a middle-aged man with distinguished silver hair and moustache waxed into perfect spirals was nursing a plate of the most succulent rabbit cassoulet.

Raymond approached slowly, snow sloughing off his grey overcoat. The diner looked up and his face, with its otherworldly blue eyes, opened up in the warmest smile. He stood and, when Raymond extended a hand, the man pulled him into a warm embrace instead. When the elder man let go of him and directed him to sit, he felt the tears of a young boy pricking in his eyes. He had not known how much he needed this.

'Georges,' he began, 'I'm grateful to find you.'

Georges de la Motte summoned Almira for an extra glass, and himself poured Raymond a measure of the darkest, richest Merlot. This he placed in Raymond's hand, folding Raymond's fingers around the glass stem himself. 'Drink, my boy,' he said gently.

So Raymond did. The wine had a warming effect. Its taste was an intoxicating mixture of red grape and cinnamon – something exotic, and of the east. He let it penetrate every corner of his body. For the first time, in a long time, he felt his muscles relax as he sank back into the chesterfield.

Georges de la Motte had just celebrated his half-centenary and, although it was showing in the silvering of his hair, he still retained that fey, otherworldly air that had first struck Raymond so many years ago. Raymond supposed Georges would have been his own age back then. There had been so much to admire in the seventh son of a French baron who'd picked him up from the taproom floor, set him on his feet and recognised, in the youngster, something of himself. Raymond had learned so much from him – not just the nuances of the double reverse spin, nor the imperceptible changes to his posture that would better create elegance in the ballroom, but of gracefulness and poise in larger life as well. It was this stability that drew Raymond to his mentor now.

'Raymond, my boy. You look like you could use an old friend.'

Raymond nodded. He did not want to seem weak in front of his old mentor, but something inside him was lost, something inside him was spinning apart. 'I'm grateful for it,' he replied. 'Georges, I need your help.'

Georges' voice dropped to a whisper. 'I told you before, Raymond. I'm here for you, whenever you need me. When you need a friend, send for de la Motte. Do you hear me?'

Raymond whispered, 'Yes.' Then, his voice more broken still, he added, 'Thank you.'

'There are no thanks needed, Raymond. It's been too long already. Two old warriors of the ballroom like us? We should be meeting every few months to drink fine wine and relive old glories. You're fortunate I'm in London,' he continued, making a steeple of his fingers. 'I received your letter, but I'm here for a precious few days.'

The truth was, Raymond hadn't expected a reply. Two days ago, he'd sent word to the Académie des Artistes and sat back in the little Holborn flophouse where he'd been laying his head, and was surprised when, the following morning, a letter came by return, from the hand of Almira the manageress.

'I'm en route to sunnier climes, my boy. Casablanca and El Jadida. Marrakesh and Tangier. Society extends thus far, and my presence has been requested. Well, who am I to say no?' He opened his palms in a resigning gesture which his upbeat eyes hardly matched. 'I've been in London for the early festive season. The Christmas dances. The tea parties in Kensington and Knightsbridge. Lord Crosby's daughter came out this summer. They hosted in her honour.'

'You didn't stay at the Buckingham?'

Georges de la Motte did not always take a suite at the Buckingham when he was in London, for there were too many lords and ladies eager to provide him a bed for the evening – and yet to see him stepping out in the Grand on the rare times he called the Buckingham home was one of the great joys of Raymond's life. Mentor and protégé, on the same ballroom floor; was anything ever as sweet?

'It had been my plan. I would have put in a call to Mr Charles. But then a certain rumour started to surface that put me in a rather thorny position. Could it be, I wondered, that Raymond de Guise had truly been . . . exiled from his ballroom?'

Raymond trembled. A week had passed since he walked out of the Buckingham, his head held high in defiance of all the eyes that bored into him. Defiance, even, of Nancy Nettleton – for who else could it have been to give up his secret, to let Maynard Charles know who he truly was?

Nancy, he thought, with such great pain. Alone in that Holborn lodging, he'd thought about her so many times. In his dreams they were dancing again, just the two of them in the little studio behind the ballroom.

After a time, when Raymond had not stopped quaking, Georges commanded him to look up – and Raymond, because inside he was still a lost little boy, did as he was told. There was something comforting in being back with Georges. Ever since he had followed him across the continent, Raymond had felt safe with him. *I would have followed him into Hell*, he thought, *just as long as Hell had a ballroom.*

'I've seen this malady before. You're in love, aren't you, boy?'

Raymond's trembling ceased as Georges' words took him by surprise – was it that obvious? He had hardly admitted it to himself.

'Yes, it's written all over you. You're in love and your head's hardly in the ballroom at all! You're in a spin, boy. But love will do that to a man. It isn't for nothing that the ancients used to call it a madness.'

Love, thought Raymond. How easy it was for Georges to read him! And yet . . .

'It's more than that, Georges. It's . . .'

How to describe it? If anyone in the world would understand, it would be Georges de la Motte. Georges had reinvented himself too. He too had cast off the expectations of his family to embrace the world of the ballroom. He too had tolerated the slurs from his brothers, the damage to his family's reputation. He too had drifted so far from them that, if ever he returned to the family estates, it was not as a prodigal son but as a stranger.

Georges leaned across the table and took Raymond's hand. 'Boy, you're suffering, aren't you?'

'I did fall in love, Georges. I know you warned me against it. A champion only has one love, and that's the love of the dance. But—'

'Tell me, boy, can *she* dance?'

'She has some talent,' said Raymond wistfully. 'Captured young, perhaps she might have danced. She is no Hélène. Her left leg holds her back, but she has . . . something special. Her body might never be a champion, but in her heart she knows music. I was ambushed, Georges, in the Midnight Rooms. They broke me. She's been helping put me back together. And now she's betrayed me.'

'Oh, Raymond,' Georges said tenderly, 'you're mixed up. Why the Midnight Rooms? You needn't go there. You're a greater dancer now.'

'I don't know if that's true,' he replied, and there was an air of genuine discomfort, real desperation in his voice. This was, Georges decided, about so much more than a girl. 'The dances there, they're . . . alive, Georges. They're changing and growing and *living* – so much more than any we perform in the ballroom. It reminds me of when I was a boy. Going to the Brancroft with my father, to the Vaudeville. I've been ignoring it for so long. And then . . . then there's Nancy. I spent so many years romancing the guests in the Grand. The princesses and duchesses and ladies of means. Then this summer my family sent me a letter. I met Nancy Nettleton. Everything changed. I thought I wanted to be Raymond de Guise, but . . .' Raymond hesitated. Then, he blurted out, 'Georges, what am I to do?'

'It's a conundrum, boy.' Georges touched his hand again, and it was enough to return Raymond to the scrawny little boy Ray Cohen used to be. It was good, he reflected, to have a father of sorts. To have somebody who understood. 'The last thing you must do is beg. Should you beg to return, you'll lose their respect. You will never have pride of place in the ballroom again unless they respect you – and unless you respect yourself.'

'Respect. Yes, that's it, Georges. I *don't* respect them. I can't. You've heard, of course, about Cable Street?' Georges' face paled at the mention of it, as if he was finally realising something about his protégé sitting in front of him. 'The British Union of Fascists marched through my old streets. They ransacked the place. My neighbours, my family, they went out to barricade the roads . . . and the police came at them with batons and truncheons and horses and fists. And only nights before, there I was, courting the same bastards in the Grand. Dancing for their pleasure, while they talked of driving people like *me* out of the country. Every night, I'm there in the ballroom. Lord Edgerton brings them in for exquisite dinners in the Queen Mary. They have the ear of Mr Baldwin and Mr Chamberlain and all of the rest – everyone who'd sell this country down the river, broker a peace with the worst of humankind. And me? I *dance* to smooth the path of their ambitions . . .'

Georges softly said, 'Politics has no place in the ballroom. You used to know this, Raymond.'

'Edgerton's turned the Buckingham into his own little embassy. Maynard Charles has rolled over and let him do it. German dignitaries fly in from Berlin and Munich to take meetings there. So many English aristocrats clamouring to take meetings with them. My brother fell upon the barricades. And all while I waltzed.'

Georges called Almira with his eyes, and she sashayed over to take his empty plate. Once she was gone, his blue eyes took in all of Raymond. 'I know your problem, Raymond. I can see which way you're pinned. The fact of the matter is you still haven't decided who you are. Raymond de Guise or that irascible young Ray Cohen I picked up off the barroom floor, so many years ago.'

Raymond drained his glass. Beads of red clung in the stubble which had grown freely, without care, in the days since he'd been banished. 'My heart says one thing, but sometimes my head says another. There are two worlds inside me. They're . . . getting closer.'

'If that is truly the case, Raymond,' de la Motte said, and for the first time there was a great sadness in his voice, 'then you're not a dancer at all – and all my work with you has been wasted. A dancer is in perfect alignment: head, heart, body and mind – it's all the same to the dancer. The dancer is whole. If you're not giving your entire being to it, you're not giving a thing. I know this more than any.'

'They have one of Edgerton's *connections* dancing the demonstrations now. He can't put one foot in front of another.'

'If that's the case, then the Grand is yours for the taking. Christmas is nearly upon you, Raymond. The masquerade at New Year. Without King Edward in the ballroom, well, Maynard Charles will need all the glamour he can find. He can't rely on somebody untested. He'll need the hotel in the society pages. He'll need to make the ball everything it was going to be and more. For that he'll need *you*. Why should the crown princess dance with anybody less?'

The King, thought Raymond. *I'd thought so little about the King. But Maynard Charles wouldn't have me in his ballroom, not after everything I said. Without the King, what is New Year at the Buckingham to be?*

Raymond pictured the ballroom at New Year, the dancers moving in formation, hidden behind their lavish masks. He imagined himself there on the dance floor, the starlight chandeliers glittering all around. There, on the balconies and tables around, stood the supposed great and good: the Queen of Norway, the crown princess, standing abreast with her benefactors and hosts. Lord Edgerton. Graf and Gräfin Schecht. Oliver White. Astors and Londonderrys and Sir Oswald Mosley himself.

How could you just stand by and let all that continue? How could you be a part of it? How could you care so wholeheartedly about dancing and not about any of this?

Under the table, Raymond's hands had turned into fists.

No. Whatever happens, whatever the fate of the Buckingham Hotel, no matter even what Georges believes, I cannot sit idly by . . . I am going to make them pay.

Chapter Twenty-six

THE GLITTERING LIGHTS OF THE chandeliers were like exploding stars. She gazed at them and the room spun and all was music and all was dance.

The ballroom might have been thronged, but Vivienne Edgerton was in a world apart. She knew some of the socialites were staring at her, but what did she care? Her lips were sweet and sticky from the cocktails they'd brought her. Her nose and throat burned from the powders she'd imbibed. She danced.

Then, suddenly, she was up and away. A pocket of time had been snatched from her. Where it had gone to, who knew? She heard someone calling her name and looked up to find herself in the great reception hall, gazing up at the enormous Norwegian fir, decorated with a thousand burning candles. The tree seemed to throb, growing bigger and then fading as she stared. She heard her name again, looked around and saw the faraway face of Mr Simenon considering her zealously from the reception desk. She gave him a dainty little wave, threw back her head –

– and then, suddenly, she was in the guest lift, draped over the arms of the attendant in his royal blue suit with golden brocade. He stood still as a statue, because to touch the daughter of Lord Edgerton was a crime punishable by immediate expulsion. She decided she would test it. She ran her arm up his arm. She touched the line of his jaw. She picked herself up, just enough that she might plant her lips on his unmoving cheek – and then she was in some other hallway. She could feel her heart pounding in her breast. She had a big heart, didn't she? She *did*. She knew that she did, because she could hear it drumming louder and louder and louder. So loud was it beating as she staggered up the hall – where was her suite? Wasn't she on the right floor? She raked her hands along the other doors as she stumbled along.

Then, the world turned again. This was her room. She was certain of it. She reeled around the four-poster, past the doors of the open armoire, and sank to her knees to upend the contents of the very bottom drawer in her dresser. Her heart was as loud as the oceans now. Its beating was all she could hear.

She threw the undergarments from her drawer aside. And there, at the bottom, her little vermillion pouch, the one she kept for nights just like these, where somehow she just couldn't get enough. Inside were two more little phials. She emptied both into the palm of her hand and, cupping it gently, lifted the powder to her face.

Her heart beat with the strength of a thousand thoroughbred horses. Then the world exploded in a fountain of colour and light.

Nancy awoke to discover she'd been crying in her sleep. In waking life you could be as strong and defiant as you were able, but in dreams . . . that was where you were exposed. She picked herself up and noticed the half-written Christmas letter she'd been composing for Frank.

This was to be her first Christmas without family around her. Frank's too. The first Christmas with their father gone. *And here*

I am. Miles from Frank. Miles from anywhere. The tinsel in the halls. The glass and paper angels. All of it was so beautiful, but none of it could compare to the decorations she and Frank made together every December.

What she wouldn't give now to get the ingredients together and make a batch of gingerbread with Frank. They were always his favourite. *Mine too. None of the Buckingham's finest confectioneries could ever compare.*

She could not forget the way Raymond had refused to look at her as he stormed out of the hotel, and she knew she never would. *What is the Buckingham, anyway, without him in it? What's a hotel without the people you love?* It felt empty.

Nancy reached for a rag and blew her nose, dabbed at her red eyes. *He's gone. He wasn't the man you thought he was anyway,* she told herself. *You came here alone. You can do it alone if you have to . . .*

Mrs Moffatt, Mrs Whitehead and the rest of the housekeeping crew would give her no quarter if she could not control her emotions. So she dressed quickly and rinsed the tears from her face, ready for breakfast.

After breakfast, Nancy turned out the stores on the first floor, filling the trolleys that the other girls marched off into the hotel interior, and – once she was done – she made haste to the fifth floor, where she was due to join Mrs Whitehead clearing out the Pacific and Continental suites. Mrs Whitehead was already half-finished polishing the brass rails of the bedstead in the Pacific when Nancy arrived.

'You might turn to the Continental,' she began, now standing on the tips of her toes to run her feather duster over the French armoire. 'The Holsteins should have already landed.'

Nancy nodded and, giving a curtsey as she turned, she returned to the hallway.

The Continental was one of the Buckingham's finest: a long barrel of a suite, with the bedroom at its apex, a half-moon lounge and a second separate study – or dressing chamber, as the occupants directed – off to one side. Consequently, preparing it for new guests often felt a Herculean task. But Nancy didn't mind. A singular task like this was one you could lose yourself in; hours might whistle by as she took care of its every nook and cranny, distracting her from all that was on her troubled mind.

Over a week had passed and there had been no word of Raymond. Only the whispers in the kitchenette at night. Only the abhorrent silence in the ballroom. Only the rumour that Rosa said she'd heard from a guest who'd heard it from a dancer down in the ballroom: *Raymond de Guise was a blackguard. They say he was bedding some poor kitchen girl and ran out on her when the management found out . . .*

She was approaching the Continental when she saw the door to one of the neighbouring rooms left hanging ajar. Chambermaids were taught that their presence in the Buckingham was not to be detected, that – for better or worse – they were to leave everything apparently untouched, no matter how unsavoury it might seem. Rosa had a story about a book of French postcards she'd observed in the suite of Elizabeth Enache, the Romanian countess who frequented in the summer season – every one of them detailing, without any shame, the beauty of a certain lady dancer from Constantinople. Almost everyone who'd worked at the Buckingham for long enough had seen something to make them blush, but the rule was simple: 'You were never there, girls,' Mrs Moffatt would say, with a nod and a wink.

Nancy had almost passed the door when she smelt the pungent tang of vomit in the air. Not even the collection of vinegars and polishes on her trolley were enough to eclipse that ripe scent.

Stay invisible! the voice in her head kept imploring her.

But Nancy opened the door to Vivienne Edgerton's suite.

The figure lying slumped on the floor at the side of the bed was none other than Vivienne Edgerton herself. Nancy rushed to her side. Perhaps she'd rolled out of bed in the night – but, as soon as she dropped to the carpet to rouse her, she knew it was more than that. The carpet was sticky with whatever Vivienne had thrown up the night before; her face was caked in orange and red. Her skin beneath was a ghostly white – and, though it barely showed through the smudged Tangee lipstick that she wore, her lips were shrivelled and paling to blue.

'Vivienne?' Nancy whispered, forgetting herself. 'Miss Edgerton?'

There was no reply. Nancy dared to touch her hair, brushing it away from her face. The girl was breathing; it was only faint but at least it convinced Nancy that she was still alive. She remembered her father. She'd found him like this once as well, the bottle of pills from the doctor half-empty at his side. The memory of it was almost as powerful a trauma as discovering him that April morning: the early spring sunshine tumbling through the window, and her father lying prone in a pool of his own filth. That had been the day she convinced him: no more. No matter what the pain, no matter what the distress, no more whisky . . . and no more dependence on laudanum.

It was as she was having this thought that she noticed the lavender purse on the carpet, itself caked in Miss Edgerton's mess. Her eyes drifted to it. The drawstring was open and, in its mouth, was a tiny glass phial. A residue remained inside: white and crystalline, like finely ground sugar, slightly discoloured with age.

'Oh, Miss Edgerton,' she whispered, 'what have you done?'

Something seized Nancy. She opened Vivienne's eyes one after another. She lifted her head, as if to open the way to her lungs. Nancy was no nurse, but she knew enough. She'd administered enough to her father in those dying weeks and months – medicines and stern talking-tos, and all the love in the world, anything to keep him dignified and alive. 'Miss Edgerton!' she called, her voice rising in pitch, 'Miss Edgerton, can you hear me?'

She pinched her cheeks urgently. Vivienne did not wake. Blood rushed to the place where her fingertips had been. *That's good*, thought Nancy. *At least her body can answer – even if Vivienne herself cannot.*

'Vivienne!' she called again. 'Miss Edgerton, I'm going to . . .'

She lifted Vivienne's head, brought it to her lap. In the same moment, Vivienne's body bucked. A single convulsion ran through the girl and erupted out of her throat. Bile was all that was left inside her. It splattered Nancy's smart apron.

Vivienne opened her eyes a fraction.

'It's going to be all right,' Nancy said, brushing her hair out of the smears on her face. 'Miss Edgerton, you've done the most foolish thing – but it's going to be all right. I'm going to get you help. Can you hear me, Vivienne?' She remembered herself, remembered her place. '*Miss Edgerton*, are you there?'

Nancy looked up and called out: 'Mrs Whitehead!'

Mrs Whitehead appeared, imperious, in the doorway. Upon seeing Vivienne Edgerton lying prone in Nancy's arms, her face twisted. 'Get up, girl,' she said. 'Quickly now!'

'No,' said Nancy – and was surprised to hear the boldness in her own voice. She caught herself, just in time. 'I'm sorry, Mrs Whitehead, but no – she needs a doctor, now, and he needs to come *here*. We can't move her, not until we know . . . She'll need water, and she needs warm towels, and she needs a hotel doctor *now*. Mrs Whitehead, I need you to fetch them.'

For a moment, Mrs Whitehead was frozen, aghast at the audacity of the chambermaid ordering her – gentlewoman, overseer, manageress – around. Then something changed. Mrs Whitehead saw the fire in Nancy's eyes, and stepped backwards out of the door.

'Stay with her, Miss Nettleton,' she breathed, and hurried back along the hall.

In the bedchamber, Nancy cradled Vivienne Edgerton's head. 'You're going to be fine,' she said. 'You *are* going to be fine,' she repeated. But Vivienne only rolled her head, retching again into Nancy's lap.

The door to Maynard Charles's office opened and Nancy nervously walked through. She had often seen the hotel director from afar. He was a corpulent fellow, the sort of indulgent man who might quickly have perished if he'd lived the same life as her father, but here in the Buckingham his rounded tummy and second chin gave him the air of a leader. In the office he was standing behind his desk, with his hands folded behind his back and his belly straining at his simple black waistcoat. By his eyes, Nancy took him for a wearied man.

'Thank you for waiting, Miss Nettleton. If you'd like to take a seat, Mr Simenon here will provide us with a pot of tea.' The head concierge, who had been lurking solemnly in the corner, turned on his heel to do as Mr Charles instructed. 'Bring the girl some sugar too, Mr Simenon. She has had quite an experience.'

There seemed a sickly pallor around Mr Simenon too. He looked over his shoulder as he left, as if to consider Nancy more closely, and then closed the door.

Mr Charles came to sit beside her. She should not have been anxious to be seated beside the hotel director – she was not some foolish little girl! – but the shock of the morning was indeed working its way out of her system. She shivered.

'You're not in trouble, my dear. I asked you to come here because I am very grateful for your service. What you did today may have been the difference between life and death for Miss Edgerton, and it does not go unnoticed.'

Nancy wanted to say that she hadn't done very much. It was by sheer accident that she'd found her. The rest – sitting with her until the doctor came, wetting her lips with water from the hem of her dress, reaching into her mouth to stop her tongue from rolling back and choking her – had been instinct.

'Is she going to be all right, Mr Charles?'

'The doctors are confident of it. Vivienne had overindulged in the ballroom last night. She has been a very foolish girl, but she will live. Whether or not she may live with the humiliation is, of course, a very different matter. And that, in a roundabout way, is why I asked Mrs Moffatt to bring you here, Nancy.'

At this moment Mr Simenon reappeared and, clearly finding it beneath him to act as a waiter, proceeded to pour tea begrudgingly for Nancy and Mr Charles. Then he resumed his place in the corner.

'Nancy, the Buckingham is in your debt. We will be in your debt further if you might do us another little service. I promise it won't take any of your time.'

Haltingly, Nancy asked, 'What is it, Mr Charles?'

'This has been a delicate business. You must know, already, how rumours can spread and change in a place like our hotel. I was here for the Spanish influenza, Nancy, and not even that sickness, vile as it was, was as virulent as a rumour in our Buckingham halls. I should like it, my dear, if you were to keep Miss Edgerton's little indiscretion between ourselves.'

She felt herself compelled to nod – the weight of expectation in the room was palpable.

Mr Charles's eyes were on her and they seemed so exacting. 'Of course,' she said, floundering for words.

Then she hesitated.

'Mr Charles, if I may . . .' *Nancy,* she thought, *what are you doing?* But the words came out of her anyway. She noted the way Mr Charles flinched as he nodded. 'I would never gossip about Miss Edgerton. But . . . Forgive me for speaking out of turn, Mr Charles, but what happened to Miss Edgerton, it isn't the sort of thing you can just sweep under the carpet. I've seen this kind of thing once before. My father *needed* his medicines too. He needed them so much he could have killed himself. And that's what Vivienne Edgerton will do, if she isn't helped. She needs a friend. She needs a chaperone. If she doesn't have those things, why, she'll . . .'

Mr Charles raised a hand, and Nancy fell suddenly silent. 'I am aware of Miss Edgerton's predicament, Nancy. I have been managing it for some time.'

'Managing it?' Nancy gasped. 'Sir, that's *allowing* it. She's . . .' Nancy didn't stop to think; the words were out before she even knew. 'She's a human being. She doesn't need managing. She needs to be *cared* for. Yes, that's it. She needs somebody to love her enough to not let her harm herself. Hasn't anyone asked where Nathaniel White was last night?'

Mr Charles's face was a mask. His nostrils flared and his face seemed to turn in on itself as he contained an outburst. *She doesn't understand,* he told himself. *Why would she? What could she possibly know about scandal and reputation? How much of our livelihood depends on us quashing the former to defend the latter. We're already to be without a king this New Year. Must we also be a cesspit of scandal as well?*

'Your concerns are noted, Nancy. But what happens next is none of your concern. I asked you here this afternoon to make this very clear. What happened to Miss Edgerton was an accident, pure and simple. She fell. She caught a fever. She is now indisposed. Only a handful of souls know otherwise, and were it to become common knowledge in this hotel, why, I believe I would know where to look. Don't you?'

Nancy stood, shivering. *You silly girl, you shouldn't have spoken out of turn.* 'Yes, sir,' she whispered.

'You will receive an extra week's wages this month in return for good deeds rendered.'

As she left, Nancy stopped in the doorway. 'I didn't do it for reward, sir.'

'Indeed not. But moments like this deserve recognition, do they not?'

After Nancy was gone, Maynard Charles gave a muted roar of fury, slamming his closed fist into his desk. 'She's right, of course,' he said to Mr Simenon – who stepped again out of the shadows in the corner of the office. 'Vivienne will do it over and again, until one day she isn't fortunate enough to be found by some passing chambermaid. And then where are we? At her stepfather's mercy, and all of us banished from the Buckingham. New Year is coming. Christmas is already here. That chambermaid speaks more sense than the rest of us combined.'

'Mr Charles, don't blame yourself. I—'

'I'm not blaming myself,' Maynard Charles snapped. 'I'm blaming whoever's helping her. A girl like Vivienne doesn't have the wherewithal to do this herself. Somebody is supplying her. Someone's trading for her in *my* hotel.'

Mr Simenon looked guiltily to the ground. 'Mr Charles, surely nobody here would dare do such a thing? Lord Edgerton is the head of our board—'

'When I find them, I'll string them up. This hotel is my life's work. I won't have it ruined by one foolish girl and her weaknesses. The girl is to receive no more packages, Mr Simenon, not without you or I having intercepted them first. Find him for me, Mr Simenon. Whoever is corrupting her, whoever is helping her kill herself – and all for a few measly pounds – find them and bring them to me. I don't care how Vivienne Edgerton wants to ruin her life – but she won't do it at the cost of the rest of us. She won't bring *my Buckingham* down.'

Mr Simenon let Maynard Charles's words wash over him. Though Maynard Charles did not see it, his ordinarily pallid cheeks were suddenly flushed full of blood. Sweat beaded on his brow as he tried desperately to work through all the permutations of what might happen were Vivienne Edgerton to tell anyone where she *really* got her secret packages from. He worked a finger under his collar, trying hard not to betray his guilt.

Then, with a sinking feeling, he said, 'I'll find them, Mr Charles. Whoever's doing this, we'll stop it now . . . before it's the ruin of us all.'

Night had fallen across London, bringing with it fresh falls of snow. The long barrel of Cable Street was criss-crossed by the footprints of tradesmen and drunks on their way home. A lone fox darted between the upturned rubbish pails, its eyes aglow.

The knock came at midnight. Alma Cohen was the first to hear it. She turned over in the bed she'd once shared with her husband Stanley, and some instinct still made her reach out for him. A knock in the middle of the night only meant one thing. Bad news. She kept an old skillet at the side of her bed for nights like these.

She was coming through the bedroom door when she crashed into her son Artie walking along the hall. 'I'll see to this, Ma,' he said. 'You get your beauty sleep. It's cold enough to freeze your knackers off out there.'

'Artie!'

'Sorry, Ma, but you've heard worse. Look, I'll deal with this. I'm the man of this house, ain't I?'

'You're not in trouble again, are you, Artie?'

If only I was, thought Artie as he tramped down the stairs. *Then I might be making us Cohens some money . . .*

Downstairs, the knocking grew in intensity. Artie braced himself, ready to deal somebody a fist of his own for having the temerity to wake his mother in the middle of the night, and opened the door.

His brother stood there, in the swirling snow of the night.

'*You*,' Artie growled.

Ray Cohen held up his hands. 'I'm not here to fight with you, Artie. I'm here to give you what you want. I can't dance for them any more. I can't stand up and dance for everything that's wrong in the world. I want to . . . what would Dad have called it? Even the scales? Redress the balance?' Ray paused, a fringe of white forming on his wild black hair. 'Get your overcoat, Artie. This night's as good as any.'

Chapter Twenty-seven

THE TWO FIGURES WHO TRAMPED through the snow of Berkeley Square were careful to stick to the shadows at the edges of the townhouses, half-cloaked by the black iron railings and tall privet hedges of the Mayfair elite. In the shadow of the Buckingham, its ornate copper crown now capped in white, they stopped and gazed up.

Raymond urged Artie up the square and down the narrow alley of Michaelmas Mews. The cobbles here were glazed in yet more white, the railings turned to spears of ice on either side. Artie's blood was getting up – but this was one enterprise in which Artie, no matter how talented he was in the subtle arts of breaking and entering, could not take charge.

At first, Artie had not known what to think when he had opened the door to his brother in the dead of night. It had taken Raymond some time to talk him around, to tell him that he was wrong, that he'd always been wrong – that when he'd said that the Grand was a world apart from the Buckingham Hotel and all its politicians and appeasers and fascists, its industrialists and aristocrats with money enough to solve the world's problems if only they *cared*, he was fooling himself. The Grand bred them, he realised now. The Buckingham attracted the very same people who would march on Cable Street and face his family down. This was not right. The life Ray Cohen had been living was *not right*. The gilded Mayfair world was one they could never hope to bring down or change – but they could take a little from it, chip away at the beast. Grand victories like Cable Street shook the world, but the little ones still counted.

But there was to be no breaking and entering tonight. The staff entrance was open at all hours, and all Raymond needed to do was perform a little distraction to get them inside. As they approached, he took Artie by the shoulder and told him to slow down. 'A fine burglar you are,' he said. 'You creep around like you're not supposed to be here.'

'I'm *not* supposed to be here.'

'Neither of us are, but we may as well act the part.'

Raymond pushed open the tradesman's door. Inside, one of the porters – a lad who lived above the Exmouth markets – was slumped in a chair, reading from one of the high-and-mighty periodicals that were scattered liberally around the hotel lounges. Startled, he looked up – and Raymond saw that he had been close to sleep. His eyes were heavy and his bottom lip shimmered where he had started to drool. Embarrassment took hold of the lad and he straightened himself. 'Mr de Guise, I know what you was thinking, but I wasn't nodding off, sir. I was just . . .'

Raymond put on his best ballroom smile. He had come dressed in his evening suit and gentleman's frock coat for this very reason. 'You can close your eyes on my account. But don't let the old man find you, it would be more than your job's worth. Still up and wandering the halls, is he?' He winked.

The boy checked the clock ticking on the wall. Its hands were inching towards 2 a.m. 'Mr Charles retired half an hour ago,' he said. 'Did his final circuit and then off to bed.'

'And you're on until dawn?' Raymond's eyes found the mug of tea sitting half-empty at his side. 'I'll wager that's stone cold, is it?'

The boy nodded.

'And it's a long winter night.'

'Six days until Christmas. My folks are travelling out west today. We have an aunt in Cornwall. I'm to follow, but not until Christmas Eve. They booked me on a train. I never took a train on my own, Mr de Guise.'

Raymond clapped a hand on the boy's shoulder. 'Go and make yourself more tea. Make yourself a whole pot. It's cold down here. Don't worry, boy. I'll look after the door while you're gone.'

The boy's face creased. 'You'd do that for me, Mr de Guise?'

'I'm not one of those who think they're better than you. But hurry – it's late enough as it is. It's time for my bed.'

After the boy was gone, Raymond opened the door for a frozen Artie and bustled him through.

'I thought you said you was banished?'

'Maybe the story hasn't got around to the porters. Who knows? But Artie, we haven't got much time.'

Raymond shepherded Artie through the interior door, directing him to one of the housekeeping stores where he waited in darkness for Raymond to return. With the boy back sitting slumped at the door, his hands wrapped around a steaming hot cup of tea, Raymond pulled Artie back out and together they headed up and out of the housekeeping hall.

This wasn't robbery like any Raymond had ever known. This was more like their Aunt May with her fingers in the till at the butchers where she cleaned on Friday mornings. *An inside job.* For a moment his resolve wavered. The Buckingham had been his home, his sanctuary, for so long; he had made so many happy memories within these walls. But, he thought, his heart hardening, that had all changed. This was not the place he had known – the Buckingham had turned on him and others like him. There were people here who were the very worst of human kind, and there were those who stood idly by while evil took hold in these halls, in *his* ballroom. And that hurt like a knife to the ribs.

The reception hall, rich with the fragrant scent of the Norwegian fir, was empty at this time of night. One of the hotel pages appeared, then disappeared just as quickly. Raymond and Artie lingered in the hallway behind the lifts, peeking out only to see one of the night managers poring over his ledger, then pacing back and forth. On occasion he disappeared through a door, to make some phone call or cross-reference some other ledger – and it was in one of these lulls that Raymond took Artie by the arm and marched him behind the vast sweep of the reception desk itself. Here another door led down to the bookkeeper's office and the door of the hotel director's office beyond.

Raymond looked up the barrel of the corridor. He reached for the door handle. Of course it was locked.

'Do your thing, Artie.'

Artie dropped to his knees. In a pouch on his belt, buried beneath his woollen coat, was a set of their father's tools. He splayed open the bag and withdrew a series of narrow metal picks, each with a tiny barb at the end.

'It's all in here, is it?'

'I said it was, didn't I?' said Raymond. 'Just hurry up . . .'

It was the work of a moment to pick the lock. Artie swept up his tools and together the Cohen brothers tumbled through, pulling the door quietly closed behind them.

The office looked small in the dark. Raymond fumbled to light the lamp on Maynard Charles's desk. Good Lord, the man was idiosyncratic. All of his pencils were arranged in a perfect row. His folders stood to attention on the deep walnut shelves that lined every wall. On the desk was a photograph, framed in silver, of some old army battalion; another image – of some army base or barracks – was scrawled with the signatures of a dozen men.

'Well?' said Artie.

Raymond heaved Maynard Charles's desk aside, revealing the little safe built into the brickwork behind it. Maynard ought to have been more careful; the thing had practically dangled open the last time Raymond marched in here. 'It's where he keeps the crown jewels—'

'What are you talking about, Ray?'

'When there's royalty in, and Hélène's to dance with some prince of the realm or other, he dresses her up in the Buckingham's finest. This world, Artie, it's all about appearances. You can't dance with a nobleman unless you're dressed like a noble lady. That means diamonds. It means silver and gold. At the masquerade ball this New Year, he'd light Hélène up in it, make her shine like a star. All so that Edgerton's dogs can ogle her all night. Well, not this year, Mr Charles. Your fascist dogs will have to look elsewhere.' He paused. 'You think you can handle it, Artie?'

'You might be a master in the ballroom, Ray, but I've got my own talents too.'

'Then quick to it. The faster we're out of here, the better . . .'

'Why don't you rough some stuff up, Ray?' Artie said, pushing past and dropping to the floor to investigate the safe.

'On what grounds?'

'It isn't a robbery if you don't rough the place up. Stands to reason.'

Raymond shook his head, but couldn't suppress the grin that spread across his face. 'And you wonder why you spent so many years locked up, Artie? Have a little class. If they don't know we've been here at all, it's the highest form of robbery there is. You wouldn't know a little elegance if it looked you in the face.'

Artie threw Raymond a wolfish grin. 'You still got that sharp tongue o' yours, Ray. They haven't completely turned you into a gent up here.' He laughed. 'It's good to have you back.'

As Artie set to work, Raymond paced the room. *Yes,* he thought. *This is . . . right.* His doubts melted away now. *Look at these plaques on the wall. The rewards for service. The golden carriage clock, a gift of the hotel board – the same board populated by Edgerton, by Astor, by poisonous, dangerous men just like them.*

You're their servant, Maynard. Taking their coin. Well, tonight that ends. And tomorrow there'll be some richer tradesmen in the East End. Anyone whose son or daughter or brother or wife was roughed up on Cable Street. Anyone who's had to struggle to survive while here we dined on venison and pheasant and caviar and champagne. There are going to be some lucky people at home tomorrow . . .

Something clicked. Artie was hunched over the open safe.

'I thought you said there was jewels in this?' Artie was frozen. '*Papers?* Ray, you stupid fool, you've had us come all this way, risk all of *this*, for . . . papers?' Artie turned around to his brother. In his hands, where there should have been the glittering necklace Hélène wore each New Year night, the pearls that would have hung in her ears and the charms that would have dangled from the bracelets on her wrist, there were bundles of paper tied up in string, and yet more tucked inside a brown leather folder.

Papers? thought Raymond. *But where are the pearls, the brooches, the diamonds . . . What use are papers? What could papers possibly be worth?*

Raymond was about to take them from his brother's hands – but another noise stopped him dead: the telltale of rat-a-tat knuckles being rapped on a door.

Raymond spun.

A familiar voice came from the other side. 'Mr Charles, is that you?'

Mr Simenon. Raymond cringed.

'Mr Charles?' The knuckles rapped again – and now, to Raymond's horror, he could see the door handle vibrate where, from outside, Mr Simenon's hand had fallen upon it. 'Mr Charles, it's one thing for us mere minions to be up at every hour, seeing to the bidding of our guests, but . . . the days when you'd have to stay up all night, every night, just to make sure the hotel woke up in the morning – aren't they over, Mr Charles? Mr Charles?'

Raymond and Artie exchanged a look, but before either one of them whispered a word, another noise silenced them both: the click of a key turned in a lock.

'Mr Charles, are you really asleep at your desk again?'

Instinctively, Raymond lurched forward – but the door was opening, too far away for him to force it shut – and there, in the doorway, appeared the sallow face of Mr Simenon. The jaw dropped. The eyes widened. 'Raymond de Guise,' Mr Simenon breathed, 'what is the meaning of . . . ?'

Then his eyes took in the rest of the room: Mr Charles's desk heaved out of its place; the man on the floor behind it; the safe in the wall, its door hanging open . . .

Think, Raymond! THINK! He knows you're expelled from the Buckingham but he doesn't know who you really are . . .

'Mr Simenon,' Raymond began, adopting his old airs, 'let me explain.'

But whatever Raymond would have said next was lost. The door slammed shut, Mr Simenon behind it. Raymond leaped forward – but then came the telltale click again, as a key was forced into the lock from outside. Raymond heaved at the handle, but the door held fast. Then he heard the clatter of panicked footsteps retreating, as Mr Simenon fled up the hall.

Artie scrambled to his feet. 'Ray, you bloody fool.'

Together the brothers threw themselves at the door.

'But you can pick the lock, can't you? We got in that way. You can—'

Artie barged him with his shoulder, gathered up his tools. 'Out of my way, Ray. You got us into this mess – and for what? some *papers*! I guess it's up to me to get us out.'

As Artie needled in the lock, Raymond stepped back, ran his fingers desperately through his hair. The office windows looked out onto the delivery yard behind. If they could get out that way, then perhaps . . .

He lifted a paperweight from Mr Charles's desk. They knew it was him now, of course. They could come looking. But Raymond had reinvented himself once before. He could do it again.

Artie's fingers trembled as he tried to force the lock. Something wouldn't give. 'He's left the bloody keys in,' he roared. 'If I can only . . .'

Artie's voice fell dead. Raymond turned slowly around, dropping the paperweight from his hand. 'What is it?' he whispered.

'Don't you hear?' said Artie, cocking his head. 'Footsteps. There's two of them now. But we can take two, can't we? Us Cohen boys. Don't you remember the Wellhorn Yard in '25? Me and you, and those Darling boys from down in Limehouse. Come to take off with those railway sleepers – and we saw 'em off, didn't we, me and you together? There's nothing that can stop us if we fight together. Besides, I fought more bastards than this on Cable Street – and that was on my own . . .' Artie leaped to his feet as his tools clattered all around. 'Back to back, Ray – just like in the old days. I'm not . . . I'm *not* going down again.'

Outside the door, the footsteps tolled. Raymond lifted his hands, clenched into fists. 'You're not going anywhere, Artie. Let me do the talking.'

'Talking? . . . *Talking?*' Artie repeated, as if he'd never heard a more ridiculous thing. 'There isn't going to be any talking, Ray. Talking's the—'

The door flew open.

Artie staggered forward. Lurching into the open door, he was quickly stopped short – for there was Maynard Charles himself, a broad barrel of a man, his evening jacket heaved shut over a dressing gown of burgundy and gold. Behind him stood Mr Simenon. Artie was driven back inside.

Maynard Charles's eyes looked past Artie, to where Raymond was standing. 'Good Lord, de Guise! What in the name of all that's holy do you think—?'

Raymond could only look on in horror as Artie took his chance. Noble fighters lost every time. Bringing his fist back, he swung right. Maynard Charles saw it early – but it had always been a feint. Artie swung past him, wrenched his body up and threw himself into Maynard Charles as he sought to retreat. The older man staggered backwards, leaving only the beanpole Mr Simenon in the door. Buoyed up, Artie threw himself directly forward. It took only a fraction of a second to realise that Simenon was no fighting man. He was almost stepping aside as Artie threw a punch – this one for real. His knuckles piled hard into Mr Simenon's chin, snapping his head around. The shock of it was all Artie needed. In moments he was through the door and away.

Maynard Charles picked himself up from the floor. 'Well,' he roared, 'after him!' But in the end, it was Maynard Charles himself who gave chase.

Artie Cohen had already erupted from the passageway, vaulted over the reception desk and was loping past the Norwegian fir by the time Maynard Charles burst into the reception hall. A gentleman guest and his lover, elegant in a sapphire gown bedecked with pearls of preposterous size, looked aghast as the ruffian launched himself into the revolving doors, then disappeared into the ribbons of snow still curling down.

Maynard Charles lingered on the hotel threshold. Through the glass, the night doorman mouthed the words, 'Is everything well, sir?', but Maynard Charles uttered nothing in reply. Instead, he turned on his heel, took a deep breath, and stomped back to his office.

Raymond was waiting, the panic pulsing through his veins, when Maynard Charles reappeared and dismissed Mr Simenon with a single, unutterable bark. The look on the hotel director's face was one that could only be classified as 'dignified scorn'. He ignored Raymond's stance, pulled out the chair from his desk and, swivelling it around, proffered it to his 'guest'.

'The open position is not a fighting stance, Ray. Let's stop pretending you're still a street fighter, shall we? You gave it up long ago, in exchange for your dancing shoes, and there's no going back.' When Raymond did not move, Maynard Charles shrugged, took the seat himself, and directed Raymond to one of the hard wooden stools on the edge of the room. 'I can summon the Metropolitan Police. But neither of us would enjoy the scandal, would we? So let's try something else, Raymond . . . and *talk*.'

Raymond dropped his fists. Maynard Charles was right; just because he'd been clenching his fists did not mean his heart was in the fight. Reluctantly, he sat.

'Care to explain what you're doing here, Raymond? Or should I make some assumptions?'

'Assume away, Maynard. You people always do.'

'Dragged one of your old "mates" along for a little petty revenge, is that it?'

'My brother—'

'Oh, I see,' said Maynard, a nasty glimmer in his eye. 'Back in the family trade, then?'

'Don't *you* judge my family, Maynard. My brother stood up to your facist friends on Cable Street. And that was just the beginning . . . So, what are you going to do with me, Maynard? There's a telephone right there. If you're going to do it, do it.'

Maynard stood, made certain the door was closed and that Mr Simenon no longer lurked outside, and marched back to his seat.

'Believe it or not, I am glad that you came here tonight. Not glad, perhaps, that you've seen fit to rifle through this office's safe, but glad because . . . Well, we'll get to that. First things first. If you are to continue looking at me in that baleful manner, this situation will end now. If you want to be treated as the gentleman you've pretended to be all these years, why, you can start acting like it. Understand?'

Raymond resisted as long as he could. Then his lips curled and he spat, 'At least I'll admit to my pretence. You just sit there, pretending to be a good upstanding citizen, and all the while eating out of the lap of those union bastards—'

Maynard Charles shook his head sadly. 'You see, *this* is why I'm glad you're here. I have wanted to explain ever since I banished you from these halls.'

'What's to explain? Lord Edgerton says jump, so you jump. Nathaniel White wants to dance in my ballroom, and he gets to. We've been entertaining these brigands for years. Don't you *know* what's going on outside – in London, in England, in Europe? Don't you *ever* look beyond your precious hotel walls? Fascists on the rise everywhere – even on your own city streets. And the Buckingham gives them a home. Artie and I came here tonight to teach you a lesson – to take what you have here in your perfect little world, and give it to them who need it. Those curs invaded *our* homes. Well, *we* can invade yours—'

'Listen to yourself. You're cleverer than this, if only you'd stop and think. I want you to listen carefully, Raymond, because I will say this once. If any of this is repeated beyond these walls – even to that reprobate brother of yours, wherever he's gone – I shall have no choice but to report this to the police – and, when I do, the ruse of Raymond de Guise will forever be exposed. Everything you accomplished. All the championships and victories you won. All the lives you touched with your dancing. Your secret will come out. Yes, the Buckingham will suffer. And, yes, I shall likely lose my livelihood. But it is what I shall do, if the occasion demands it. Do you understand me, Raymond?'

Raymond. At least he still calls me by my chosen name. That has to mean something.

'I understand.'

'There is a reason I cannot simply eject Nathaniel White from the ballroom, and it is not – as you seem to think – my slavish devotion to Lord Edgerton and his friends in the British Union of Fascists. White is here under their patronage, yes, but it remains *my* ballroom and my hotel. It may take a little *management*, yes, and sometimes members of the board – Lord Edgerton included – demand a little persuasion. But I have not lasted near twenty years in charge of an institution as vast as the Buckingham Hotel without learning how to get the very best.

'Nathaniel White is here because *I* want him here. I want him here because his family want him here. It *is* in my interests to please these people, Raymond, but not in the way you have imagined. Here. It is, perhaps, best if I show you . . .'

Maynard turned to crouch down at the safe and, cursing under his breath at the broken mechanism, lifted out the bundles of papers inside.

'I haven't used this safe to store the Buckingham's jewels for two whole years, Raymond. I've needed this space for something so much more valuable.'

Peeling off the first page, he handed it to Raymond.

8 September 1936

Graf Schecht in Queen Mary, 8 p.m. Duck breast and port sauce.

Graf Schecht invites Lord Edgerton and wife to the family townhouse in Munich. Charles Londonderry is to be in attendance. Graf Schecht believes that, if enough of London's aristocrat class are sympathetic to the aims of Mr Hitler's government, they can successfully persuade the Right Hon. Mr Baldwin to agree formal peaceful terms.

14 October 1936

Lord Edgerton is in attendance in the ballroom and invites Dr Bernhard Weber, new attaché at the German embassy, to drinks in the Candlelight Club. Weber and Edgerton are later joined by Mr Oswald Mosley of the British Union of Fascists. Mr Mosley impresses upon Weber that a pact between the British Crown and the National Socialists in Germany can be effected. Gossip indicates a pact will soon be formalised between Germany and Italy. Weber suggests this be seen as a model for how an agreement might be worked between Great Britain and her German cousins. Would the King not be amenable? Weber asks. Lord Edgerton is certain he would and, by the end of the evening, has promised to send an invitation to the King via his private secretary.

3 November 1936

Felix Kraus (of Kruger-Kraus Holdings) dines in the Queen Mary. Mr Chamberlain's personal secretary

Frederick Dunn is in attendance. Kraus passes a 'belated anniversary' card to Dunn for transference to Mr Chamberlain. Message intercepted in hotel post room: an invitation to high tea at the German Embassy.

30 November 1936

Dr Weber dines with German nationals, Herr and Frau Mayer. Herr Mayer's son is liaison to the Hitler Youth movement (see papers filed June 1935). Current estimates membership of five million boys of good German stock. Conversation recorded is only partial – my boy feared he had been caught eavesdropping – but understanding is that, before Christmas, membership of the Youth will be compulsory to all true-blooded German boys. No Jews or so-called 'inferior races' are permitted membership. All Youth will be trained in arms. FIVE MILLION German boys are being trained as basic-level soldiers. Sirs, Nazi Germany is not only rearming. It is CONSCRIPTING.

Raymond's eyes drifted up from the pages, each of them typewritten and initialled in the corner with two florid letters: MC. *Maynard Charles*.

'What are these?' he whispered.

'I need Lord Edgerton's set in the Buckingham as often as possible, Raymond. *That's* why I don't object to Nathaniel White strutting around our ballroom as if he owns it. Not because I'm desperate to please our lord. Because I'm—'

Raymond uttered, 'You're a . . . spy.'

'Not a spy,' said Maynard Charles, and for the first time he seemed agitated. 'I dislike the word. It conjures up so much slipperiness. And I am as straight and by-the-book as they come. But, yes, ever since Lord Edgerton took majority control of the board, I have been collecting ... intelligence, you might say. Things overheard. Things whispered in the privacy of our hotel. Lord Edgerton knows many men of interest – not just his union friends, the Astors, the Londonderrys, but all of his associates from the continent. When they come to our hotel, it is my obligation – no, my responsibility – to *listen*. In some small part, because of the intelligence I have gathered in this hotel, the British Security Service were forewarned of the Nazis marching back into the Rhineland in March – enough time for them to get their agents out of there. Because of the "gossip" I have collated from our dining rooms and Candlelight Club, and combined, one can only assume, with that of my counterparts in other institutions, we are aware of a plot within the Establishment itself to broker terms with Herr Hitler as soon as the political class allows. This might look like it's merely a luxury hotel, but it is, in fact, an open front in a war we are fighting – a war which, if we are not good enough, may yet consume us all. So when you call me a fascist dog, Mr de Guise, I am at once proud that my deceptions have gone undetected – and filled with rage. For I am anything but.'

Raymond had so few words. He opened his mouth but all that he could say was, 'I thought you were just a money man.'

Maynard Charles decided to take this in the good humour in which it was almost certainly not intended. 'I'll take that as a compliment. I am, as you say, a money man, Raymond – but it is not *all* that I am. I have my values too. I have my private life to protect.' It was the first moment he'd shown any vulnerability; his voice trembled, until he conquered himself once more and his reserve returned. 'You must understand this dangerous business, Raymond. I don't tell you it lightly. I shouldn't tell you it at all. Yet, when you stormed in here and accused me of lying down in bed with the very worst in this world, well, something in me snapped. You're too young to have fought in the Great War, Raymond, but I am not. I spent myself in Flanders and France. I bled into the earth and watched my boyhood friends tumble, one after another. I won't see it again. Lord Edgerton and his ilk, they're manoeuvring towards a kind of peace. They think there are terms we can come to that might stop Mr Hitler landing his soldiers on English beaches. If the right ministers can be put into the right positions, if the men on the street can be whipped up into wanting it – why, we might have Mr Hitler taking tea with the King on the lawns at Buckingham Palace. They'd sell my country – *our* country – to the worst of all men. The way they see it, there'd be no war at all – because it would be over before it even began.' Maynard paused. 'It's happening, even now. English aristocrats flock to Berlin to meet their German cousins. Even King Edward of old might have been swayed. But an England united with that host across the water? The cost of it is too much to bear.'

'So you sell their secrets . . .'

'Their secrets belong to the Buckingham. They are mine to sell, should I choose. I am doing what little I can, Raymond. But the Great War enveloped us all and so will a new war, if it comes to pass. I would not see my life ruined twice over. I am still fighting *my war* – but I'm fighting it in a different way, the only way I know how. I will have peace, Raymond. I won't see a generation slaughtered again.'

'You'd be fired if they found out.'

'Worse, Raymond. Much worse. That is why they must never find out. It is not just my livelihood at stake. The meetings that take place in this hotel may seem inconsequential, but they are but pieces of a puzzle. Together they build a picture – and that picture might be the difference between war and peace in Europe.'

'You can't possibly do all this on your own, Mr Charles. Why, you'd have to be in twelve different places at . . .' Raymond's words petered out, as a realisation hit him. 'Billy Brogan. The hotel pages. You aren't the only spy in this hotel . . .'

Maynard Charles cringed. 'I've told you how distasteful I find the word.'

'But you have a network.'

'I have need of it. Pages and chambermaids can slip by unseen. In and out of a guest's room, should the need arise. Billy Brogan has proven indispensable, though I'm quite certain he doesn't yet understand how or why. And now I have need of another.'

Raymond hesitated. 'Wait there, Mr Charles. I'm exiled from my ballroom, aren't I? And now you intend to . . . what? *Enlist* me?'

'Your brother out there fought them, didn't he? He did it in the only way he knew how: boorish, with his fists and knives. Well, you have more wiles about you, de Guise. Good Lord, you've kept up a bigger deception than mine for half of your existence. Yes, thinking about it now, you're more cut out for this line of work than I am. And Nathaniel White is in our ballroom. Exorcising him is the wrong thing to do. But so too is ignoring the fellow, leaving him to his own devices. He has grown . . . fond, shall we say, of Vivienne Edgerton. What they do with their bodies is of no importance to me. But what they say might be. Nathaniel is privy to gossips from his family that might prove invaluable. He must let things slip. I want those things heard. I want them recorded and observed. I want somebody in the ballroom who knows what I know. Someone who has his wits about him. Somebody like you. So, what do you think, Raymond? If I was to scratch your back, perhaps you would scratch mine?'

Raymond lifted himself in his seat. 'You'd put me back in the ballroom?'

'I'll admit I was a little . . . rash in ejecting you so summarily.' Maynard Charles betrayed just a hint of embarrassment. 'I was too emotional in my reaction. I felt attacked, you understand. But then I came to my senses.' He paused. 'It is expedient for us both. I'll have Brogan release a rumour that you were merely absent for a few days, recuperating the last of your health. Then, when you step out in the ballroom again, it can be an event. *The Return of de Guise.*'

'Nathaniel White won't be happy.'

'I don't give two hoots about how happy he is. He will not relinquish his position. You may need to be seen to play second fiddle. Just for a while. Just watch him for me, Raymond. Christmas is already on us. The New Year's ball is two weeks away. In less than a week our suites open to the great and the good.

Without the King in attendance, we must still put on a show. And, of course, Lord Edgerton is gracing us with his presence for New Year. All of his compatriots will be here with him. Mr White, Senior. Mr Mosley.'

Raymond thought: *yes, I can dance for them. I danced for those bastards before. I came here tonight to get one up on them, didn't I? To balance the scales. But what's a little stolen and redistributed treasure compared to this? They've riches enough they might hardly notice . . . But Cable Street was just the beginning, wasn't it? Another step down that road, a couple further, and suddenly the world could change. What if I can help stop that? What if I can do what's right for my country, for my people, for my family by staying right here in the Buckingham Hotel, by spying on them just like Maynard Charles wants? Gossip, he calls it. Intelligence. Information. Well, it's all of those things, but it's something else as well – it's power. It's the power to do what's right. To protect people who need protecting – not up on the barricades like my brother, but in my own way.* 'It's time to pick a side,' Artie had said. Well, now, at least, Raymond was being given the chance to prove it.

'I'll do the work for you, Mr Charles,' he said with a dark finality. 'But there's still the problem of Artie. My brother.' *And Nancy*, he thought, then pushed the image of her to the back of his mind.

Maynard Charles darkened. 'Yes. This, I haven't forgotten. You brought your brother here so that you might steal from me. Am I simply to let it go unpunished?' He seemed to muse on the idea. Then he crouched again and, opening a locked drawer in his desk, came back with a roll of banknotes in his hand. Delicately, he peeled off the top layers, slipped them inside an envelope, and sealed it. 'Artie Cohen was never here.

He won't be seen here again because I'm giving the doormen explicit instructions that, if he is seen here, they are to deal with him in the way doormen all over the world deal with intruders. And, of course . . . Raymond de Guise doesn't have a brother, does he?'

Raymond accepted the envelope, staring in disbelief at Maynard Charles. 'You'd overlook it, just like that?'

'Use this money wisely. I need you, Raymond. There are other worlds inside this hotel. I feel I must balance them. In spite of tonight . . . you are one of the good souls. The world needs good souls, so let us stand beside one another. So –' and here Maynard Charles paused, doubt creeping into his voice for the first time – 'make Artie listen, Raymond. Make Artie see sense. But if he were ever to set foot in this hotel again . . .'

'You'd do that for a petty thief, Maynard?' asked Raymond, with a twinkle in his eye.

Maynard Charles nodded. 'It wouldn't be the first time. I'll write it off as an unaccounted loss – replacement of a guest theft, perhaps. Well, you don't think you're the first to come here and try and rob my hotel, do you?'

Nancy Nettleton was composing a letter to Frank when there came a knocking at her bedroom door. Proudly – because she had not yet let Rosa and Ruth or any of the others see her cry and she didn't mean to tonight – she stood and opened it.

And there stood Raymond de Guise, dishevelled in clothes that could hardly have been his own, while over his shoulder – in the kitchenette where she had gone to make a soothing cup of tea after she had woken in the night – Rosa stood gawping.

'Rosa!' Nancy gasped. Now was not the time. Now was not the moment to tell them everything. 'Rosa, please, I'll explain . . .'

'Nancy,' Raymond breathed.

'What's *he* doing here, Nance? *Nancy Nettleton*, of all the *things* I've seen in this hotel!' She was crowing with laughter now, the strangest mix of bewilderment and hysterics that Nancy had ever heard. 'You – you little country mouse!' she said with glee. '*You're* the scandal! Ha! Here, Ruth! Agatha!' Rosa spun around to call along the hallway to the other girls' rooms. 'Get out here! You won't *believe* who's turned up at Nancy's door . . .'

I'll get fired, Nancy thought. She was sure she could already hear the girls stirring behind their doors, roused from sleep by the promise of some scandal. *Raymond, you bloody fool.*

Nancy reached out, took him by the arm, and hauled him within. As she slammed the door, she caught Rosa's eye – and braved the slightest smile. '*Please*, I'll explain . . .'

Inside the room, Raymond towered over her. She stepped forward, shaking, drew back her arm and slapped him once across the cheek hard. Raymond winced.

'I deserved that,' he said. 'Nancy, I behaved badly towards you and—'

'You deserve more.'

For a moment, there was silence.

'You can't just walk in here! The girls saw you. What if Mrs Moffatt . . .'

I can hear them outside the door already . . .

'I should have come to you before I left. I'm sorry. I thought you'd betrayed me. I wasn't thinking straight, Nancy. I haven't been thinking straight for months. I didn't know who I was. Whether I was Raymond de Guise or Ray Cohen. Whether any of it mattered at all. But what I hadn't seen, what I should have seen weeks ago is . . . even when my head's been in a chaos, even when my worlds have been colliding, there's one thing I *have* seen straight on. And that's you . . .'

Nancy was silent.

'I know it *wasn't* you, Nancy. Somebody betrayed me to Maynard Charles, told him who I really am. It wasn't until tonight that I realised – Billy Brogan was in his pocket. Brogan brought me a letter from home, so Brogan knew too. It *must* have been Billy. And do you know what? I can't blame him. The boy has a family, doesn't he? We all have families to support – and it's a dark world out there. It's growing darker by the day. Nancy,' he whispered, 'I'm sorry.'

He leaned forward, as if to kiss her, but Nancy withdrew. 'You don't win me over as easily as that, Raymond. I'm not the desperate little country girl people seem to think I am. And I have other things on my mind than what's happening to *us*.'

Nancy stared at him for a moment then strode to her dresser, opened one of the drawers and produced from it a little lavender drawstring purse. She'd cleaned it up since she'd found it on the floor of Vivienne Edgerton's suite, but the two glass phials still rattled within. She upended it and spilled them into Raymond's open palm.

'I've seen addiction before, Raymond. You know I have. The ruin it made of my father's mind was so much worse than the disease that was ruining his body. And that's what it's doing to Vivienne Edgerton. I found her, Raymond. Sprawled on her suite floor, lying in her own filth. She might have perished, right there, with no one to hold her – and all because of *this* . . .'

Raymond was reeling. Of all the things he'd expected coming here, this was the most surprising. 'Vivienne's a wreck of a girl,' he said, 'but she does it to herself—'

'*NO!*' Nancy took the phials and slid them back into the lavender pouch. 'Vivienne is wanton and Vivienne is cruel. Vivienne's a drunk and all of these things people say, but they've never given her a chance, have they? I'm the one she stood there and openly mocked and threatened, but I'm willing to see past it. Why isn't anybody else? All they see is the stupid, pretty little rich girl desperate for attention down in the ballroom.' Nancy paused. 'Well, I see her for what she really is. She's an addict. She's lonely and lost and she's scared and, if she's cruel and destructive and she doesn't care, well, that's the reason why.'

By now Nancy was breathless. She resisted Raymond's arms and steadied herself until she could speak once more.

'You've got that look in your eye,' said Raymond. 'Nancy, what do you mean to do?'

'Why, isn't it obvious?' she replied, folding her fist so tightly around the lavender pouch that the glass phials inside shattered with a satisfying crunch. 'I'm going to do for Miss Edgerton what I did for my father. She's too far gone to do it herself, so . . . I'm going to help her out of it, and there isn't a thing in the whole of the Buckingham Hotel that's going to stop me.'

Chapter Twenty-eight

MAYNARD CHARLES SLAMMED HIS OFFICE door and prowled the room, stopping only to pour a stiff brandy from his decanter. He drank it in one, then poured himself another. The first was to relieve all of the tension that had been pumping through his body as he faced Raymond de Guise. The second was to take the edge off the sudden wooziness that hit him as he drank back the first. By the time he poured himself a third, he had reached some equilibrium again. He was calmer, more self-possessed; the doubts that he had done the right thing were beginning to fade as the brandy's warmth spread around his body.

He stood at the window. He'd made a mistake here, somewhere. A hotel director was supposed to be a master tactician. He was supposed to be able to move his pieces around the board with the skills of a chess grandmaster, deploying his bishops and knights, quietly advancing his pawns until they, too, could take positions of influence in the vast hotel engine.

He ought to have known about de Guise before Brogan spoke up. Somewhere along the way, his eye had been somewhere else – and he'd overlooked every sign that the dancer was not truly who he said he was. Thank the Lord that Billy Brogan had the good sense – or was it self-interest? – to have copied down the contents of that letter. A hotel director had to know every secret, every skeleton in every cupboard, because there was only one thing that could fell him: scandal. He had to know what scandals were coming and contain them.

De Guise – he would continue to call him de Guise; it would pay to buy into the legend – was right, of course. The Buckingham could be an unseemly place. When Lord Edgerton descended with his pack of fascist friends, his cousins in high society and their associates from overseas, something had changed. But he was in no position to ask anybody to leave the hotel; to do as much would have been unthinkable – even if it hadn't been for Mr Moorcock and the other spooks like him who had found, in Maynard Charles, the perfect tool.

He didn't realise until he spilled brandy above the rim of his glass that he had started shaking. Just the idea of Mr Moorcock's threats was enough to make his blood boil. He drank what brandy remained in the glass and left the office, locking it behind him. Not that this had done any good once the Cohen boys had wandered into his hotel. He would not be able to reprimand the boy who'd let them in – to do so would have risked exposing the pact he'd made to keep Raymond here – but he would make certain, from now on, that he was not left alone at the staff entrance. Weak boys could be bought. He was sick and tired of people being bought and sold, traded like pawns, in this hotel. He was sick and tired of being the one doing the buying and selling.

But then he thought of Mr Moorcock again, and the only thing that could stop him screaming out loud was the walk he took, up through the housekeeping halls, into the service lift and up, up, up – not to his own quarters, but to the sixth storey and the unmarked door of the Park Suite.

Maynard had no need to knock. He kept a key on a silver chain in his pocket. He slipped it into the lock and, opening the door just enough to squeeze through, he entered the suite.

The smells hit him at once, as always they did: the light and woody oriental smell of cologne imported from the East; the smell of roast coffee beans and peppermints in the silver bowl on the dresser.

He stood for a moment and took in the suite. *No*, he thought, *all the brandy in the world couldn't have the same effect as simply standing here, breathing it all in*. Just stepping through the doors made him feel lighter, freer, as if Mr Moorcock and all of his MI5 acolytes didn't exist at all. If only he could stay here . . . and not have to march out each morning to battle with the Buckingham, nor retire each night to his own quarters, just in case he was seen creeping around and questions started to be asked. There were already enough rumours about the permanently locked abandoned suite on the sixth floor. One day soon he would have to perform an elaborate act of misdirection and silence them all again.

The suite's lounge room was small but cosy, with an ornamental fireplace around which three armchairs were arranged, and a wireless which ordinarily buzzed with news from the BBC. Radio was a godsend; it opened one up to so much of the world. These newfangled television sets might be a novelty, but they would never replace radio in Maynard Charles's view. Who would want a pair of eyes staring back at you from a little box in the corner, as they read out the news? But the radio – the radio could be a comfort, through the long, lonely days.

The trolley was still waiting, where Mrs Moffatt had left it, ready to be picked up in the morning. The grouse they had eaten for dinner had been superb, and the spiced plums for pudding had made Maynard think of Christmases in long gone, happier times. He fancied he could taste them even now, as he crossed the little lounge and went through the archway into the bedroom.

The wheelchair was up against the wall, where he had left it. Two single beds dominated most of the room; by the side of the bed closest to him was the medicine cabinet and, by that, an oxygen tank, now spent, that Doctor Evelyn Moore routinely delivered. The sounds coming from the first bed were only gentle snores, and this made Maynard's heart soar – because it meant that everything was all right.

Quietly, so as not to disturb the sleeper, Maynard Charles took off his dressing gown, crossed the room, and climbed under the covers of his own bed. Moments later, the figure in the bed alongside him startled. Inwardly, Maynard cursed. He himself had long been a light sleeper, after the years he had spent sleeping in foxholes in the earth. He hadn't slept a night uninterrupted since the Somme in 1916.

The figure picked himself up, as if expecting attack.

'Shhhh,' Maynard began. 'It's only me.'

'What happened?' said a voice.

'Oh, Buckingham business. Another fire that needed extinguishing. It's—'

'Not Moorcock again?'

'Not this time,' whispered Maynard. He leaned across and kissed the figure on the forehead. Then, 'Aubrey, get your rest. You'll feel hellish in the morning if you don't sleep on.'

But the figure beside him was restless now. He reached out for the cord that dangled at his bedside, drew on it, and a lamp illuminated the room.

Aubrey Higgins was several years older than Maynard Charles. Almost entirely bald, he nevertheless had a beard of striking silver. Though he had once been broad and powerful, now his body was slight; he appeared to sink into the bed sheets, and the ribbon that dangled around his neck was attached to a mask that was itself attached to the oxygen tank at his side. He paused to put the mask over his lips, drew in deeply, and then removed it again.

Maynard sat up and looked at him fondly. 'You've been doing so well.'

'I can smell brandy, Maynard. You haven't been having a little tipple without me, have you?'

'I needed it, Aubrey, like you wouldn't believe.'

Maynard climbed out of his own bed, crossed the room to perch on the other and touched his companion's shoulder. Aubrey Higgins: the secret of the Park Suite.

They'd met in '15, that summer when the entrenchment was hardening across the Western Front and what had been thought of, the year before, as temporary measures were rapidly becoming permanent constructions. Both were Warrant Officers, both old in the regiment. Maynard had signed up in 1914. At the age of thirty-nine, he might have avoided the front altogether if he'd played his cards cannily enough – and at the time, night manager at a Bristolian hotel of some growing renown, there was even a chance he could call it a reserved occupation. And yet . . . Maynard had no family, no wife and children and no prospect of either to keep him in England. He was a man of principle and a man of duty and, when people asked him why a handsome, well-to-do, esteemed fellow like him had not yet dignified the holy seat of marriage, he had any number of tactics to evade the question. Love had not found him, he was fond of saying, but the fact was that love had found him several times over, but Maynard consistently pushed it away – whether out of shame, or propriety, or fear, he had never been able to say.

Yet when he met Aubrey Higgins, all of that changed. It happened in stages, as all the best love stories do – and, though it had crept up on them both, there was no less passion in it for that. Aubrey was the first man whom Maynard Charles had outwardly admitted he loved; Maynard the first for whom Aubrey would surely have lain down and died. Later, Maynard had told Aubrey that it was because he expected to die out there – that it freed him enough to live his life the way he wanted to live it, for he knew it would not last long. For Aubrey it was different – the culmination of a lifetime seeking someone worthy enough.

They made it, together, as far as Passchendaele in that bitter year of 1917. It was in that blasted landscape, shorn of all life, that Aubrey had fallen. First, his lung punctured; then, corroded by the reefs of acrid yellow gas that floated over the battlefields. He was invalided home and nobody expected Aubrey to live. Maynard had made his goodbyes, right there in a hole in the earth, before the Red Cross crews fought their way out to bear him away. And yet, in 1918, when the Armistice came, Maynard Charles was repatriated to Britain to discover that Aubrey still lived, bedridden, but in the care of an elder sister. One of his lungs was ruined, the other under enormous strain, but by the sheer fortitude of his heart he survived.

When Maynard got the job at the Buckingham, a plan was hatched: the Park Suite, smallest of the Buckingham's suites, was closed for refurbishment – and never reopened. It was a simple thing to smuggle Aubrey and his cases within. And here he had remained ever since. Aubrey had once spoken of himself as a princess locked in a tower – but, oh, what a tower! In springtime he could look down on the verdant green of Berkeley Square. In winter, the fire roared. The hotel provided all that he needed, in life and in love. Here he lived and here, when the time came – as surely it would soon – he would die. It did not matter to him, as long as Maynard was at his side.

Aubrey leaned over and snuffed the light again. 'It will all look better in the morning, dear Maynard.'

'I have asked Raymond de Guise back to the Buckingham,' Maynard said, into the dark. It seemed something of a confession.

'You have?'

'I told him,' Maynard said. 'About Mr Moorcock. About what I do here, in the Buckingham.'

Aubrey Higgins tensed. 'My dear, is that wise?'

'I had no choice, Aubrey. I won't be called a fascist in my own hotel. I won't be a sympathiser. You recall the last time I met with Moorcock, down there in the Candlelight Club?'

'I do.'

'The Schechts are still hoping to meet Mr Chamberlain here, in our hotel. They're still planning on bringing over what dignitaries they can from Berlin. They want to engineer peace – a peace with that monster in the Reichstag. There's a war coming, Aubrey, and they're using our hotel to help Britain choose a side that will keep her out of the way of the aggressors' progress. Well, I want to be on the right side of history. I fought for Britain once. We both did. Look what it did to you, Aubrey. All of that will not be in vain. So I'll fight them again, here in my hotel.'

For a time there was silence – until finally Aubrey asked, 'Did you tell him . . . *about me*?'

Maynard reached over and took his hand. 'I wouldn't. I couldn't. Raymond is a good soul, but if he were to know the real reason I'm in Mr Moorcock's pocket, why, I'm not sure he'd understand. Much better, I think, that he thinks me a rabid man of principle, one of the last upstanding men.' There was some element of joke in this; Aubrey laughed in return. 'I can't risk you, Aubrey. You need a roof over your head. You need somewhere warm and safe. And I need to be close to you. I won't have you living in any less than this.'

Moorcock – that bastard . . . He'd appeared in the Candlelight Club one evening in '32, while the sale of hotel stock to Lord Edgerton was still going through, and insisted on buying Maynard Charles a drink. He'd detailed his interest in certain guests at the Buckingham and had passed Maynard an envelope crammed with notes of various denominations. Maynard handed it straight back. But all that changed in the Christmas of 1932, when Mr Moorcock settled himself in the Pacific Suite for an evening – the bill settled, of course, by the Ministry itself – and, in the evening, placed a phone call to reception, requesting to have a private dinner with the hotel director himself. When Maynard Charles appeared in the Pacific, all it took were two words to change the complexion – and the very direction – of his life. 'Park Suite,' Mr Moorcock had intoned. 'What do you think might happen, dear Maynard, were your new lord to realise what goes on in the Park Suite? Why, this sort of thing – appropriating hotel accommodation for your own illegal pleasures – might count as scandal, mightn't it? How might that fall out for you, dear boy?'

From that moment he was theirs. There was nothing more important in this world than making sure Aubrey was tended to, that Aubrey had a safe place to live. Nothing more important than making sure Aubrey was loved.

'You've done the right thing,' said Aubrey, distant now as sleep came back to whisk him away. 'By your very nature, Maynard Charles, you've done the right thing.'

But long into the night, Maynard Charles wondered: *have I? How long can I keep up this dance? How long can England? We're all waltzing, waltzing like they do down there in the ballroom, waltzing while the world around us teeters on the brink. How long can any of this go on?*

For long hours he lay awake, safe in his secret world, and listened to the rattle in Aubrey's lungs – while, outside the Buckingham Hotel, the snow continued to fall.

Chapter Twenty-nine

Another night had fallen but, in Vivienne Edgerton's suite, it did not matter if it was night or day. She had spent the first day after that fateful night in bed; the second she had pottered around the room, staring glassily out of the windows and nibbling at the platters of food the housekeeping staff had arranged for her. It wasn't until the third day, when her body was beginning to feel robust again, that the boredom had truly set in – but, when it did, it was more powerful than any drink or drug that had ever flowed through her system. She tried on every one of her ball gowns. She summoned room service to bring her a collection of the latest *Vogue* and *Harper's Bazaar*. She put countless records into her gramophone. Sometimes the snow fell so thickly that it completely occluded the world outside and it was then, a prisoner in her lonely tower, that Vivienne Edgerton truly began to feel like a captive.

She tried the door, but it was still locked.

She dozed and, some time approaching midnight, she saw the door open – and in slipped Nathaniel White. He had come last night too, the key procured for him by no less than Billy Brogan himself. Resplendent in his evening suit, his hair perfectly coiffured, he came to sit beside her on the bed. Still reclining, she reached out a hand.

'You came.'

'I promised I would.'

'How was the ballroom tonight?'

'In true flight,' said Nathaniel joyfully. 'The Christmas guests are in full attendance. Archie Adams played a list of classics. They jingled all the way.' He paused. 'I would have come sooner, Vivienne, but Hélène and I spent today choreographing our new routines to launch the masquerade ball next week at New Year. I have a spectacular planned, if only Hélène can learn it in time. Sometimes she seems so reluctant. And I am told she is not to be here, in the hotel, for *four* days over Christmas. Why Maynard Charles might acquiesce to such foolishness, only the heavens know. If Hélène is not here to take my instruction, then how are we to provide a night to remember at New Year?'

'Is it the same without me, Nathaniel? I mean . . . down there in the ballroom?'

Nathaniel paused. 'It's been mere days . . .'

'But even so. I hate the thought of you facing *them* alone. The only saving grace is that Raymond de Guise is gone and never to return.' Vivienne did not notice the look that flickered across Nathaniel's face – or, if she did, she was so wrapped up in herself that she thought nothing of it. 'I'll be back soon, Nathaniel. I could have danced with you tonight, if they'd let me out of this damned room. They think I'm some delicate flower but . . .' She would have gone on, but her throat was parched and suddenly she was racked with coughs. Nathaniel poured her water from the glassware on the room service trolley and helped put it to her lips. 'They'll have to let me out at Christmas. My stepfather is sending a car for me. I'm to have Christmas dinner in Suffolk. With my *mother*.' She used the word like a curse, because that was what it was. How long had she been in England, and how often had she seen her mother in this time? The two were so far apart that it seemed a vast chasm yawned open between them. 'When I get back, they won't be able to confine me again. Not when my stepfather finds out—'

'You can hardly speak with your father of this, Vivienne. Mr Charles is doing what he can to protect you—'

'Protect me?' Vivienne protested, hoisting herself up.

'What do you think Lord Edgerton would think if he knew his daughter—?'

'Well,' Vivienne snapped, finding her fire at last, 'the first thing he'd do is ask who joins me in my . . . indulgences. And who might that be, Nathaniel?'

For a time, Nathaniel was silent. Then, thinking twice, he wrapped his arms around Vivienne and kissed the nape of her neck. 'I'm only thinking of you, Vivienne. What if something worse had happened to you? Where would I be then?'

The words made Vivienne soften; it was exactly what she'd wanted to hear. 'I took it too far, Nathaniel, that's all. We can still have a good time, can't we?'

His lips on her neck had stirred something in her. She drew back from him, just enough for there to be air between them, and tried to kiss him full on the lips.

Nathaniel turned his head.

'Nathaniel?'

He hesitated. If Vivienne had had more wits about her, perhaps she would have seen the scorn in his eyes. It was the scorn a boy has for a plaything he no longer needs, a toy tarnished and best left forgotten. 'You're not . . . strong tonight, Vivienne. You need your rest. If you're to dance at New Year, you should recuperate properly. Don't push your body.'

'I just wish I had a little something to take the edge away. Good God, even a cocktail would do. A gin rickey or a bee's knees, one of those I used to drink with the girls back in New York. Or . . . I need Mr Simenon. I wouldn't have to indulge. Just a little sugar so I can sleep.' Vivienne paused. 'But if I can't have that, well . . .' Her fingertips ran up Nathaniel's thigh, closer and closer to his body – until, at the last moment, he got back to his feet.

'Get your rest, Vivienne. I'm glad you're still among us.'

Only as he disappeared through the door did she find the breath to utter, 'Nathaniel, what's wrong? What have I done?' But Nathaniel had already gone.

Then Vivienne's eye was caught by something glinting in the lamplight.

Quite by accident, Nathaniel had left his key.

Mr Simenon was up, as he always was, with the dawn. In the head concierge's office, he folded the calendar from the twenty-first of December, the winter equinox, to the twenty-second. Routine made a man like Mr Simenon happy. He was the sort of man who wakes daily at sunrise, whether he has an alarm clock or not; the sort of man who has laid out his clothes – identical every day – the evening before; the sort of man whose morning ablutions happen like clockwork.

He was scanning over the hotel guest list, preparing himself for the possibilities of the day ahead – in spite of his love of order, Mr Simenon enjoyed the impromptu missions he was sent on by the Buckingham's most high-profile guests; if a man could please lords and ladies and assorted gentry, he was a fine man indeed – when, without warning, the door opened behind him.

He turned on his heel to see Vivienne Edgerton.

She looked pale. Her cheeks were still washed out and her eyes, devoid of any make-up, seemed black and sad. But she was standing here too, and that meant she had rediscovered something of her old self.

'You're supposed to be recovering from your little ordeal. Miss Edgerton, what do you think you're doing here?'

'I need your help.'

Mr Simenon kneaded the bridge of his nose, with just an air of deliberate melodrama. 'Vivienne, you need somebody's help, that's for certain. A doctor of medicine, no doubt. You do understand that Mr Charles has charged me – *me* – with unearthing the supply of your little indulgences. What am I supposed to do here, Vivienne? You might have died. You might have brought ruin on us all and—'

'I need a special delivery. I'm not asking for much. I know what I did and I know it was wrong, but I'm pent up, Mr Simenon. I don't know where to turn. Maynard Charles is looking over me like I'm a baby deer, unable to do anything for myself – but he would better be reminded where I come from, and who I am. I *need* your help, Mr Simenon.'

'Vivienne, you must think I'm a simpleton. I won't be responsible for the death of you.' He stopped. 'You're a sweet girl and what you do to yourself is nobody's business but yours. But I value my place in the Buckingham Hotel. I've been here longer than Maynard Charles himself. I intend to retire my position here only when I'm too old to be of use to anybody. I won't risk it for—'

Vivienne snapped, 'You've already been risking it.'

'I'm a concierge. I fulfil my guests' requests.'

'Then fulfil this,' said Vivienne coldly – and Mr Simenon noticed the colour of anger rushed to her cheeks. 'If you're not able to help a girl in her hour of need, well, a little bird might whisper in Maynard Charles's ear. The hotel director might be *very* interested to hear where his lord's daughter has been acquiring her particular poisons. If there's a scandal here in the Buckingham, you're it – so why don't you help a poor girl out? I am, Mr Simenon, your guest, after all.'

As Mr Simenon's jaw worked frantically to come up with a reply – but found only silence – Vivienne Edgerton stepped out into the reception hall and back towards her suite.

As she marched out of the lift, it was all she could do to hold herself together. She'd been feeling so cold, too cold for these halls where thousands of cubic yards of hot water and oils pumped to keep the hotel warm. She could feel the goose bumps all over her flesh – but that, she realised, had nothing to do with the season. It was her body calling out for it. Something to pick her up, something to make her whole. If only Nathaniel had lain with her. If only he'd tricked room service into bringing her one of her cocktails, a bottle of Moët, something to take her away from this place where she didn't belong.

She reached her room and fumbled to unlock the door, her hand shaking. Was it really so much to ask? There was Christmas to survive. Christmas with the *family* – a family who loved her so much they'd rather she boarded here, alone, in the Buckingham, than under their own roof. And even if she survived that – well, what was there to look forward to? More of this intolerable hotel. More of this . . .

All she wanted to do was step out on New Year's Eve, resplendent in her gown, with Nathaniel on her arm – and remind her mother that she existed. A night like that was worth all of the rest. A night like that would be something to look forward to, a diamond in the rough of her life.

But Nathaniel hadn't even wanted to touch her. What was she – *dirty* to him now?

She fumbled the key into the lock and stepped through. At first she did not notice the envelope that had been slipped under the door – but, as she flailed forward, it caught the end of her foot.

Dear Miss Edgerton,

We may not have seen eye to eye in the past, but perhaps we can set this to one side. You may not have been told, but it was me who found you and brought your predicament to the attention of Mr Charles and his staff. I have been instructed to keep my own counsel, but I have seen the ruin addiction makes of a person and my heart goes out to you. Perhaps we can talk? I am sure I can be of some assistance.

Your friend in a time of need,

Nancy Nettleton

Nettleton? thought Vivienne. The chambermaid with the lame leg . . . and the eye of Raymond de Guise? Vivienne supposed she ought to have been grateful for what she'd done, but that girl really was above her station. To suppose *Vivienne* needed *her*? She stood and stared at the letter. Then she took it between thumb and forefinger and tore it into a wealth of tiny pieces.

She didn't need cheer. She didn't need pity. All she needed was for Mr Simenon to do what he was told.

Why, then, did her mind keep going back to Nancy's words – *my heart goes out to you* – and why did they bring the shimmer of tears to her eyes?

Billy Brogan had hoped never to attend the Midnight Rooms again – and yet here he was, trudging back through the slush and snow of Soho in winter, with a little lavender pouch tied up in his back pocket. The Midnight Rooms did a roaring trade in winter. Christmas and New Year were the most indulgent times of year.

Afternoon was curdling to night, and Christmas only days away. Billy looked forward to Christmases in Lambeth. His brothers and sisters still bought into the magic of the season. He longed for the chicken on the table – because, unless he was wily enough to pilfer one from the hotel kitchens, the family could never afford a goose – and the family gathered around; the presents wrapped in newspaper they would open and the songs they would sing. He had been siphoning off his money from Mr Charles all autumn, and back home the cavity underneath his bed was crammed full of all the books and toys he'd bought for his brothers and sisters.

And here he was, bringing the risk of death back to Vivienne Edgerton's door.

His heart was beating wildly as he crossed the Buckingham and made his way to her suite. He hadn't been there to see what had become of Vivienne that night – but nothing escaped Billy Brogan. As he reached up to knock on the door, he couldn't help but wonder at what he was going to find inside.

All he found was Vivienne, wearing an ivory gown, pearls around her neck. She had called out for Billy to enter and now he stood there, nervously, at the end of the bed.

'Mr Simenon saw sense then, did he?'

Billy didn't know what kind of sense it was. All he knew was the way Mr Simenon had seethed as he delivered Billy his instructions; all he could remember was the warmth of the spittle that had showered down on him as Billy began to protest. 'You're not here to question me, Brogan. You're in the thick of this, just the same as I am. If little Miss Edgerton rats on me, who else do you think's in the firing line? So go get her the powders, boy – and I'll throttle you if you breathe so much as a word . . .'

Billy reached into his back trouser pocket and produced the little lavender pouch.

'I'll take my leave, if I might, miss.'

Vivienne wheeled around, positioning herself between Billy and the door. 'You may certainly *not*,' she returned, pinning Billy in place. For some reason, the hotel page was refusing to look in her eyes – perhaps, she thought, for fear of what he might find there. 'Billy, look at me, won't you?'

Against his will, Billy lifted his eyes.

'What is it, miss?'

'You've been a good friend. I don't forget my friends. Here,' she said, and unstrung the pearls from around her neck, 'take these, won't you?'

Whether he wanted them or not, they fell into Billy Brogan's cupped hand.

'I've a favour to ask of you, Billy.'

Billy was uncertain. 'I did everything Mr Simenon asked.'

'Oh, *that*,' she said. 'Not *that*. No, my favour's more particular – and less troublesome, you might say. I don't want you to procure me anything, Billy. Anything but . . . information.'

Information was a hotel page's stock in trade, but there was something about the way Vivienne spoke that still gave Billy Brogan pause. He could see her hands shaking as she spoke.

'You see and hear everything in this hotel, don't you, Billy? And you want to stay here, don't you?'

Billy blurted out, 'I'm only doing as I'm told, Miss Edgerton. That's all I've ever done. Whether it's for Mr Charles or Mr Simenon or Mr de Guise, or even for you. I've only ever done what's asked. I didn't know you was going to get sick. It's not what I wanted—'

'Shhh,' said Vivienne, softly – and dared to touch Billy on the shoulder. 'You don't need to fear, Billy. Your *procurement* secrets are safe with me. I'd just like a little something in return for keeping quiet, that's all.' The shaking from Vivienne's hand must have been contagious, for in that moment Billy started shaking too. 'Hélène Marchmont. Nathaniel says she's vanishing for four days over Christmas. She vanishes every so often, leaving the ballroom to Sofía LaPegna and all of the rest. What I want you to find out, Billy, is *where* does Hélène Marchmont go?'

The tension in the room was thick as treacle.

'I know you deliver letters for them all, Billy.'

'Why would you want to know, Miss Edgerton? Why would you care?'

Vivienne smiled. She could see, already, in the way he fidgeted, that she had won. 'That's my business, Billy. All you need to know is this: you're going to promise me you'll find out the truth – all of it – right here and right now, or I'm going to put in a call to Maynard Charles – and all that money, all those secret payments you take back to that rotten little family of yours, plus any prospects of good future employment is going to come to an end. So,' she whispered, 'what's it going to be?'

Chapter Thirty

IN THE FINAL DAYS APPROACHING Christmas, the atmosphere at the Buckingham Hotel had changed from one of ruthless order to one of barely controlled chaos. It seemed to Nancy that the very fabric of the hotel was changing. The guests who came were of a different order: the businessmen and dignitaries visiting on official business had retired to their country estates for the season, while the guests who arrived were cut from a different cloth. They came, not to use the Buckingham Hotel as a home away from home and explore the sights and sounds of London town, but to revel in the luxury and splendour of the Buckingham itself. For a week now, the kitchens of the Queen Mary and the Buckingham's other dining rooms had been on high alert, everyone from potboy to head chef working long into the night to prepare for the Christmas Day to come. Eighty prize turkeys from a Gloucestershire farm had been delivered to the hotel cold stores. One hundred wood pigeons, pheasants and grouse were strung up by their feet in the cold larders, waiting to be plucked by the army of sous-chefs drafted in for the occasion. An inventory of the cold room would have shown six whole red deer, butchered and dangling from spikes, along with forty suckling pigs and a succession of haunches of beef big enough to feed a battalion. Nancy had caught sight of the cauldrons of gravy that had been slowly simmering since the equinox, and the Christmas puddings – baked en masse in August and left to mature in the dark kitchen larders – were now being unearthed and fed with yet more brandy for the occasion.

Nancy was worried about Frank. Mrs Gable would put on a Christmas spread for the boys who stayed in the boarding house, but Nancy did not like to think of him waking up on Christmas morning without his family. She had arranged for the hotel post room to send him a set of postcards of London's most magnificent sights: the Tower and the Thames, the rolling green splendour of Regent's Park and the majesty of St Paul's. All of these things she meant to show him one day. It did not seem right that he should be lonely on Christmas morning.

Nancy lingered in the reception hall, in the shadow of the Norwegian fir, watching as Hélène Marchmont stepped through the revolving doors, straight into a waiting Hackney carriage. The last of the pre-Christmas guests were making a steady stream through the doors as well – and there among them stood Vivienne Edgerton. She was dressed sombrely for a day like this, with a simple sky-blue day dress and a day bag at her side. She looked drawn, thought Nancy. Drawn and old. Nancy had to remind herself that *she* was the elder of them by four, maybe five years. Vivienne was only a girl.

The letter hadn't worked. In truth, she had known it wouldn't. The letter was cowardly, and Nancy Nettleton was no coward. So, with the blitz of departing and arriving guests still fizzing around them, she made her approach.

'Miss Edgerton?'

Vivienne turned around, but seemed to look directly through Nancy.

'I'm sorry, Miss Edgerton. You may not know this, but it was me who found you when . . .' Nancy's words petered into silence. She had seen the look of horror on Vivienne's face. It only hardened.

'I've got to go,' Vivienne uttered coldly – and, hailing the doorman, disappeared out of the door. One of her father's fleet of gleaming black Rolls Royces was wheeling around the square, ready to pick her up. Behind her, Nancy could do nothing but stare.

In the Rolls Royce, Vivienne shook. How dare that chambermaid approach *her* in the reception hall? How dare she call her by her name? Was that what was becoming of the world? Was all decorum lost? All sense of propriety gone? As if she needed *reminding* of how undignified it was to be found, lying on the floor of her suite?

The chauffeur was trying to speak with her, but Vivienne closed her eyes and ignored him, as if to do so was to shut out the rest of the world. Her hands were quaking and, of their own accord, they wormed their way into the day bag on her lap. There they discovered the little lavender pouch brought courtesy of Billy Brogan. Inside, the two phials of powder remained intact. *As long as they're intact, I'll have something to escape to; I don't have to listen to my mother fawning over my stepfather all through Christmas dinner, or even tolerate them talking about The Problem of Vivienne Edgerton.*

Yes, Christmas Day was going to be an intolerable affair, but at least she was out of the confines of the hotel and as long as she had the promise of her powders she would survive it.

'What do you think, Sybil?' asked Hélène, carrying the child out into the small, frosted yard behind the Archers' home. 'Your first snow.'

It had not fallen as thickly along Brixton Hill as it did in Berkeley Square and the royal parks of London, but the red-brick wall was capped in white, and underfoot the snow lay deep enough to leave lasting footprints wherever Hélène stood. Nervously, she crouched and helped Sybil – wrapped up in the woollen coat Noelle had stitched for her – totter off into the white. Watching her walk was a revelation, thought Hélène. Every time she came here, Sybil was less her baby girl and more her growing daughter. This time, Hélène thought, her face was less rounded. Her eyes were changing colour. Her hair had a new wildness to it. She reminded her so much of Sidney.

'That's enough, girls,' called Noelle Archer from the doorway. 'You don't want to catch a chill.'

Inside, a log fire was burning beneath a mantel bedecked in cards. The Archers always went to great lengths to decorate their home at Christmas. It stemmed, Hélène knew, from those first years after they emigrated – because to embrace a country's traditions was to embrace the country itself, and there was nothing their children enjoyed more than the English tradition of Christmas, so different to the Christmases they were used to back in Jamaica. The portraits of Sidney, Samantha and Joseph were now framed with tiny paper snowflakes. It made Hélène's heart ache to think of Noelle sitting here, peacefully drawing them with Sybil looking on. All the little moments of magic, the waking up to wonder and enchantment that she was missing while she toiled in the ballroom. At least for today and tomorrow she might not think of that majestic place at all. She might forget the clammy touch of Nathaniel White . . .

Noelle brought down the box of card, ribbons and string she had secreted away, while Maurice Archer busied himself with his shovel and stepped out into the front yard.

'That man thinks he can fight winter itself!' Noelle shrieked. Then, seeing the way Hélène was staring at the home-made decorations, she leaped to attention. 'Let's make more. We can all do it together. Sybil, you can help. But stay away from your grandmother's scissors, girl, or they'll come a-snipping after you.'

Helping Sybil clutch a pencil; cutting out the strange, many-pointed stars she somehow managed to draw; seeing her giggle with delight as Hélène dangled them above her, only just out of reach. *These things make all the tensions of my other life ebb away. All I really want is you, Sybil.*

Hélène could almost imagine that New Year was not going to happen at all. Across the last days, Nathaniel had been instructing her in his new routine. It was a showy, ostentatious thing, a dance that kept Hélène firmly in the background while Nathaniel showed the world exactly what his body could do – but it was not as impressive as he seemed to think; a dance could only ever inspire real awe when two people were working together. But what Nathaniel White wanted, Nathaniel White got. He had even instructed her in the gown she was to wear, and what Venetian mask would cover her face.

The boy barely looks at me while we dance. He looks at the audience instead, the onlookers, the spectators, standing in front of me, eclipsing me, like he's the only one they should see. I didn't train for so long for this.

'Something's bothering you, my dear. Hélène, you can fool yourself but you can't fool me. Come on, girl. You can tell your second mother.'

'It's nothing, Noelle,' Hélène lied. She refocused on the decorations and tickled Sybil under one of her manifold chins. 'Do you remember,' she went on, 'how nervous I was when I came here that first Christmas?'

Noelle's eyes lifted to the picture of Sidney on the mantel. She had made an extra effort to crown Sybil's father in snowflakes. In the picture he was nineteen years old and holding on to his trumpet. He looked angelic, as if he existed outside of time.

'I remember you were *terrified*,' said Noelle. 'But you had no need. Hélène, you did beautifully.'

Two years ago – a whole lifetime . . .

Hélène could clearly remember the first morning she'd known she was pregnant. The Christmas tree was being hoisted up in the Buckingham reception. The tinsel and baubles appeared overnight, the hotel staff slaving long past the midnight hour. Dawn found her with her head in the bowl of the toilet at the end of the dancers' hall. She had never known a sensation like this. By the time she arrived in the ballroom for the afternoon demonstrations and took Sidney to one side, she knew that her suspicions were right. There was a baby inside her, curled up and waiting for its mama to introduce it to the world.

Three weeks later, on the night of the winter solstice, Sidney had brought her to this very door. He'd first kissed her a summer before, one night when only she and he remained in the rooms behind the ballroom. From that moment on, Hélène's life had lit up. She had known romances before, but always with men who sought to own her, to define her, to box her up and package her away for their eyes only. Sidney was not like that. Sidney burned bright and his passion for her was matched only by his passion for his trumpet. She loved how much he knew about music. She loved how much he knew about dance – although, on the rare occasions he'd stepped out onto the dance floor, it was obvious that, though a natural musician, dance did not come as easily. She loved how he breezed through life, thinking only of the day, not caught up in the trap of the future like so many others. And she loved, most of all, the way he had touched her that first night they lay together, up in her room in the Buckingham Hotel. The secret was theirs alone, and it had intensified all year, just like their love.

Now, though, love felt different. It felt like sickness in the bottom of her stomach. It felt like faintness when she demonstrated a particular dance with Raymond de Guise. It tasted like last night's dinner, forever lurking at the back of her throat.

The moment she stepped through the doors and Sidney introduced her, his family fawned around her. They made her tea. They buttered hot teacakes and presented her with all manner of biscuits. They made her feel more at home than her own family ever had. And she knew, in an instant, that she had a new family now. Perhaps it was a family the world might never know about – but it was a family all the same.

That Christmas had changed her life. She'd lain in the back bedroom here, with Sidney next to her, and wondered at the baby budding inside her. She'd been here at New Year too, when the Archie Adams Band played for Prince George, the Duke of Kent, who was entertaining his continental friends at the Buckingham's famous Masquerade Ball. Sidney had kissed her goodbye on the doorstep and set off into the snow with his trumpet case at his side.

He'd never come home, for as he left the Buckingham late that night – drunk, perhaps, on what a beautiful turn his life was taking; drunk, too, on the brandy that Archie Adams had shared around while the festivities were at a high – he stepped out into the path of an omnibus slewing around in the snow.

The horror of the moment when Louis Kildare appeared on the doorstep in Brixton to break the news . . . The fraction of a second when she thought he was playing some terrifying joke and that Sidney would appear from around the corner, his trumpet in his hand. Then the yawning realisation that this was real, that Sidney was gone, that Hélène's whole world was being torn into fragments around her. All of these moments were like photographs. She remembered them so starkly. But no moment would ever be imprinted on her consciousness as vividly as the moment Louis presented her with the trumpet that had been found just a few yards from his body, still safely tucked up inside its case. One day, she would give it to Sybil – the first and last gift from her father.

Hélène had sat at his funeral while their baby turned somersaults inside her, unable to reveal herself as Sidney's lover, able only to shed tears as a member of the Buckingham Hotel who'd known him for his music. She'd hidden the pregnancy well, flanked on one side by Louis Kildare and the other by Raymond de Guise, the only two men she'd trusted enough to tell. With their support she had managed to keep in the tears until nobody could see. Then, in the churchyard, she'd felt the bite of the wind and realised that she'd never hear him playing his trumpet again, that she'd never wake to see him grinning at her, that she'd never tell him that, when she danced in the ballroom, it was *him* she was thinking about, no matter who was in her arms. The devastation was absolute. Hélène's world was a different shade of grey. When people spoke to her, she heard them only as if from a distance. The sun was gone, and in its place there was endless night.

It was only later that year, when Sybil gave her first cries and Noelle Archer herself lifted the mewling baby to Hélène's breast – that sound, more real and beautiful than anything she'd ever heard in a ballroom – that she'd felt the grief subside. *My daughter,* she'd realised. The revelation was unique. The child had been growing for nine months – but only when she could see her face, touch her and feel her, did she understand. *I am a mother – for now, and for the rest of my life.* The enormity of it, the love and the fear that mingled in her, was almost too difficult to grasp. But she lay there that night and she knew just how right it was.

'He would have been proud of you, Hélène,' said Noelle. 'Proud of you both. Let's make it a Christmas to remember. He always loved your English Christmases. He'd want that for Sybil too.'

At that moment, Maurice Archer burst back into the room, brandishing not only his shovel but the most glorious smile. 'Come and see!' he said, and together the family followed him out to the yard.

In front of the house, where he'd cleared the path, the snow was piled high in what Hélène first took for a simple hummock. It was only as she carried Sybil around it that she looked down and saw it for what it was: a giant trumpet, sculpted perfectly from the fallen snow. It was the most wonderful thing.

By the time the first suppers of Christmas Eve were being served in the Buckingham Hotel, Billy Brogan was loping back across the river. Over his shoulder was a haversack and, wrapped up inside, the perfect Christmas surprise: a single suckling pig. He could almost taste it now.

The lights were on at home. Billy gambolled through the door and, in an instant, was mobbed by his brothers and sisters. They seemed to think him Father Christmas himself, and nothing could have given Billy greater joy. With a half-dozen pairs of hands clutching him, he allowed himself to be carried through to the living room, where the tiny tree his parents had put up appeared a mere bough when set against the majesty of the fir tree standing in the Buckingham hall. And yet the presents piled up around its bottom in their higgledy-piggledy pyramid seemed greater than any gifts that would be exchanged in the Buckingham tomorrow morning. Billy's heart soared.

'I'm about to make your night even better,' he announced. 'Stand back, you bairns. Wait until you see what we're eating tomorrow . . .'

The pig was wrapped in baking parchment. When Billy unfurled it on the floor, his sisters cringed away – all except Roisin, with the ruddy cheeks, who joined her brother Patrick in poking the poor dead thing with the tip of her finger.

'And I got this too, for those that's grown up enough.'

The next surprise he produced was a big cut of meat, dark and red with barely an ounce of fat on it. 'It's venison,' Billy announced. 'It's what them who's better than us eat. Well, I say, tomorrow we Brogans are just as good as the rest of 'em. So tomorrow we're going to eat like kings and queens.' He paused. 'What do you think, Ma? Stick it in the oven, thing'll cook, won't it? They eat it red and bloody in the Queen Mary, but—'

'Billy Brogan,' she said, 'you're a wonder. But what about that chicken I got sitting out there?'

'Chicken, for the whole lot of us!? No, Ma, let's treat ourselves. It's but once a year. And we ain't paupers, are we, Pa?'

Billy's father nodded and, in silence, returned to his newspaper.

'What's the matter with him?' Billy asked as he and the other Brogans scrabbled into the kitchen to see their ma stow the fresh meat in the larder.

'Oh, don't you bother with him,' said Billy's mother. 'He brought us a turbot tonight. It'll do nicely alongside all this. Good Lord, we could feed the whole parish.'

'Let's not,' grinned Billy. 'We Brogans got to look out for ourselves.'

But even while he played with his brothers and sisters, fashioning a den out of old chair legs and blankets, then telling Christmas stories and stoking them full of magic for the night to come, Billy had a nagging feeling in the back of his head as his father continued to sit in silence.

The Brogan children went to sleep early that night, though for long hours afterwards Billy could hear them clattering out of bed to gather at the windows and watch the snowy skies above. Billy stayed up later. His mother and father had hidden more gifts in the cranny at the back of the kitchen larder, and as she went off to dig them out, his father brought out a bottle of bourbon he kept hidden for celebrations like this. He poured a measure for himself, then one for Billy as well.

'Drink up, son. There's something I want to talk about.'

Billy tasted the bourbon, pretending not to wince as it burned the back of his throat. 'Some of the Buckingham's finest, eh, Pa?'

Billy's father nursed his drink. 'That's what I want to speak about, son. Now, I *know* you. I know you better than anyone, excepting your ma, so don't go getting up in arms about this. It needs saying. I need to get it off my chest.' He paused, steeling himself with a breath. 'I don't know how you get your suckling pigs and venison. I don't know how you get these bottles of bourbon and half-bottles of Moët et Chandon. I don't know how you bring such big tips every time you come home. Now, don't get me wrong, son, it isn't that I'm not grateful. I got eight of you bairns, and your mother to think about too. What you do for this family, it's appreciated more than you'll ever know. But . . .'

'Pa, what is it?'

Billy's father sensed the wariness in his son's voice. He hesitated before going on.

'I'm worried for you, son. That's what it is. You don't fool me. We look the other way, but maybe that's not right either. Maybe we're all complicit. Robbing from where you work, it's . . . not the Christian thing. There's right and there's wrong. Now, what those toffs of yours are throwing away, well, maybe that's not theft. Who knows? Maybe that hunk o' red deer got dropped on the kitchen floor, and your dandies are too proud to eat it, all because of a bit of dirt. Well, I'll never say no to that. I'm a proud man, but not so much as I'd deny my children. But . . . there are lines in life, son. Do you know what I'm saying? There are lines we mustn't cross, not if we're good, God-fearing people. And, son, when you come home with your pockets full of silver—'

'Oh, Pa!' Billy exploded. 'It's Christmas night! You might just say thank you and—'

'Now, Billy—'

'No, Pa. *You* listen. I'm helping. I want to help. Those bairns deserve everything I got, and more. So do you, and so does Ma. So why don't you just *let* me? I'm sorry, Pa. I'm sorry if I'm doing better than y—' Billy stopped. His father's face was suddenly crestfallen. Perhaps he had taken it too far. He set his glass down and muttered, 'Sorry, Pa, this bourbon's stronger than I reckoned. It's gone straight to my head. I'm going to bed now. It's Christmas in the morning. I always loved Christmas.'

Billy did not turn back, not even as his mother came back into the room. Upstairs, he threw himself onto his bed, with fists clenched at his side. Through the walls his brothers and sisters were still chattering. By God, he missed the pure innocent magic of Christmas.

Innocence. Now, there was a word. Billy tried to ignore it, but he could still hear his father as he closed his eyes to go to sleep. *There's right and there's wrong*. Well, Billy had always known it. And taking tips from Mr Charles for eavesdropping on Lord Edgerton and his Fascist Union friends, copying down the contents of a few envelopes passed here and there, taking careful note of what Graf and Gräfin Schecht said about Mr Baldwin and Mr Chamberlain when they gathered for drinks in the hotel bars, had never seemed so very wrong to him. Billy was too young to remember the Great War, but he was not young enough that he couldn't see the impression a war like that left on his father. Who would want the world to slide into another war like that? And if the titbits he picked up in the hotel might help Mr Charles in whatever glorious endeavour he was engaged in, well, Billy was proud to do it.

But then he thought of Vivienne Edgerton and Mr Simenon, his illicit trips to the Midnight Rooms, the phials he brought back. He thought of how she had cornered him in that suite, and the look of neediness and desperation on her face.

And the thing he had promised to do, all so that she would not tell.

Serving Mr Charles and whoever he was working for was one thing. That was a noble secret. But being in the service of Vivienne Edgerton? Betraying his friends, so that he himself might not be betrayed? Well, that was quite another.

What if I don't do it? he wondered. The thought kept him awake long into the night. *If I say no? Well, then she tells Mr Charles who's been supplying her, and then . . . then it's my neck on the chopping block, then it's me being marched out of the Buckingham without even a letter of recommendation to my name.*

Then it's me coming back home, empty-handed every night. No wages. No little extras. No treats saved from the dustbins being brought back to feed that lot through there. And . . . Billy thought of his father, all of the days he'd come back from the fish market not knowing if there would be work for him the next day, the next week, the next month. The world was cruel out there. The well-fed one day were starving the next. *All those faces, depending on me. How could I let one of them go hungry for even one night? What does right and wrong matter when there's hungry children to be thinking about?*

Somewhere out there, over the rooftops of London, Big Ben began to toll midnight. Christmas Day had come.

Chapter Thirty-one

Earlier that same night and the chambermaids of the Buckingham Hotel ought to have been in bed long ago. Yet here they were, gathered in the staff kitchenette, all clamouring for a story. 'Tell us!' the girls said. 'Every . . . last . . . detail!' they insisted. Nancy Nettleton craned around, taking in each of their faces in turn. Rosa and Ruth. Agatha and Frances.

'We know how it started,' Rosa laughed. 'Dance lessons. And then—'

'What did he do, just kiss you?'

'You ever been kissed before, Nance?'

'I reckon she has! Girl from a mining town like that. You'd have been fighting 'em off, were you, Nance?'

'Wait, wait, wait!' Nancy cried out. 'I'll tell you,' she said – and there was an audible gasp around the room. 'But you have to promise me. This is our secret, girls. *Please*. If Mrs Moffatt were to find out . . .'

'Oh, rot!' Ruth cackled. 'She's only a dragon half of the time. You think you're the first serving girl, Nancy Nettleton, who's fallen for somebody she shouldn't in this hotel? When I first got here, there was Suzanne. Now, Suzanne and this guest, Lord Some Such or Other, they were found in—'

'Oh, *hush now*, Ruth! It's Nancy's story we're after.'

Nancy inhaled deeply, taking in all of the expectant faces around her. *You can't lie now, Nancy. They've seen. And . . . look at them. You thought they'd scorn you for it. You thought they'd mock and . . . what? Use it against you?* No, looking at them now, Nancy didn't see a group of girls scrabbling for some gossip just to spread it around. She saw them thrilling alongside her. She saw them eager for a little romance, a little adventure, a little love.

So she told them. Every last bit.

Later, much later, when all the girls were off to bed, Nancy silently crossed the darkened Buckingham halls and knocked on a door. Moments later, the door drew back – and there, still in his evening suit from his night spent in the shadow of Nathaniel White on the ballroom floor, stood Raymond de Guise.

Nancy held up her hands. In them there was a little package, wrapped in crêpe paper and tied with an emerald ribbon.

'Come in,' Raymond whispered, with a smile.

Nancy looked quickly up and down the corridor. Tonight, with her story finally shared, she felt as light as the air.

When she was certain there was nobody to see, she darted inside.

'I told them,' she blurted out. 'Rosa and Ruth and the others. I—'

'And they're not going to—'

'Gossip?' Nancy grinned. 'Oh, they'll gossip. I'm certain of that. But they'll gossip with each other. They'll natter away. They're my friends, Raymond. At least I think . . .' She passed him the gift. 'Please,' she said, 'open it.'

'It's not Christmas morning.'

Somewhere, far away, the bells of St Stephen's Tower were tolling. 'It is,' said Nancy, 'so open it! I want to see your face.'

Raymond's hand trembled as he worked at the ribbon. *Why are you so nervous?* he asked himself. But he already knew. There was something on the tip of his tongue, something that he wanted to say.

The crêpe paper came apart and fell to the ground at his feet. Inside, there was a little wooden box, decorated with spirals and swirls. It smelt of beeswax. Raymond had no idea what he was looking at but he smiled all the same; it came from Nancy, and that was all that mattered.

'Well,' she beamed, 'open it again.'

Together they perched on the end of the bed and Raymond opened the varnished box. Almost immediately, a motor started whirring. The box rumbled in his hands as, from its centre, two uniquely sculpted figurines arose: two dancing figures, holding each other in a classical pose.

'A music box.' Raymond grinned, and listened to the melody. 'A Viennese waltz.'

Nancy smiled. 'It's Christmas. It had to be elegant. I didn't think a cha-cha would do.'

'I love it,' said Raymond. 'I . . .'

He fell silent. Was Nancy mistaken, or was he embarrassed? *There's something on his mind,* thought Nancy.

Raymond produced a gift, wrapped in scarlet paper and finished with a bow. 'For you, Nancy.'

She unwrapped it gently, not wanting to tear the paper, until she had revealed a black taffeta evening gown. She unrolled it, held it up against herself. *It's so unforgettable. Something Hélène would wear.* It had exaggerated peaked sleeves, sheared down the centre and puffed up to perfection.

'For when we go dancing. Because, we *are* going dancing, Nancy, you and I. Might be we disappear off to the Hammersmith Palais, down to Margate, to Brighton – somewhere they don't know us. Somewhere where we can be us. Away from Buckingham eyes.'

Nancy was too full of emotion. 'I love it,' she whispered.

'There's something I have to say.'

Nancy was caught off-guard. 'You don't have to say it again. You already said it. I know you're sorry, Raymond. I know what you were going through. You don't have to—'

'It's not that.'

Nancy froze. *Something's happened,* she thought. *Maynard Charles or Vivienne Edgerton . . . Something's wrong.* 'Raymond, what is it?'

Raymond leaned forward, clasping Nancy's hands. 'Nancy, the last few months – I think they've taught me more about life than any before. The world's changing. There's something coming – something . . . dreadful, or magnificent, something that's going to change everything. It's happening about us now . . . But Nancy, my eyes have been opened—'

'Raymond,' she said with a tremble in her voice, 'you're frightening me. What is it?'

Raymond drew her to him and kissed her, long and hard.

'It's that I love you. Here and now I love you, and that's never going to change.'

There were two separate Christmas mornings in the Buckingham Hotel. Across the hotel the guests would rise before eight and make their way to the dining rooms, where Christmas breakfast

– a spectacular continental affair of extravagant pastries, succulent cheeses and cured meats – was waiting to be served. But for all those who worked at the Buckingham, Christmas morning began in the pitch hours of night. Outside, London slept on – but here in the Buckingham, ranges were being warmed, tables were being laid, boilers were being stoked and a flock of turkeys pre-basted with butter and sage. For the guests, Christmas was a luxury; for the staff, it could feel like a forced march through the snow.

The alarm clock trilled and Raymond reached out to silence it. As he rolled back into place, he realised that the space beside him was empty. He squinted up. Nancy must have been so in tune with the rhythms of the Buckingham that she had stirred moments before the alarm. She was already sitting on the bedside, pulling her apron over her pinafore.

Raymond picked himself up, draped his arms around Nancy's shoulders. 'Not yet,' he said teasingly. 'A little longer?'

'Raymond, I can't. Mrs Moffatt will be waiting. It's Christmas . . .'

'Well, quite,' said Raymond. 'But if you can't rest on Christmas Day, when can you?'

Nancy slapped his wandering hands away and pushed him back onto the bed. 'There are two worlds in the Buckingham – you dancers might waltz between them, but you can't deny it. Christmas Day is for those who can afford it. For the rest of us, Christmas has to wait till the work's done.' She was almost at the door when she turned back; the sight of him lying there was enough to make her face glow in a smile. How strange life was, and how quickly it could change. 'You won't be as smug this afternoon, when I've hung my shoes up for the day and you're still entertaining guests in the Queen Mary.' She rushed back to his side, planted her lips tenderly over his.

The clock on the wall read a quarter to five.

'Merry Christmas, my dear Raymond,' she whispered.

Raymond did not lounge for long. As soon as Nancy had vanished, he rose and paced the length and breadth of his quarters. Then he began his routines: stretching first his legs, then his back, then his arms, his shoulders, his neck. The press-ups were for the strength in his arms; the sit-ups for the core muscles that directed the dance. The squats and stretches he performed were the same exercises that Georges had shown him all that time ago. He had stuck to them like a religious rite ever since. If Nancy were still here, and if he had dared ask, he would have performed each stretch with her balanced over his shoulders – anything to make sure his body was right, that he was strong enough to show the dancers in the ballroom what they had been missing.

The sweet scent of Nancy was still on his bed sheets. After he had finished his routine, he reclined for a moment on the bed and remembered her. It was, he decided, the most miraculous thing. *Somebody who knows who I am, every last inch of me, for better and worse. Somebody I . . . love.*

When, at last, the sun was shining its pale winter light across the Buckingham Hotel, he dressed in his smartest day suit and brogues, turning himself into the gentleman he most certainly was not. As he studied himself in the mirror, he wondered if his mother, his aunts and Artie were keeping to the old traditions today: turkey at noon, and then drinking in the social club through the afternoon, all crowned off with an argument of epic proportions. There was, he admitted, a part of him that wished he was there. If he looked at himself askance, he saw Ray Cohen; if he looked at himself face on, he was Raymond de Guise. Perhaps, after what he and Artie had done, they'd even expected him to be there – back where he belonged. He'd sent word, just as Maynard Charles had asked. He'd delivered the banknotes, made a promise that there was more to come – that all Artie had to do was get on with the business of being alive, and that everything would be all right. He hoped it had bought them a good Christmas – good enough to keep Artie out of trouble, at any rate. But a little piece of him still pined for the snow falling over the rooftops of Whitechapel, the dirty footprints snaking up and down the Commercial Road.

Raymond shook off the feeling and strode out of his quarters and into the golden lift. Nancy might have been working since long before dawn, but she was not the only one who had to serve the Buckingham this Christmas Day. The Grand Ballroom would be closed until evening, when the Archie Adams Band was due to play its Yuletide extravaganza, but until then Raymond had other duties to perform.

Mid-morning, and the Queen Mary was a hive of activity. The champagne breakfast was served but, everywhere, the diners remained – and here they would stay until the clocks tolled noon and Christmas luncheon was served. Raymond hovered in the doorway, watching the diners. In the heart of the room was the ceremonial serving station where the first of the Christmas turkeys would be carved by Maynard Charles. Many of the diners here were day guests, descending on the Buckingham for lunches and dinners – the whole of the Brazilian embassy had turned out at the management's invitation to celebrate the season – but Raymond saw staying guests among them too: Mr Perez, the star of the Parisian stage; Belikov and Blokin, the Russian playwrights who, it was rumoured, were personal friends of the old king.

Maynard Charles bowed between the tables and, as Raymond sashayed through, they met alongside the sweeping mahogany bar.

'Time to employ that characteristic charm of yours, Mr de Guise. Fraternise, my good man.'

Raymond looked around the room. Archie Adams was holding court at a table where guests were enraptured to hear stories of his time in the hotel bars of New York and New Orleans. It did not surprise him to find Nathaniel White in attendance at the neighbouring table. The odious young man, with his blond hair styled in a magnificent flourish, was dressed in a silver waistcoat and sitting alongside his father and a collection of men from the German embassy on Belgrave Square. Maynard Charles tipped his head towards them and whispered, 'You'd do worse than fraternise there, Raymond. Consider that an order.'

Raymond held himself tightly. 'Mr Charles, it's Christmas—'

'Be that as it may, we are still at work. And, now that you know what manner of work I am bound up with, you might consider lending your assistance.' He kept his voice low. Maynard Charles, Raymond was beginning to understand, was a man who could keep a secret. Raymond wondered what other secrets the private man might have kept. 'My colleagues will know the ambassador came here, and who he came with. I must give them something. And Billy Brogan is not here to undertake his duties for me. So do your best for me, Raymond. There's a good chap.'

There was a seat alongside Nathaniel, and Raymond slipped into it. He was practised at hiding his disgust, and – in spite of Nathaniel's razor glare – quickly found ways to charm his way into the conversation. There was snow in the Black Forest, the ambassador was saying. Berlin itself was a picture of perfect white. The Berliners and the British, Nathaniel's father interjected, they were not so very different. And Raymond – in spite of himself – found himself agreeing, if only for something to say. Raymond had been to Berlin. He had danced in the ballroom at the Hotel Adlon with its dramatic elephant fountain and grand piano in the lobby. 'The ballroom there is a marvel of mahogany and marble,' he said. 'And the dancing girls . . .'

'Yes,' the ambassador grinned with a gleam in his eye, 'nowhere in the world are there dancing girls as in Berlin.'

In this way, an hour and more passed. The champagne was in full flow. Raymond could feel himself light-headed already, though trying to remain alert to the exchange of information. Then, suddenly, silence spread like a wildfire, from one table to the next. Raymond looked around, following the eyes of his fellow diners.

At the back of the hall, the doors to the Queen Mary service kitchen opened. A procession of waiters marched out. Then, as if on military parade, they formed a guard of honour along which the head waiter and his second-in-command appeared, bearing the first of the enormous Gloucestershire turkeys on a silver platter. A rousing cheer went up from the nearest tables, and the turkey was taken to the centre of the room, where Maynard Charles stood with his carving knife at the ready. Raymond watched as he sliced through the golden skin, revealing the moist flesh underneath. Then, all at once, the ceremony was complete. While all eyes were on Maynard Charles, the waiters had returned to the kitchen – and now they flocked out, bearing platters and plates, trays on which champagne glasses were fizzing and overflowing. Somewhere, a cork popped, arcing out over the diners. Somewhere else, Christmas crackers were pulled, revealing slim silver wristwatches and golden cufflinks within. The air around Raymond was heavy with the scent of butter-basted turkey, the salt of bacon wrapped around fresh sausages, the sweet tang of cranberry sauce. He had forgotten what it was like to eat quite so handsomely, and his love for the Buckingham Hotel was suddenly renewed when a steaming hot plate was laid down in front of him. Raymond felt a sudden flush of pride at all the hundreds of people devoted to keeping the Buckingham alive. *Maynard Charles was right. The Buckingham can't wane. The Buckingham can't fall. Too many of us depend on it.*

He looked up. Nathaniel White was pontificating to the ambassador and his staff on the intricacies of the double reverse spin and his elevated place in the ballroom – but Raymond looked straight past him, over the heads of the other diners, to the very doors of the Queen Mary itself.

He felt as if his heart would stop.

There, hovering in the doorway, stood his brother, Artie. Their mother, Alma. Aunts May and Rebecca lingered behind. *They look as out of place as Lord Edgerton would in the markets on Cable Street*, Raymond thought. *Or Maynard Charles grifting scrap metal in the yard with my old man.* They were gazing with faces crinkled up in nerves, Artie shifting from foot to foot in awkwardness. *It isn't many of us who can slip from one world to another . . .*

Raymond was still staring at them when he felt fingers drumming on his shoulder. So frozen was he that, at first, he did not turn around. The sheer incongruity of seeing his family here in the Buckingham had rooted him to his seat – so that he only looked up at all when he felt the moist breath in his ear, and the words, 'Get rid of them, Raymond, and do it without anyone noticing. Do it *now*.'

He looked up. He had almost been able to feel Maynard Charles's whiskers tickling his ear. 'Excuse me, gentlemen,' he said to the table – and then, braving their inscrutable glances, he marched across the Queen Mary and, throwing his arms open as if to embrace them, ushered his family back out of the room.

In the hallway outside, Raymond stopped dead.

'What are you . . . ?'

'You look like you seen a ghost!' crowed Mrs Cohen. 'A ghost at that feast of yours. Well, did you think we was going to forget you on Christmas Day, Ray? After what you done for Artie? After what you done for us? Well, we were all sitting there – Artie, your aunts and me – and we thought . . . Christmas is for families, Ray. We ought to be together. Your pa always sorted you brothers out when you was fighting. What would he have thought of the way we been carrying on?' She paused. 'Well, Ray? Aren't you gonna invite us in?'

Raymond looked over his shoulder. He fancied he could still feel the glaring eyes of Maynard Charles boring holes in his back. Through the portholes in the door he could see that somebody was making a speech.

He ought to have been there too. Raymond should have been waltzing between the tables, putting on a performance every bit as flamboyant and dramatic as his demonstrations down in the ballroom.

'I'm sorry,' he said. 'I can't take you in.'

Artie's face turned to thunder. 'I thought we'd got an understanding, Ray? I thought we was good . . .'

'No,' Raymond grinned, 'I won't take you in there, but *I* won't go back either.' He opened his arms, directing his family back up the corridor, to the reception hall. 'Come – there's somewhere else, but you'll have to hurry. Mr Simenon's sloping around here somewhere, Artie. You remember the last time you met Mr Simenon?'

'I remember,' said Artie, 'that he couldn't keep a Cohen boy down.'

'Yes,' said Raymond with a smile, 'but let's not tempt the fates, shall we?'

The doors of the housekeeping lounge opened wide and into the chaos of music and drinking stepped Raymond, his brother at his side.

The housekeeping was finished for Christmas Day. The porters were left with so little to do – for Christmas Day was the one day in the year when guests neither arrived nor departed from the Buckingham Hotel. The chambermaids, the laundry staff, the members of the Archie Adams Band not grand enough to take their places in the Queen Mary; all were here, where the glasses were overflowing with whatever cheap alcoholic delights the grandees in the Queen Mary could not withstand. In front of Raymond and his family was a scene more reminiscent of the Midnight Rooms than the Buckingham Hotel itself. A small contingent from the Archie Adams Band, led by Louis Kildare and his soaring saxophone, were playing something that sounded, to Raymond's ears, like American swing. On the tables, pushed against the walls, Sofía LaPegna and her friends were dancing, baring their ankles for all the room to see.

'Artie,' he said, 'Ma, Aunt May. Rebecca.' He opened his arms wide. 'You don't want to be up there with ambassadors and doyennes. Where's the fun in talking politics and high society with that lot of old toffs? No, you want to be here. Welcome,' he beamed, 'to the beating heart of the Buckingham Hotel . . .'

Raymond watched them fan out, his mother and aunts reticent to join the hubbub, Artie's eyes drawn slavishly to Sofía LaPegna and the rest, shimmying up on the tables. He had the most disorientating feeling of his worlds colliding; the whole of the Buckingham Hotel seemed different somehow. For a moment, panic ripped through his body – with just a few words his family could bring the truth of Raymond de Guise crashing down around him. But he shook himself – if you couldn't trust family, who could you trust? He watched as Artie took a swig from one of the bottles left on display, then spun himself in a circle to capture the hand of one of the kitchen girls. Moments later, he was spinning her around. Raymond had quite forgotten that Artie was no slouch on the dance floor; Stanley Cohen, he remembered, was a part of them both. And here was his ma, drawn into conversation with one of the housekeeping mistresses. Aunts May and Rebecca were already stripping off their coats and looking for partners with whom to dance.

Raymond beamed, giddy as a man who'd been drinking champagne since before breakfast. He'd spent so long denying he had any family at all. Was it possible he'd been wrong, all this time?

And was Artie charming Sofía LaPegna *already*?

At that moment, he felt a hand snake around his waist and looked down to see Nancy standing there, with a glass of champagne in her hand.

'I thought you had duties to attend to?' she asked, with a wicked grin.

Raymond shrugged. 'My seat is going cold up in the Queen Mary.' He paused. 'I'd rather be here,' he said – and, at that moment, a rousing cheer went up. A string of chambermaids and the younger concierges had formed a conga and began to snake up and down the lounge. Raymond saw Louis Kildare, saxophone still in hand, at its head. It seemed a revelation, at last, to admit it to himself: upstairs, with the dukes and duchesses and other men of means, he was a day-tripper; downstairs he was at home. 'Oh,' he said, spying his mother re-emerging from the crowd, 'and there's one more thing . . .'

'Who's this then, Ray?' Alma Cohen asked, looking Nancy up and down. Nancy was not certain whether the look on her face was genuine inquisitiveness or sneer. 'This another reason you been holding out on us, is it, boy?'

Nancy looked, aghast, between Raymond and the eerily familiar stranger.

'Nancy,' Raymond began, in his boldest declarative voice, 'may I introduce you to—'

Alma Cohen gave a deliberate splutter. 'The name's Jones,' she interjected. 'We used to carry Raymond's bags, back in his continental days. We was your . . . retinue. Wasn't we, Mr de Guise?'

She raised her eyebrows imperceptibly, as if inviting him to join the charade – and, in that moment, Raymond felt such a surge of love and gratitude. All of the disappointment and distance there had been between them – and now this . . . To pretend she was not his mother, to help him maintain his facade even when it meant denying her firstborn son – somehow this seemed the greatest act of love Raymond had ever known.

'No,' Raymond said, gently placing a hand on her forearm. 'Nancy, this is my mother. Alma Cohen. Ma, this is Nancy Nettleton. She's the real reason I'm staying here at the Buckingham Hotel. Ballroom or not, I'm here for her.'

Alma Cohen looked Nancy up and down. Then, with an approving nod, she said, 'More beautiful than any of those toffs up there in that fancy restaurant of yours. Well, Nancy, I'm charmed.' Then, out of the side of her mouth, Alma whispered, 'Dance well, does she?'

'Like an angel,' said Raymond, and squeezed Nancy's hand.

The conga swept by and Raymond reached out to join its tail as it passed. It was then, with Nancy and his mother behind him in the line, that the real Christmas celebrations began.

Christmas night, and at last all was quiet in the Buckingham Hotel. The ballroom lay still and serene. The Queen Mary had served its last meal. The Candlelight Club was closed to all but the most privileged guests – and Maynard Charles had finally handed over the keys to the bronze revolving doors to his night manager for the evening. Now he stepped out of the golden lift, walked his familiar circuit to his own quarters – just in case he was being observed – and, doubling back, arrived at the doors of the Park Suite.

At the little dining table in front of the fire, Mrs Moffatt and Aubrey Higgins looked around as Maynard entered. Aubrey raised his glass of cognac and gave Maynard the most sympathetic smile. Christmas Day was hard toil; Maynard looked as if he needed yet another stiff drink.

Maynard took off his evening jacket and draped it over the back of a chair. By the time he reached the table, Mrs Moffatt was on her feet and tidying her plate away. Maynard touched her tenderly on the arm. 'I'm grateful, Emmeline,' he said. 'You've been such a good friend to us, over the years. Thank you for being here for Aubrey when I cannot. Christmas Day would be the worse without you.'

'Nonsense,' Mrs Moffatt declared, collecting her own coat from the stand in the corner. 'Christmas is for family and friends. I consider you both. That goes for you as well, Mr Higgins. Besides, I'm too old for whatever shenanigans they'll have been up to in housekeeping.' At the table, Aubrey gave her a salute. 'He's a monster at rummy,' Mrs Moffatt whispered. 'He had me gambling for matchsticks. I lost my fortune.'

'Yes,' said Maynard, 'he's always been a hustler,' and he lifted the lid from the silver platter on the room service trolley. There was dinner enough here for him. 'Emmeline,' he said, 'from the bottom of my heart – thank you.'

Mrs Moffatt's face turned an unlikely shade of crimson. 'That's the last I'll hear of it,' she said. 'Happy Christmas, gentlemen.'

After she was gone, Maynard poured them both a glass of cognac.

'To one more year,' Aubrey began, raising his glass for a toast.

Maynard said, 'It isn't over yet.'

'There's something bothering you,' said Aubrey. 'No, don't deny it. I've known you too long, Maynard. I can see it on your face. You get a single crinkle between your eyes. You're lost in thought. Has –' he hesitated before going on – 'something happened, my dear Maynard? Was Christmas Day a catastrophe?'

Maynard paused. How to describe the feeling that had been building in him all day? How to put something as intangible as this into words? The day, he reflected now, had gone exactly according to plan – as he had known that it would. The Christmas luncheon had been a triumph. The Grand had been a magnificent affair. Even when Raymond's secret world arrived unannounced in the Queen Mary, there had been no disaster. Raymond had handled it with considerable aplomb.

Why, then, did Maynard Charles get the feeling he was sleepwalking, sleepwalking into something from which there was no return?

Was it how close they'd come, in the past week, to inviting Lord Edgerton's wrath, his stepdaughter found half dead on the Buckingham floor? Was it how Nathaniel White strode through the ballroom, a colossus with connections to the most dangerous Englishmen in London? Was it his last meeting with Mr Moorcock, and the fear he had felt for so many years – the fear of exposure, the fear of being *found out*? Was it only that New Year was on the horizon and, without King Edward to grace his hotel, the extravaganza on which so much of the hotel's future rested was suddenly so much more of a risk?

Or was it something more? This feeling he couldn't escape, that not only the Buckingham, but the whole of England itself, was marching onwards into thc dark? That the titbits he gathered for Mr Moorcock were but the tip of the iceberg. That the England he loved and had fought and lost so many friends for was standing, brave but alone, in the path of a coming storm?

Maynard Charles drained his glass. If they were dancing to disaster, he decided, there was nothing to do but dance on. The world had to keep turning. He was but one man, and a hotelier at that. How could one man do anything to change the world?

He reached out and took Aubrey's hand gently.

'It was,' he declared, 'a triumph.'

But all that night, and into the long morning after, the thought would not leave him: *every day was another day closer to the end.*

Chapter Thirty-two

THE CLOCK TICKED DOWN to the masquerade ball. Across the hotel, not a soul escaped the pounding headaches and aching bones as they returned to their early morning duties. And as Mrs Moffatt marshalled her girls to overturn the rooms being vacated by the Christmas guests, Nancy Nettleton realised, for the first time in her life, that pleasure and pain were inextricably interconnected. *It's little wonder that Father struggled so much to free himself from his laudanum at the end. It's little wonder that Vivienne Edgerton is so in thrall to her powder.* A little drink, a little something, to push the pain away for another day would have been most welcome right now. But instead Nancy pushed on, with Rosa and Ruth, Mrs Moffatt, Mrs Whitehead and all of the rest.

Billy Brogan had not been here to see the Buckingham in its revelries, but as he sloped through the staff entrance and kicked the snow from his heels, he had a similar sinking feeling in his stomach. He was relieved to see that Mr Simenon was not at his post and slipped into the concierge's office. Returning to the Buckingham Hotel had always been such an exciting endeavour. But now? He started at the sound of the familiar tread of Maynard Charles as he made his rounds. It was not right to be spooked at every little sound. The Buckingham seemed different somehow. Surely it was not what his father had said to him? The feeling had been growing in him all Christmas. Where once every suite had promised a bounty – either an errand he might run for a few coppers, or a titbit he might find and trade back to Maynard Charles – now they seemed traps designed to ensnare him. He was, he decided with his heart beating wildly, in the pocket of too many different people. Serving Maynard Charles was one thing. Eavesdropping on conversations, snooping in some noble's suite while he was being entertained in the ballroom – these things had always thrilled Billy. But he realised now: he ought not to have read Raymond de Guise's letter and traded its contents back to Maynard Charles. He ought not to have scurried off to the Midnight Rooms so regularly, bringing back harm with him to the Buckingham halls. Possibly the only thing he was proud of was delivering Hélène Marchmont's letters back to that address in Brixton so that they did not have to go through the hotel post room – but even then he recalled the moments he had slipped his finger into the envelope, eased it open so that it might be resealed, and read what lay within. Maynard Charles had taught him that secrets were currency, but a new thought had occurred to Billy: *secrets are a poison. They're poisoning me now.*

And here was the reason. Composing himself, he stepped out of Mr Simenon's office and saw the revolving doors open on the other side of the reception hall. From them, a porter already carrying her bags, stepped Vivienne Edgerton. Billy's heart leaped. She looked as elegant as ever, in a flowing felt coat of forest green and with a pin in her hair, but Billy had long since stopped thinking about her beauty. No, his heart soared for one reason only: Vivienne Edgerton was still alive, and that meant that the powders Mr Simenon had sent him to procure for her were either still tucked away in her bags, or that they hadn't poisoned her at all.

Billy tried to avoid her gaze, but soon Vivienne's eyes had found him. There seemed something defiant about her today. She waved the porter past and he paused at the guest lift, holding the door open for her. Vivienne made him wait. Instead, she approached the check-in desk behind which Billy lingered and fixed him with a glare. 'I'll need to see you, Billy,' she said, 'and soon. I'll be in the ballroom at noon. Make certain to find me there . . .'

Billy floundered for words. He'd been lucky once. The last thing he wanted was to be sent back to the Midnight Rooms for more. His father's words rang in his head.

'Billy?'

'Yes, Miss Edgerton,' he whispered, and could not stop himself shaking until the lift doors were closed with Vivienne inside. *Perhaps,* he wondered, *it's time. Time to run. There are other jobs. Other hotels. Maybe, if I'm lucky, I won't need a reference at all. There's a whole world out there. They always needed pages at the Savoy and the London Ritz. There are hotels in Paris and Berlin, hotels in New York and even further afield.*

Anywhere, he thought, where the secrets and promises battling each other in his head might not be poised to expose him.

Vivienne Edgerton strode into her room, found it arranged to her satisfaction, and dismissed the porter with neither thanks nor tip. Then, with the door locked behind her, she spilled the contents of her suitcase onto the bed. The Madeleine Vionnet gown could go back into her wardrobe, the rouge and perfume onto the dresser. The pearls had been a gift from Lord Edgerton. He would expect her to wear them at New Year, she supposed, and perhaps she would indulge him; her hatred of her stepfather did not extend to the expensive jewellery he foisted on her – all those gifts, just so she wouldn't put up a fuss at being kept here. Besides, her mother would attend the ballroom for the New Year celebrations as well – and, if it was the last thing she did, Vivienne intended to be noticed by her mother at New Year. Nothing else would do. Nothing else mattered.

She looked down at the bed. There, among the gifts she had not asked for and the cards her old friends from New York had sent to the Suffolk mansion, not knowing she'd been banished to the Buckingham all this time, was the little lavender drawstring pouch. She upended its contents into her palm. The two phials of Midnight Rooms powder were still intact. She gazed at them for a long time.

It wasn't that she hadn't been tempted. But she'd stayed strong.

She looked around her. These same four walls. The same telephone by the bed, by which she'd call for the same meals from the same room service. No one to talk to. Still no formal introduction to English high society, and no way to make friends here without one. It was no surprise she'd found solace in these little drawstring pouches. But . . .

The chambermaid. The disgrace of it all. Being peeled off the carpet, sponged clean by that girl with the lame leg. Vivienne meant to be noticed, but not like this. *And they'll all be gossiping, of course. You can't trust a chambermaid to keep her lips sealed. She'll have told anyone who'll listen – as if being trapped here at the Buckingham Hotel wasn't bad enough already.*

Well, at the Masquerade Ball, I'll stand up and be seen. Not for the wreck they all think I am. Not as the spoilt little rich girl they all loathe. I'll stand in front of them all – talented and elegant, with poise and grace. Somebody to reckon with. Somebody to . . . love.

And then? Then, when my mother's finally seen? Well, then I'll tell them. I'm leaving. I'm leaving with Nathaniel. I'll follow him to the continent. I'll follow him to the other side of the world. Wherever his stardom takes him. Anywhere but here.

She had been staring at the phials of powder too long. Temptation grew stronger the longer she stared. In a sudden moment of clarity, she dropped them back in the lavender pouch and buried it in the pile of clothing at the bottom of her armoire.

Then she sat at the bedstead, produced an ink pen and pad of hotel notepaper, and began to inscribe the words she had been thinking about for so long.

It was time to put her plan into action.

By prior arrangement, the ballroom was to be closed between the celebrations of Christmas and the ball at New Year. This morning an army of chambermaids and porters had gathered to strip back the Christmas decorations and begin hanging the adornments for the ball.

The sprigs of holly with plump red berries and woven ropes of mistletoe were replaced by brass braziers in which blue and green flames would burn. The smaller Christmas trees which had sat in the corners of the ballroom were taken away as kindling, and in their place stood proud mannequins dressed in Venetian finery: startling white frocks with ostentatious frills and lace, great velvet capes bedecked in emerald feathers and tall headdresses.

Beyond them, the stage where the Archie Adams Band would welcome its guest singers was being transformed into a palace of glittering silver and gold leaf.

The main doors to the ballroom were open as workmen filed in and out, so it was simple enough for Vivienne to slip through. Maynard Charles was here too, surveying the carpenters, joiners and painters embroiled in their tasks. Maynard Charles came to stand at her side as Vivienne looked down on the dance floor where Raymond de Guise was practising a few simple moves with the Spanish girl Sofía LaPegna.

'It's good to see you on your feet, Miss Edgerton.'

Vivienne disliked the insolent reminder of her disgrace, so she nodded sharply.

'I was sorry to miss Christmas at the hotel,' she said at last. 'I have imagined it a magnificent affair.'

'I'm certain you had an extraordinary Christmas of your own?'

'Extraordinary is not quite the word. Mr Charles, I believe I know what you're thinking. I have been a hindrance to your good work in my stepfather's hotel. I hope you know how much I appreciate your discretion. You are going to see a changed woman, Mr Charles. By New Year, you will see – I promise.'

Maynard Charles hesitated. The doors to the dressing rooms had opened and out onto the dance floor came Nathaniel White and Hélène Marchmont, no doubt practising the routine with which they would open the Masquerade Ball. Maynard Charles remembered last New Year, when Hélène had returned from her sabbatical and he had watched her dance with Raymond. The ballroom had come to a standstill to watch them turn around each other. One of the guests had remarked that it was as impressive an affair as watching Alicia Markova or Margot Fonteyn at the Royal Ballet. Sofía LaPegna and all the other girls in the troupe had marvelled at everything they saw, the emotion of it as Raymond and Hélène danced, each of a piece with the other – and perhaps it had inspired them all to greater deeds, too, because in the months afterwards the ballroom had been more alive with magic and light than Maynard could remember. *And we need that this year, we need it more than ever.*

But the sad fact was that watching Nathaniel throw Hélène around was not the same. It was showy and ostentatious and some of the things they were doing seemed improbably ambitious, but there was something more mechanical, less elegant, about it as well. Hélène's face seemed locked in a rictus of concentration.

Vivienne's eyes were on them too. Maynard Charles sensed her imperceptibly hardening.

'We can manage almost any scandal here at the Buckingham, Miss Edgerton, but were anything untoward to happen where I cannot disguise it . . .'

Vivienne wrenched her eyes away from Nathaniel – was she wrong or did his hands not *have* to rest so low in the small of Hélène's back? – and faced Maynard Charles. 'You will see me for who I really am, Mr Charles.'

Maynard was momentarily at a loss, the silence following her declaration difficult to interpret. He simply nodded and stepped aside.

After he was gone, Vivienne fingered the hotel notepaper she had secreted in her hand. Her eyes were fixed on Hélène, the way she stiffened and then softened as she and Nathaniel danced. Yes, Vivienne thought, there was nothing here that was beyond her. Nathaniel had shown her enough. All she wanted – all she *needed* – was for the world to listen. Everyone deserved to be heard, didn't they?

She was watching them still when she heard the patter of footsteps behind her. Billy Brogan had appeared. He was wearing one of his sheepish looks, as if to say he didn't want to be here at all. But what did that matter?

She handed him the paper. 'Arrange it for me, Billy. Do this one thing and we'll say no more about the Midnight Rooms.'

Billy opened the paper, took in the words Vivienne had written, and felt as if a crevasse was opening up underneath him, earthen hands reaching up to drag him down.

Billy folded the letter and scurried away.

Chapter Thirty-three

Maynard Charles woke with a start, his heart and head pounding as he clawed his way up from some feverish dream.

It was dark in the Park Suite. Maynard trembled as he reached for the water he had left at the bedside, then stood and peeled back the blinds. Fat, lazy snowflakes were drifting down across the square. London was a perfect vision of white. He could not have asked for a more magnificent setting for his New Year celebrations.

Why, then, is my heart beating like a panicked bird?

Why, then, was the Buckingham Hotel crumbling to dust in my dreams?

He'd felt like this only twice in his life before: the first, his boarding school days, and those long, empty hours sitting outside the headmaster's office, waiting for a thrashing; and the second, the battlefields of Flanders and France, waiting with his bayonet in hand for the whistles to start sounding and the boys to start pouring over the top.

Outside, the snow kept falling.

'Hurry up, de Guise, the entourage is already here!'

Raymond sat in the dressing rooms behind the ballroom, wrapping the bandages more tightly around his chest. The ribs had healed, he was fairly certain of that – but the hours he'd put in, practising in the ballroom, had shown up in new bruises along the lines of each rib. Last night Nancy had run her fingers along each one. A mid-morning vermouth had dulled the ache for an hour, but there were less than ten hours between now and the moment the Archie Adams Band would strike up their first song, announcing the beginning of the great Masquerade Ball. It was not long enough, but it was all that he had. He wrapped the bandages tighter. All they had to do was sustain him for one more night. His foot had healed but that didn't mean it had stopped aching. He would worry about the ruin he was making of his body tomorrow.

Nathaniel White turned on his heel and marched to the dressing-room door. 'It's your funeral, de Guise. It's not *you* who's dancing for their pleasure tonight.'

Raymond took a deep breath. Nathaniel could say what he wanted; on the dance floor, it was not words that mattered. Raymond fastened the remaining buttons on his shirt. He would dance more stiffly trussed up like this – but the irony was he would still dance more elegantly than Nathaniel. The crowd would see that, even if White did not.

In the reception hall, the Buckingham gathered. As Raymond made his way up from the ballroom, he could see the kitchen staff turned out in their perfect whites, standing like a phalanx with the Queen Mary's head chef at the front. The other hotel departments were arranged in similar military fashion. Mr Simenon had his concierges drilled and standing to attention. Mrs Moffatt had organised her chambermaids in pristine uniforms. Raymond caught Nancy's eye as he marched past, giving her an almost imperceptible wink. *I'm going to be OK, Nancy. You made it that way.* The truth was, he felt the pain in his ribs like a needle being worked around under his skin. But New Year was only one night. He would survive it and put on a show, even if it was the last thing he did.

In front of the Norwegian fir tree, Maynard Charles and the heads of department were lined up in order of rank. The night managers, the bookkeeper, the director of finance and accounts; all of them were turned out in their finery – and at their head paced Maynard Charles himself. The hotel director was turned out in a pinstripe suit of black and grey, his hair scraped back with pomade. A golden pocket watch dangled over his lapel, and silver cufflinks glistened at his wrists.

On one flank stood the assembled musicians from the Archie Adams Band. On the other, stood the demonstration dancers. Louis threw Raymond a smile as he marched over to join them, the needling eyes of Nathaniel White on him all the way. White was standing at the head of the party, with Hélène at his side. She turned to him as he came to stand directly behind her, alongside Sofía and the rest of the dancing girls.

'Are you . . . ?' she whispered, turning over her shoulder despite Nathaniel's ugly look.

'All's well,' Raymond returned. 'You may be picking up my broken bones from the dressing rooms this evening, but all shall be well. You can have faith in that.'

Hélène was about to reply when the revolving door turned. The first figure to appear was bedecked in a long black coat, and upon his head a tall top hat. Lord Edgerton himself. Behind him, like faithful retainers, came a succession of porters, who mingled with the assembled Buckingham crowd until they had almost disappeared. Meanwhile, the revolving door kept turning – and through it stepped a tall man in his sixties in full military regalia, a tall beaverskin hat on his head. His face was adorned by magnificent whiskers, and his bright blue eyes stopped to take in the assembled crowd.

Maynard Charles stepped forward, Lord Edgerton by his side.

'King Haakon,' he began, 'it is my pleasure to receive you once more. Might I tender my hotel at your service?'

'Mr Charles,' the King of Norway replied, his English accented with the harder sound of the northern landscapes he called home. 'The pleasure shall be ours. We have looked forward to our attendance.'

King Haakon had the look of an elderly headmaster, thought Raymond. Behind him, the bronze doors kept revolving. Next to step through was the King's wife, Queen Maud. A sexagenarian herself, she was draped in fur – and, as she had done all of her life, seemed to suit the royal accoutrements less well than her husband. A princess of Wales, Maud was the daughter of England's own late King Edward VII; for her, London was a homecoming. She took in the familiar sight of the Buckingham hall and Raymond was certain he saw her visibly relax.

No sooner had she stepped through and been introduced to Maynard Charles, than the doors turned again. Now came the crown princess, Princess Märtha Sofia, a glamorous beauty with short dark hair and simple pearls in each ear. She appeared on the arm of her husband, Prince Olav, the heir apparent to the Norwegian throne. Raymond watched as Lord Edgerton and Maynard Charles welcomed them, as yet more porters marched in behind, bearing suitcases and trunks.

As the Buckingham waited, Raymond cast his mind back to the New Year celebrations of times past. He'd seen Georges de la Motte put his arm around Queen Maud's waist and lead her out onto the dance floor. Two New Years past, Georges had waltzed for the first time with Princess Märtha in the ballroom at the Savoy. He felt a stabbing in his chest that was nothing to do with the state of his ribs. If it weren't for the Midnight Rooms, it would have been him twirling around the ballroom tonight with the queen and the crown princess and the rise of the fascist influence in this hotel would have had one more barrier to keep it at bay. His eyes drifted up, to where Nathaniel White was standing with his chest swollen with arrogant pride.

At Maynard Charles's signal, the assembly parted and a royal procession began, down through the reception square to the golden lifts – where, one after another, the royal family disappeared into the Buckingham interior. In the reception hall, the crowd let out a collective breath. Mrs Moffatt clapped her hands, summoning her girls back to their duties. Mr Simenon hissed at his concierges; the head chef barked orders, sending his underlings scurrying back to their kitchens. Meanwhile, Nathaniel took Hélène forcibly by the hand and turned her back towards the ballroom. 'We've only hours,' he declared. 'It has to be *perfect*.'

Hélène tore her hand away from him – but the clock was ticking, and she followed him all the same.

At 6 p.m., the doors to the Grand opened.

Billy Brogan lingered in the reception hall, beneath the boughs of the glorious Norwegian fir, and stared through the ballroom doors. He had never seen it look as beautiful. The cavernous interior was bedecked in hanging masks, the chandeliers lit up in radiant array. The dance floor itself was lacquered so that it reflected the lights. *It will be like they're dancing on an ocean,* thought Billy.

Tonight would prove if the Buckingham could withstand removal of the English king's patronage. Billy hovered anxiously in the reception hall as Lord Edgerton's associates arrived. Graf and Gräfin Schecht were already in attendance. Nathaniel White's father, Oliver, appeared with his family in tow, and a horse-drawn carriage wheeled around in the snow to deliver Lady Edgerton, Vivienne's mother, to the marble stairs. *The great and the good,* thought Billy. *We call these the great and the good.* Why, then, did he feel so dirty?

Soon, guests milled between the tables in the ballroom. The popping of champagne corks could be heard echoing in the ballroom's magnificent rafters, as waiters pirouetted across the expanse serving the canapés that the Queen Mary's sous-chefs had spent long days preparing. Billy thought about venturing down there. Hidden behind one of those fanciful masks, perhaps he might even go unnoticed. But then he looked at the revolving brass door, and the snow strafing down across Berkeley Square. The temptation to run out into it, to bury himself in the pure white, was almost overwhelming. He took two faltering steps in that direction, but then he stopped. The die had already been cast. His fate was already sealed.

Sickened, he turned back towards the ballroom.

In the dressing rooms, the excitement was threatening to turn into panic. Sofía LaPegna could not find the ribbon that matched her gown. Raymond was steeling himself against the pain in his ribs with the best Martini the Candlelight Club had been able to provide. Nancy kneeled at his side, sorting out the bandages he meant to bind himself in before the first dance. Louis Kildare was polishing his saxophone clean on the hem of his very best shirt, while Archie Adams welcomed one of the guest singers for the night – a dapper young man in a white cocktail suit, who went by the name of Alfredo Bianchi – and the rest of the orchestra ran through their set list with increasing intensity. In the midst of it all, Nathaniel White hovered over Hélène Marchmont as she stared into the looking glass, painting delicate lines around her eyes. Ordinarily, Hélène had the steadiest of hands – but tonight, even she was trembling.

'You *must* remember how it goes exactly,' Nathaniel intoned. 'Once the number comes to an end, release me at once. That's when I shall approach the crown princess.'

Hélène paused, still applying her kohl. 'It's drilled into me, Nathaniel. You can be certain of that.'

'My father is out there tonight.'

'I know that too,' she retorted, exasperated.

'Lord Edgerton and all of the rest. I've choreographed this specifically for them, Hélène. When we go through those doors . . .'

The kohl pencil snapped in Hélène's hands. Her eyes flashed up. She saw the state of herself in the mirror, the way she was holding herself so tensely. She paused, fought to regain her composure. Then, as serenely as she could muster, she said, 'Nathaniel, we've rehearsed for weeks now. It's perfect. Now, if you wouldn't mind—'

Hélène never got the chance to finish that thought, for in that precise moment, knuckles rapped urgently on the dressing-room doors – and, without waiting to be invited in, Billy Brogan crashed through. The look on his face was pure desperation. He took in the banks of staring faces, the way Archie Adams scowled at him for intruding, and paid it no mind. In moments he had loped across the dressing room to the place where Hélène was sitting. 'Hélène,' he said, 'can I—'

'Can't you see we're in the middle of something?' Nathaniel snapped. 'This is an important night, you bog-brained cretin. We're trying to—'

Hélène flew to her feet, wielding her eyeliner like a sabre. She stared at Nathaniel through the mirror. Then, softly, she said, 'Come with me, Billy,' and shepherded him back to the dressing-room door.

At the door, Hélène asked, 'What is it, Billy? He has the ear of the Edgertons. You mustn't upset him . . .'

Billy's face was scarlet – either with embarrassment or shame, Hélène could not say. He reached with some trepidation into his back pocket and produced a single folded sheet of paper. He held it out for Hélène to take.

'The telegram boy came to the tradesman's door. He asked for mc by name. I'm sorry, Miss Marchmont. I read it. I know I oughtn't to have done. But Miss Marchmont? Miss Marchmont, you've . . .'

Hélène's face had turned ashen as she took in the contents of the letter. Then she started to shake. This was so much more than the frustration she'd vented when faced with Nathaniel White. The tremor started in her hands and worked throughout her body.

'I'm sorry, Miss Marchmont. I'm—'

'Who else has seen this?' she suddenly demanded.

'Not a soul, miss!'

Hélène caught herself. She bent down, planted a single kiss on Billy's cheek. 'Thank you, Billy,' she said – and then, without once looking back, she pushed past him, up and out of the dressing rooms.

Billy watched her go and felt, for a moment, as if he might faint. He could still feel the impression of her lips upon his cheek. It was the most shameful thing.

High above, Vivienne Edgerton stood at her open balcony window, allowing the bitter cold of Berkeley Square to flood in. She had been waiting hours already. She had been waiting too long. The lights below lit Berkeley Square only in small halos, but it was enough. As she hovered there, she saw the tiny figure of Hélène Marchmont canter out onto the square, wrapped up in a thick coat. She stumbled, caught herself before she plunged into the snow, righted herself against one of the townhouse railings, and disappeared off the square.

Vivienne smiled.

It took great effort to close the windows against a sudden onslaught of wind, but Vivienne battled them back and marched to her wardrobe. Inside hung a sky-blue gown, a spectacular creation of chiffon and lace. Yes, she thought, this was as elegant as anything Hélène Marchmont ever wore. She picked it out, held it up against herself and gazed into the mirror. She would look beautiful in this – and anyone who said otherwise could hang.

She looked up from the mirror, back at the window panes, and something caught her eye. With the dress still held against her, she staggered over and looked back out. Another figure was hurrying across Berkeley Square. Another figure she knew. She clenched her jaw – but then, thinking again, relented. What did it matter if he was gone, after all? The poor fool had already done everything she asked. He could freeze out there for all she cared.

Billy Brogan tore across Berkeley Square in his shirtsleeves. A dozen horses and carriages were wheeling around the snowy expanse in the heart of the square, bringing their guests to the ballroom for the night. Stopping while one of the carriages sailed by, Billy felt the bite of the wind. He thought he saw Hélène striding purposefully along one of the roads leading to Regent Street, but by the time the carriage had passed, all he could see was the snowy dark.

He looked up at the towering facade of the Buckingham Hotel.

He remembered his father's words.

He tore back across the square.

By the time he reached the staff entrance, he could feel the chill in his bones – but he did not stop. He clattered on, up through housekeeping, around the reception hall where more guests milled, and burst back through the dressing-room doors.

Nathaniel rounded on him at once – 'What did you do to her, Brogan?' – but Billy sidled past, to the corner where Nancy and Raymond still sat.

'Nance,' he said. 'Nance, I've—'

'Spit it out, Brogan!' roared Nathaniel, gripping him by the shoulder.

At once, Nancy stood. 'Don't manhandle him, Mr White. Can't you see he's—'

Nathaniel stepped back. 'You can get out of here too. You can't bring your *pets* down here, de Guise, not on a night like this.' He turned. 'If Hélène isn't here in one minute, Brogan, you've some explaining to do.'

Nancy put an arm around Billy and escorted him back to the dressing-room door.

'I shouldn't have done it. I know it. I'm not proud. I . . .' The words were pouring out of him in an unstoppable torrent. Somewhere inside Billy Brogan a dam had burst, and now the waters were running wild. 'You have to believe me. I should have taken my punishment, whatever was coming to me, but . . . She has ways, Nance. She does. She looks into you and it's like . . . she can see *everything*. It's my own fault. I know it is. I should never have—'

Nancy gripped him by the chin, forced him to look into her eyes. 'Take a deep breath, Billy. You'll have to start at the beginning.'

'But that's just it. I don't know how it started. I've always run favours in this hotel. Always made drop-offs and collections for people. I didn't know, the first time I went to the Midnight Rooms, what I was going there for.' Nancy's face furrowed. She remembered how Billy had confidently led her down the Midnight Rooms stairs, how he'd stepped so easily through that door, but she'd thought it the first time he'd been there too. Had she been wrong? 'It was Mr Simenon who sent me. He did it as a favour to Miss Vivienne Edgerton. What she asked for, she got. Only it's below Mr Simenon to go to a place like the Midnight Rooms, so he sent me. And I'd bring them back for her, those powders she has. The cocaine . . .'

Nancy's face drained. She stepped back from Billy.

'You'd better go on, Billy,' uttered Raymond. 'What in God's name have you done?'

'After what happened to Miss Edgerton, after how you found her, Nance, we was meant to stop procuring powder for her.

And we did – for a little while, at least. Only . . . she said she'd tell. If I didn't get her what she needed, if I didn't help her out, she'd go ratting to Maynard Charles and . . . Scandals, Nance. Any sniff of a scandal and the management have to stamp it out. I can't get stamped out. What'll happen to me without the Buckingham Hotel? What about all my brothers and sisters? So, Lord help me, I did what she asked. I told her. I told her where Miss Marchmont goes.'

Raymond was about to grab Billy by his collar when Nancy, sensing his anger, stepped between them.

'You know everyone's secrets, don't you, Billy?' snapped Raymond. 'You were happy enough passing mine to Maynard Charles—'

'You'd better tell us,' Nancy said, more softly. 'Tell us everything.'

'Miss Marchmont has a daughter. She lives south of the river, off Brixton Hill. Nobody's meant to know because—'

'Because what, Billy?'

'She's black, Nance. Hélène and Sidney, he used to be in the orchestra, the devil with a trumpet. The one who died. Hélène had his daughter and she lives down there, with Sidney's parents. It's me who delivers them messages back and forth. And . . .' Billy steeled himself, and Raymond had the distinct impression that here came the most terrible secret of all. 'Once Vivienne knew, she made me make another promise. She wants to dance tonight, you see. She wants to be on the dance floor, behind her mask, for everyone to swoon and gawp over, for everyone to think she's the star . . . And then she wants to rip off her mask and reveal herself – all so's her mother and Lord Edgerton get the shock of their lives. So she wrote a letter. She made me deliver it. She made me deliver it to Miss Marchmont . . .'

Raymond looked over his shoulder. From the other side of the dressing room, Nathaniel was still staring at them, his hands placed squarely on his hips.

Raymond looked back at Billy. 'I think,' he said, 'you'd better tell us exactly what that letter said – before it's too late.'

The omnibus was already driving off by the time Hélène reached out for its doors. By some strange mercy, the driver noticed her and slowed the engine. 'Climb aboard, love. There you go. Don't want you stuck out on a night like this, do we?'

Hélène was still quaking as she found a seat. Pressed up against the window, she opened up the telegram and scoured its words again.

Hélène, come at once. Sybil woke last night with a fever. You must come at once. It has a hold on her, Hélène. Come at once. She needs her mama. There may not be another chance.

The paper strained where she held it. Sybil was so near, and yet a lifetime away. What did the ballroom matter, what did any of it matter? A winter like this could kill the strongest of men. What hope for a little girl with an infection racking her chest? She looked up through the window at the endless white as Regent Street turned into the Circus at Piccadilly. The great billboards peered down, advertising all manner of wares, and it was all Hélène could do not to scream, and scream, and scream.

At the ballroom dressing-room doors, Raymond froze.

'Billy, you bastard. Billy, you fool. Go after her. Go *now*. Well, you're the only one who knows where she's gone, aren't you?'

Billy nodded. There was anger in Raymond's voice, but there was purpose as well. 'I'll get her back,' he said. 'She can still dance tonight. She can still—'

'To hell with the dancing, Billy. Bring her back here and . . .' He looked at Nancy. 'I'm going to find Vivienne. And when I find her, I'll . . .'

Raymond flew through the dressing-room doors, strode like a colossus past the dance studio, up and up towards the reception hall. Vivienne was not in the ballroom itself. That left only two places she could possibly be. Either she was lining up the cocktails in the Candlelight Club or she was in her rooms, preparing to sashay down the stairs and present herself. A thousand thoughts hurtled through Raymond's mind. No doubt Nathaniel White was in on this. No doubt that was why he'd spent so long with her, training her in the studio, dancing with her on countless nights in the ballroom itself.

He reached the service lift and rang the bell to call it down. At the sound of hurried footsteps behind him, he turned and saw Nancy, face flushed, rushing towards him.

'I'll kill her,' Raymond spat. 'I'll kill her for what she's done . . .'

The lift doors opened, revealing the attendant. Raymond reached in and heaved him out. Before the poor man knew what was happening, the doors were closing and Nancy was slipping inside after Raymond.

'NO!' Nancy exclaimed, grappling with Raymond's arm. 'You don't know why she did it, Raymond. You don't know . . .'

'I know it was jealousy, pure and simple. People like Vivienne Edgerton, it's bad blood through and through . . .'

The lift soared, counting one floor after another.

'Listen to yourself,' Nancy cried. 'Bad blood? You don't really believe in bad blood. If you do, you're the same as the rest of them. As Lord Edgerton and all his fascist set. No, there's no bad blood, Raymond. There's only . . .' Nancy paused. They were almost at Vivienne's floor. 'If you'd seen what my father was like, then maybe you'd understand. If you'd seen the way his addiction changed him from being the most wonderful, caring father – into someone who cared only about where his next dose was coming from. It turned him into something else, Raymond. If not a monster, then a ghost. I didn't matter to him. He barely remembered I had a brother.' She stopped. The lift had come to a halt, and with the ring of a bell the doors slid open. 'It wasn't *him*, Raymond. That's my point. He did the most terrible things, but he wasn't himself.'

Raymond stepped out. From around the corner he could hear the footsteps of yet more guests as they were all drawn down towards the ballroom. A clock on the wall showed the hour inching towards 7 p.m. The evening's performances were about to begin.

Nancy reached out, took him by the arm once more.

'*Please*, Raymond. You have to listen. What Vivienne did is abominable. What Hélène's going through isn't right. But she'll get to Brixton Hill, she'll find her daughter, she'll know it was all a lie – and her life, *their* lives, will go on. But Vivienne . . . Vivienne didn't do it out of evil. She did it out of desperation. You heard what Billy said – she wants to dance. She wants to show her mother, her stepfather, that she *matters*. It's why she asked you to teach her and why she took it so badly that you would not. It's why she fell in with Nathaniel White. Maybe she needs it. Maybe she needs something to cling on to, something to steady her – anything so she can face the world. Vivienne isn't the enemy here, Raymond. All of the damage she's been doing, to herself, to the hotel – why, even to *me* – she's been crying out for help all this time. And who was answering? Only Mr Simenon and that poison of his.' She stopped. Raymond had already surged ahead, bound for Vivienne's room. 'Raymond. *Ray*. You have to listen. It wasn't Vivienne who did this, not really. It was the poison . . .'

Chapter Thirty-four

THE DOOR TO VIVIENNE EDGERTON's suite burst open, the door jamb splintering beneath the force of Raymond de Guise's boot. Raymond was the first to crash through. Nancy followed in his wake.

Vivienne's suite was empty, the wardrobe hanging open. Raymond looked inside it, to find a succession of ball gowns pushed aside and a single hanger empty in the wardrobe's centre. All around him was that familiar scent of Chanel.

'Where is she?' Raymond uttered. Then realisation hit him square between the eyes. 'The ballroom.'

The doors of the Grand Ballroom stood wide open. Vivienne Edgerton, a glittering tiara in her hair and a simple black mask in her hand, stared down the sloping hall and into the ballroom itself. Men and women gathered in small groups, their gowns ostentatious, their suits adorned with strange flourishes and swirls, alive with colour. Guests were still arriving, brushing past Vivienne as, masks of animals and princesses and unreal spirits in hand, they made their way to the celebration. She was certain she caught sight of her mother, face hidden behind black satin, and stepfather – one of the few wearing only a plain evening suit – in the turning crowd, but then they were gone.

She was going to do this.

Her heart was beating as fast as a baby bird's. She felt light-headed and found herself craving something, anything that might take the edge off what she was feeling. She would need confidence tonight. She would need fire. The phials Billy Brogan had procured were still upstairs. A part of her wanted to fly back there, inhale everything she could, and then return to the ballroom with the conviction she felt every time she indulged. But she could see the ballroom filling up. She looked up to find the clock above the check-in desks. It was almost seven o' clock – the time when the band would strike up, the first clarion call of the trumpets flaring, and the dressing-room doors would open for the dancers to sweep out. She had seen what Nathaniel had planned. She had marvelled at it.

No, she thought, *there's no time to hesitate now. Lives are transformed in moments like this. I'll do it whether I'm feeling fearless or not. I'll do it all for myself, without any false courage fizzing in my veins . . .*

She turned on the spot, marched around the lifts and down to the back doors of the ballroom. The dressing-room door was ajar so, without breaking her stride, she strode on through.

The atmosphere was electric.

Archie Adams and his orchestra were already crowding the doors to the ballroom itself. Sofía LaPegna and the dancers were scattered around, still tending to each other's gowns, still painting their faces with white paints and rouge. Just the scent, just the *feel* of the place, made every nerve in Vivienne's body tingle. The air was alive with expectation.

Nathaniel White was up by the ballroom doors. As Vivienne approached, she saw the look of agitation on his face. That, she supposed, was only to be expected. Her heart, which until now had been quickening, suddenly slowed. She was going to make this better. It hit her with a clarity she had not expected. For the first time in her life, everything was going according to plan.

She reached out to caress his arm. 'Nathaniel?'

Nathaniel looked over his shoulder to find Vivienne standing there.

'Vivienne,' he said, 'I can't talk. Not now. Marchmont's absconded. She's done it to spite me – you can be certain of that. She knows what this means to me. If she isn't here by the time the orchestra plays—'

As if on cue, Archie Adams clapped his hands together to make an announcement. Louis Kildare and the rest of the band followed suit. At Archie's instruction, they formed a line, ready to march out and begin the celebrations.

'God damn it,' Nathaniel uttered. 'God damn *her*.' He craned around. 'LaPegna!' he hissed. 'LaPegna, it'll have to be you. Follow my lead and don't—'

Sofía LaPegna was about to reply – 'Where's Hélène?' – when Vivienne interjected, '*I'm* here, Nathaniel.'

'I can see that, Vivienne, but they're about to—'

The dressing-room doors opened. One after another, the band members began to march through to the ballroom itself. The ballroom fell silent. Then, after a pregnant pause, the applause began. In the corner of her eye, Vivienne could see Louis Kildare and the rest soaking up the worship of the crowd. Then, one after another, the orchestra took their places upon the stage.

Nathaniel White's eyes were on Sofía. Vivienne stepped in front of him, obscuring his view of everything else.

'I can do it, Nathaniel. You know I can. I've watched you dance it. You showed me the steps yourself. We've danced almost every night out there in the ballroom.' She smiled warmly, her eyes full of anticipation. 'I *can* do it, Nathaniel. You're the one who taught me . . .' She was almost laughing now. Vivienne Edgerton had never believed in destiny, but this felt like destiny tonight. She reached out, trying to clasp Nathaniel's hand. Perhaps she should have been perturbed when he did not immediately entwine his fingers with hers, but she was too high on the moment to notice. 'Imagine it, Nathaniel – you and me—'

Nathaniel snatched his hands away.

'You?' he hissed. 'Dance in the Grand? Dance for the lords and ladies out there? Dance for a king and queen? A crown princess?' He had started out disbelieving, but by the time he was finished he was braying with laughter. 'Vivienne, how much have you indulged yourself tonight? You told me you weren't going to do that any more, not after you nearly killed yourself the last time . . .'

Vivienne's eyes were still full of hope. 'You'll lead me, Nathaniel. I can do everything Hélène Marchmont can. The way we dance together, it's—'

'Child's play,' scoffed Nathaniel. His eyes darted back to the dressing-room door. The applause was beginning to die down as the band settled onto the stage.

'Yes!' Vivienne beamed. 'We make it look so easy—'

'Not like that,' snapped Nathaniel. 'The way we dance? It's like dancing with a three-year-old, Vivienne. Like balancing somebody's baby daughter on your feet and *pretending* you're on stage at the Folies-Bergère. It's all make-believe. Oh, Vivienne,' he laughed, 'you're not *serious*, are you? You don't really think I could take you out there? I'm to put on a show. I'm to romance the crown princess of Norway herself. I couldn't let *them* see *me* dancing with someone like *you*.'

The malice in his words finally touched Vivienne. The effect was like putting a lit match to spilled paraffin. The flames caught instantly. Her eyes grew fat with tears. Her jaw trembled. One moment she had felt as big as the world; now she felt as diminutive as a child.

'Somebody . . . like . . . *me*?'

'An untalented little junkie, barely fit to visit the ballroom, let alone perform in it. Oh, Vivienne, you silly little girl. What did you think all this was for? You girls and your wild romances. A ballroom isn't for romance, Vivienne. It's for the cold, brutal, realities of life. You think it's all beauty and starlight, but you're wrong. It's *war*.' Nathaniel's eyes roamed the room, desperate to see Hélène stride back through the doors. He was coiled like a serpent ready to strike. 'Good God, Vivienne, this night's about to fall apart right in front of me – and what do you do? Did you *really* think a few weeks of dancing could turn you into somebody worthy of the world stage?' He barked one last time. 'I like you, Vivienne. We had our fun, didn't we? You helped me get my foot in the ballroom and I gave you what you wanted in return. I danced with you, didn't I? Not just out there, but *up there* too. But how could you even hope to compare with somebody like Hélène Marchmont? Girls like you are good for just one thing, Vivienne – and it isn't for kings and queens . . .'

The whole of the dressing room was a blur. Vivienne staggered backwards, flailing over her own feet. *Good for just one thing,* she thought. The words echoed mercilessly in her ears. Yes, good for just one thing – and that thing, it was waiting upstairs, right where she had left it.

She wanted it now. She *needed* it now.

She took another step backwards, crashed into whatever was behind her. As she turned, she felt arms picking her back up. Raymond was standing there, his arms around her. His chambermaid was with him, her eyes full of fury. *Do they know what I've done?* Vivienne wondered. She could not stand that now. She did not want to know.

Raymond set her back on her feet, then strode past her. His face was set hard. His eyes were full of fire. He reached out and clapped one of his meaty hands on Nathaniel's shoulder. It was strange how little Nathaniel seemed compared to Raymond. She hadn't noticed it until now.

Through the doors, the band had started playing. Sofía LaPegna and the other dancers leaped up and out of their chairs, preparing for the first dance. Yet the door to the ballroom was being blocked by Nathaniel.

Raymond brought his hand back. Vivienne saw it clenched into a tight fist.

'She might be a spoilt little rich girl,' he said, 'but she's *our* spoilt little rich girl.'

His fist flew forward, connecting with Nathaniel's chin. Nathaniel's head snapped back. He reeled. Still dazed, he did not notice as Raymond wheeled around with a second fist. This blow caught him on the side of the head and he dropped, unconscious, onto the dressing-room floor.

Raymond loomed over him. 'Our ballroom isn't for your glory,' he uttered, 'no matter who your father is.' Then, without turning around, he said, 'I see it now, Nancy. Vivienne, you'd better—'

'Vivienne, no!'

At Nancy's exclamation, Raymond finally turned around. Vivienne had already taken off, up and out of the dressing room. For a moment, Nancy stared into Raymond's eyes. 'After her,' he said. 'What she said to Hélène, that can wait. Nobody comes into our hotel and treats people like that. Our ballroom isn't about war. It's about magic.' He was tempted to put a boot into Nathaniel, but Sofía LaPegna and the other dancers were already clamouring round. The band had been playing too long already. 'Go!' he cried out, and Nancy took flight, rushing after Vivienne.

Raymond bent down, put his arms around Nathaniel and heaved him aside. His mind was still buzzing. Hélène was somewhere out there in the snow. Billy Brogan had gone after her, but there was no hope of her coming back in time – there never had been. Maybe Nancy had been right. People connived and cheated and lied for all manner of reasons. The bastard unconscious underneath him – he'd connived and lied and led people on, all for his personal glory. Was it really possible Vivienne was a victim in all of this?

There was no time to debate the goods and evils of it. His eyes scanned the room, picked out Sofía LePegna. Dropping to his knees, he picked up the black mask that Nathaniel had dropped when he fell. Its strap was still intact. He slipped it over his own eyes.

'It's a quickstep,' he said, listening out for the music. 'Watch me for the rhythm changes, and follow my lead . . .'

In the ballroom, the guests had got to their feet as soon as the dressing-room doors opened and the orchestra walked out to take their places. Then, as soon as they were assembled, a single spotlight flared, picking out the dressing-room door. The doors swung open again – and, into the halo, stepped Archie Adams himself. It was then that the applause went up, filling the ballroom with appreciative thunder. The legendary bandleader paused to soak it up – this was his moment, the finest of the year – and walked purposefully to the stage. The applause was still rolling as he settled behind the gleaming white lacquered grand piano. His orchestra were arranged around him, resplendent in their snowy white jackets and golden collars.

The first tune struck up, to be met by a wall of applause. The band would begin the evening gently, with their 'Californian Serenade'. Maynard Charles had heard it a hundred times before, but tonight it was only the *hors d'oeuvre*. He himself had signed the invoices to pay for the guest singers. Alfredo Bianchi had played the game well, countering the Buckingham with an offer he'd received from the Savoy. Tonight, the music would be perfect. The guests here could dance until the band played their big band version of 'Auld Lang Syne'. Then they could dance on into the dawn.

The band played on, but no dancers had appeared.

Maynard Charles cast his eyes around the room. The longer the music played, the more bewildered the glances that came his way. He crossed the ballroom to where Lord Edgerton reclined with his wife at his side and his entourage around him. The royal party themselves were on their feet, waiting for the doors to open and the dancers to appear. Until they did, the night had not formally begun.

'Is something the matter, Mr Charles?' Lord Edgerton intoned.

'Nothing, sir. The Buckingham runs like clockwork.'

'You are behaving in a most skittish manner for someone who believes there is nothing wrong, Mr Charles. Need I remind you . . .' Lord Edgerton's eyes rolled over to where the royal party gathered. The crown princess was a vision of vermillion, holding her mask on a stick in front of her eyes. 'Find out what's wrong,' Lord Edgerton hissed. 'Music in a ballroom without dance is a farce, not a celebration.'

Maynard nodded. He felt the sweat gathering at his collar. He cast his mind back, to Aubrey sitting up high in the Park Suite, to the visions of foreboding he'd had last night. Somebody would know what was going on back there. Where was Billy Brogan when you needed him?

Maynard Charles stomped across the ballroom – but he had not gone halfway when the doors at the head of the Grand burst open, and from them appeared two dancers, frantically turning around each other until they reached the centre of the floor. Behind them came the rest of the troupe. Each partnership spiralled away from the others in a flourish, perfectly synchronised.

The band struck up a new song. The guests were suddenly on their feet. Couples rushed to the edge of the dance floor, eager to see the performance before they too could get lost in the music. Maynard muscled through them to do the same. But there was something bothering him about the two principal dancers who had led the others out onto the ballroom floor. They were wearing masks so he could not see their faces, but there was something about the way they held themselves, something about their statures and shapes. He lifted his half-moon spectacles up from the bridge of his nose.

His jaw dropped. No, he was not mistaken. He glanced feverishly around, in case Lord Edgerton too had noticed. The atmosphere in the ballroom was thrilling at last – but the two dancers leading the show were not Nathaniel White and Hélène Marchmont.

Vivienne had already crashed into the guest lift by the time Nancy reached the reception hall. She saw its golden cage closing as a sobbing Vivienne disappeared into the uppermost reaches of the Buckingham Hotel. Nancy careered across the red and black chequered tiles, hurling herself through housekeeping until she reached the service lift. The cage itself was nowhere to be seen. Perhaps it was being loaded on one of the other storeys. She prowled the corridor for only a second, before deciding that any second she waited here was a second too long. There were still stairs. Her leg would not like her for it, but the pain would not last for ever; and, no matter what she'd done, no matter what kind of girl she was, Vivienne Edgerton needed a friend now.

Nancy reached the stairwell, took the steps two at a time. *Miss Edgerton, please. Please wait. You don't need your drugs. All you need is . . .*

By the second storey her leg was already putting up a protest, but she hurried on. By the fourth, she had slowed. The staircase seemed interminable. She clung to the banister and heaved herself up – and, by the time she reached the sixth storey, her leg was throbbing with pain.

No matter. Vivienne's suite was only yards away. She could see its door hanging open.

In the moment before she reached it, Nancy had a terrible vision: Vivienne lying pale and white on the bed, all of the life drained from her body.

Is it that bad, Vivienne? Is your life really that bad?

Nancy crashed through the open door – and there she was. The drawer from the bottom of her dresser had been upended on the bed. Vivienne was manically rifling through it. As Nancy staggered to the foot of the bed, Vivienne found what she was looking for: a little lavender pouch. She opened it up and emptied its contents into her palm: two tiny phials of crystalline powder.

'Vivienne.'

Vivienne looked up. Her face was red and raw. Her eyes were smears of black where her make-up had been kneaded away. She was beautiful, thought Nancy, but she was feral as well.

'What are you doing here? Get out. *Get out!* I'll have Maynard Charles summoned. I'll have you fired. I'll—'

'No,' said Nancy, her voice barely a whisper. 'Vivienne, I'm not going anywhere.'

'You'll call me Miss Edgerton, or you'll—'

'Your name is Vivienne. I'll call you Vivienne. Vivienne, you can summon Mr Charles. You can make it so that I never set foot in the Buckingham Hotel. It doesn't matter to me. All that matters is . . .' She hesitated. 'Would you put them down, Vivienne? You don't need to do this. You're better than it. Stronger.'

'Stronger?' she gasped. '*Better?* What does it even mean? I am what I am. Look at me. Here I am. This is *me*. This is *all* there is.'

Nancy inched around the edge of the bed. 'That isn't it at all. That stuff in your hand, it's not *you*. I said it to my father once and I'll say it to you now. You can take those powders, or you can throw them away, be done with them forever. That choice – *that's* what you are.'

Vivienne wheeled around. The top of her dresser was a chaos of Maybelline face powders and Guerlain lipsticks, the bottle of Chanel, all the little odds and ends she'd been given for Christmas. She swept it all aside, glass shattering and powders puffing into the air as the bottles and boxes hit the floor. Then, settling down, she took the stoppers out of each of the phials and carefully laid a trail of the white powder on the surface of the wood.

Nancy dared come no closer. There was a look of such concentration on Vivienne's face.

'You didn't deserve it,' Nancy blurted out.

Vivienne froze.

'Nathaniel White. He used you to get into the ballroom. He cheated and he connived. You didn't matter to him. Nobody does. And Vivienne – you didn't deserve it.' She enunciated the last words so clearly that they seemed to punch their way through Vivienne's armour. She turned away from the intoxicating drug for the first time. 'You've been resisting it, haven't you?' Nancy ventured. 'Billy Brogan procured you those drugs before Christmas. And that means . . . You *want* to stop, don't you? You know you nearly died right here – *right here on this carpet!* – and you want to stop.'

'I should have died here,' Vivienne trembled. 'If it wasn't for you, I would have. And then I wouldn't feel like this, would I? I wouldn't feel anything at all. And God knows, I don't want to feel it. I don't want to feel a thing . . .'

Nancy had been holding back, but something told her that now was the moment. She stepped forward, sat on the bed at Vivienne's side.

'Why would you help me? Why would you pick me up off this carpet? What are you doing here, even now? I was horrible to you. I was wicked.'

'I know,' said Nancy. She dared lift an arm and put it around Vivienne's shoulder. 'But it doesn't matter. It's only words. Words can be undone. But this thing? This thing you're about to do? That *can't* be undone, Vivienne. And, Vivienne, the world doesn't want you to die.'

'The world doesn't want me at all. You don't know what I did . . .'

Nancy was still.

'I sent that poor girl out into the snow. I made her think her baby was dying. And for what? So that he might dance with me? So that it might be *me* out there in the ballroom? So that, for just one evening, my mother and the others might have *seen* me, thought something *good* of me, realised what she did when she chose *him* over *me* . . .'

The sobs erupted out of her in a great geyser. She crumpled, and at last she was in Nancy's arms.

'I hate this hotel,' she uttered. 'I hate being here, in this country, where I don't know a soul. I hate my stepfather for bringing me here. I hate my mother for letting him. I hate it every time I breathe *them* in, those powders Mr Simenon brings. I hate it every time I ask for another cocktail in the Candlelight Club and some waiter comes running. And the men. They don't want me for me. I . . .' For a moment she was lost for words. She sank further into Nancy's arms. 'I hate myself,' she sobbed – and after that she said no more.

Nancy held her softly, then held her tighter still. Vivienne's body quaked up against her until, after a time, she was as still as a child.

The dance was almost at its end. The two principals turned, came apart, and came back together again. The male lead swooped his partner forward, then back, lifting her from the ground as they spiralled together, hitting the final beat in perfect harmony. Then, in a fanfare of trumpets and Archie Adams' hands ricocheting up and down the piano, the music came to an end. An explosion of applause erupted. On the ballroom floor, the dancers stopped, breathless, each couple clasping hands and bowing towards their principals.

The masked male lead released the hand of his partner and strutted along the gleaming wooden squares, the rest of the dancers forming an aisle around him. As he reached the edge of the dance floor, his chest puffed out – and, from the balustrade where he watched, Maynard Charles thought that he held himself like a hero from classical myth.

At the very head of the dance floor, the Norwegian royals stood together, proudly joining in the applause. Märtha, the crown princess, was up against the balustrade, beating her hands more fervently than the rest. The lead dancer stopped at the bottom of the stair. He bowed and, upon rising, extended his hand to her.

'Your Highness,' he ventured, 'shall we?'

The orchestra were striking up another tune. The guest singer Alfredo Bianchi had emerged from the ranks to stand beside Archie Adams. He crooned the opening words of Archie's first ever hit.

The crown princess took the principal's hand – and it was then that, with his free hand, he reached up and took the mask from his face. Dark almond eyes stared out. Black hair sailed wild around his perfectly imperfect face.

'Your Highness,' the principal dancer began, 'my name is Raymond de Guise. Welcome to the Buckingham Hotel. For the rest of the evening, I remain at your service.'

All across the dance floor, the professional dancing couples came apart as the guests streamed down to meet them. Still at the balustrade, Maynard Charles watched Raymond de Guise guiding the crown princess to the dance floor. And, in that second, all of the worry, all of the anxiety, all of his fear for the future of his hotel and country, evaporated away. Whatever had happened backstage at the Buckingham ballroom, and whatever was coming, outside in the real world, could wait. For now, Raymond de Guise was where he belonged, the king of the dance floor, putting on the performance of his life – and, if only for a fleeting moment on this most tempestuous night, everything was right.

Chapter Thirty-five

BY THE TIME THE OMNIBUS reached Westminster, Hélène Marchmont knew it could go no further. The snow that tumbled down had turned the abbey into a castle plucked straight out of the pages of the fairy tales she used to read – the fairy tales she one day wanted to enjoy with Sybil – but it had transformed other things too. London was swiftly becoming iced in white, and the windows of the omnibus were plastered in snowflakes so that she could barely see the streets outside. 'We're not going over the bridge,' the driver said in his gruff Glaswegian accent, stepping outside to see the state of the road for himself. 'I'm taking her back to the depot before I have to spend the night with her. *All change!*'

Some of the rag-tag of other passengers put up a protest, but Hélène did not have the time to lose. Reeling out into the falling snow, she pulled down her cloche hat – it provided so little comfort from the cold – and peered up and down the Horse Guards Road. Ribbons of white were twirling everywhere, St James's Park itself hidden behind the shifting veil. As the rest of the passengers fanned out, some bound for Westminster Bridge, some back the way the omnibus had brought them, Hélène looked desperately for a hansom cab. But it was all so futile. It was New

Year, and London was a fantasia of white. She may as well have looked for a single specific snowflake among the many millions that fell.

She stopped dead. She wanted to scream. She wanted . . .

She needed to get to Sybil before this night was out. Anything less and all of this – the secrets, the lies, the double life she had been living – was in vain. Anything less and she was not fit to be a mother.

She turned to face the river. The Palace of Westminster was above her, crowned in ice. If there were no more taxicabs, she decided, she would just have to walk. She took her first steps, felt the chill of the snow creeping up over her feet. She looked down. The snow was clinging in clumps to her dainty dancing shoes. She'd left in such a hurry that she hadn't thought to take them off.

The snow hardened as she stepped out onto Westminster Bridge. High above, Big Ben began tolling out the hour.

Over the river, through the warren of Lambeth town, there was at least some shelter from the snow. From the taprooms she passed she could hear the sounds of music, of song and dance and cheer, and fleetingly she cast her mind back to the Buckingham and the Masquerade Ball. It would not have taken long for them to realise she was gone. She could imagine the panic that had ricocheted around the dressing rooms. She could imagine the way Nathaniel White's face would have paled to think that his routine, his chance at glory, was being scuppered. But Hélène cared nothing for that. Better out here, the cold already deep in her bones, than quickstepping around the ballroom on the arm of one of Lord Edgerton's cronies.

She was fighting her way down the Albert Embankment when she became aware of the headlamps behind her. She looked over her shoulder, uncertain what to expect, and saw the cab grind to a halt. Out of the window, a voice cried out, 'Where are you going, love?', and Hélène called back, 'Brixton Hill!'

'You'd best hop in then. You'll catch your death out there.'

Hélène thought that was true. The fire in her heart still burned brightly enough, but her fingers, the tips of her toes, all of them were numb.

By the time the cab slid past the great grey churches of Brixton Hill, Hélène's heart was beating hard.

Finally, they came to the corner of Sudbourne Road. There were lights on in the Archer place. She could see the silhouette of their Christmas tree up against the curtains. Was it really only a week since she'd come here, since she'd held her darling Sybil in her arms?

'Is something the matter, love? Is it anything I can help with?'

Hélène froze. She would not look up.

After a time, the taxi driver said, 'Have you got plans, love? I promised the wife I'd be home for midnight so we'd see it in together. For the kids, you know. Have you got any children yourself?'

Hélène crumpled the telegram in her hand. All of those nights, waltzing in the ballroom. All of those afternoons demonstrating dances alongside Raymond de Guise. All of those dignitaries and statesmen who requested her by name when they came to grace the Buckingham Hotel. What was it all for, if not this? She closed her eyes and, fleetingly, imagined life as it might have been: she and Sidney and Sybil, in a little house of their own. In her mind, Sybil was toddling along a burgundy carpet, and Hélène was in the kitchen – no longer a dancer, nor a model staring out of the pages of a magazine. Simply a mother. An ordinary, decent, loving mother . . .

The taxi driver was waiting. Hélène steeled herself. 'Please,' she said, 'let me . . .'

She was fumbling in the pocket of her woollen coat for whatever payment she could find, when the taxi driver put his hand over hers and whispered, 'Off with you, now. You don't owe me a penny. Happy New Year, Miss.'

Moments later, Hélène heard the car wheels whining as the driver took off. She stood in the snow and looked up at the face of the house, afraid of what she might find.

She knocked.

She knocked again.

She knocked, harder and harder, so hard that lights came on in the neighbouring houses.

Her heart was beating a thousand different rhythms.

There came a clatter of footsteps on the other side of the door and it drew open, spilling the light from within. Noelle Archer was standing there with the most inscrutable expression, as if she hadn't expected Hélène at all.

'Noelle, I got your message. Am I . . . Am I too late? Noelle, is she…'

Hélène wanted to say more, but the cold had robbed her of all breath. She strode through, Noelle's face opening wide as she floundered past, and took off up the hall . . .

. . . and there lay Sybil in her crib, softly snoring in her sleep.

Hélène was hanging over the crib, unable to understand, when Noelle and Maurice appeared in the doorway behind her.

'Hélène?' Noelle gasped. 'What's happened? Why aren't you dancing?'

Hélène reached into the crib and put the back of her frigid hand to Sybil's head – but her daughter slept soundly, without any fever at all.

The baby opened her eyes. It took her a moment to take in the scene around her. Then, when her eyes found her mother, Sybil began to babble, reaching out with both pudgy arms.

'Dadadadadadadadadaaaa!'

Hélène took her baby in her arms and cradled her to her chest. Sybil shrieked and squirmed where Hélène held her against the snowmelt on her coat, but she held on to her all the same.

With her daughter in her arms, she marched back past Noelle and Maurice, into the living room where two glasses had been laid out, with a bottle of rum in anticipation of midnight.

'Hélène, something's happened,' said Noelle, hurrying in their wake. 'You're supposed to be dancing. You're supposed to be putting on a show. What changed?'

Hélène thought of the letter in her pocket. If Sybil really was well, it meant that somebody had connived against her tonight. Somebody had tricked her. Somebody else was spinning across the ballroom in her place.

Some time later the little carriage clock on the mantel began to toll midnight. Sybil's head craned around to listen. Through the walls, Hélène could hear the sounds of 'Auld Lang Syne' being sung in a drunken baritone. In the ballroom now, a thousand voices would be joined in chorus. Up and down the Buckingham Hotel, princesses and queens would sing in concert with concierges and chambermaids. The dances would go on and on and on, into the deep, still hours of the night; there was still time to get back – but what did that matter to Hélène Marchmont? What did Nathaniel or the Edgertons, or even Maynard Charles matter to her? She carried Sybil to the window and showed her the snow falling down. Sybil gaped and cooed, reaching out a fist as if she might catch a snowflake through the glass.

'Mama . . .' Sybil gurgled, for the very first time. 'Ma . . . ma . . .'

No, thought Hélène, *none* of it mattered. Not the elegance and the grandeur. Not the two-step or the quick. Not the joyful rhythm of the Archie Adams Band or the spectacle of the hotel dancers performing for the adoration of the crowd. You could keep all the riches and the intrigues in the Buckingham Hotel. You could keep all the kings and queens and crown princesses who came to grace its beautiful ballroom. All of that was just dust when compared to standing here, surrounded by family, with her child in her arms, while one year faded, and another, full of possibilities, began.

She leaned down and placed her lips gently on the top of Sybil's head. On an enchanted evening like this, there was no other place she would rather be.

Epilogue

January 1937

A New Year

NANCY NETTLETON OPENED HER EYES.

The fifth day of January and, at last, the snow across Berkeley Square was starting to retreat. As soon as she was dressed, she hurried to the kitchenette where Rosa, Ruth and all the other girls were kneading the sleep out of their eyes. 'Another day, another duchess's sheets to change, eh, Nance?' Rosa joked as, linking arms, they gazed from the window across the rooftops of Mayfair. It was the start of a new year, a fresh beginning, and London was waking up . . .

But the work of the Buckingham Hotel, from upstairs to downstairs, from on high to low, still carried on.

Mrs Moffatt was waiting for them in the housekeeping lounge. As Ruth dished out the tea and the girls listened to Mrs Whitehead reading out the tasks ahead, Nancy tried not to crease up with laughter at the way Rosa, with the simplest crinkle of her features, could mimic Mrs Moffatt exquisitely. There was, she knew, a new spirit in the girls since New Year – and not only because of what they'd learned of her secret *friendship* with Raymond de Guise. It seemed to Nancy that the discovery of her secret had meant so much more. The girls knew her now. She'd told them about Raymond, yes, but she'd told them about other things too: her mother, her father, the brother she'd left behind and hoped one day to bring to London. And they, too, had shared stories of their own. Nancy had even spent enough time in the little kitchenette that she'd been victorious in her very first game of backgammon. 'And that's a sign.' Rosa had grinned. 'You're one of us now.'

After breakfast was done, Nancy tried not to show how anxious she was when Mrs Moffatt beckoned her over. *I wonder what she knows? Of New Year and everything that happened. Of Raymond de Guise . . .*

'I've an extra job for you, Nancy.' Nancy must have looked startled, because, before she carried on, Mrs Moffatt looked at her gravely. 'Is something wrong, Nancy?'

'No, Mrs Moffatt,' she breathed in relief, 'nothing at all. What . . . what kind of job, Mrs Moffatt?'

'It's a little unorthodox, and of course you'll have to complete your other jobs today as well, but there's been a personal request. From Miss Vivienne Edgerton.'

Nancy's heart stilled. It seemed to take an age for it to start beating again. And when it did . . .

'It seems Miss Edgerton has made a request of management, and Mr Charles has asked me to relay it to you. Miss Edgerton has made it known that she wants no other chambermaid, nor even one of the housekeeping mistresses – not even me, you understand – to be responsible for her suite.'

There was silence in the housekeeping lounge as Nancy tried to process what was being said.

'Nancy, do you understand? You, and only you, are to be responsible for Miss Edgerton's quarters from this moment on. She won't tolerate anybody else. It seems she's taken *quite* a shine to you. There'll be a little extra in it for you, of course. As I say, highly unorthodox, but Miss Edgerton is who she is and we are left with little choice in the—'

'I'll do it!' Nancy blurted out.

Mrs Moffatt stepped back. 'As I say, we aren't left with any—'

'No, Mrs Moffatt. Mrs Moffatt, I *want* to do it.'

I really do, thought Nancy as Mrs Moffatt dismissed her with a knowing twinkle in her eye, and she hurried out into the hall. *What happened at New Year changed Miss Edgerton, but it changed me too. Miss Edgerton needs a friend. Everyone does. What else is there in the whole of the world?* Mrs Moffatt was right when she said it was highly unorthodox – but then, Nancy Nettleton had never been the most orthodox kind of girl.

The other girls had already disappeared up in the service lift, so Nancy wandered alone up the housekeeping hall and to the red-and-black chequered reception where the Norwegian fir had already been stripped down. It wouldn't be long before they started thinking about the next Christmas, thought Nancy; in a hotel as vast as this, time passes by so quickly. *But how much can change in a year? Last year began with a new king and ended with his abdication. This year we'll crown another new king. There's still war in Spain. And in Germany . . .*

Nancy stopped herself. *Well, who knows what the future can bring? So much happened in a year, for the world as well as for me . . .*

Billy Brogan was lurking – yes, there was no other word for it – by the reception desks, where the night manager was filling out his end-of-shift reports for handover to Mr Charles. When Nancy appeared, Billy caught her eye and, flushing crimson, promptly looked the other way. There had been something shamefaced about Billy since New Year's night. What he'd helped Miss Edgerton do to Hélène was unconscionable. *But everyone deserves a second chance. And Billy did the right thing in the end, didn't he? What's right and what's wrong – he knew the difference, when it mattered. We're all just trying to live our lives, to make them work, in the best way we can.*

But Billy hadn't spoken to her since New Year's night – and that wasn't right either.

'Billy,' she said, hurrying to his side. 'Billy Brogan, you're going to have to speak to me some day. The Buckingham's big but it isn't big enough that—'

Billy's eyes flashed up, opened wide. He lifted a finger to his lips, urging her to be quiet, then stretched it out, past the check-in desks to the hotel director's office beyond. Nancy followed his gaze.

Mr Simenon had appeared.

Nancy turned, as if she might scurry instantly away – but then she felt Billy's hand on her arm. 'Wait,' he whispered – so waiting was what she did. She waited as Mr Simenon approached. She waited as he loomed over her, his great beak nose in the air and his sallow eyes narrowed. She watched as he stopped dead, his heels clicking, and cut Billy to the core with a devastating look. She listened as he seethed, 'You'll pay for this, Brogan. It may be when you least expect it – but, one day, you'll pay . . .'

Then she watched as he donned a long woollen coat and marched directly out of the revolving brass doors.

Bewildered, Nancy wheeled around. She had not noticed it until now, but Mr Charles had appeared from the corridor directly behind Mr Simenon. He was standing, half-hidden by the check-in desks, with his hands folded in front of him and a satisfied look on his face. When Mr Simenon had vanished down the hotel's polished marble steps, Mr Charles nodded firmly at Billy. 'On with your work now, boy. We're all done here.' Then he turned on his heel and disappeared once more.

'Billy,' Nancy gasped, 'what happened?'

'Oh, you know what Mr Charles does.' Billy was trying to be dismissive, but a smile was playing in the corner of his lips. *And it's good to see Billy Brogan smile*, thought Nancy. 'He protected the Buckingham's reputation. Isn't that the job of a hotel director? To make the scandals go away, no matter how big or small they are? Well, the Buckingham needed protecting. Somebody was bringing it into disrepute. Somebody was risking everything, just to make a few extra pounds for themselves. Somebody was giving Miss Edgerton whatever she wanted – even if it was going to kill her in the end.'

'How did Mr Charles find out who it was?'

Billy shrugged, giving a wink. 'People whisper in this hotel, don't they, Nance?'

Nancy felt such an outpouring of affection for Billy that, unprompted, she threw her arms around him. Then, into his ear, she whispered, 'I'm glad you're still here, Billy.'

'I thought I wouldn't be, Nance, not after what I did. I didn't know if I could show my face. But then I thought: running away's not right, is it? Not when you done something wrong. The only thing that puts anything right is to stay where you are, on your own two feet, and hold your hands up to it and take what's coming. So I went and found Miss Marchmont. Crack of dawn, New Years' Day. I went and stood on her doorstep and told her everything I done, and why I did it. I swore I'd never set foot in the Buckingham again, if that was what she wanted.

But, well, it's Miss Marchmont, isn't it? Miss Marchmont's heart doesn't work like that. She seemed to understand . . . Everyone's just trying to do the best for the people they got, aren't they, Nance?' For a fleeting moment, Billy's shame crossed his face. Then he brightened. 'Miss Marchmont said she'd see me here, ready to start the year anew. Well, she can't give up either, can she? Not with a mouth to feed. Not with her secret safe . . .' Billy paused. 'At least that old serpent Simenon won't be going after you every time he sees you now, will he Nance? You see, I was your knight in shining armour after all . . .'

'Billy, you have the best heart. Don't ever change.'

In an instant, Billy's face was bright red with embarrassment.

'Billy,' Nancy said, 'there's something I wanted to ask . . .'

This seemed to perk Billy up. 'If it's another trip to the Midnight Rooms,' he joked, 'maybe you can ask somebody else?'

I'm just going to concentrate on whatever Mr Charles needs, he thought, *because there's bound to be something, isn't there? War still going on in Spain and the National Socialists on the march in Germany. More and more blackshirts on the city streets out east. New Year's gone, but the world keeps turning. There'll still be secrets. There'll still be spies. There'll still be guests coming through this hotel that need watching . . .*

'Nothing like that.' Nancy grinned – though, privately, she wondered if there might be a trip to the Midnight Rooms again, one where she could dance openly with Raymond, far away from the prying eyes of the Buckingham Hotel. 'It's only that . . . I wondered if the Buckingham might ever want more pages? There's so many of you already but maybe there's room for another? It's my brother. I left him at home and I promised . . . Well, families should be together, shouldn't they? It doesn't seem right not to have your family around.'

Billy drew himself tall, bursting with pride. 'I'll find out, Nance. I'll put a word in. Well, what could be better? Two Nettletons in the same hotel! Nance,' he announced, 'you been a good friend to me. I'm at your service.'

Nancy beamed as Billy hurried on.

It was almost time for the day's work to begin. If she were to dally a moment longer, Mrs Moffatt was sure to find out – and then, whether she was suddenly Miss Edgerton's personal chambermaid or not, there were certain to be stern words. *You've got to know your place*, Nancy reminded herself.

But perhaps there was time for one more moment . . .

Nancy scurried down the hall that snaked around the ballroom, and tentatively opened up the door to the little dance studio behind. The music of the gramophone was quietly playing – while there, on the makeshift dance floor, Raymond de Guise and Hélène Marchmont turned a simple tango, limbering up for their rehearsal to come. For a time, Nancy watched them dance. Indeed, so silent was she, so respectful, that the song had come to an end before Raymond and Hélène had even noticed her at all.

When his eyes found her, Raymond's face lit up. His almond eyes glimmered, his lips opened up in a smile still faintly crooked after the brawl of the Midnight Rooms three months before. Every last piece of him was beautiful to Nancy.

The gramophone was clicking into another song. Raymond moved as if to step out of the hold he was in with Hélène, but Nancy softly shook her head and mouthed the single word, 'Later.' Raymond understood. He returned to Hélène and, as the beat of the music increased, their gentle steps turned into something more strident, something faster and more demanding. Nancy watched as they crossed the room, turned, crossed it again, weaving their magical signatures across the studio floor. The music lifted Nancy up, filled her with as much joy as if she was out there in the ballroom on New Year's night itself. And there was Raymond. *Her Raymond*. It was enough to simply stand here and watch him dance.

The year was only just beginning.

The End

Acknowledgements

My heartfelt thanks to my marvellous editorial team – Sarah Bauer, Kate Parkin and Eleanor Dryden for all of your support, energy, inspiration and enthusiasm for me and my imaginary world of the Buckingham Hotel. Ever since the day we first met and discussed my ideas and inspiration, I've known it would be the perfect pairing. I've had tremendous fun throughout the process – thanks for all your hard work and for never saying no!

Thanks for your copyediting and proofreading prowess Jo Gledhill, Marian Reid and Steve O'Gorman. And to Richard Barber, for spotting an anachronism we'd missed.

I'd also like to thank my publicist, Francesca Russell, and the whole team at my publishers, Bonnier Zaffre. I've learnt that it takes a lot more than an author and an editor to make a book! Every single person I've had the pleasure of working with or meeting at Bonnier Zaffre has been absolutely amazing, so passionate and hard-working. I feel like a very lucky author.

I am hugely grateful to Melissa Chappell, my agent at I Will Know Someone, but more importantly, my friend. Without Melissa's support, advice and keen eye, incredible projects like this wouldn't happen. Thank you too, to Kerr

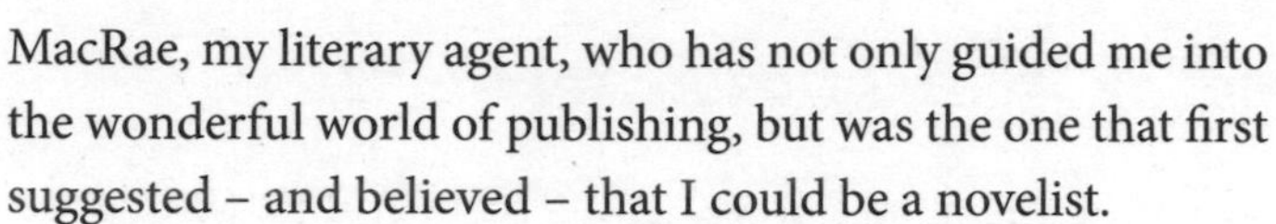

MacRae, my literary agent, who has not only guided me into the wonderful world of publishing, but was the one that first suggested – and believed – that I could be a novelist.

Ballroom dancing is a partnership and writing this book was no different. As a debut novelist I couldn't have written this without the support of my wonderful writing collaborator. Thank you for all that you've done, it's been a pleasure. Over many hours and weeks you guided me and helped me turn my story ideas into this finished book – a dream of mine that has now come true.

A lot of the ideas that this novel grew from were inspired by all the fascinating, talented, inspirational and eccentric people I've met and the places I've had the great fortune to have visited or performed in during my years in this magical world of dance. Thank you to every one of you.

And finally, but most importantly, thank you to you – my readers. Without you there would be no novel.

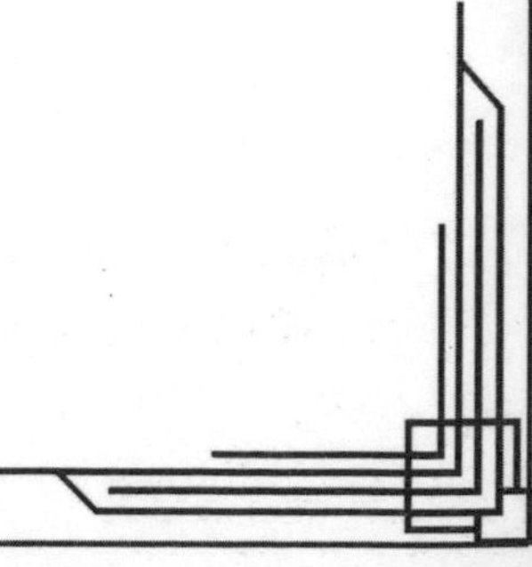

Hello my loves,

As I write this it still doesn't quite seem real that it will be going inside my book. My book. I still get excited saying that. I'm an author now, don't you know? It feels tremendous and I am so pleased that you've got it and, hopefully, have read it!

I just wanted to write this little note to say thank you. As some of you may know I've always loved books and reading and it has been a dream of mine to write a novel, which is why I am so thrilled about this one. But it couldn't have happened without you – my readers. If you've bought this book, thank you. If you were given this book as a gift, thank you (and the person who bought it for you), frankly I don't mind how you got a hold of the book, thank you for reading it.

I won't give anything away in this letter, in case you've skipped straight to here but I will tell you a bit about the inspiration behind it. The first half of the last century is truly the most fascinating period. So much happened in the world during this time – even without the two World Wars – it is a part of history that I truly love. Back then the ballroom truly was central to your social life, they really knew how to dance back then! Plus dance was evolving, people were starting to travel more and bringing with them new styles of music and, in turn, new styles of dance. The Latin dances we know today were just gaining popularity and were seen as very risqué.

I always knew I wanted to set the book in a London hotel, not only because of their magnificent ballrooms but because it gave me an opportunity to bring together characters from all of the world and all walks of life. Where else would a cockney lad meet a Princess from Europe? And so much happens in hotels, there's so many private corners for deals to be struck and gossip to be shared. Raymond De Guise – one of my main characters is a demonstration dancer in the Buckingham's Grand Ballroom. He gets to see it all – hobnobbing with the highest of society, whilst living in the staff quarters and hearing all the goings on. Not to mention, he's dashingly handsome and extraordinarily charming – not unlike myself!

The dancing, London scene, the hotel, the intrigue, the romance, all the characters, the band, bandleader; all of these creations have featured in my life, in some form, at some point – to varying degrees. Well, except for the period, of course. I wasn't around in 1936.

I truly hope you enjoy reading about the world of the Buckingham Hotel as much as I enjoyed creating it!

For all the latest news about my novel (and *Strictly*, too, of course!) do sign up for my mailing list, details for which you can find on my website: http://www.antondubeke.tv/

Love,

Anton

P. S. Don't forget to follow me:

@TheAntonDuBeke
@MrAntonDuBeke
www.facebook.com/antondubeke/

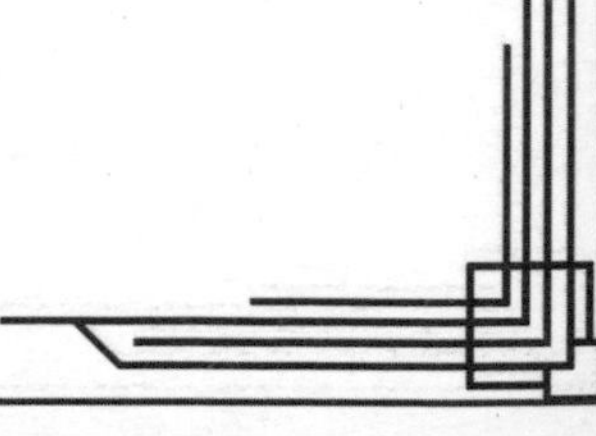

Return to the Buckingham Hotel
in Anton Du Beke's next
enchanting novel . . .

Moonlight Over Mayfair